Taylor Caldwell's moving tragedy of parenthood

LET LOVE COME LAST

Driven by hatred for the employer who exploited him, William Prescott used all his brilliance and forcefulness to take over the lumber mill where he had started as a clerk. With superhuman will, he turned it into one of the industrial giants of a burgeoning America.

Fabulously rich, he was obsessed with becoming richer—solely to give his children everything he himself had been denied.

But instead of gratitude, he only reaped their contempt. And their complicity in a plot that would shatter forever his titanic dream . . .

"AN EXTRAORDINARY FEAT OF MISS CALDWELL'S LEGERDEMAIN!"—*Saturday Review of Literature*

"The lofty peaks of best-sellerdom . . . are traditionally difficult to scale. . . . But there are three American novelists who have climbed to the top not once or twice but over and over again. In so doing they have established themselves as an *élite* among U.S. fiction writers. . . . All three are women: Edna Ferber, Frances Parkinson Keyes and Taylor Caldwell."

Life Magazine

LET LOVE COME LAST

TAYLOR CALDWELL

"Let love come last, after the lesson's learned;
Like all things else, love also must be earned."

PYRAMID BOOKS ▲ NEW YORK

This book is dedicated
with compassion
to all who are parents
and to all who hope to be

LET LOVE COME LAST

A Pyramid Book
Published by arrangement with Charles Scribner's Sons

Scribner's edition published August 1949
Pyramid edition published February 1965
  Tenth printing, March 1975

The characters and events in this novel are fictitious.
Any resemblance to actual persons or events is coincidental.
If the name of any actual person has been given to
any character it was unintentional and accidental.

ISBN 0-515-02885-1

Printed in the United States of America

PYRAMID BOOKS are published by Pyramid Communications, Inc. Its trademarks consisting of the word "Pyramid" and
the portrayal of a pyramid, are registered in the United States
Patent Office.

Pyramid Communications, Inc., 919 Third Avenue, New York,
New York 10022, U.S.A.

EPILOGUE

"—My dear and beloved Children—"

The words had a grave resonance, like the opening of the funeral Mass, like the organ sound of limitless mourning and the last murmur of futile tragedy. They were an epilogue to a man's life, thought Ursula Prescott, her bent head throwing a shadow upon the paper in her hands. But then, was there ever prologue or epilogue? In the beginning the end was already inherent; one might almost say it was simultaneous.

Ursula's fine and delicate hand touched the paper gently. She was not a woman who cried easily. She was not really crying now; she knew this. Not crying as a woman often cries, copiously and emotionally, and with a bursting relief.

She folded the paper slowly, but not before she had again read the two terse words: "—my wife." Those words struck her with fresh suffering for a moment. Then she said aloud, as a mother would say to a tormented child who at last begs for forgiveness: "Yes, yes, my darling. I understand. It doesn't matter." Nothing mattered, but that William might have peace. She had never been a religious woman. She had hoped, at one time, for personal immortality. But now, almost with passion, she hoped that William had found complete annihilation, complete darkness and nothingness.

She stood up, went to the somber casement windows, and glanced out. The small private park swept before her, darkening steadily under the dark opal of a winter sky. The naked black trees were daubed with snow; the ground glimmered spectrally. Far off, she could just see the low gray wall that surrounded the grounds. Beyond them, the street lamps burned with a fugitive and blowing yellow. How often, through how many years, she had stood at this window, and had seen this exact scene, and had felt its desolation! She had hated it, for she had found something inimical in the sight, just as she had found something inimical in this house which she was leaving forever in less than an hour. She had always hated this huge and echoing house, dark and forbidding in its long narrow corridors, its false turrets and towers of swart and heavy stone, its grim walls and slits of high windows.

5

Her thoughts ran on. She thought of Oliver, who would be coming with Barbara very soon, in that horrible bright-red automobile which they had just purchased, and of which they were inordinately proud. Involuntarily, and with sadness, she smiled. But the loud thunder and roar of the automobile would be a pleasant sound to her now, for all its stink of gasoline, and its smoke. Oliver, she thought.

Ursula pressed her aching forehead against the cold leaded window. She strained for a first glimpse of the vivid red monster which would carry her away from this house forever. Behind her lay shrouded rooms, with only a single light burning far down in the entrance hall. The servants had all been dismissed. She was alone in this mansion, where four of her children had been born, and where William had died. She could hear the dull booming of vagrant echoes, which were not the echoes of anything living. The room in which she stood, her bedroom, was growing cold; the fire had died down to a heap of ash and sparks.

Dear, dear Oliver. Had it not been for Oliver, this last night in this dreadful house would have been the most final of despairs.

Restlessly, out of her intense weariness, Ursula walked back and forth before the great casement windows, watching for Oliver, listening for the sound of his bright infernal machine. She passed the table where she had laid the paper. She put her hand over it, quickly, protectingly. "Yes, dear," she said, aloud, very gently, and as if comforting.

The great house boomed and creaked. She had a vision of its many rooms, shuttered and arctic, the mirrors and the immense furniture covered with dust cloths. She saw again the white, the dark-blue, the brown, marble fireplaces, before which she would never stand again. She shivered.

She heard a loud and staccato series of explosions. She turned to the window again. A pair of fiery eyes were rushing up the broad driveway. Oliver and Barbara had arrived for her. They would rescue her, and take her away.

It would be a beginning again. Not the beginning of youth, with joy and anticipation. It was only the beginning of age. For her, however, it would, perhaps, also be the beginning of peace.

PART ONE

"*Let parents, then, bequeath to their children not riches, but the spirit of reverence.*"

PLATO

CHAPTER I

IF ALL HER LIFE had indeed been complete from the first drawing of her breath, Ursula, in later years, often thought that a kind of beginning had taken place on a cool white twilight in late March, 1879, in the city where she had been born—Andersburg.

Andersburg was never to grow larger than one hundred thousand souls. In 1879, it boasted a population of fifty thousand. There had been no impetus for any enormous growth, for Pittsburgh was less than one hundred miles away. Foothills, covered with fine forests (much of it first-growth timber), gave it a natural beauty, and even endowed it with the reputation of being an excellent summer resort for those curious creatures who must often fly from their fellowmen lest they kill them in a moment of frenzy, or of complete understanding. Even in 1879, many "lodges" had been built in the foothills, summer homes of refugees from New York, Philadelphia, Pittsburgh, and even of Bostonians who were tired of the quaint New England countryside. New England eyes automatically expected to see the clean white steeples, set among neat severe houses and gardens, to which they were accustomed. But even seen from the hills, Andersburg had a sprawling and untidy character, a burliness of brown stone, and its houses had an air of heavy crudeness and stolidity. The city was not too far from rich coal fields, and many of the owners lived here in mansions indescribably ugly and formless, but very opulent.

Andersburg had a very small middle class, composed of small manufacturers, shopkeepers, wholesalers, merchants, bankers, lawyers, doctors and teachers. It was a smug and tight middle class, though it had little money. In compensation, it invented prestige, and affected, on the one hand, to despise the workers, whom it feared, and, on the other, pretended to laugh at the rich "outsiders" who drew their fortunes from coal and oil and rents and land.

Ursula Wende's father had been a teacher in the small private school in Andersburg; he had also been a philosopher. "There are only two ways a teacher can escape mass-murdering his

9

pupils," he had once said. "He can acquire a healthy hatred for them, or he can become a philosopher about them."

His pupils came, almost without exception, from the middle-class families. He acquired a philosophy about the middle class, also. He did not go so far as Aristotle in his admiration of this class, but he did believe, sincerely, that their survival was distinctly necessary to the survival of a nation. "As they are without imagination," he would say, "they often smite like a good sound club, on the delirious brains of fanatics and malignant idealists who would destroy any order for the mere love of anarchy. And they serve another harmless purpose: they furnish material for writers; they are the straw-men who can safely be knocked about by lunatics with missions, without harm either to themselves or to society in general."

August Wende had come of a sound "Pennsylvania Dutch" family, and as he was not completely free from affectation himself, he affected to find his antecedents "amusing" and rather base. But, in truth, they had been a people remarkable for solid common sense and shrewdness, and with a respect for learning which August had found "pitiful." Pitiful or not, their square and sturdy homes had been filled with books and musical instruments, much talk of Schiller and Goethe, much disgusted argument about Bismarck, and much delicate mysticism.

Much of the family fortune had been lost during the war, and when August died, in June 1878, he left his daughter a small fieldstone house in Andersburg, a large plot of uncultivated land just beyond the suburbs to the west, eight thousand dollars in cash, many objets d'art, and multitudinous books. There was nothing else, unless one also added a fine capacity for self-understanding, a clarified serenity of mind, pride, reasonableness, and a balanced ability to observe the world and its doings without overmuch heat.

"I suppose, my love, that you'll have to become a teacher yourself now," he had remarked on his deathbed, with regret. "You will need to remember one thing, and remember it always: Nothing very singular ever turns up anywhere. Consequently, one should never become excited, either over a strange student or a strange event. For there is nothing strange, and, really, nothing very interesting, in all the world."

Even in the moment of her deepest grief, as Ursula had looked down upon her father slowly dying, she had thought: "He is really dying of ennui." For some weeks after his death, she felt that his ennui had had in it elements of tragedy, and so, a certain splendor.

Eight thousand dollars, even when augmented to ten thousand dollars after the sale of some of the objets d'art, would not last her a lifetime. She was twenty-seven years old, a "confirmed" spinster. Fortunately, she had no relatives to support. Her mother had died when she, herself, had been a child of ten. She was comparatively healthy. She did not particularly dislike her fellowmen, so that she contemplated teaching with no aversion. Though August Wende had made fun of his parents' thriftiness, he had been exceedingly thrifty himself, and Ursula was a competent and frugal housewife, a bargainer in the food shops and the clothing establishments. As she had always made her own clothing, she was a clever dressmaker and milliner. She had, therefore, three choices of a way of making a comfortable living. She did not consider teaching better than either of the others, for she was without false pride. She decided to take some months or even years to consider. Teaching had "prestige," to which she was indifferent, but dressmaking and millinery might bring in more money.

She went alone, scandalously, to New York, enjoyed a few operas and plays, walked endlessly, studied the bonnets in the fine shops, and the rich gowns, garnered many ideas and much refreshment, and returned home in calm and rejuvenated spirits. She worked in her pretty garden all summer, preserved jams and jellies in the autumn, made handsome frocks of the materials she had purchased in New York, through the winter, set her garden in the spring. Then she began to think of what she must do for a living. Her capital was sacred. That must never be touched. She knew her ideas were middle-class, and was proud of them.

Once, in her early twenties, she had considered marriage. But though she had attracted a number of young men, she had never been overly attracted to them in turn. She had had a happy and tranquil life with her father, and, as she was a keen observer, she had not believed the marriage state, as exemplified among her friends, to be particularly ecstatic, or even satisfying. At twenty-seven, she had only one suitor.

She finally decided that she would accept a teaching post. She had been offered a teaching position in a small, girls' school, with a salary large enough to take care of her very modest requirements. This, then, was the best way open to her.

The small fieldstone house, set on a quiet tree-lined street, had an old loveliness. She would not sell it, though good offers had been made to her. It was her refuge, with its little library full of books, with its excellent old furniture, its three bedrooms with sloping ceilings, its ancient elms and perfect small garden, its leaded windows and strong plank doors, its flagged walks and hedges, its good paintings of plump ancestors on the panelled walls. Both she and her father had had exquisite taste. There was not an ugly or a cheap note either in the house or in its grounds. Her front windows looked on the narrow cobbled street, but the rear windows, from the bedrooms, had a view of the distant lavender foothills, and of the gardens.

Here Ursula could entertain her very few friends, but not too frequently. She was happiest when alone. There was nothing morbid in this. She had the contemplative mind, poised and still and lucid. She did not pretend to dislike people, as August had sometimes pretended. There were moments when she felt quite warm towards her friends.

Now it was March, pale, white, sterile March, with its wan cold twilights and its silences. She would often stand in the wet brown garden, her shawl over her shoulders, and listen for the first sound of life, drawing the chill pure air into her lungs. Nothing, she thought, will ever change. She was not sorry.

Yet on the twenty-eighth of March, with spring definitely established, things changed for her forever. The change came with William Prescott.

The jonquils massed themselves in cold golden pools near the rear wall of the house, strong, watery, and vigorous, shining even in the pale twilight. The wind from the hills ranged over the garden, and it raised a burst of fecund scent, as lustful as a mating animal. The ground had darkened; in the west, over the hills, lay a dull brazen lake, filled with the black rags of approaching clouds. Above the lake stood the slender silver of the moon, a curve of ice glimmering and sharp.

Ursula had not as yet lit a lamp in the house; it waited for her, dark and silent, with a low red fire in the parlor. She was cutting an armful of the jonquils, and thinking, with a tranquil sadness, of her father, who had preferred these flowers above all others. Perhaps it was because, like himself, they had so little perfume. There was nothing heady about them, like the roses, nothing passionate, like the tiger lily, nothing sweet and intense, like the lilac. They pleased the eye; they did not disturb the spirit. They had a simple perfection of petal—and they were soon gone. Ursula sighed. Regretfully, she concluded that her father, after all, had not been even a philosopher.

She would put the jonquils into water tonight, enjoying the mass of them against her walnut walls; tomorrow, she would carry them to his grave. Of course, he was not really in his grave. He was not anywhere. But she would allow herself the brief sentimentality of pretending to believe that he was aware of the jonquils, and of herself. There were times when it was almost soothing to pay lip-service to conventional belief. One or two of her neighbors would see her in the cemetery, and remark on the jonquils, and would think more highly of her for it. Ursula smiled faintly. She did not, truly, particularly care about the opinions of others. But if she were to be commented upon, she preferred that the comments be kind, rather than malicious.

My life is closing in upon me, she reflected. It does not matter. I am an old maid. Even that does not matter. I have a peaceful fire waiting for me, and books, and I have eight thousand dollars in the bank, and no one can disturb me. If I choose to indulge myself in hypocrisy, then I can do so without reproachful eyes fixed upon me.

The curve of the moon brightened, and now the wind became colder. Even the jonquils faded in the darkening twilight. But a white and spectral light hovered in the branches of trees, still bare and waiting.

It was then that she heard the brass knocker sounding loudly on her front door. Echoes bounded back to her. The whole street would hear that peremptory summons. She could not recall that any of her friends were rude enough to sound her knocker so noisily. One did not do that. In this sedate city, still brooding under Quaker traditions, one did not do that.

Annoyed, Ursula thought of heads appearing at windows along the street, staring down at the gray cobblestones and at her door. She entered the house through the rear door, laid the jonquils on the bare scrubbed table in the kitchen, which was lined with knotty pine, thrust a spill into the still glowing coals in the stove, carried the wavering light into the parlor, and there lit a lamp. Whoever stood outside must have seen the warm flare against her undrawn curtains, for he again struck the knocker a resounding blow, impatient and imperious.

Her cat, black and sleek, rose purring from the hearth and rubbed himself against her skirts. She felt the annoyed hardness of her lips, and forced them to part. She laid down her shawl, passed her hands over her hair, went composedly to the door, and opened it to the rush of the dark night air.

The gas-lamps along the street were already flaring in the dusk, yellow and glowing. They outlined the tall broad figure of a man. She could not see his face, only his head, with the hard round hat still upon it. He did not remove his hat for several moments; she could feel his eyes staring down upon her. Then, as if reluctant, he took off his hat, and said, in a cold, quick voice: "Mrs. Wende?"

"Miss," corrected Ursula, as coldly.

There was a ruthless urgency about this stranger, and Ursula had a swift thought that she was glad that she had no relatives who might be ill, no friends whose calamities could really stir and strike her, no fear of any summons to death or suffering. Otherwise, facing this stranger, she might have been alarmed. Now she could observe him on her own invulnerable threshold, and feel only irritation at his brusqueness.

"What is it you wish?" she asked. She had a clear, chill voice, the voice of a born spinster, as she had often wryly commented to herself.

"Miss Wende," said the stranger. He paused. He was trying to be polite, she saw. Then he went on: "You have a plot of land, fifteen acres, to the west of the town. I want to buy it. What is your price? I understand it is for sale. Someone told me an hour ago."

Ursula wanted to laugh. But she was still exasperated. Her first impulse was to say: "The land is not for sale," and then shut the door with finality. Yet that was absurd. She wished to sell the land; she had a price already fixed. Mere pique must not do her out of a sale, no matter how she disliked boors.

She said, closing the door a trifle: "You must see my lawyer. He manages all my affairs. Mr. Albert Jenkins, in the Imperial Bank Building, on Landmeer Street."

She saw that discreet heads were already bobbing at the windows of the nearest houses. Her door closed even more. "Mr. Albert Jenkins," she repeated, firmly.

"Nonsense," said the stranger. "Why should I wait until tomorrow? I saw the land this evening, and I immediately wanted it. I can't go to bed without having bought it. I don't want to diddle with lawyers. You sound like a sensible woman. Why pay your lawyer the commission?"

"Simply because he is my lawyer," replied Ursula, obdurately.

"If I go to your lawyer," said the stranger, with a most absurd threat in his voice, "I'll offer him five hundred dollars less than he asks, and then you'll pay his commission to boot." He paused. "I suppose I was mistaken. You aren't a sensible woman after all."

"But why does it have to be settled tonight?" asked Ursula, with a sharp edge to her voice. "I can't bargain with you on the doorstep——"

"Then you can invite me in." His own voice softened, as

if he were smiling. "I'm harmless, and I'm in a hurry. You don't need to be afraid of me."

"I'm not in the least afraid," said Ursula, with cool impatience. She hesitated. The heads were still at the windows. If she admitted this man, this stranger, the news would be told at breakfast in every house on the street: "Ursula Wende had a male caller last night; she allowed him to enter her house, though she had no female friend with her. Of course, everyone knows that Ursula is the soul of discretion, but still——"

Suddenly, Ursula was sick of discretion. Besides, she was by nature respectful of money. Extra dollars would not harm her in the slightest. The land was worthless. It adjoined no farms; it was in the least fashionable of the suburbs, and no one wanted it for new houses. She resented the taxes she had to pay on it, small as they were. She thought of the grasping Mr. Jenkins. She opened the door wider, and said, briefly: "Come in."

The man promptly followed her into her tiny warm hall. She had a moment's nervousness as she closed the door and found herself alone with him. She remembered newspaper stories of lone women murdered in their beds. But I am not in my bed, she thought to herself with faint humor. She restrained a desire to hurry into her parlor and place herself close to the poker near the fireplace. She led the way sedately into the room. The lamp had a heartening light. It revealed the walnut panelling on the walls, the faded Aubusson rug in its blue and rosy tints, the well-polished ancient chests, chairs and tables, the cat on the hearth, the darkened portrait over the mantelpiece, the Chelsea porcelain figurines and ormolu clock below it. It all had an exquisite look of loving care and taste, fastidiousness and elegance.

The stranger stood in the center of the room, and looked frankly about him. He smiled. He had a dark saturnine smile. There was about him an atmosphere of force and ruthlessness. All at once, the parlor seemed to Ursula too dainty, too attenuated, too refined, a woman's room, for all her father had furnished it, had chosen each article from the houses of his deceased relatives.

"A nice room," said the stranger. Ursula eyed him narrowly. Was he making game of her? But she saw, after a moment, and with surprise, that he was sincere. He was admiring the room, and everything in it. To Ursula, this seemed grotesque. He was such a big man. He was neither old nor young. She guessed his age as thirty-two or three.

"I always thought there must be such rooms," said the stranger. "I, myself, though, prefer heavier furniture, and thicker rugs. But I know what is here is very good. Probably priceless." There was a suggestion of a query in his voice. Exasperated again, but just a little amused also, Ursula replied: "I really do not know. Everything here belonged to my father's people. He chose what he wished."

"Old, and priceless," said the man. He was well dressed, in an excellently cut coat of the best black broadcloth and discreetly striped trousers. His waistcoat was of heavy silk. His black cravat boasted a good pearl pin. He carried a fine greatcoat on his arm, and his boots were handmade and brilliant. A malacca cane hung from his other arm. His clothing proclaimed the gentleman. But Ursula, with the instinct of her breeding, knew he was no gentleman.

She felt an unfamiliar curiosity, and studied him with more interest than was usual with her. He had a large but narrow head, with thick, straight, black hair, well-combed and neat. Below it was a knotted forehead, brown as if it had been repeatedly, and vulgarly, exposed to much sun. Eyebrows, thick, unruly and very black, almost met over deep-set and restless gray eyes. His nose was predatory, thin and curved, with flaring nostrils. His wide thin mouth was set tautly; he had a sound hard chin with a deep dimple.

With more and more surprise, Ursula said to herself: He has an eloquent face, and very expressive. I do not know whether I like what it expresses, for I do not know what it is. But though his face is eloquent, it has a quality of earth. How can features be so eloquent of so many things, and yet be so coarse? The coarseness, she decided, with astuteness, must come from some quality of his nature.

"Won't you sit down, Mr.——" she suggested, and hated her voice for its note of primness.

"William Prescott," he said, and sat down, after laying his hat, greatcoat and cane on a nearby sofa. He glanced at the fire, then before she could say anything, or make a move, he was up again, was tossing coals on the red embers, and was vigorously stirring them up. "I hate to be cold," he remarked. "I like heat, plenty of heat. I suppose that is because I was so often cold in my life, and could not get warm."

Nonplussed, Ursula watched him, and listened to him. She sat down, feeling quite numb, and waited until he had seated himself again. He gave her his cold, unfriendly smile; she noticed that he had strong white teeth. He should have made her uneasy. But, on the contrary, the queerest excitement stirred her.

She observed he was studying her candidly. She could see herself through his own eyes. She saw her tall slenderness, her narrow waist and high breasts under the russet wool frock, her thin thighs and neat and narrow feet. She saw the white lace collar at her throat, fastened with her mother's cameo brooch circled with seed pearls, and the white lace at her strong but narrow wrists. A ruby ring sparkled on the ring finger of her right hand. The left was ringless. All at once, she did not know why, she was glad that she had fine white hands with the "philosopher's" prominent knuckles, and fingers that tapered. She had no vanity, and she knew that she was not beautiful. Still, friends had commented upon her long oval face, so smooth and cool and colorless except for the rather inflexible mouth of a pale coral tint. She knew that she had a delicately Roman nose, arched and somewhat arrogant, a nose which had caused her secret tears in her girlhood, when she had compared it with the little retroussé or straight noses of her friends.

Her hair and eyes were faultless, she admitted frankly. The hair was smooth and heavy and waveless, very long and thick, and of a deep russet color, like an oaken leaf in autumn. She had eyes to match. Her father had said they reminded him of the best sherry, for, though aloof, they were liquid and bright, flecked with golden brown, and set in strong russet lashes. Ursula never cared much for passing style. She wore her beautiful hair parted in the middle, over a very high white forehead, and drawn back austerely to a large knot on her nape, with never a curl or a coquettish fringe.

She dressed discreetly, but with taste, and she had about her an unbendingly composed air, sometimes a little stern but invariably self-possessed. Once, her father, feeling more affectionate than usual, had told her she was a great lady, and he speculated, audibly, how such a great lady could have sprung from his sturdy, "Pennsylvania Dutch" ancestry. "There is something Spanish aboout you, my pet," he had said. Then he had added, with a little malice: "But there is nothing Spanish in your temperament."

She had been pleased. But now the memory disturbed her, made her vaguely resentful. What had her father really known of her, and her potentialities?

William Prescott said, with another of his unpleasant smiles: "You think me precipitous coming like this, hardly two hours after seeing your land?"

Ursula was exasperated at her own emotionalism, and she replied in a cool tone: "It does seem extraordinary. You were not expecting to build on it tonight, were you, Mr. Prescott?"

He laughed suddenly. The laugh was hoarse, and as disagreeable as his smile. "Strange to admit, but in a way I was. I never wait. I've found that everything that is ever accomplished is done by precipitate people."

"I prefer people who take a little thought," said Ursula.

He looked at her, still smiling. His small grey eyes were very penetrating and hard, like bits of stone. "I take plenty of thought. But I do it faster than the average person. When I saw that land, I had not only bought it in my mind, but I had built upon it what I wished, complete to the last detail."

She thought: He is a conceited lout.

He continued: "I have been looking for such a piece of ground. Isolated. Large enough, not too large. And cheap. It is the cheapest suburb of Andersburg."

Ursula was again irritated. "You haven't even asked the price. I am not prepared to sell the land cheaply."

"How much?" he asked. She became aware that there was always a demand in his questions. She began to dislike him more and more. She hesitated. She had placed a price of one thousand five hundred dollars on the land. She said indifferently: "Two thousand dollars."

He stared, then glowered. "Two thousand dollars! That's exorbitant. I could buy a fairly good small farm for that."

Ursula smiled frigidly, but said nothing.

"I had expected to pay no more than one thousand five hundred, at the very most," said Mr. Prescott. "Even that is too much, and you know it. There is nothing around it of any value, and you know that, too. I understand they may even put up workmen's shacks all about it! If they do, you won't get a thousand for the whole fifteen acres."

"Mr. Prescott," said Ursula, formally, "I did not solicit you to buy what I own. You came here yourself."

"But you saw I wanted the infernal land, so you put up the price," he said, with a very nasty inflection in his voice. His words were offensive, yet Ursula, incredulously, saw suddenly that his expression was almost admiring.

"I am not going to argue about prices," she said. "I have given you the price I will take. If you do not wish to pay it—or cannot," she added, with a sudden and subtle awareness that with this she could cut him sharply, "then we need not go on with the discussion."

She saw she was right, for he turned an ugly brick-red. "You know nothing of my financial condition," he said rudely. "You know nothing about me; you never saw me before."

So, he was vulnerable. This made Ursula smile with pleasure.

"You are quite correct, Mr. Prescott." She made her voice haughtily insolent. "Who are you? Are you a stranger to Andersburg?"

Now he glanced away from her, and his mouth tightened. "I was born in Andersburg, Miss Wende. On Clifton Street. But, of course, you know nothing of Clifton Street." He said this with an insolence that surmounted her own.

"Oh, yes," remarked Ursula, with repellent pleasantness, "I know all about Clifton Street. The Ladies Aid of my church makes up Christmas baskets for the unfortunate inhabitants. We also gather up discarded clothing, mend and patch and clean it."

All at once, she was disgusted with herself, for she saw him involuntarily glance down at his rich clothing as though it had turned abruptly to rags. The disagreeable expression went from his face, and was replaced by one so gloomy that she hated herself.

"I'm sorry," she said, with real humility and regret. "I ought not to have said that."

He laughed shortly. "I have that effect on people," he said.

He said this, not with apology, but with a kind of hard bitterness and defiance. Then he added: "I no longer live on Clifton Street, Miss Wende. I am temporarily living in the Imperial Hotel." He watched her closely, then smiled. "You aren't impressed?"

"Should I be? Should I admit that I know that the Imperial Hotel is very expensive?" Her words were unkind, but her voice had become gentle at the last.

"I have the best suite," he said, frankly, and his own voice was almost humorous. His eloquent face expressed amusement at himself, and now it lost its earthy quality and took on a vivid liveliness. "When I was a very young fellow, I promised myself I should have that suite. I worked in the hotel for a while, as a waiter."

He watched her narrowly for a look of disdain. But she was gazing at him with that new gentleness. "How nice that you realized your ambition," she commented. Something warm was spreading in her, something she did not recognize as pity. She had never before really pitied anyone, for she had never cared enough.

"My mother kept a boarding-house on Clifton Street, for the men who worked in the Leslie Carriage Shops," he said.

"Of course, this is of no interest to you, Miss Wende, and I don't know why I am telling you this. But I might say that I am a lumber man, now. After I was a waiter, I began to work for the American Lumber Company."

Ursula knew Mr. Chauncey Arnold, president of the American Lumber Company. The acquaintanceship was distant, for Ursula had always considered Mr. Arnold to be very gross. The gentleman had tried to cultivate August Wende, without notable success.

"I shan't bore you with all the details," said William Prescott. "Ladies, I know, are not interested in commerce, or money. Except when they try to get the highest price for a poor piece of land," he added, smiling.

Ursula returned the smile. "Mr. Prescott, I'll bore you with a few details of my own. I am an unmarried woman. My father came of a wealthy 'burgher' family, but they lost their money after the war. My father was a schoolmaster. He died less than a year ago. He left me a sum of money, but it is not enough to keep me for the rest of my life. I have found a position as a teacher. The salary is small, even if just enough for my needs. I like to think that I have a small, secure principal. I am quite healthy, and may live a long time. You are, obviously, a gentleman of means. You will forgive me, then, for driving as good a bargain as I can."

She was amazed at her unique retreat from habitual reserve.

She added, with angry pride: "I originally put a price of one thousand five hundred dollars on the land. You may have it for that, if you wish."

He looked down at his big thin hands, brown and strong, and he was thoughtful. "I'll take your original offer of two thousand," he said.

Ursula could not endure this. She stood up. He raised his eyes to her. Then, apparently, he remembered that gentlemen rise when ladies rise, and he, too, stood up. They faced each other on the hearth.

"Mr. Prescott," said Ursula, "my price is one thousand five hundred. I shall take no more. So, let us end the matter."

He inclined his head indulgently, after a moment's study of her. "One thousand five hundred, then." He put his hand in the inner pocket of his coat and drew out a purse of the best Florentine leather workmanship. His fingers rubbed it almost lovingly. "I will give you a deposit, now, of two hundred, and take your receipt. Within a few days, you can give me the deed, and receive the balance of the money." He looked at her steadily. "Or shall I call on Mr. Jenkins?"

Ursula, for all her irritation, could not help laughing.

"Never mind Mr. Jenkins," she replied. "As you said before, why should I pay him a commission? Only last week he told me that I would never sell that piece of property."

Smiling in answer, William Prescott extended two gold-backed bills to her. She took them. Her fingers brushed his, and a strange thrill ran down her arm, struck at her heart. This so bemused her that she stood there, staring at him in confusion.

"I'll give you a receipt at once," she stammered. She stepped back a single pace; she could not look away from him. He said nothing, but now his eyes were keener than ever. He was frowning, as if disturbed.

She turned suddenly, and went to her delicate rosewood desk in a distant corner of the room. She sat down quickly. Now her eyes blurred. She began to fumble in the drawers of the desk.

She heard his voice beside her. "Let me light the lamp for you," he was saying. He had taken a box of matches from his pocket. He took the chimney off the desk lamp, then lighted it. The little flare trembled as if a breeze had touched it. He had some difficulty with the flame of the lamp. She watched him, as if in a dream, her mouth parted. Then he replaced the chimney. "There now," he said, with absurd triumph, as though he had accomplished something of tremendous difficulty and importance.

She wrote out the receipt. Involuntarily, she managed to brush his fingers again. They looked at each other, hypnotized, as he folded the receipt without glancing at it, and put it away in that resplendent purse. She sat there, and he stood there, for a long time, in utter silence.

He said, in a stupid tone, dull and shaken: "You ought to have gas in this house. It isn't very expensive. And quite safe. I have gas-lights in my suite. Very convenient. Much better light, too, and better for the eyes. Some people object to the glare, and say the smell is more offensive than that of oil. I don't think so. Of course, one has to keep a window a little open. The fumes, you know."

"I've heard about the fumes," said Ursula, faintly, leaning back in her chair. "I understand they give you a headache. I don't think I should care for gas."

"But you must have gas!" cried William Prescott. He appeared quite excited. "One should progress." Then he fell into silence. He stared down at Ursula. The smooth, cool pallor of her face was suffused. She was beautiful as she had never

been beautiful before. The light brightened her russet hair
to a ring of gold about her head. She felt a warm swelling in
her breast, a richness in her thighs, an urgency all through her
body.

He turned abruptly and went back to the hearth, and stood
there, looking at the fire. Slowly, Ursula got to her feet. She
returned to the hearth, sat down. They both stared intensely
at the leaping flames that crackled all over the fresh coal.
William Prescott, though standing too near her, did not move.
There was a somberness about him, and something like a deep
silent anger. She could feel this. But she was not alarmed, or
dismayed. Something excited rose in her. For the first time
since her childhood she was feeling, and not thinking, and the
experience was primordial.

The delicate ormolu clock between the Chelsea figurines
chimed a sweet clear note in the silence. William Prescott actually started a little. He said, in his strange dull voice: "It
is nine. I must be going." He turned away to the sofa, picked
up his greatcoat, hat and cane.

Ursula rose. "Yes," she said, dimly, "it is nine o'clock."
Something was beating strongly in her throat. "May I ask,
Mr. Prescott, what you are going to build on that land? A
mill?"

He paused. He did not look at her. There was a cold brutality in his manner. "Why? Does it annoy you that I might build
a mill? What have you against mills, Miss Wende?"

"I have nothing against mills!" she cried, with asperity.
"Why should I? It's your land, now. Do what you want with
it." It was stupid to be trembling like this, as if she were afraid.

"I have no objection to telling you," he said. "I am going
to build a house upon it. The biggest house in Andersburg."

It was worse than stupid to experience such a sick shock,
thought Ursula confusedly. It was surely nothing to her that
he was building a house! But when one built a house, one had
a wife, or intended to have one very shortly.

"Mrs. Prescott will be pleased, then," she murmured. She
rested her hand against the mantelpiece. I feel quite odd, she
thought. I must have gotten a chill, standing so long in the
garden.

William Prescott put on his coat before answering. Then
he said, with hard denial: "There is no Mrs. Prescott. I am
not married."

"I see," said Ursula, in the most imbecile way.

William Prescott's loud voice filled the room: "I want the
house for myself! I want room after room, storey after storey!

I am going to fill every corner! I am going to have what I've always wanted, and be damned to everybody!"

Ursula was silent.

"If and when I marry, the woman won't matter in the least," said this peculiar man. He looked at her now, almost as if he hated her. "I shall marry only for children. I want to fill my house with children. A woman, to me, has no other reason for existence."

They regarded each other in a thick silence.

"I'll pick the best," said William. "Nothing but the best for me. Because of the children. A lady. But I am not ready yet. I shan't be ready until the house is built. Then I'll do my searching."

There was a kind of virulence in him, an alien quality which Ursula had never before encountered. She felt a blinding rage against him.

"I wish you good luck," she said distinctly, "though I am sorry for the lady."

Without another word, he turned away from her, and went out of the room. Ursula waited to hear him open and close the vestibule door. But the door neither opened nor shut. She felt him there, in the small closed darkness, as if he were lurking, like some great and inimical beast.

Then she heard his voice. "You don't need to be sorry for the 'lady'," he was saying. "She will know why I am marrying her. She will know there is no sentiment in it." He stopped. "I expect to marry a sensible woman."

"Good night," said Ursula, quietly.

He did not answer. Now he did open the door. He slammed it behind him.

The whole house shook and echoed after that enormous gesture of turbulence. Ursula stood by the fire and listened to it. Her cat came from a corner and rubbed against her skirts. She did not bend and pet it as usual. She continued to gaze at the doorway to the vestibule.

"Why, the horrible man," she said aloud, in a sick, wondering voice. "The horrible, horrible man! He is quite insane. I do hope I'll never see him again."

She would notify Mr. Jenkins tomorrow to see Mr. Prescott. Let Mr. Jenkins take care of the final negotiations. Let him have his commission. It was nothing to her. She could not bear, under any circumstances, to encounter that dreadful man again. It was not to be borne.

The little exquisite house was so still all about her, as still as though a storm had passed over it and it was left alone, safe and quiet from all recent batterings. The lamplight flared; the fire muttered; the cat mewed questioningly. It was a good house, this, but something violent had assaulted it. The violence had gone, without inflicting damage. Life could go on serenely, as usual.

Serene—and empty. Empty as a skull. Full of books and quiet, and empty as death.

CHAPTER II

MR. ALBERT JENKINS sat and beamed humorously at his charming visitor, Ursula Wende. He was a widower. Three years ago he had been relieved of a remarkably repulsive wife, and a year later he had proposed for his old friend's daughter. He had considered himself a catch of no mean attributes; he was one of the richest men in Andersburg, a stockholder in three of the most prosperous mercantile establishments, not to speak of a directorship in the American Lumber Company. He was not yet forty-five, not, he thought, too old for the spinsterish twenty-eight-year-old Ursula. Nor was he physically distasteful to other spinsters, and widows—a short, lean red-faced little man with a great reputation for amiability and shrewdness. Moreover, he had no children. He also possessed, and lived in, a very handsome home on Crescent Road, a most fashionable and exclusive street. His habits were impeccable; he neither smoked nor drank, nor was he ever heard to utter a word not entirely acceptable in mixed company. The minister of his church regarded him as a most estimable man, which no doubt he was.

Ursula did not consider him a great catch. She did not consider Mr. Jenkins at all, though there was nothing about him to repel a fastidious lady. She had refused him gently, and with a faint surprise. She rather liked him; he was courteous and friendly, and had rescued some of the old Wende fortune for August. But she could not bring herself to think of him as a husband for herself.

She knew him for an avaricious man, who could always "turn a good penny." She did not hold this against him. After all, sensible people liked money, and wanted it; only fools professed a fine scorn for the delightful commodity. So, it was not his avarice, his shrewdness bordering on cunning, which made her refuse him. Once or twice, thinking of her own precarious state, she wondered at her lack of worldly wisdom. But the thought of sharing Mr. Jenkins' house with him, and, candidly, his bed, bored her.

Mr. Jenkins did not become her remorseless enemy because of her lack of sense and her apparent unawareness of what it would mean to be Mrs. Jenkins. He liked Ursula very much. Even though she had refused him, he thought her a young woman of immense distinction and character and good judgment.

Now, as she sat in his office, he thought how superior she was to other ladies of his acquaintanceship. No fussing; no fripperies; no flutterings and aimlessnesses. To be sure, her costume was a little dull, but she gave refinement and gracefulness to it, and extraordinary taste. She was all in brown, from her woolen frock with the white collar, the neat plain cloak, the exquisite gloves, to the bonnet with its inner ruching of tulle, and its brown ribbons. Mr. Jenkins always declared that he disliked ladies who had a streak of the blue stocking in their characters, but, perversely, he liked to talk with Ursula, who understood everything, and never stared vacantly, or protested that all this "legal talk" was quite beyond her delicate mind. Ursula always understood very well.

Ladies of mental power were often "rebels," Mr. Jenkins would think dolorously, licking his late wounds. Mrs. Jenkins had been a "rebel." She had even dared assert, in open company, that women ought to have the right to vote. Only Mr. Jenkins' unassailable position in finance had kept husband and wife on the best calling-lists after that outrage. But Ursula, though a lady of education and intelligence, had no such enormities and peculiarities of character. She never antagonized anyone.

All in all, Ursula would have been perfect as Mrs. Jenkins the second. In the meantime, it was pleasure to see her, and to talk with her. Moreover, gossip never touched her, which was a happy circumstance.

This morning, Ursula had been telling Mr. Jenkins of William Prescott's visit. Naturally, with her customary taste and prudence, she had refrained from imparting all the circumstances. She had only hinted, carefully, that Mr. Prescott had revealed himself to be a most extraordinary man, hasty, savage, impulsive and without a single gentlemanly instinct. She managed to convey all this without the actual words, by a delicate amusement and a wry gesture or two.

"Well, my dear Ursula," he said, leaning back in his chair and beaming at her, "at least you are rid of a most unprofitable piece of land. And at a very good price. You will remember I advised you to sell it for a thousand. But you have sold it for one thousand five hundred. I always considered you a very good businesswoman, you remember."

The cold bright April sunshine struck into the handsome

office, with its fire, its leather-covered desk, its good chairs, and its wall of legal books.

Mr. Jenkins surveyed his visitor admiringly. "A very good bargain," he said. "And so Prescott wants to build a house on it, eh? Well, it is just like him, the scoundrel." For a moment, Mr. Jenkins' amiable countenance puckered in an ugly way. "I'm glad you sent him to me for the final details."

"Yes, I wrote him a note, at the Imperial Hotel," said Ursula, without much interest. "I thought the final negotiations had best be conducted by you, Albert."

"A very good thought," admitted Mr. Jenkins, approvingly.

Ursula looked at her gloves.

"It is just like him," repeated Mr. Jenkins, with some sudden passion, "to rush out to you the very night he had seen the property, and demand it. None of those who know him will be in the least surprised."

"Oh," said Ursula, guilelessly, "then he is known in Andersburg?"

"Known!" cried Mr. Jenkins. The chair creaked loudly as he sat up. Now his face showed disgust and repulsion and a black resentment. "Do you mean to say, dear Ursula, that you never heard of him before? Why, *The Clarion* has written about him every week! He is notorious, the rascal!"

"I don't read *The Clarion* often," admitted Ursula. "Papa always got the Pittsburgh and Philadelphia and New York newspapers, and I have kept up the habit. And none of my friends ever mentioned Mr. Prescott to me."

"His name is not fit to be mentioned in decent company!" exclaimed Mr. Jenkins, with great excitement. His sharp red face became almost purple. "A thief and a felon like that! Surely, you can't be unaware of what he did to Arnold, of the American Lumber Company? Why, Arnold was like a father to him. And he ruined Arnold, it is said. I don't know all the details as yet, but *The Clarion* intends to publish the whole nefarious story very soon, and I assure you it will shock Andersburg to its heart."

Mr. Jenkins knew all the details, hence his excitement and his hate-filled voice, loud and harsh in the room. "Ruined Arnold," he repeated. "And it may have terrible consequences for the Company's stockholders." He paused. "Fortunately, I had some hint of this a few months ago, and I may sell out my holdings."

"How clever of you, Albert," murmured Ursula.

"Just a weather eye, my dear Ursula," he said, with an air

of self-deprecation. Then he became virtuous and purple again. "But there are a number of my friends who will be involved in this; it is enough to make a man ill."

Ursula gazed at him ingenuously. "How sad that you were not—sure—Albert, a few months ago, and could not tell them what you already guessed, so that they might salvage a little from their investments."

There was a sudden brittle silence in the office. Jenkins stared at Ursula, and his small eyes narrowed.

Ursula's calm gaze remained very candid, and gentle, upon him. An unpleasant thought came to him. He had often remarked to acquaintances that Ursula was "smart as a whip." Why had he said that? Was it some instinct? If she was as smart as he had thought—and he could not just now remember why he had thought it—then she was suspecting something.

He said, almost incoherently: "I—I'm not sure, my dear. It was all done so undercover by that scoundrel. A feeling, let us say. You ladies could call it intuition." He smiled at her indulgently. She inclined her graceful bonneted head, and smiled back. He breathed easier. "Smart as a whip" some women might be, but, fundamentally, they were all fools. "One does not rush to one's friends without proof, you see——"

Ursula still smiled. All at once, Mr. Jenkins almost disliked her.

"You did not do so badly, yourself," he said, with a rich chuckle. "If you had got five hundred dollars for that slum, I should have congratulated you. But to have got one thousand five hundred——" he spread his hands. "My dear Ursula, you are a financial genius! If you were a man, I should ask you to be my partner, at once! How did you manage to force him to give you all that money?"

Ursula in her reflective voice replied: "Yes, it is a slum, is it not?" She waited, then added, as if making an insignificant remark: "He offered two thousand."

He gaped at her, confounded and incredulous. He could not believe it. He spluttered: "Two thousand? You are not joking? The man must be insane!"

For a few moments Ursula did not answer. She had led a sheltered existence, but she had not been unaware of life. Villainy, through books and hearing and observing, was no new thing to her. She was not disturbed by it. She asked herself, now, very sharply, why she had not been disturbed. Why had she not been made indignant by it, and angered, if not embittered? It is, she thought, only because I have always been so supremely selfish and self-centered, so abominably egotistic.

This man before her was a villain, if only a small and a petty one. Yet she had looked at him and had felt only a faint disdainful amusement. Amusement! She had not known then, but she knew now, that such tolerance could be an evil thing.

She became aware that Albert Jenkins had been laughing incredulously, and that he had said something. She spoke quickly: "Forgive me, Albert, I am afraid my thoughts strayed for a moment. Please, what did you say?"

"I said, it seems impossible that he should have offered you two thousand dollars, and that you should have refused it."

Ursula smiled artlessly. "But, Albert, that would have been dishonest, you see. I knew the land wasn't worth that."

He loved her afresh for this idiocy. "Well," he said, magnanimously, "one thousand five hundred is one thousand too much. I have already made out the deed, after receiving your note. He is to call for it tonight. I understand that he has actually begun operations on the land. No one knew what his intention was. You tell me he wishes to build a house. Right next door to chicken coops and shacks and stony fields! Well, well!"

"I wonder why he wanted that land?" asked Ursula.

Mr. Jenkins scowled. "I'll tell you why! Because nobody, after hearing the—rumors—and knowing what he was, would sell him a single clod of earth anywhere!"

"He tried to buy land somewhere else?"

Mr. Jenkins frowned again, and rubbed his chin. "Well, I can't just say. Not for sure. Never heard of it." He became thoughtful, and stared into space. "Now why should Prescott buy that particular piece of land? Very strange."

Ursula smoothed her gloves. "Andersburg can't move farther east, because that is the industrial section, where all those factories and mills are, and no one would care for that, and good land beyond that area is too far from the city. It can't move north, because the hills are there, like a barrier, and most of the land is in estates. It can't move south, because of the river, and the docks, and the farms nearby. So it seems odd to me that no one ever thought that it might move west. I suppose that is because Andersburg hasn't grown much recently. But if it should suddenly start to grow, the west is the only place, isn't it?"

If Ursula had been a man, Mr. Jenkins would have sworn suddenly and violently, and would have called himself an idiot, and his friends also. Of course, it was obvious! Just because Andersburg had hardly grown since the war was no reason why it shouldn't do so now. Of course, the farmers along the river and slightly inland would eventually be induced, by high offers, to sell the land for suburban or city development. But the prices would indeed be high! To the west, however, the stony and undesirable land lay, cheap and unwanted, waiting only for a clever man to buy it, or a group of clever men of vision, anticipating the future. One could buy all the land one wished, from the miserable squatters and grubby truck-gardeners and artisans who lived there——

Mr. Jenkins dropped his eyelids, to conceal the sudden sharp gleam in his eye. It was an instinctive gesture, even before Ursula, who could not possibly understand such things as speculation in land. Mr. Jenkins' heart began to beat very fast. The suburbs, the desirable ones, were already becoming crowded.

Then he had a sickening thought. Someone had already thought of all this. William Prescott. It was to be expected. William Prescott, ugly rat from Clifton Street, despoiler of better men, thief and liar and conniver and scoundrel! Mr. Jenkins stammered, watching Ursula closely:

"Did Prescott mention buying any other land in that vicinity?"

Ursula knew very well what was transpiring in Mr. Jenkins' mind. Her old habit of faint amusement tried to assert itself. Instead, and she felt this with a kind of exhilaration, contempt came to her, clear and vivid.

She said, as if in vague wonder: "No. But then, our interview was very short, really. I found him most disagreeable. We concluded our arrangements, and he left."

Suddenly, she remembered him beside her, at her desk. She saw the spill shaking in his hard brown hand. That hand became intensely visible to her now, in the light of the remembered sudden flare of the lamp.

She heard Mr. Jenkins sigh with relief. He had taken up a pen. He was tapping it thoughtfully against his teeth. He said, quite loudly: "It was only because he could not buy elsewhere."

Ursula's shoulders moved under her cloak in something like a shrug. She wanted to go. But the thing, the obscure but powerful impulse which had brought her to this office today, held her in her chair.

"I suppose you are right, dear Albert," she said, encouragingly. She paused. "A most uncivil man, Mr. Prescott. And, from what you have told me, apparently disreputable. Odd, too."

"Insane," agreed Mr. Jenkins, emphatically. "Do you know

what he did a year ago? He adopted a brat left in a slum hallway by some slut, some unknown female, of whom the less said, in the presence of a lady like yourself, the better. The brat was about a year old, then. Origin unknown," said Mr. Jenkins, using legal phraseology. "The orphan asylum is very crowded and wretched, so he had no difficulty. It was in the papers. Made quite a stir. Everyone laughed at him, and properly, too. But now the wretch has a nursemaid for the brat, and has rented the best suite in the Imperial Hotel. And he is paying a pretty penny for it, too!" Mr. Jenkins chuckled enviously, thinking of his friend, the owner and proprietor of the hotel. "Well, dishonestly come, easily go, to paraphrase the old saying about money," he added.

"He is a rich man?" asked Ursula, innocently.

Mr. Jenkins bristled. "No one knows! He doesn't bank here, or I'd know from Bassett. Banks in Pittsburgh. Probably not, though he will be," he added, with a return of his original infuriated malignance. "But I do know this: someone is backing him, to the extreme limit. And I know who the 'someone' is. An outsider."

Ursula appeared bewildered, and Mr. Jenkins did not enlarge.

"It was a kind thing, at least, to adopt the child," she murmured.

Mr. Jenkins laughed shortly. He was about to make an insinuating remark, but refrained, remembering his visitor's sex. He said: "I told you he was insane. Do you know what else he did, a week ago? He gave the orphanage five thousand dollars, for a new wing!"

Ursula's wine-colored eyes became very bright and intent, as they regarded Mr. Jenkins. Suddenly, without knowing why, he flushed sullenly.

"I suppose," he said, with elaborate carelessness, "there are some who would approve of that. I, myself, think he intends a strong attack on Andersburg society in the near future; he believes he will ingratiate himself this way. He will be sadly disillusioned, I am sure. No one worth anything, socially, will ever have anything to do with Bill Prescott, even if he endows a college or a dozen orphan asylums. We know him too well for what he is, and when the whole story comes out he will be more anathema than ever—the trash!"

"But why, until the story is known, is he held in such low esteem?" asked Ursula.

Mr. Jenkins became quite excited. "My dear Ursula! Who *is* the man? The son of a woman who kept a noisome house for the workers in the mills and factories! A man who is nobody! An upstart, a climber, from the slums! A former waiter, if not worse! He hasn't a friend in the city! No schooling, nothing——"

"He speaks like an educated man, if he does not have an educated man's careful accent," said the daughter of a schoolmaster.

Mr. Jenkins shrugged. "There is some rumor that old Cowlesbury—that ancient quack doctor who died about ten years ago—took an interest in him, let him read his books, bought him books, actually, and tutored him in his spare time. But everyone knew about Cowlesbury. He was more than a little mad, himself, living off there in the woods, after his retirement, with a pack of dogs. He had about two thousand dollars when he died, and he left it—with all his books—to Prescott."

Ursula vaguely remembered Dr. Cowlesbury, who had been a town "character" for many years. He must have been almost a hundred years old when he had died. Whatever esteem or position he had ever commanded had been forgotten twenty years before his death. Ursula had never seen him, but had sometimes heard his name mentioned.

She rose, and Mr. Jenkins came to his feet with gallant alacrity.

"My dear Ursula," he said, grateful that she was leaving, so that he could concentrate on his glorious new idea, "please let me send you home in my carriage. I can send for it immediately. It is in the stables around the corner."

Ursula was about to refuse, as usual. Then, all at once, she was very still. She stood and looked at Mr. Jenkins, and her eyes became quite brilliant.

"Thank you very much, Albert," she said. "Though I intend to drop in at Mrs. Bassett's tea, and it is only a few steps from here, as you know. But I do feel rather fatigued."

CHAPTER III

MR. JENKINS' carriage, while not the finest in Andersburg, and distinctly not of the class of some of the elegant carriages that, in the summer, conveyed the exquisite families of the rich coal mine owners and oil barons and land aristocracy about the streets of the city on their calls, had yet about it a solid, middle-class soundness and comfort. No dainty appointments marked the carriage's interior, nor was the coachman uniformed in maroon or black or dark-blue. The only concession to splendor on the part of the coachman (who was also Mr. Jenkins' gardener, handyman and messenger) was a sober cap with a visor.

The carriage robe, while not of fine fur, was of thick wool, and for this Ursula Wende was grateful, for the early April afternoon had turned chill. A hard and relentless wind poured down from the hills; the light had become bleak, robbing every house and street of its third dimension. The sun had retreated behind determined clouds, so that no glass shone on shopwindows, and no shadow stood under bare trees. A sky of gray and ugly faint brown lowered over the city. Andersburg, never a handsome town, appeared preternaturally ugly in this spring light, and the "square," as Ursula rolled past it, had an untidy and disheveled look; even its statue of a Civil War hero stood amid a melancholy litter of straw, paper, twigs and other debris.

It was no day for an excursion, especially an "unreasonable" and impulsive one, Ursula reflected. Few other carriages were taking the air. She, herself, ought now to be sitting by the cosy fire in Mrs. Bassett's drawingroom, genteelly sipping tea and softly exchanging news and scandal. Not that one could really call scandal what transpired among the polite females of Mrs. Bassett's acquaintance. It was not that juicy and fruity, though a reputation or two might be slightly damaged or impugned by those dainty and chirping voices.

Ursula, with a quite inexplicable complacency, began to wonder whether her friends, now probably murmuring questioningly about her absence from the tea-party, might not be scandalized if they knew where she was going at this moment, and why. But then, I myself, she thought, truly do not know

why. Everything, including my thoughts, has become so remarkable to me during the last few days. I presume that if
I should sit down quietly, and really concentrate upon the
matter, I might come upon a clue.

Her cheeks suddenly became warm, and she pushed aside
the robe a trifle. Oh, how absurd this was, how very cheap!
She would call to the coachman and ask him to take her to
the Bassetts', after all. Her gloved hand lifted; then, very slowly, it subsided. Her cheeks remained hot, but her mouth set
itself firmly, and her eyes, under the bonnet-ruching, glinted
with a strong and outlandish excitement.

"It is only curiosity," she murmured aloud. Then, because
she was very seldom capable of total self-deception, she laughed,
ironically. The coachman turned his head in inquiry; Ursula
pretended to be returning the bow of a lady in a passing carriage. The necessity irked her; a week ago, she would not have
given the gesture a thought, for it would have seemed only
proper. What a smug dolt I have been all my life, she remarked
inwardly.

These are very fine thoughts indeed for an incipient schoolmistress, she thought, as the carriage rolled through streets
becoming less and less respectable. I must learn to keep them
from showing on my face or I shall not survive a single term.
Sad, in a way. The young ladies in the forms might learn something real and valuable were schoolmistresses permitted a
few original comments of their own, not prescribed in decorous
school-books. But honesty in schoolrooms, as in civilized
society, must always remain a dream, lest anarchy result. Was
it necessary to make men dull in order to keep them from murdering each other?

Ursula was so engrossed with her extraordinary thoughts
that she looked up in bemusement when the carriage stopped
and the horse halted along the side of the cobbled road,
which ended at this place. She knew this plot of land very well,
and she remembered it with distaste. She had last seen it in
February, broken, uneven, blotched with dirty snow and pud-
dles of brown water. Now the snow had gone, but the water
lay in larger pools on the land, and the pools were partly filled
with rubble and trash of all kinds. Far beyond, at a considerable
distance, clear and small and busy in the hard and waning April
light, Ursula could just discern a veritable hive of workmen
with shovels and buckets. Near them loomed enormous heaps
of tossed wet earth, which they had thrown up. Carts and wagons tilted and heaved near by; men were filling them with earth,
and with the shale which had already been dug from beneath

the surface. Ursula, surprised at all this activity, guessed that a huge foundation was already in process of being dug, though the deed to the property was not yet signed. Now, she was no longer surprised. She smiled. It was something to be expected of the precipitate Mr. Prescott.

Except for the workmen, the land was empty. Beyond its boundaries stood barren shacks in haphazard formation, smoke pouring from tilted chimneys. Scattered little houses spread behind them, in patches of land used for truck farming later in the spring. Then, with gardens rich and crowded, the scene did not appear as desolate as it did now, in this fugitive and shadowless light of fading afternoon, with the gray and lowering sky bent over it, and a rising wind ruffling the tops of the cold brown pools of water.

The coachman, who had not received his training at the hands of "fine people," directed a question at Ursula, half turning on his seat: "This where you wanted to go, ma'am? Your land, ain't it?"

"It was, Bob. It isn't, now," replied Ursula calmly. "I sold it a few days ago to a Mr. William Prescott."

"Bill Prescott?" Bob turned to her fully now, his old red face staring. "You mean that trash from Clifton Street, him who's trying to rob his betters? Him that's no better than a jailbird, ma'am?" His reedy voice was incredulous.

Ursula's face, out of habit, began to settle into prim cold lines. Then she deliberately forced the expression from her features. She smiled up at the old man. "Oh, Bob, come now, he isn't that bad! And you mustn't believe everything you hear, you know. People will talk." She paused. "Especially envious ones. What if Mr. Prescott was poor once, or what work he once did? He is rich now," she added, tentatively, "and is making quite a name for himself."

Bob Willard snorted. "Well, ma'am, getting rich that way, quick and fast and sure, can't be honest," he said, darkly, "even if you don't pay much attention to what folks say."

Ursula privately agreed with this. She remembered Mr. Jenkins. It was very disreputable of her, she knew, that she should regard Mr. Prescott's mysterious derelictions so tolerantly, and be so annoyed with Mr. Jenkins. But there was an enormity inherent in Mr. Prescott's predatoriness; huge and criminal manipulations appeared to her just now, for no adequate reason at all, less dreadful than the mean and petty ones. I apparently share this opinion with millions of other people, she thought, ruefully, otherwise we should not tolerate wars so benignly, and hang a man with one mere murder to his credit.

Sitting in the carriage, and looking absently out over what had once been her land, she let her strange new meditations have their way with her. She had been a very young girl when the Civil War had ended, but she remembered clearly the distress and misery of the years that followed, the high prices which deprived millions of bread and shoes and clothing and houses, the vast national uneasiness and nameless dismay, the fear, the formless hatred, the restless and sullen faces on the streets and in the shops. The air of the country had been weighted with a kind of speechless dread and suspicion. All men had been aware of it. They explained it vaguely as "the usual aftermath of war." It was more than that. It was a kind of soul-sickness, a smothering sense of guilt.

Could it be, wondered Ursula, that man instinctively knows that to kill his brother is the highest atrocity, not only before God, but before himself? Was it because man subconsciously knew that it was expected of humanity that it resolve its problems without murder? If man knew this, how did he know? It was instinct, just as the Bible, itself, was only instinctual apperception.

She started when she heard the rumble of wheels, and quickly glanced to her left. A very resplendent carriage, which made Mr. Jenkins' comfortable victoria appear most humble and commonplace, was drawing up beside her. It was a closed vehicle, all glass, black and red lacquer, all silver harness, and drawn by two black horses beautifully groomed. The coachman wore a smart black uniform, with touches of red, to match the carriage, and he was a young and apparently well-trained man.

Ursula flushed deeply, and fervently hated herself for being in this place. She had an impulse to tell old Bob to drive on, and remembered, just in time, that this would only add to the humiliation she had brought upon herself. So, flushed as she was, she merely waited with every appearance of serenity as the coachman sprang down, walked importantly to the side of the other carriage, and opened the door.

CHAPTER IV

WILLIAM PRESCOTT descended from his carriage with gravity, and without haste, ignoring his coachman's courtesies. He stood for a moment and gave the desolate land he had bought, and the workers upon it, a quick and casual glance. Of course he knows I am here, thought Ursula, vexed. How very silly of him to pretend to be unaware of me.

Mr. Prescott turned and came towards Ursula's carriage, and he did not simulate any surprise. She saw his face in the thin shadowless light, which gave an odd clarity to everything. And again, she was excited by the contradictions in that face, the mingled eloquence and coarseness, refinement and brutality, power and wariness. Now she detected what she had missed before: a sullen uncertainty in his small hard eyes. But he was smiling, and he was openly curious.

Ursula was accustomed to the conventional dictum that ladies never explained, and gentlemen never asked them to explain, so that she was not prepared when he said: "Miss Wende? Come to look your last on your property?"

For a second or two she was at a loss, then replied: "Good evening, Mr. Prescott." She paused, to let him meditate on his impoliteness. But he was not at all conscious, apparently, that he was acting like a lout. He merely came closer to her carriage, and stared at her with open question, and. in spite of his fixed smile, it was a question inexplicably full of hostile implications.

She could have touched him from where she stood, and her heart began to beat thickly. Why, the man seemed to pervade the atmosphere for a good distance about him! It was not a pleasant thing to feel, neither was it unpleasant. She looked at him in silence, and did not know that both her lips and her eyes had opened very wide. She looked down at his hands, remembering them as she had seen them in lamplight. They were gloved now. Something like keen disappointment came to her. She forced herself to smile again and to speak calmly, but she detected the falseness in her own voice.

"I am out for a drive," she said. "The first dry day, you see."

Her head swirled with confusing thoughts. She knew that all the strange ideas which had come to her during the past days had been because of this uncivil and disagreeable man, that he had, unwittingly, forced her to think honestly for the first time in her life. And the strangest thought of all came to her at this moment. She saw that in spite of the honesty he had aroused in her, she could never be honest with him.

She saw that she was quite right in this, for the hostility, or resentment, with which he had recognized her began to fade, and was replaced by a heavy awkwardness. He did not know what to say next, and she graciously helped him, feeling more in command of herself:

"You have not wasted any time, Mr. Prescott, in beginning your house."

"I never waste time," he said. In another man, this might have been boasting. But, in Mr. Prescott, it was simply an irritable stating of fact. He studied her with hard candor. What feeble men you must have known before, he seemed to be saying contemptuously. He went on: "I have hopes that it will be finished within six months. I have all the furnishings ordered from New York, and am importing others. Then I shall move in." He scowled, and Ursula was taken aback. He gestured roughly towards the workmen. "That is, if this cattle decides to do an honest day's work for an honest day's pay. But that, I suppose, is more than one could expect."

Now his face turned ugly and common, as if with hatred, lost all its eloquence and fluidity, and became unfinished and rude. This man had come from "the people." Yet he had neither understanding nor kindness—nor forgiveness, perhaps —for them. Ursula drew the woolen carriage-robe closer about her.

She said, coldly: "They appear to be working very hard." She hesitated before speaking again, and then said something she would never before have dreamed of saying to anyone, or even of thinking: "After all, their wages are poor. They look thin and worn to me, and I am very sorry for them. I wonder if their food is adequate."

She regarded him directly, and the lids of her eyes were stiff and hard.

He was genuinely surprised at this. He laughed shortly. "I see that you know nothing about this kind of people, Miss Wende. But I do. I have the advantage of you in this respect. My mother cooked for them."

"Indeed," murmured Ursula.

"Just animals, let me assure you," he continued, and now

he was looking at her with dislike, and again she detected contempt in him. He put one of his polished boots on the step of the carriage, and leaned towards her. "Miss Wende, I'll make it very brief for you. Quite often a self-made man is condemned by others because he 'forgets' or 'oppresses' the very people from which he came. No one ever considers that he perhaps both 'forgets' and 'oppresses' because he understands, and has reason for what he does."

Ursula replied cuttingly: "I am sure, Mr. Prescott, that you know all about these poor people. And why should you not—certainly?"

She was so positive that even he would understand this full insult that she began to raise her hand to Bob, who was listening ardently. But she had hardly lifted her hand halfway when Mr. Prescott laughed openly and loudly. Her hand dropped back.

She was baffled. There was actually an amused twinkle in his eyes; he was almost cordial, and all the eloquence had come back to his face. This protean quality in him confused her.

"Anyway," he was saying, "I don't 'oppress' them. I pay them more than the prevailing rate. The contractor didn't approve of it. Bad precedent, he appeared to think. What is sacred about a precedent, either good or bad?"

He put his foot down on the ground, then looked at it thoughtfully. All at once, she knew he had forgotten her. When he glanced up again, he had every indication of faint surprise, as if he had expected her to be gone. This freshly annoyed Ursula. Also, she noticed for the first time that he had not removed his hat, had not even touched it in slovenly recognition of the conventions.

"You don't care for precedents, Mr. Prescott?" she heard herself saying.

With renewed mortification, she saw he had recognized her inanity, for he merely shrugged. He was looking again, over his shoulder, at the dismal tract of land. The skies steadily darkened, and now the wind had become definitely cold. Ursula waited. She saw that Mr. Prescott did not intend to answer her foolish question. Something spiteful rose in her.

"A very unlikely spot for a fine house, don't you think. Mr. Prescott?"

He returned to her, smiling disagreeably. "Not for very long, however, Miss Wende. You see, I have bought up a great deal of the land all around it, at least seventy acres more."

"No!" cried Ursula, forgetting everything now. She thought of Mr. Jenkins, and then began to laugh. She could not stop herself. Once, she put up her gloved hand to her lips. But she could not stop laughing. Mr. Prescott stared at her, frowning, waiting for her to finish.

"I'm glad I have amused you," he said, sullenly, when she could catch her breath. And he smiled, with some dark amusement of his own. "I suppose you would not tell me if friends of yours have become interested in the properties around here, since I have bought yours?"

"Oh, I should not, really I should not!" exclaimed Ursula, with delight.

"I see," he said, and they smiled at each other with huge enjoyment. He continued: "What fools they are, to think I'd be such a fool, myself. Of course, I know that Andersburg must grow this way, and that all property in this area will eventually be very valuable." He waited, but Ursula only smiled. "I bought your land first. Then, in the last day or two, I bought up the rest. Yours was the key plot, and naturally it had to be bought first. I don't mind telling you that I intend to use only your fifteen acres for my house and grounds. The rest will be retained by me for a high price, and will not be sold for any purpose other than houses comparable to mine."

He shrugged again, a coarse and heavy gesture. A hand tapped on the window of his carriage, and he glanced in that direction. He returned to Ursula. He said: "Would you like to see my son, Miss Wende? He is in my carriage." His expression was almost friendly.

"Your son?" asked Ursula, opening her eyes innocently. "I thought you were not married, Mr. Prescott."

"Of course I'm not married," he answered, with impatience. "But I adopted a child some time ago. A little boy. He is now two years old, and a very likely little fellow."

"I should like to see him, indeed," said Ursula.

Without another word, this peculiar man beckoned to his coachman and spoke to him curtly. The servant promptly got off his seat, jumped lightly to the ground, and opened the carriage door. Ursula saw a flurry of feminine petticoats, the swirl of a cloak, and the outlines of a bonnet. She sat up straighter on her seat, and a little thrill of fear went through her. But when she saw that all this finally subsided into the figure of a young woman in the uniform of a nursemaid, the fear disappeared.

The young woman was carrying a child in her arms, a child richly dressed. She came diffidently towards Ursula's carriage. Even before she looked at Ursula, she looked at Mr. Prescott, and her fixed and obsequious smile could not hide the hatred in her large blue eyes. She was quite a pretty creature, but it was quite evident that Mr. Prescott did not see either her prettiness or her sex. For him, she was only a convenience. She had hardly reached him before he snatched the child from her arms. He dismissed her with a movement of his head, as if she were an importunate dog. She retreated from him, then stood waiting. Ursula caught a glimpse of the look that passed swiftly between her and the young coachman, and the look made her brows contract.

Mr. Prescott had forgotten all about the nursemaid. He held up the child for Ursula to see, and now, to her utter bewilderment, he was all gentle tenderness. There was about him an air of almost idolatrous absorption, a kind of exulting pride and triumph. "His name is Oliver!" he was saying. "Look at him, Miss Wende. Is he not a fine boy?"

Ursula politely attended to the child. She was not fond of children. She was too well acquainted with them, for her father's students had often come to the house. Yet, in spite of herself, she immediately became interested. The little boy was rather larger than usual for his age. He wore a round fur-trimmed hat. But under that absurd hat, entirely too ostentatious for a baby, was a full and rosy face, full of shy intelligence. The features were not the average baby's features, all rosy bluntness and vacuity. They were not sharp or keen, either; rather, they expressed an awareness beyond their age, and a firm delicacy. There was strength in the eye-sockets even now, and the forehead was good and clear. The child's eyes, large, dark, fearless and smiling, caught and held Ursula's final and complete attention.

"What a dear!" she said, involuntarily. Quite without meaning to, she held out her arms, and took the boy from Mr. Prescott, lifting him into the carriage and settling him on her knee. She gazed at him with pleasure, rubbing his cheek with her gloved finger. She had never kissed a baby before, but now she impulsively bent and kissed that red cold cheek. "A dear!" she cried again, holding the baby close to her breast. He looked up at her, no longer smiling, but intent and very quiet. He showed no inclination to discourage her demonstrations.

"I see you like children," said Prescott, and with such gentleness that Ursula was startled out of her preoccupation with little Oliver. She held the child against her breast, and regarded Prescott thoughtfully. She had been about to say: "Certainly not. I do not dislike them, but I am a mature woman and so cannot help finding children extremely boring." But with her queer awareness that she could never be honest with this man who had made her honest, she answered evasively: "Who could help loving this darling?"

Apparently he had not detected her evasion. He came closer to the carriage, rested his elbow on the side, and stared at her with deep penetration. Again, she felt the power in him, the magnetism which both drew and repelled her. She bent her head over the baby. The child smiled at her gravely and steadfastly, as if he understood her.

Ursula, though she did not turn away from the baby, spoke softly to Prescott: "I heard, only today, of your kindness to our orphan asylum. All of us know it is in a fearful condition, but inertia, or selfishness, or indifference, has kept us from doing much about it, ourselves."

"Yes, I know," replied Prescott, bitterly. "The children are poorly clad, they eat the food of beggars, they have little or no medical attention, they are forgotten and abandoned, then hired out at an early age at work unsuited to them. It is my intention to put a stop to this, at the earliest possible time."

Ursula was intensely moved. She smiled softly at this man of so many amazing contradictions. "You must be very fond of children, yourself," she said, wonderingly.

To her faint alarm, a look of concentrated fanaticism flashed into his eyes. "I am fond of them because they are the only decency in the world!" he exclaimed. "The only cleanness and goodness. They are what men were intended to be, and are not. There is no evil in children, no cruelty, no madness, no greed, no heartlessness."

Astounded, Ursula could only keep an incredulous silence, but it was a silence maintained with difficulty. Again, she thought of the children of her friends, the pupils of her father. Remembering this, she wanted to exclaim, in answer to Prescott: "Oh, what nonsense! Children are only people, except that mature men's natural instincts are kept in precarious restraint, while children's are not."

Again, she held herself back, but with some effort. She might often have been a prig; to herself she had rarely been a hypocrite. Since knowing this man, she had learned to think honestly; she saw now that she must also learn hypocrisy. Despising herself, therefore, she made herself say in a sweet tone: "There are so few who understand children or care to know them."

How was it possible for a man so obviously intelligent to be so fatuous and so silly?

His face was so eager and so stirred, that her sudden repulsion died away. He said: "Yes, that is completely true. Miss Wende, I have told you that my mother boarded workers from the mills and from the ditches. They were a disgusting lot, and vicious. They cuffed me about, and kicked me, teased and tormented me. I grew to hate them, and their kind—the smell of them, the shape of their faces, their voices." His own voice changed, became quietly savage. "There are some people, stupid people especially, who grow rapturous about the man with a hoe, or a shovel, or at a machine, and think that any virtue the world possesses lives in these. I know better. I'd like to take the nice advocates of the poor," and now his voice became louder and more excited, "and force them to live for a while with those they pity and admire so much. That would cure them, I warrant you!"

What an extraordinary man, and so full of obvious inconsistencies, thought Ursula. She wondered at the huge blind spot in his thinking, and knew, then, that while he might work with complete objectivity, he thought with his emotions on any matter connected with other men.

All at once, she was tired, and her head began to ache. The vitality he exuded confused her; her reactions to him, for all their excitement, were both novel and wearying. She held little Oliver out to him with only one thought: to go home and sit by her small fire and watch the evening come on.

He took the child and held him almost fiercely in his arms. Oliver looked up at his face with intense gravity.

"I want to do what I can for children, all children," said this preposterous man, staring at Ursula as if he were defying her. "I want to give them everything they want, to make the world a happy place for them, and a clean one."

"And you think that by denying a child nothing, by giving him his way, by refraining from disciplining him and teaching him responsibility, that he will be happy?" asked Ursula.

"A child has a right to everything," replied Prescott, and again he was fanatical. "Nothing should be demanded of him, but everything should be demanded of his parents. He owes nothing to anyone, but everyone owes everything to him. He is the world's responsibility."

Really, thought Ursula, the man is not only a barbarian, he is an egotist. Of course, it is easy to see that he is thinking of his own childhood and the deprivations and mortifications he must have suffered at the hands of the cruel. He does not love children so much as he loves the memory of his helpless young self, whom he now wishes to avenge. I wonder if all altruism, charity and devotion does not really stem from hidden memories of undeserved suffering and injured vanity?

Only a short time ago she had been thinking that the men she knew were colorless, lacked form and substance compared with this man. Now she saw them as calm and safe and reasonable civilized human beings with whom it was pleasant to talk even if the conversation were something less than stimulating. She sighed, smiled wearily.

"It is very kind of you to feel so strongly about children, and to care for them so much," she said, with mendacity. Prescott did not answer. He was busy fastening a button on little Oliver's coat, and he did this with absorption. Ursula raised her voice. "I really must go home," she said.

He had heard this. He gave her a smile so open, so friendly and gentle, that she was more startled than ever.

"Yes, of course. It is getting cold," he said. He shifted Oliver to his left arm, held out his right hand to Ursula, without bothering to remove his glove. She hesitated. Then she gave him her hand, and she felt the warmth and strength of his fingers. They looked at each other in an odd and sudden silence.

"Good night," he said, and then again, in a lower voice, mysteriously troubled, "good night." But he did not release her hand. He looked down at it. "Oliver likes you. He is very reserved with strangers. Perhaps I could bring him to call on you soon?"

"By all means," said Ursula, faintly. "I am always at home to my friends on Sunday afternoons."

He released her hand now. Again, the dull resentment was thick on his features, and they had stiffened.

Ursula murmured a word to Bob, who flicked Mr. Jenkins' horse with his whip, and drove on. Ursula fell back on the leather cushions. Her fingers tingled a trifle. She was very tired.

Then Bob said, without turning on his seat: "Funny fellow, that Mr. Prescott, ain't he, ma'am? But a lot brighter'n I thought. Common sense, he has."

Ursula came to herself, disbelievingly. She wanted to say: "But, Bob, he was denouncing your kind! He is dangerous to you, and to all those you know, who work with their hands and have nothing!"

However, she did not say this. She could only marvel at the stupidity of the human spirit, at its natural tendency to hate its own kind. Or, she reflected grimly, perhaps each man believes himself unique and extraordinary and set apart, so that the very denunciations of himself are believed to be directed against others. "Not me. You mean my brother," he replies to all attacks.

Perhaps man's belief that he is not as others, that he is superior to his replicas, is of ominous portent to the rest of humanity, thought Ursula.

CHAPTER V

THE SPRING THAT year, Ursula always remembered, had been unusually balmy and warm, so that it was hardly past the middle of April when the lilacs bloomed.

Ursula was extremely fond of gardening, which usually calmed any slight ruffle in her mind, any vexation or trifling anxiety. It was not until this spring that she began to suspect that she was always serene because misfortune had never touched her, because emotion of any kind had never invaded her house. Years of complete tranquillity, of complacent absorption in herself and, to a lesser degree, absorption in her father, had enabled her to withstand August's death with what her friends dubiously called "remarkable fortitude."

She busied herself with planting and transplanting in the garden this year, as usual. But now, it was not "calming." The very rush and murmur and bursting of spring heightened almost unbearably the novel restlessness from which she had begun to suffer. Mysteriously, however, this very restlessness made her natural love and awareness of spring more poignant, and the scents of the earth meaningful as they had never been meaningful before. She found herself pausing, in the very act of digging about a plant, to look at the hills, warm purple and intense blue, which stood in the distance behind her house; she would often lift her eyes to the sky, to watch a transfixed cataract of radiance plunging eastward between the clouds. And as she did so, her heart would rise on a sudden wing of mingled ecstasy and pain, as if, for the first time, she had discovered profound significance in everything.

Always, a pang came with the rapture, a hunger, a yearning, a passion for something which she had never experienced. It was this which gave purport to the smallest thing: a new leaf, a bud, the sight of a tiny brown root wet in the ground, the notes of a robin at twilight, the red shadow of her fire in a darkened room, the sound of rain against the windows of her bedroom, the call of the wind in the eaves. They all urged her to see what she had never seen before.

She became conscious that, though she was not in first youth, she was still young, that she was a woman, that her flesh was warm and firm. She had taken her feminine attributes for granted, but now, as she worked in her garden, she was aware of the strong thrust of her breasts against her bodice, the bend of her thighs, the suppleness of her ankles. When at night she brushed out her long russet hair, she would swing it before her lamp, and bemusedly watch the play of dark gold and copper in its smooth and living lengths. She would study the curve of her lips, her profile, the lines of her throat. And as all this happened to her, as it had never happened when she had been a girl, a strong ecstasy would snatch at her throat.

One twilight, when she was examining the first red tips of the peonies which had pierced the wet cold earth, she stood up, stared before her, really shocked, and very still. She remembered that a kind of urgent excitement had begun to rise in her every Thursday, that it heightened on Friday, that on Saturday her restlessness became almost unendurable, that on Sunday at "teatime" she often trembled when she heard a knock on the door. But Sundays always passed placidly, with an old friend or two dropping in for a brief chat and a cup of tea, and then the evening would come, and she would be alone before her fire, with the church-bells ringing softly and plaintively through the spring twilight. How lonely she would feel then, how yearning and saddened!

"No!" she said aloud to the heliotrope sky, with a kind of quiet fierceness in her vehemence. Not to have known. And why do I not now know that I have been even more stupid by unconsciously waiting for him, that awful barbarian, that impossible and dangerous man? She went swiftly into her house, closed and locked her door, as if to shut out something grotesque and threatening. She heard her breath in the dark kitchen, and it was loud and hurried. She carried a lamp into her parlor, and it shook in her hand. She set the lamp on a table, stirred up the fire, then sat down before it, her fingers tautly laced together. She began to cry as she had not cried even when her father had died. But her tears could not wash away this huge hunger, this sadness, this loneliness, this passion, now acknowledged, to see William Prescott again.

She did not want to see him again; she did not want to think of him. And so she forced herself, deliberately, to think of the most humdrum things, to prepare for her position as schoolmistress. She brought out her sober lengths of brown wool and black cloth, she commenced to transform these lengths into proper garments for the schoolroom. She worked on them diligently. Then, one day, she remembered the rich blue silk her father had given her only a week before he died. She brought out the silk and, after long contemplation, she flung aside the brown wool and black cloth, and began to fashion a handsome gown.

She was beginning to learn not to think or to study her thoughts. Under her swift and skillful fingers, the silk began to take on shape. She remembered a dress she had seen in one of the great shopwindows on Fifth Avenue in New York. The bodice was plain and closely fitted; she added rich buttons of crystal, purchased in New York, which marched from high throat to waist in a close sparkling blaze. The skirt was molded, yet formed of rows of full ruffles to the floor; the rear was a cascade of draped full softness, so arranged that it caught the light in a mingled flow of brilliant and darker blue. She made the sleeves tight, so that they shimmered, then broke into wide ruffles at the wrist. She worked almost feverishly, sometimes forgetting her garden. When the gown had been completed, and she stood before her mirror, she saw how the color brought out the copper in her hair and made her eyes appear to be of a deep amber shade, and she saw that she was a woman, and young, and desirable.

She put away the gown firmly, wrapping it in a sheet. Immediately afterwards, she was overcome with exhaustion.

It was the next day that the "terrible" news about William Prescott burst out in thick black headlines in both the Andersburg newspapers. There were editorials, too, which, while they did not cry "robber" and "swindler," implied these things very forcefully.

The papers went into the story extensively, and imaginatively. From them, Ursula learned much of a strange industry, the lumber business. It seemed that William Prescott had started as a clerk in the offices of the benign Mr. Arnold, "a gentleman well known to most Andersburg residents, and respected and admired by all." Mr. Arnold, "always benevolent and interested in the welfare of his employees," had taken much interest in the young Mr. Prescott of ten years ago. "Almost a son," wailed *The Clarion. The Clarion* acknowledged, reluctantly, that Mr. Prescott had demonstrated a "natural ability," and therefore Mr. Arnold had taught him the ramifications of the lumber industry, to the learning of which "Mr. Prescott had applied himself with an assiduousness which might have been admirable had it not been with a sinister intent." Mr. Prescott had learned to be a lumber surveyor, and had very frequently been sent by Mr. Arnold to survey virgin forests in Michigan, and "other Western states," there to buy up options for the American Lumber Company. The forests of Pennsylvania had begun to show signs of ruthless depletion, and it was necessary to find new sources of special woods.

Only a year ago, Mr. Arnold had sent his trusted employee to Michigan to survey a certain region of forests and to discover whether the wood were suitable for our expanding railroads. Mr. Prescott had returned, had uncompromisingly reported that the wood was of no consequence, and had advised Mr. Arnold not to take options on the forests. However, in a very underhanded and reprehensible fashion, he had taken up options in his own name on ten thousand acres of the choicest forest lands in Michigan, lands which the owners wished cleared. It was "rumored" that he had paid a dollar an acre for options, "the money having been earned during his years of employment under his benefactor, Mr. Arnold."

This was an evil enough thing, but worse followed. Mr. Prescott had gone slyly to New York, and in some way had "forced" Mr. Jay Regan, the great New York financier, to see him. Apparently, he had persuaded Mr. Regan to finance him. He had shown Mr. Regan the options, and Mr. Regan, through the network of bankers extending from city to city, had verified that Mr. Prescott was indeed a man of experience. "The eminent Mr. Regan apparently overlooked the despicable flaw in this man's character, or was unaware of it. We cannot believe that a gentleman of Mr. Regan's renown would have lent himself to so base a scheme." Whether or not Mr. Regan had known, or had been unaware, he had "backed" Prescott, who, still working undercover, had set himself up as the Prescott Lumber Company, incorporated only two months ago.

The snowball of this man's evil had begun to enlarge. It seemed that Mr. Arnold had offered a certain large railroad a tremendous load of lumber. The railroad officials had practically promised to buy the wood. Suddenly, and without warning, this New York company had politely rejected the offer, and had placed its order with the Prescott Lumber Company, of which Mr. Prescott was president, and, as yet, sole officer. Moreover, Mr. Prescott had bought up several saw-mills near Andersburg, had placed large orders for coal, and had begun to hire men. Immense modern machinery was, at this writing, already arriving in Andersburg.

In the meantime, Mr. Prescott had not been idle. He had gone again to Michigan, and to other states and had, with Mr. Regan's money, bought up more options on endless forests.

He had also returned with certain selected lumbermen who were to supervise the mills. Further, he had purchased saw-mills in Michigan and in other states.

The American Lumber Company, small but prosperous, had felt this terrific blow. It had fully counted on the order for wood from the New York railroad. It was in no position to sell wood as cheaply as the Prescott Lumber Company, backed by Mr. Jay Regan, could sell it. One by one, other orders fell into the hands of the contemptible Mr. Prescott, "this man without honor or gratitude or morals." The stock of the American Lumber Company had begun to drop dangerously in the market. Dozens of local businessmen, who had invested in that company, would be almost if not entirely ruined. "The savings of a lifetime are threatened!" cried *The Clarion*. The paper implied that Mr. Prescott was not only a scoundrel, but a despoiler of widows and orphans, a betrayer of his benefactor.

This, then, was the story of William Prescott, a penniless unknown, the son of a woman who had kept a boarding-house for factory and mill workers, the man without a friend in Andersburg, the man who had succeeded by treachery, chicanery and double-dealing, the man who had been able to hoodwink his "noble employer and friend" and persuade the august Mr. Regan of New York to finance him. "Let Mr. Regan beware!" exclaimed *The Clarion*. "He has taken a viper to his bosom!"

Ursula said aloud, after she had finished reading this history of infamy: "What an unprincipled scoundrel!" She sat back in her chair, and tried to summon up intense moral indignation. Certainly, the story was bad enough. Certainly, the man had acted with cold-blooded mercilessness. Certainly, he had deceived, exploited and betrayed his employer. Even discounting the fervent righteousness of the newspapers (one of which had been financed by Mr. Arnold), the tale had in it elements of disgusting truth.

The reprehensible part of it all was that Ursula, try though she did, could feel neither revulsion nor contempt. She knew Mr. Arnold quite well, and she knew that his own hands were "soiled," to use a delicate local expression describing some of that gentleman's own chicanery and avarice. No, she had no pity for Mr. Arnold, and she doubted very much whether he had ever been a "benefactor" to anyone. If he had trusted, advanced, and paid William Prescott an excellent salary—so excellent that he had been able to save ten thousand dollars in ten years—then Mr. Prescott had been worthy of his hire, if not more. Given the same opportunity, a thousand Mr. Arnolds would have done as Mr. Prescott had done.

But, thought Ursula, if I had never met the man I should have been very indignant. She stood up, walked about the room restlessly, refusing to admit what she knew. Moment by moment, she became more agitated. She put on the kettle to brew a cup of tea for herself, and then walked to the kitchen window. It was two o'clock in the afternoon; the hills had become a deep and brilliant green under the mild spring sky. The lilac bushes in the garden frothed in white and lavender and purple near the window, and a puff of their perfume came to her as she pushed open one side of the casement. The poignant odor aroused that strong yearning which was becoming familiar to her, and she turned away and went back to the stove.

Her cat rubbed himself against her skirts. She looked down at him, and said disdainfully: "How they harp on the fact that his mother kept boarders! That seems to infuriate them more than his manipulations, the silly fools! Let a man succeed, and all the envious dogs begin to yap about his antecedents. If he becomes rich, they howl that he was once poor. If he attains fame of any kind, a dozen people who knew him in his meagre days snarl about his once-shabby clothes, and resentfully recall that he was often hungry."

I wish, she thought with exasperation, that I had never seen the man. He has upset my whole life, disordered all my ideas. I must remain home as quietly as possible until I am in control of myself again.

She heard someone strike the knocker on her door. She stood very still near the stove. The caller was undoubtedly a friend, come to discuss the horrid news with her. It was well-known that she had sold Mr. Prescott her land, and that he had visited her. Doubtless, too, old Bob had let it be known that she had talked with Mr. Prescott that day earlier in the month. The fact that no one had mentioned it to her had given her some moments of uneasiness. As her knocker sounded again, she said aloud, irritably: "I wish Papa had left me more money!"

She opened the door, and with a rush of relief saw that her caller was a young man shabbily dressed, who held a letter in his hand. He pulled off his cap, and mumbled: "A message from Mr. William Prescott at the Imperial Hotel, ma'am. He says I am to wait for an answer." He stared at her curiously.

For a moment or two, Ursula could not take the letter, and when she did so, it dropped from her trembling fingers. She bent for it swiftly, before the dull young man could reach it. Then, caution coming to her again, she raised her eyebrows, and said, in a bewildered voice: "Mr. William Prescott? Why should he write to me? I think you ought to have taken this to my lawyer, Mr. Albert Jenkins, who is taking care of the sale of my land."

Apparently, she saw with relief, her acting had deeply interested the young man. He said awkwardly: "Mr. Prescott wanted an answer, personal, ma'am. He didn't say to give this letter to no one else."

Ursula said, clearly and primly: "I certainly have no business with Mr. Prescott. I can't imagine why he should write me. My lawyer manages all my affairs." I hope I am not overdoing this, she admonished herself. She sighed loudly. "Well, if Mr. Prescott insists, I shall read the message, and you may wait for my answer."

She left the door ajar, and went into her parlor. Her fingers were thick and shaking as she tore open the envelope. There were only a few lines scrawled in a large, black and arrogant hand: "Oliver and I should like to call upon you at six o'clock this evening, on a matter of importance." There was no salutation; Mr. Prescott had signed his name at the end of his message without any of the accepted and polite conclusions.

Slowly Ursula refolded the note. She had to sit down. She held the note in her hand, and bit her lips. She really must control herself, she thought, sternly.

The young man shuffled on her doorstep, and coughed. Ursula made herself get up and go to the door. She said, coldly: "Please tell Mr. Prescott that I cannot change any of the terms agreed upon between him and Mr. Jenkins, and that if he is not satisfied I shall be glad to tell him so, myself."

"Yes, ma'am," said the messenger eagerly. He walked away, and Ursula closed the door. Would William Prescott understand? She was really trembling quite ridiculously. What if he did not understand, and did not come? What would he think of such an extraordinary message? But there was nothing else she could have done, with safety.

AT FOUR O'CLOCK, Ursula Wende was extremely incense with herself for her folly and for the ludicrous anxiety sh was experiencing. She tried to force herself to work in the gar den. But a silvery rain had begun to whirl down from the hills and was beating into the grass. A mist rose to meet it from the earth; the hills became vague dark shapes swathed in va por. Little traffic sounded from the street, as all housewive or their servants were busy in the kitchens; only once or twic did a wagon or a carriage rumble over the cobblestones. Th wind was blowing from the proper direction, and Ursula coul hear the wailing of the daily train from Pittsburgh. A fair light, like quicksilver, shone from the sky. With the rain chill had come into the spring air, and Ursula made a fres fire in her charming little parlor.

Her thoughts no longer shocked or vexed her. She sai aloud, slowly and wonderingly: "I love him." She heard he voice in the warm silence of the kitchen, and she caught he breath. This emotion was too strong, too profound, too nake and stark, to insult it with a call upon "common sense." Fo the first time, she realized that common sense might sometime be a mean and petty thing, a thing without imagination o passion, artificial compared to the poignancy of powerfu emotion.

She pushed aside her kitchen curtains; the gardens wer afloat in mist; the trees were ghosts under the polished pewte of the evening sky. Except for a dripping of the eaves, all th world lay hushed and smothered in this spectral half-ligh Ursula thought: It is not possible that he might come to lov me. Why should he? I have seen him twice, and each tim he looked at me with sharp dislike, each time we ended b quarreling in the most stupid and incredible fashion. We ha only to face each other, and something like the strongest antip athy or enmity sprang up between us.

She turned away heavily from the window. Her eye fe on the newspapers she had been reading, and she saw agai the black headlines. He had aroused in her so many alien

53

latent instincts, she could not rid herself of an immense premonition of disaster.

I wish, she thought again passionately, that I had never seen
him!

William Prescott had wrecked all the carefully nurtured serenity of her life, all the consciously guarded tranquillity. What
if these were more than a trifle precious and selfish? At least
she had been invulnerable to disorderly passions, to superficial
and bedraggled emotions.

Slowly and wearily, she went upstairs. She lighted the lamps
on her dresser, and studied her face and somberness. She spoke
to that face honestly and simply: "Even if he does not love
me—and surely, he does not, for he could never love anyone, I
am certain—I shall never forget him. If I never see him again,
I shall never forget him. I have never loved anyone but myself;
I see that now. Therefore, I have no resources, no consolations,
no possibility for healing. Yet I prefer this pain, even though
it will last all the rest of the years I have to live, to a return
to that death-in-life I knew before."

She put on the new blue gown, fastened the crystal buttons.
There was a great pounding all through her body, a desperate
elation. She opened the bottle of French scent which her father,
just before he had died, had given her for her birthday; it
had never been used before. With a new artfulness, she touched
her ears and her hair with it, and let fall a drop on a lace-
bordered handkerchief.

All at once, she was conscious of the utter stillness of her
small house. She stood and listened to the stillness; clear and
sweet, she heard the chiming of the little clock on her mantelpiece. It chimed six times. He will not come, thought Ursula.
Carefully she blew out the lamps, went down the stairs, slowly,
quietly.

She had just reached the bottom of the winding curve of
white stairs when she heard a carriage roll to a stop before
the house. Her heart jumped so violently that she pressed her
hands to her breast. Then, before she could control it, the habit of a lifetime reasserted itself: "Why am I permitting this
indiscreet thing? I ought to have had a woman friend in the
house with me. If he knocks on the door, a dozen heads will
be at windows, and I shall be ruined."

Before the knocker could be sounded, she ran to the door
in a loud rustle of silk. She flung the door open. William
Prescott's carriage stood outside, its lamps burning in the
misty street; the wet cobblestones gleamed in the yellow light
of the street-lamps. Ursula stood on the threshold, and a strong

gust of wind blew inward against her, bringing with it the almost intolerably sweet smell of the living earth.

William Prescott was alighting from the carriage, which his coachman had opened. He was carrying the child, Oliver. He carefully tucked the collar of the baby's coat around his neck, and though Ursula could not see his face, she knew at once that it wore that doting expression. Oh, it was absurd! A child was only a child, only a human being in an amorphous state. It was not a special species, an angel, a delicate and impossibly valuable creature above humanity. It carried in itself all the ugliness, viciousness, evil, good, indifference, brutishness and intelligence, or the lack of it, of all its ancestors, time out of mind——

For the first time, then, William became aware of her. The light behind her fell full upon him, his face changed instinctively, and she saw, again, that look of dull withdrawal which had so repelled her before, that suspiciousness in his small gray eyes, in the hard wariness of his mouth.

"We have come to see you," he said, in his flat and toneless voice, which told her nothing.

"So I see," she answered. Her throat was dry and stiff. She glanced at the carriage. The coachman was huddled on his high seat again. So, Mr. Prescott did not expect to stay long; he had not dismissed his carriage; he had evidently told the coachman to wait.

Mr. Prescott entered the little vestibule, and he filled it, and once more Ursula felt him there, ominous and lurking. She closed the door behind him, then led the way into her parlor. She could not speak. She stood in the center of the room, her hands clasped before her. She watched William Prescott remove his hat and coat, and toss them on her sofa. He then removed Oliver's absurdly expensive cap and coat, and revealed the child in an even more absurd little frock of wine-colored velvet and lace. While he did this, Oliver stared at Ursula gravely with his large dark eyes. He studied her for a moment, then smiled. Involuntarily, she smiled back, and took a step towards the child.

Without waiting for her to seat herself, William sat down in August's favorite chair near the fire, lifted Oliver on his knee, and looked at his hostess. He appeared less unfriendly now; his smile was almost kind. "I understood your message, of course," he said. "And the reason for it. It must be dreadful to be a lone woman at the mercy of gossips."

She was freshly surprised at his subtlety. Something tight relaxed in her. She sat down, and laughed. The laugh was more than a trifle unsteady. "Well, I must preserve my reputation, if I am to teach the young ladies of 'the best families'," she admitted.

Though she knew him to be completely unpredictable, she was, nevertheless, startled when he said: " 'The best families'!" He regarded her so penetratingly that she felt herself impaled. "Do you really consider them 'the best'? And, if so, on what evidence?"

Why was it not possible to conduct a conversation with him that had reality and pleasantness? Was he really so ignorant that he did not know how to carry on such a conversation?

That anger which always stirred her when he was near her filled Ursula again. She spoke slowly and clearly: "What is 'the best'? I should say it is to be found in people who are kind, considerate, polite, well-intentioned, with a respect for civilized amenities, with a code of honor——"

He interrupted rudely: "I agree with you. But I have never met such in this town, or anywhere else, for that matter."

She was silent, her lips pressed together.

Then he said awkwardly: "Except you, Miss Wende."

She could hardly believe that he had said this. She stammered, all her anger foolishly draining away from her: "I beg your pardon?"

He flushed. He pretended to be engrossed for a moment with straightening Oliver's frock. "I think you heard me," he replied.

Then, abruptly, he set Oliver on his small feet. "That is Miss Wende, Oliver," he said. "A very nice lady. Go to the lady, Oliver."

Ursula wanted to respond hysterically to this overture. In the leap of her elation, she wanted to act the hypocrite. She wished that she might cry out softly to Oliver, woo the man through the child, pretend delight at the thought of the baby's approach, and urge him to come to her. But she could not. The silence filled the room like a portentous presence, a waiting. The eyes of the man and the woman fixed themselves intently upon the child, who was dubiously swaying on his feet, and peeping shyly at Ursula.

A few moments ago, Oliver had smiled at her, wisely and gravely. He was not smiling now. If the child did not come to her, all was lost. It was ridiculous and nightmarish, but this man had arranged it so, this capricious and dangerous man! Ursula felt a flash of rage and humiliation.

Oliver clung to his father's knee, doubtfully studying Ursula. She saw his eyes so clearly now, intelligent and search-

ing, as if he were indeed weighing and considering her. That
was not possible; he was too young. Now that his fur cap had
been removed, his hair, like a dark soft vapor, floated about
his large round head and against his cheeks. Ursula could see
the pulsing in the little throat. She had never before considered
children vulnerable, or touching. All at once, without her volition, her heart opened painfully towards Oliver, with a kind
of sad yearning and tenderness.

Oliver dropped his arm from his father's knee. Ursula had
forgotten William Prescott. Slowly, but firmly, the child moved
towards her; his eyes had fastened eagerly on her face, and he
had a look of listening, of hearing and understanding what
she had soundlessly cried to him. Now his steps quickened,
stumbled. With one last spurt he had reached her, had flung
his small arms on her knees. She bent and caught him up swiftly, holding him so that he knelt on her lap. She pressed him
against her, and kissed his forehead, his cheeks, his hair. He
was warm and strong and small in her arms; she pressed him
tighter against her breast as if to quiet the yearning and love
and sorrow she felt for him, and the huge hunger. The child
did not move as she caressed him and murmured to him, her
lips against his cheek. Again, he appeared to be listening; his
arms were about her neck, and she felt all his trust, all his
surrender to her love.

Ursula actually started when William said, in his loud flat
voice: "Oliver!" There was a jealous intonation in the one
word, in the call. Ursula lifted her head and looked at him.
He was smiling in gratification, but he was also apparently disturbed in his own egotism. The baby clung more strongly to
her, and chuckled wisely.

Ursula gently loosened his arms. She was flattered at the
baby's affection, and deeply moved by it. But she also loved
the man who was his adopted father. She understood his jealousy and, again, she was saddened by her compassion. Here
was all he had, and it was in her arms. She set the baby down,
and said: "Go to Papa, darling." Oliver peeped up at her mischievously, and then it was as if he comprehended, for he
shouted once, gleefully, and ran to his father, throwing himself
lavishly into the man's arms, and kissing him. A subtle child,
thought Ursula, smiling; a darling, the dearest thing.

Mr. Prescott held the child to him tightly, his thin dark
hand smoothing the baby's hair tenderly. He said, smiling at
Ursula with that peculiar blend of jealousy and pleasure:
"It is plain to see that Oliver likes you, Miss Wende."

Ursula wanted to reply tartly: "That is what you wanted

to find out, isn't it?" Being a sensible woman, she only smiled.

She said, with care: "Naturally, I am flattered. I have known many children, and I have never seen one as sweet and intelligent as Oliver. You are to be congratulated, Mr. Prescott."

"Oh, I don't know," he remarked, attempting to be judicious and appraising. "I imagine most children are like Oliver." He added: "Or they would be if their parents, and other adults, did not corrupt them, and make them into images of their own cruelty and viciousness."

Ursula suddenly remembered seeing a group of the neighbors' children playing in the street that morning. Their parents were civilized and kindly people, and had certainly not taught their children any savagery. Yet the children were delightedly, and with an extreme absorbed pleasure, torturing an injured kitten they had found in the gutter, the victim of some wagon. Remembering, it was on the tip of her tongue to say with scorn: "Do not be ridiculous,, Mr. Prescott!" But again, she caught it back. Her smile, however, was a little artificial.

Then she remembered another unpleasant thing. August had once indolently observed: "Avoid the man or woman whose tenderness pours out in an extravagant flood upon children and animals. These are dangerous people. For they can justify the atrocities of war, the burning of cities, by some vague and specious explanation; they can, in silence, or with vague dissent, look upon injustice, and feel only indifference or, worse, some perverted pleasure."

As she thought this, she studied Mr. Prescott with sharp somberness. Her father was quite right. This man was not only dangerous; he was full of hatred. The doting passion and adoration with which he regarded the child in his arms confirmed her opinion. It was not Oliver he was embracing; it was his own image as a child.

He became aware that she was silent, and stiff, in her chair. He scrutinized her closely, with that uncompromising stare of his. He smiled, disagreeably, shifted Oliver to a sitting posture on his knee. He said, still stroking the child's head: "I presume you have seen the newspapers, Miss Wende?"

"Yes," she answered coldly.

Again, he scrutinized her. He could read nothing in her face. Her eyes did not avoid his. But he saw that there was no condemnation, no repulsion, in them. Curious, he leaned towards her.

"What did you think?" he asked.

This bald question affronted her. She did not know what to say.

"Would you prefer I denied the stories?" he asked.

"I should like you to deny them, if they are not true," she said, vexed.

He was obviously amused. "And if they are true?" he suggested, tentatively.

Ursula, very weary again, shrugged. "What concern is it of mine? But I see you prefer a direct answer, Mr. Prescott. I will give it: Though I am a woman, and have led a quiet life, I am not ignorant of the world. The saga of entrepreneurs is the saga of a rising America. I am not saying that such entrepreneurs are either good or bad. I know only that they seem to be a natural phenomenon, and that civilization, and the building of a nation, appear to be dependent on their inventiveness, exploitation, violence and energy. So I suppose they serve a valuable purpose."

He concentrated on her reply with extreme thoughtfulness, his head bent, his expression brooding. It might have been some abstract and novel concept which she had presented to him for his consideration. At length, to her great surprise, she saw that, in some oblique fashion, she had pleased him, for he began to smile.

"I don't suppose you really mean to flatter me," he said, in a quizzical tone. But he watched her closely. "At any rate, I can tell you this: On the surface, the newspaper tales are true." He waited. "You are not shocked? After all, what I have done doubtless affects many of your friends."

Ursula ought to have thought of half a dozen of her friends agreeable and gentle and honest people, who had been injured by this man. She thought, instead, of Mr. Albert Jenkins.

She said, with constraint: "I think that you did not particularly have it in mind to injure so many people. It was unavoidable. They were merely in the way of what you wanted." She paused. "But there was someone whom you not only needed to injure, but whom you wanted to injure, was there not?"

She had spoken as bluntly and crudely as he spoke; she saw his swift look of lowering surprise. After a long moment, he carefully set little Oliver down on the chair beside him. He took considerable time for this. Then he glanced at Ursula again, and there was an ugly exaltation in his eyes.

He said, very quietly: "Yes. You are quite right. I always knew you were an intelligent lady, Miss Wende." He stopped. "I needed, and wanted, to injure Mr. Chauncey Arnold, of the American Lumber Company. My employer. My 'benefactor'." He did not sneer, or descend to any other pettiness as he quoted the newspaper.

"You know Mr. Arnold, Miss Wende? He is a friend of yours?"

"He tried to be a friend of my father's," she replied, faintly.

He nodded. "I see. Well, you must know him. A fool, a braggart, a blusterer, a conceited, damned idiot. Worse, he is a thief on a small scale, a little mean liar and rascal. Had he been a big thief, a prodigious liar, a great scoundrel, one might almost admire him. But, of course, you do not know what I mean."

Ursula, recalling her own thoughts, on the day she had visited her land, could not answer.

Mr. Prescott became belligerently excited. His hands knotted on his knees. He regarded Ursula with inflexible attention, as if challenging her.

"When I went to work for him, over ten years ago, the American Lumber Company was about to become bankrupt. I saved it, Miss Wende. You are a lady, and it would be no use to tell you the details. I made it a flourishing concern; it flourished even during the Panic of '73. I learned all about woods, and not from Mr. Arnold, who was grossly ignorant. I learned all this by experience, and because I had a plan in mind." He stopped for a moment. "The newspapers made much of my having the ten thousand dollars with which I worked my 'betrayal' of Arnold. In ten years, he had not paid me that much. I made it by small investments, by surveying forests for other lumber companies; also, I had received a legacy of two thousand dollars from old Dr. Cowlesbury. It was all he had; he left it to me." Now his face changed, became sternly gentle; saddened. He sighed. Then he continued: "I saved the American Lumber Company, and Arnold finally was paying me nine hundred dollars a year. Nine hundred dollars! For rescuing him from bankruptcy and enabling him to buy the handsomest house in the city, and to own three carriages, and to stuff his bank accounts! And, all the time, the fool thought that I was an idiot, meek, benighted, witless, without the intelligence to know that I was being exploited."

You would never forgive that, thought Ursula.

"Yes," she said, gently, and now her eyes were golden and soft and pitying in the lamplight.

"Eh?" He did not understand. He frowned, looked down at his knotted hands. Then he laughed, shortly.

"If it will help at all, Mr. Prescott," said Ursula, "I think Mr. Arnold is a crass dolt. I have rarely been in his house, though his wife has repeatedly asked me. My father despised him, and knew what he was."

All at once, her love for him was a huge and surging thing in her. It shone like a brilliance on her face, and in her smile. He looked at her, incredulously.

"You really think all that?" he asked, and there was a hard suspicion in his voice.

She became impatient.

"I should not have said it, if I did not think it," she answered, a little hoarsely.

"Then you do not condemn me?"

His words were childish, yet to Ursula infinitely touching.

"No. But why should you care, Mr. Prescott, whether I condemn you or not?"

He stood up, very abruptly. He took a step towards her, then turned away, went to the hearth, and looked grimly at the fire. Little Oliver glanced from Ursula to his father. He sat very still on the sofa, his little legs stuck stiffly out before him. There was a foreboding silence in the room. Ursula leaned forward in her chair.

Say it! she cried to him, soundlessly. Say what I have waited all day for you to say, all the days I have known you, all the years of my life! You can say it with truth; I have seen the truth on your face. You love me; you have only to say it.

She did not know that she had stood up with swift exultation and yearning. She did not know that she had taken two steps towards him. She only knew this when he turned his dark and furious face towards her, so almost hating in his helplessness against her, that she retreated, aghast.

He said, with quiet and bitter wrath: "Why should I care? Because I came here tonight to ask you to marry me."

Ursula could not move. His extraordinary expression, the tone of his voice, terrified her. You love me, she said feebly, to herself, you love me, and you hate me because you love me. You never intended to love any woman.

"Well?" he said. "Can't you speak?"

Ursula felt for her chair, and sat down again. She turned her head towards the fire, and gazed at it blindly.

"You have a most singular way of proposing to me," she said, her voice very low.

He ignored this. "You have not answered my question. I shall understand if you refuse. But I want you to consider what I am offering you. You are not a rich woman. I am a rich man, and I shall be richer. There is nothing you might want but that I can, and will, give it to you."

Ursula turned her head to him, and regarded him steadfastly.

"Why do you want to marry me, Mr. Prescott?"

Now his expression became as she had seen it that day near her property: dull, coarse, brutal. "Because Oliver needs a mother. Because I think you will be a proper mother for my children. Because the house I am building needs a mistress." He threw the words at her insultingly, but she realized he was defending himself against what he instinctively knew, and yet would not admit, because he had never wished to love her, and hated her for it. He continued furiously: "I intended to marry some time. I intended to marry a woman like you, a lady, of good family. I had hoped to marry a woman with money. It is unfortunate that you are poor. Yet I still wish you would marry me."

Ursula turned scarlet with affront and indignation. "Mr. Prescott!" she exclaimed.

He stared at her implacably. "I am being honest with you. I am, I repeat, a rich man. I want money; a very great deal of money. I had hoped to marry it. I might have married it in New York, or Pittsburgh, or Philadelphia, eventually——"

Ursula rose, and she was astounded at her own rage.

"You still have time," she said, in umbrage and scorn. "Why do you waste your time here, with me, in this city? Why are you in this city at all?"

Suddenly he smiled. "A very intelligent question, your last. I really ought not to stay in Andersburg. My work will take me away very often, to Michigan and Illinois, and to other Western states. But I must live in Andersburg, for a very good personal reason of my own." He would stay here to triumph, to reduce the city to humbleness, and admiration of him, and fear. It was petty, thought Ursula, with a sudden loss of her anger. But it was human.

He was speaking again: "You will not be annoyed too much by my presence. Oliver will be with you. You will still have your friends."

"I don't believe that—if I marry you," said Ursula, helplessly, and wondering if she were not in some grotesque dream.

He nodded his head, and smiled his familiar, unpleasant smile. "Oh, yes you will." He waited, then asked with renewed impatience: "Well? Will you marry me?"

She walked away from him. She went to her desk. She put her hand down upon it, and leaned against it. "Yes," she whispered.

He could see her eyes from that distance, and they were wide and strained. For a long time, they looked at each other across the length of the room.

"Thank you," he said.

Then, while she stood so far away, and silent, he dressed little Oliver again. He put on his own hat and coat. He did all this swiftly, without fumbling. He lifted Oliver in his arms. He hesitated. Now he went towards the vestibule. He stopped there, turned his head over his shoulder to see Ursula.

"Shall we make it almost immediately? Say, next Monday?" he asked.

Her voice was almost inaudible: "If you wish."

He was actually leaving her. She did not move. He opened the outside door, and the sound was loud in the silence.

Then he put little Oliver down swiftly, on the step outside the door. He returned quickly to the parlor. He came rapidly across the room to Ursula. Suddenly he grasped her arms and pulled her to him. She did not resist, for she was too weak, too shaken. He bent her head and kissed her lips with so much fierceness that they were pressed against her teeth, and bruised.

"Ursula," he said. And again, as if he were moved: "Ursula."

He released her as suddenly as he had seized her. He was going away. He did not look back. He picked little Oliver up in his arms, and the door closed after him.

A few moments later she heard the carriage drive away.

The next morning, when she arose after a sleepless night, a messenger arrived with a small package for her. She opened it, to find a brilliant emerald ring resting on golden velvet. There was a small note in Prescott's handwriting: "I bought this for you a week ago, in New York."

CHAPTER VII

ONE OF THE HANDSOMEST houses in Andersburg was the home of Mr. and Mrs. Ezra Bassett. It was not a mansion, in the true sense of the word, for it contained only fourteen rooms, but it had a solid massiveness of dark-red brick and stone which made it appear larger than it really was. All Andersburg approved of it, with its mansards and turrets and little useless stone balconies, its pretty formal gardens, its flagged walks and driveways and stables and conservatory.

The townsfolk had watched the building of the house, immediately after the war, with some dubiousness, for money was "scarce," and the making of the Panic of '73 was already under way. There were trouble-makers who professed to be anxious about their deposits. Mr. Bassett eventually ended all anxieties by allowing to be published in the local papers, with no modest fanfare, the fact that many wealthy depositors from nearby communities, and even from Pittsburgh, were now doing business with him. Mr. Bassett was indeed a shrewd and expert banker; he had an uncanny ability whereby he was occasionally able to purchase apparently slow or obscure stocks, of which few had ever heard and, within a year or two, have the satisfaction of seeing them boom preposterously, with happy results for all.

Mr. Bassett had his sources of information, which he never divulged. Smiling, short, fat, and full of jokes, he could keep his own counsel while maintaining an outward aspect of open-hearted joviality and candor. Not even his wife knew anything about his affairs, but by some process of osmosis she had acquired her husband's hard and hidden shrewdness, and much of a banker's mentality. None of her friends felt this, for she was much like her spouse: sweet-tempered, discreet, forthright about unimportant matters, hospitable, and sympathetic. Like Mr. Bassett, she had a short round plumpness all dimples and rosiness, a pair of steady blue eyes, a friendly smile, and an air of sympathy. Like all good ladies, she was an excellent gossip, but she never repeated, not even by insinuation, anything which might antagonize a depositor or investor. However, compared with Mrs. Bassett, the two newspapers of Andersburg were very poor vendors of news, indeed.

Mrs. Bassett had a nose for news. When she received a little note from her dear friend, Ursula Wende, asking for a "quiet hour of tea and conversation, alone," she "smelled" something excessively important, and eagerly sent off, by messenger, a cordial invitation for that very afternoon. It was no secret in town that that frightful and odious Mr. Prescott had paid Ursula two visits, and while it was virtuously admitted that this was doubtless because Mr. Prescott had business with the young lady, there was still some delicious if rigorous speculation.

In the meantime, Mrs. Bassett, thoroughly enjoying the speculations and the condemnations and all the innuendoes, added nothing to the scandal, though her friends had wondered if she had had any "news." Mrs. Bassett shook her head regretfully. If there really was anything, she promised, she would not refrain from divulging it. When Mrs. Bassett received Ursula's note, then, she was extremely excited, and announced to a number of friends that she might have something to tell them the next day. Her manner was mysterious and fateful, and her friends received the impression that the news would be very exciting, indeed.

Every lace curtain on Englewood Street was discreetly and formally in place when Ursula arrived on foot at Mrs. Bassett's house. Behind every curtain was an alert and eager face. Ursula's costume, it was noticed, was very quiet, even for Ursula. She wore the black bombazine which had been her mourning garb, but her bonnet was obviously new, and very smart, formed of black velvet and bugle beads, tipped with a black ostrich feather, and tied under the chin very smartly with a black satin bow. Her light spring cloak, of black broadcloth, was also new, and very chic, heavily embroidered at the border by Ursula's own clever hands, and fastened with black jet buttons ringed with crystal. She moved, quietly yet swiftly, up the stone steps of Mrs. Bassett's house, and it is truly a comment on the exquisite powers of perception on her watchers' part that not a detail of Ursula's costume went unnoticed. Nor was it unobserved that Ursula was indeed very pale and subdued, her mouth troubled, her head slightly bent.

The door closed behind Ursula. The whole street heard it. There was not a lady who did not ardently wish that she might be present at the interview. But one must wait. In the meantime, the ladies speculated excitedly among themselves.

Mrs. Bassett received her guest with the gravity and formality befitting the occasion. The drawing-room had been thrown open, though Mrs. Bassett was accustomed to hold her teas in the small cosy morning-room in the rear of the house. Now a low fire sparkled on the marble hearth, and glinted on the silver and china of the small tea-table. The draperies had been partially drawn, not only to exclude the sun which might fade the carpets, but also to lend to the room an air of solemnity. This might have been the hour for the reading of a significant will or the setting for some somber discussion about intimate family matters, too doomful for a less elaborate atmosphere. The wax flowers were dim shapes under the dull gleam of the glass dome on the great walnut table in the center of the room; in the half-light, the red plush of the enormous sofas and chairs became funereal. Though the air was soft and mild outside, a chill lurked here, hung down from the high white ceiling, swathed the red damask walls, like a cold vapor inhabiting some vault.

Mrs. Bassett, a cheery little person ordinarily given to bright colors, ruffles, fichus, sashes and bangles, had dressed herself to add weight to this hour. She, too, wore black, her best silk, bought for the funeral of her husband's brother hardly six months ago. Even the frills were black, unrelieved by a sparkle of jet or crystal. She was not given to caps, but today she wore a cap on her graying curly brown hair, a cap as punctilious and grave as her gown, a dignified creation of lace and black ribbons.

Ursula, who had indeed been troubled and subdued before her entrance into this room, gave one quick look about, glanced at her hostess, and immediately had difficulty in keeping down the corners of her lips. It was fortunate that Mrs. Bassett did not see the dancing in her visitor's eyes; her own were downcast with majestic sorrow. While the maid took away her cloak, Ursula had a moment or two in which to compose herself. She sat down at a little distance from Mrs. Bassett, who had already murmured greetings.

Good heavens, thought Ursula. One would think there was a body about. She understood very well the reason for all this fatefulness and ponderous atmosphere; she understood Mrs. Bassett's black gown and lace cap, and irritation mingled with her amusement. But, with humor, she saw that if this was her own hour, it was also Mrs. Bassett's, and she had too much kindness to want to destroy the imposing climate of this room. Her irritation vanished; she even entered into the

spirit of this play, folded her hands over each other on he
lap, and even bowed her head a trifle. Sitting thus, her sligh
figure, draped in black, took on a helplesss and piteous attitude.

A little silence fell on the room, broken only by the sobe
crackle of the fire. Ursula mischievously refused to speak firs
so that at length Mrs. Bassett raised her full blue eyes and fixe
them upon her guest.

"Dear Ursula," she murmured, mournfully, "you do no
seem at all well. So very pale, my dear. Only this morning
had a premonition that all was not well with you, and whe
your note arrived, I was certain of it."

Ursula wanted to say, briskly: "Nonsense, dear Jemima
Don't be a fool." But, of course, she murmured in reply
"Dearest friend, I have need of your help. I could think o
no one else but you, for have you not been a sister to me fo
many years?" By these words, she not only followed Mrs
Bassett's sorrowful lead, but tactfully overlooked the twelv
years' difference in their ages. Mrs. Bassett, warmed by botl
these graciousnesses, smiled at Ursula tenderly.

"Indeed, darling Ursula, I should have been most grieve
had you solicited the aid of any other but myself." Her voic
melted yearningly as she spoke, but her eyes gleamed in th
dusk, and she leaned forward towards her visitor as if to clasp
her to her plump bosom. "To whose heart but mine could yo
have come in your—your hour of need?"

Ursula bit her lips severely. She bowed her head even more
and sighed.

"You know my orphan state," she said, with sadness. "M
unprotected condition."

Mrs. Bassett clasped her hands together passionately; the
were plump, white little hands, well-tended, but ringless toda
except for her massive wedding-band.

"Ah!" she exclaimed, "have I not thought of this many times
my poor dear friend! I have often reproached myself tha
I have not offered you shelter under—under my wing, in m
own home, but I knew your pride——"

Oh, dear God, thought Ursula, quite hard-heartedly. Sh
managed to utter a sound that could pass for a dry sob; sh
also managed to touch her eyes with the corner of a whit
handkerchief.

She sighed again, to cover her thoughts. "Pride," she admit
ted, "often has its penalties. But it is a fortress against weak
ness, dear Jemima."

Mrs. Bassett, who had begun to suffer some consternatio

over her recent hasty words, and who had visions of a guilty Ursula seeking refuge in the immaculate Bassett ménage, drew a deep breath of relief.

"You were never weak, dearest Ursula," she said, her voice shaking after so narrow an escape from disaster. "You were always so strong and composed, so independent——"

"Nevertheless," breathed Ursula, "I have come to you for help, on this occasion. Who is there, but you, darling friend, to announce my approaching marriage?"

"Your——" began Mrs. Bassett. She sat upright with a loud creak of stays, and her round full face was a white glare in the dimness.

Ursula nodded heavily. "Yes, my marriage. You see, my dear, I have engaged myself to Mr. William Prescott. The name is familiar to you? Hardly, I am afraid."

Mrs. Bassett could not speak. She had not known what she had expected Ursula to say. She had been half-prepared for some confession of an indiscreet but essentially innocent nature; she had thought that because of her behavior Ursula had been notified by the head schoolmistress that her services would not be required in the autumn, and that Ursula was coming to her today to beg for her intercession. Mrs. Bassett had been prepared to listen with stern sympathy, to administer an elder-sisterly lecture of some length, to offer some uncompromising advice, and then rid herself of Ursula in order to satisfy the intense curiosity of her waiting friends.

Mrs. Bassett's head whirled. Not only was Ursula not confessing some outrageous conduct, and imploring help and shelter, but she had uttered completely incredible words. She had actually announced an approaching marriage with a man whose nefarious machinations were rumored to have made him one of the potentially richest men in Andersburg, if not *the* richest, if one were to credit febrile speculation!

She stammered feebly: "You—you said Mr. William Prescott, Ursula?"

Ursula was enjoying herself more and more, but she merely allowed herself a dolorous nod, and dropped her head even lower on her breast.

"Yes," she whispered, "he proposed to me two days ago. I know I ought to have referred him to you, dearest Jemima, as my closest friend, and to Ezra, as your husband."

Again, Mrs. Bassett could not speak.

Ursula went on in a deliberately pleading voice: "Of course, you do not know of Mr. William Prescott, Jemima, or, at least, you have not met him. There have been some completely unfounded and libelous statements about him in the public press, but you, with your love for truth, would not read such things. I assure you, dear Jemima," she went on, allowing her tone to rise, "that Mr. Prescott has been cruelly maligned! I know him well; he is the best and worthiest of men, and he tells me he is quite rich, though, naturally, I am not concerned with that."

Oh dear, she reprimanded herself, I am really behaving and speaking very extravagantly. This is a little too thick, for even Jemima to swallow.

It was not "too thick." Mrs. Bassett swallowed it all in one huge gulp. Moreover, her thoughts were beginning to form some pattern out of the chaos. Very clearly, she remembered her husband's bitter comments on Mr. Prescott. Ezra had denounced the gentleman as a rogue and a thief and an utter blackguard. But he had been less censorious about Mr. Prescott's crimes than he had been about Mr. Prescott's failure to do business at his bank.

"He, an ignoramus, a dolt, might have had the decency to respect my advice, which is always waiting to be of assistance to anyone who requires it, and he—we—I mean, Jemima, we might have turned a pretty penny—but an honest one, you understand—together," Mr. Bassett had said.

Mrs. Bassett stared feverishly at Ursula. Ursula was about to marry this man. And Ursula was not one to forget her friends, her protectors against a cruel world. Ursula would have influence with her husband-to-be—dear, dearest Ursula! Mrs. Bassett gulped loudly in the silence. Her voice came, shaken, with an attempt at loving severity:

"It was indeed imprudent of you, my dearest, not to have sent the—the gentleman to your friends, before accepting his proposal. But how imprudent!" Then, frightened that she might have affronted Ursula even a little, she stammered: "But it must all have been so very sudden, and how very trying, for you!" She clasped her hands together and rolled her eyes effectively.

Her eyes filled with tears. She rose with a rapid crackle of skirts, rushed over to Ursula, dropped on plump knees beside her, and drew the young woman's head to her bosom, all in one fervent motion quite astonishing in one of Mrs. Bassett's avoirdupois. Ursula allowed herself to be embraced; she even managed a tear or two. Over and over, she begged her darling friend's forgiveness, and meekly asked her help. Mrs. Bassett kissed her in a quite delirious transport.

"You are breaking my heart, my dearest!" cried Mrs. Bassett.

"All is forgiven!" She wiped Ursula's eyes with her own kerchief, then rocked her in her arms. "We shall never speak of it again; it is gone, forgotten! What a naughty rogue that Mr. Prescott of yours is, indeed, to have stolen so quietly behind our backs, and to have robbed us of our treasure! And how precipitous, and sudden——"

"Yes," sighed Ursula, humbly. "I can hardly believe it, myself. We have met but a few times. But we understood each other at once."

"How could he have failed to be enraptured with you, dear," said Mrs. Bassett, ardently, seeing impossible beauty in Ursula now. "One can understand his recklessness, in proposing so soon. And, of course, no one really believes in the stories about him. It is all envy, and jealousy, and other unChristian emotions." She sat back on her heels, and gazed on Ursula, enchanted.

It was then that Ursula revealed her ring, the great emerald which she had turned in towards her palm after removing her glove. She displayed it artlessly. Mrs. Bassett caught her breath, seized Ursula's hand, and with unChristian emotions of her own she turned the ring about, to catch the faint light in the room, which, though feeble, could not dim the deep-green sparkle and sea-colored glow. Never had Mrs. Bassett seen such a gem before! Never had it been possible to conceive of such a jewel! Mrs. Bassett's thoughts actually stammered: Why, it—it was a king's ransom! It was the treasure in a crown! If—of course—it was real.

She glanced up, then, at Ursula's smiling face. She still held her fingers about the ring, loath to release it, loath to believe it was genuine, but bitterly convinced that it was. She smiled with pale difficulty. "A lovely stone, my dear," she said. "It is, certainly, a——?"

"An emerald," replied Ursula, with immense indifference. "From Cartier's, in New York. I have the box." She laughed sweetly. "I do declare, the box is as handsome as the ring itself!"

Then, it was real. Cartier's lofty name was well known to Mrs. Bassett. She went back to her chair, to catch her breath, to compose herself, to control her very uncharitable emotions. She studied Ursula intently, to discover how it was that a man able to buy such a ring could ever have become enamored of her dear friend.

As from some giddy distance, Mrs. Bassett became aware that Ursula was speaking: "It is so impetuous of dear William, is it not, to insist upon our being marrried on Monday!"

"Monday!" gasped Mrs. Bassett. "This coming Monday?"

"Indeed," sighed Ursula.

Mrs. Bassett's head again went into a mad spin. Then, out of the chaos, a glorious plan rushed into her mind, a plan which would not only be magnificent for Ursula, with her poor little house, but which would, immediately and completely, fortify Mr. Bassett's position with Mr. Prescott, and put the latter gentleman forever in the debt of the amiable banker.

"My dear, dear child! This cannot be! You cannot be married with such unseemly haste! Mr. Prescott would not wish you to be placed in such embarrassment! You have only to impress this upon him, Ursula. After all, he has—will have—a high place in the society of Andersburg. You must insist, my dearest one, in being married at the home of your best and most devoted friends, at my home, and Ezra's. That will take at least two weeks to manage; the best wedding-cake, of course, Ezra's best wines——" She stopped, overcome with her own visions. She put her hands to her plump breast. "And there is the matter of your wedding dress, your trousseau—the guests, the dinner——"

Ursula, alarmed, was about to decline all this at once. She paused. She remembered William Prescott's expressions of scorn for Andersburg's "best" citizens. But now, very suddenly, she knew that he did not intend to remain the town's pariah, that it was his own full plan to establish himself firmly and with conspicuous eminence in the ranks of those who pretended to despise him, or who still genuinely despised him, and to lord it over them with grandeur. She glanced down at her ring. It was not a gift of a man who wished to live in splendid isolation, his aggrandizements a secret to himself.

Now her face was deeply troubled. She turned the ring slowly on her finger. He, William Prescott, had known that Ursula had a considerable position of her own in Andersburg society; she was a lady; she had influential friends. Mr. Prescott would not be unaware of all this; in fact, Ursula very clearly knew that he had been well-informed. Well, she attempted to chide herself, it is only human. What did I expect? What did I believe? That he wished to lurk like a hermit in the house he is building, with all windows and doors shut? How very foolish of me.

Yet, a chill, and still another, ran over her. It was absurd, but she had believed he might be superior to her friends in character, as he was superior to them in energy, imagination and ruthlessness.

Without her own conscious volition, she began to draw the

ring from her finger. Then her cold fingers halted.

She saw him, lonely, fierce, and hating, and she wanted to go to him immediately and put her arms about him, as if in protection and consolation.

"Dear Jemima, it is so very kind of you. I accept. Mr. Prescott will agree, with gratitude, I know. If I could send him a note at once——"

Mrs. Bassett became wildly animated. "At once, my love! At once!" she cried. She clapped her hands together, and stared at Ursula. "And, dearest one! It would never do for you to remain alone in your house, now! A companion must be found for you. I know the very lady—Mrs. Templeton, the widow of our late minister. I shall approach her on the subject this evening, and I know she will be delighted. Oh, Ursula, how incredible, how marvelous, all this is!"

A maid interrupted with hot tea, and Mrs. Bassett, her hands shaking with the glory of the occasion, served tea and cakes to Ursula, whom she now regarded as the most adorable female of her acquaintance, the one most esteemed and most loved. The ladies sat and drank delicately from their cups, and nibbled at the little cakes, and Mrs. Bassett's tremendous joy and delight gushed out like a small cataract. Ursula listened, in pale and smiling silence, the great cold emerald pressed tightly in her palm. It cut her flesh.

CHAPTER VIII

THE NEXT DAY, BOTH the Andersburg newspapers carried, in a prominent position, this interesting item:

"Mr. and Mrs. Ezra Bassett have the pleasure of announcing the betrothal of Miss Ursula Wende of Englewood Road to Mr. William Prescott, who is residing temporarily at the Imperial Hotel. The marriage will take place on May 20th, at the Bassett residence. Miss Wende has chosen Mrs. Bassett as her Matron of Honor, and Miss Rose Bassett and Miss Lily Bassett as her bridesmaids.

"Miss Wende is the only daughter of the late Dr. August Wende, Ph.D., well known to all Andersburg as a scholar of extreme eminence, and instructor in English Literature at Mr. John Landsdowne's School for Young Gentlemen. Mr. Prescott has recently founded the Prescott Lumber Company in Andersburg.

"Until Mr. Prescott's mansion on Schiller Road is completed, he will continue to reside at the Imperial Hotel where, after her marriage to him, Miss Wende will also reside."

Andersburg was thrown into the utmost excitement and turmoil after this announcement. Nothing else was of any significance, or worthy of discussion, except, perhaps, that Mr. Jenkins remained away from his office for two days thereafter and returned, on the third day, with a marked pallor. Friends attempted to gain his opinion, but the usually garrulous gentleman was strangely silent.

Ursula had sent her note to William Prescott. She had also mentioned the fact that Mrs. Martin Templeton would be her companion until the day of the wedding. She felt some trepidation about this. But Mr. Prescott replied immediately:

"I consider that you have acted with extreme prudence in all matters." Ursula read this, and her mouth became somber, and just a trifle cynical. She had not been mistaken in her conjectures then. With something quite heavy in her breast, she read on: "I am leaving for New York day after tomorrow morning, and shall not return for two weeks. Thereafter, I am at the disposal of your friends."

73

The answer was accompanied by a most enormous sheaf of red roses bearing Mr. Prescott's card: "From Oliver and your ever faithful servant, William."

Mrs. Templeton, newly installed as Ursula's companion and chaperone, exclaimed ecstatically over the roses. But Ursula turned away from them, slowly tearing the card to shreds.

What did she want? She did not know. Her emotions and her actions were inexplicable, even to herself. Once she thought: He is a hypocrite. But she could not believe this.

If Andersburg had been electrified at reading the news in the morning, it had another exciting event to discuss, later in the day. For, at noon, precisely, Mr. William Prescott was observed entering Mr. Bassett's bank, the First National of Andersburg, and it was afterwards reported that Mr. Bassett had received him with the warmest expressions of regard and had personally conducted him into his private office.

Two hours later, Mr. Prescott emerged, his dark face smiling but taciturn, and Mr. Bassett accompanied him to the very door of the bank. Mr. Bassett's arm was linked cosily with Mr. Prescott's, though Mr. Prescott walked stiffly and rigidly. If Mr. Bassett felt some lack of response on the part of his visitor, this was not evident; his unctuous banker's voice held that nice blend of obsequiousness, warmth, brotherly intimacy and devotion reserved only for the most important clients. His round and rosy face was more pink than usual; his full blue eyes glowed upon Mr. Prescott with tender delight. Like Mr. Prescott, he must have been so engrossed with whatever had been told him in his inner sanctum that, unaware of the absorbed attention of a score of clerks and depositors, he rubbed his hands together after Mr. Prescott had closed the outer door behind him, and capered once, as if unable for sheer rapture to compose himself.

Mr. Bassett was besieged the next day with callers at his bank. The eager clerks observed that he received with coldness many whom he had formerly received with affection, and that others, formerly coolly treated, were escorted within, arm over shoulder. Some emerged from his office with elated faces, some deeply downcast. Among the latter was Mr. Chauncey Arnold, of the American Lumber Company. Mr. Bassett's voice, from the depths of his office, was heard to say, to the retreating back of Mr. Arnold: "And again, Chauncey, I want you to remember that the man has shown a lot of damned Christian magnanimity in all this!" Mr. Arnold did not reply. He slammed the door after him, and his complexion was gray and ashen.

What had transpired in that office that day was not to become public property until just before the marriage of Mr. Prescott and Miss Wende. In the meantime, the town simmered.

The late afternoon before Mr. Prescott went to New York, Ursula received a note from him. Since the announcement of their betrothal, he had not attempted to see her, and this, while it obscurely relieved her, had disturbed her. His note read simply: "It is my wish that you become more accustomed to little Oliver, so that when we are married he may not feel strange with you. So, by your leave, I am sending him, with his nursemaid, Lucy Jones, to remain with you at your home until I return in a few days."

Ursula was both dismayed and chagrined at this note. Her first impulse was to send a prompt message that this would not do at all, that she had a small house, and had acquired a chaperone. Moreover, she resented this high-handed method of burdening her without consulting her wishes.

I am certainly bewitched, she sighed to herself. She wrote a note in which she tried to express pleasure at Mr. Prescott's arrangement. She sent off the note by messenger. Mr. Prescott's carriage, containing Lucy and Oliver, arrived promptly. Ursula received them with graciousness, and installed them in August's bedroom, where there was a couch as well as a bed.

Mrs. Templeton, a tall, spare, meek-faced woman, childless and lonely, was quite delighted at this invasion. It was just what dear Ursula needed, and it would be so good for this darling of a child, whom Mrs. Templeton, though an austere minister's widow, could not help but regard with fascination as a creature personifying wealth and power. She busied herself carrying in fresh linens and blankets to the pretty if sulky Lucy, and once she even dared to embrace little Oliver. Ursula, somewhat grim, watched these proceedings from the doorway.

"You will be quite comfortable, Lucy, on this couch," prattled Mrs. Templeton, laying on the narrow sofa the linens and blankets assigned to the nursemaid. (She had already chosen the softest and most scented linen and the fluffiest blankets for the big tester bed in which August had slept and died and in which, it was now taken for granted by Mrs. Templeton, Oliver would sleep.) "The darling baby will so enjoy this bed," said Mrs. Templeton with an air of sprightliness.

Lucy was silent. She had removed her bonnet and shawl, and her pretty yellow ringlets fell to her shoulders. She was undressing Oliver, who was surveying all this with intense solemnity. Lucy gave the couch a brief and indignant glance, but did not speak. Lucy was a full-sized girl; the couch had not been meant for prolonged sleep, being hardly more than five feet three inches long, while its width would not permit of much turning. It was adequate for a child; certainly not for an adult. Ursula, speaking for the first time, moved quietly into the room.

"Lucy," she said to Mrs. Templeton, "cannot possibly sleep on that couch. She will occupy my father's bed. The baby will have the couch."

Mrs. Templeton straightened up from the bed, which she was tenderly making for Oliver. She looked at Ursula with pale eyes that protruded with astonishment. "But Ursula," she protested faintly, "the little one——"

"The little one will be comfortable on the couch. He is very small," said Ursula, firmly.

"But—but he is Mr. Prescott's child," stammered Mrs. Templeton.

"And Lucy is a young woman whose comfort is very important if she is to do her tasks competently," replied Ursula. Her mouth drew together in a thin line. "Bertha," she continued, still gazing at Mrs. Templeton with that hard look, "a full-grown human being is more important than a child."

Mrs. Templeton was speechless. Her thin worn hands fluttered impotently. Lucy hid a discreet smile behind Oliver's head. Little Oliver, sensing something exciting, bounced on Lucy's knee, chirped and beamed. In spite of her annoyance, Ursula could not help smiling at him. She went across the room, picked up the child, and kissed him with sincere heartiness. Lucy looked on with appreciation. She had been prepared to hate Ursula, as she hated her employer, but now she looked at Ursula as if in speculation and surprise.

"I'll be quite suited on the couch, ma'am," she ventured.

"Nonsense, Lucy," said Ursula, gently pinching Oliver's cheek. "You know you won't. And why should you be uncomfortable? Why should anyone be uncomfortable for anybody, especially when it isn't necessary?" She returned the child to Lucy.

Lucy became uneasy. But before she could protest again, Mrs. Templeton found her voice, and it came forth in a wavering and indignant squeak: "I think you are forgetting, Ursula, that the child is—is the son of Mr. Prescott, while this young woman is—is——"

"A servant?" interrupted Ursula, tranquilly. She looked at Mrs. Templeton, and her eyes were a chill amber. "Does not a servant have flesh and bones that would protest if laid on a cot fit for a child? Is not a servant a human being?"

Mrs. Templeton's wits swirled together in confusion. She could not understand. She was a good Christian woman, but everyone knew that servants should be satisfied with the most meagre of accommodations, and the poorest of food, and should be content with the lot which God had ordained for them. Ursula was certainly not behaving in a proper and Christian manner.

She said, almost weeping: "I think you are forgetting, Ursula, that my late dear husband was a minister, and that for years I was his wife, in the parsonage——" She gulped, then stammered on: "I think I might be considered an authority on Christian behavior."

"You might, dear Bertha, I admit," said Ursula. "But in this case you are not demonstrating your knowledge."

Mrs. Templeton was dumbfounded. Ursula studied the couch critically. "We can push a chair or two against it," she observed, "so that the baby won't fall off."

Lucy was alarmed. "Mr. Prescott would not like it," she muttered.

Mrs. Templeton found her voice: "He certainly would not!" she cried. A dark unhealthy flush appeared on her lean and sunken cheeks. "He would be outraged, and with good reason! Whoever heard of——"

"Mr. Prescott," interposed Ursula, tartly, "does not live in this house. It is mine. He did not consult me about the sleeping arrangements. As mistress here, I shall insist on making what arrangements I deem most satisfactory to everyone." In spite of her outward calm, her heart was beating with angry vigor.

Mrs. Templeton, struggling for dignity, but with the dark color still high on her cheeks, went out of the room with a rustle. Ursula smiled slightly. She sat down in an old rocking-chair, and with a pleasant expression surveyed Lucy.

"Oliver seems to flourish in your care," she said, kindly. "I hope it is your intention, Lucy, to remain with him after I marry Mr. Prescott."

Lucy stared at her with shy devotion. All the sulkiness had disappeared from her pretty, common face. "Oh, yes, ma'am! I did hope you would have me!"

Ursula gave her a quizzical smile. "Why not? I know nothing about children, Lucy, and I am not overly fond of them. In fact, I find them quite tiresome, and their company tedious. I have friends who profess to be fascinated by what they call a child's 'mind,' but I suspect they are only being affected, and want others to believe that they are exceptionally discerning people."

She waited. Lucy did not comment. Her fair brows had drawn themselves together in a puzzled fashion. She smoothed Oliver's tumbled hair absently.

"Have you not discovered that those who are elaborately devoted to children are generally hard-hearted and suspicious and without real character?" asked Ursula.

Lucy colored. She straightened Oliver's frock. "Well, now, ma'am, I never thought of it before, but it's true," she replied, with sudden impulsiveness. "Not that I don't like babies, Miss Wende," she continued earnestly. "I do. In their proper place. And it's cruel to the children, ma'am, to push them out of their proper place. They don't understand. So it makes them mean and bad-tempered, and they don't know what it's all about, and no one denying them anything——" She caught her breath, then burst out quickly: "It's wrong for the children, ma'am! They've got to be taught their place, and how to control themselves, so that people won't hate them, as they always hate children who've always had their way, and no discipline!" She turned crimson.

Now she became frightened at what she had said. She hugged Oliver against her plump young breast, and stared at Ursula pleadingly. "But Oliver's not spoiled," she stammered.

Ursula sat back in her chair, her face grave. "No, I see he is not," she murmured. Then she added: "Lucy, you know I am about to marry Mr. Prescott. You may trust me, my dear. Does Mr. Prescott try to spoil Oliver?"

Lucy hesitated. She was close to tears. "Well, yes, ma'am, he does. Very bad. If it was any other baby but Oliver, Oliver would be ruint. Toys all over, ma'am, so you can't walk. Never a 'no' to the baby, when the master's about. Oliver must have what he wants. If he doesn't want to eat, he mustn't eat. If he doesn't want to sleep, then he must be sung to, until he sleeps, instead of being made to sleep natural. If Oliver has a cough, Oliver must never be left an instant; he must be read stories to, and played with, and dandled, instead of learnin' to bear his misery as he'll have to some day, anyway. If Oliver's naughty, then he mustn't be punished, because punishment is 'barbaric.' That's what Mr. Prescott calls it, ma'am: 'barbaric.' If Oliver tears a book, then the book must just be taken away, and his fingers mustn't be slapped, as they should. If he stamps and shouts, when crossed, then no attention must be paid. All must be pleasant, as if he hadn't stamped and shouted. You know what that does to a child, ma'am?" asked Lucy.

"I think I know," smiled Ursula. "It thwarts him, not to have his naughtiness noticed."

"Yes, ma'am," said Lucy. "It kind of sets a baby back on his heels when he isn't punished when he knows he should be punished. It makes him feel helpless, kind of. A baby wants to feel his father cares if he's naughty, and he wants to feel his daddy is a strong man, and standin' no nonsense. And if a baby don't have that—that——"

"Safety," said Ursula.

"Well, yes, ma'am. I guess you'd call it that. If he don't have that feelin' of strength in his parents, he just goes all a-twitter inside, and that makes him act up like a little frightened fiend, and he's a nuisance, and everybody hates him. They don't know he's just scared and doesn't know what's right or wrong." She paused a moment. She added quietly: "And he gets to hate everything and everybody, and his whole life is ruint."

Ursula had listened with profound and serious attention. She regarded Lucy now with respect.

Ursula said: "You've had other charges besides Oliver, Lucy?"

"Oh, yes, Miss Wende. I've been in service for six years." Her round face darkened a little, and she sighed. "I know children, ma'am. There was eight of us, and I was second eldest and brought up a whole mess of brothers and sisters. Then I worked for three years in Philadelphia, for Mrs. Enright-Dawson. You know her, ma'am?"

"I've heard of her." Ursula's attention was again caught.

Lucy sighed. "They was very rich people. They had five children. They couldn't keep a nursemaid, or a governess, or a tutor, and even the cooks kept leavin', and the butler and the chambermaids. It was the children. They had everythin' their own way, all the time; spoiled to death. Even when company came to the house, they was permitted to race around like—like hellions and such—all through the drawing-rooms, and stick out their tongues at the guests, or shout, or bully, and their ma thought it was high spirits, and then she'd get mad if the guests didn't like it, and there was the old lady, Mr. Enright-Dawson's mother, who came one Christmas, and then went home in her carriage half-way through the Christmas dinner, saying she'd never again set foot in that house until the children's ma had come to her senses. That's what she said, Miss Wende, and Mr. Enright-Dawson was so ashamed. You see, he'd try to control the children, but it was no use, and his mother walked out of the house sayin' that that's all he deserved."

Lucy continued, with evident distress: "There was Lawrence, the eldest boy, sixteen. His ma called him 'mettlesome.' But, ma'am, it wasn't that. He was just rotten spoiled, and had a bad temper, and never learned any manners, because, his ma said, he wasn't to be 'brutalized.' He wanted a horse of his own, and his pa said no, he didn't know how to treat any creature, human or animal, but his ma bought him the horse. Then he'd go a-tearin' around the country, like wild, and he didn't care what was in the way, and he rode down a little girl, a farmer's child, and killed her."

"How terrible!" said Ursula, shocked.

"Yes, Miss Wende. It was terrible. His pa was all for lettin' him suffer the consequences, but his ma came rushin' to the rescue. I don't know how it was done, but the farmer got some money, and Lawrence, against all his ma's tears, got packed off to school. I left soon after, because little Godfrey kicked me hard in the knee when I was tryin' to get him to mind, and I'd had all I could stand, anyway. So I came back home to Andersburg, and I've been with Oliver ever since Mr. Prescott 'dopted him."

During all this, Oliver had sat quietly, as if listening intently. His great dark eyes wandered from one woman to another, and when he caught a glance, he smiled gravely. Ursula looked at him.

"But Oliver has not been spoiled," she remarked.

"No, ma'am, and it's a miracle why he hasn't, everybody bein' ordered not to cross him, but to give in to him. 'I'll not have him warped,' Mr. Prescott said, when I came to work for him. 'Nobody is going to cripple this child's mind or break his will.' As if anybody with sense would want to break a baby's will, whatever that is! But in spite of everything, Oliver is good, so good, ma'am! Children can be so mean, ma'am, you've no idea," added the girl, anxiously.

"Yes, I know very well," said Ursula encouragingly.

"Well," sighed Lucy.

Oliver smiled contentedly. He gently took one of Lucy's yellow ringlets and gave it a playful tug. His eyes sparkled gleefully at her when, in mock anger, she shook a finger at him and released her ringlet. Ursula laughed. But the old sensation of impending calamity came to her, and she had the strangest thought: I ought not to marry William. What if there are other children? What will he make of them, with his perverted convictions?

"Not that Oliver's an angel," Lucy went on, oppressed by Ursula's sad face. "He's a healthy baby, and has his tempers, but you can talk to him, little as he is. You can tell him what's right and wrong. But only behind Mr. Prescott's back. He wouldn't stand for it. But I do my best."

Ursula was very moved. "You are such a good, sensible girl, Lucy!" She went on: "I do hope that you'll never leave us."

Again, Lucy's face darkened, and her soft blunt features became obstinate. "I hope I never have to, ma'am. But——"

"But what, Lucy?"

"Oh, ma'am, I shouldn't be talkin' to you as I've been doin', you about to marry Mr. Prescott and all! It's not my place." Now she was horrified.

"Lucy," said Ursula, very quietly, "I have asked you to talk to me. And why isn't it your place? What foolishness. You see, Lucy, I want to know. I remember that day when I first saw you."

At this, bright distrust leapt into Lucy's eyes, and a hard wariness. She scrutinized Ursula, her lips pursed together, her head on one side. She did not answer.

"Lucy," pleaded Ursula, "don't look at me like that. I beg of you to trust me. I know you think this conversation very extraordinary. But I must know everything possible. Won't you have faith in me?"

Lucy colored again, dropped her eyes. "Well, ma'am, it is kind of funny to be talkin' to you like this. I shouldn't be. It's impudent." She looked up swiftly, and said, with recklessness: "If you want me to talk, Miss Wende, I will, and I do trust you! I never heard of Mr. Prescott until I came back here a year ago, but I've heard talk. He comes from plain common folks, like me, and they say he hates us all." Resentment flared on her face. "I wouldn't mind if it was puttin' on airs. Poor folks who get rich always put on airs, and it makes the rest of us laugh, and we don't mind much. But Mr. Prescott don't put on airs. And he pays good money to everybody who works for him, sometimes more money than they've ever seen before. But he looks at us as if we're lower than dirt." She seemed bewildered. "Why should he hate us, ma'am? He's one of us, even if he did get rich."

Ursula rose and went to the window. The hills beyond were plum-colored in the twilight.

Lucy got to her sturdy feet. "And now, ma'am, if you don't mind, I'll go down and give Oliver his dinner. It's almost time for his bed."

CHAPTER IX

ON MAY 10TH, William Prescott returned from New York, and went immediately to the large room at the bank, which Mr. Bassett reserved for conferences. As prearranged, he found there, waiting for him, a beaming but secretive Mr. Bassett, Mr. Albert Jenkins (whose thin and ruddy face was now exceptionally pale and drawn), ex-Judge Oscar Muehller, Mr. Hazlitt Leslie, of the Leslie Carriage Company, former State Senator Kenneth Whiscomb, Dr. Eli Banks, Chauncey Arnold, and a somber recording-clerk who showed, by his expression, that he realized the immense importance of this event.

William Prescott, dressed in the latest and most elegant costume, recently purchased in New York, entered the conference room and, with one accord and quite involuntarily, every gentleman but Mr. Arnold rose with embarrassed, gloomy or respectful alacrity to greet him. He stood for a moment on the threshold and every eye studied him warily and intently, with hatred, interest, suspicion, secret contempt, or dread, according to what each man expected of this command interview.

Mr. Prescott made a most impressive figure, there on the threshold. Some hidden excitement and triumph made his face most expressive and eloquent; his small, flat gray eyes glittered. He gave out an emanation of extraordinary vitality and power, and his features, on certain occasions so dull and coarse, today were alive and mobile. Each man, looking at William, felt himself thick, clumsy, insignificant or old, sensations not inclined to warm the heart towards this alien and dangerous man.

"Gentlemen," said small, plump Mr. Bassett sonorously, with a wave of his hand in a manner suspiciously histrionic, "Mr. Prescott. Mr. Prescott, sir, I believe you know Mr. Chauncey Arnold (here William tried not to smile), Senator Whiscomb, Mr. Hazlitt Leslie, Judge Oscar Muehller, Mr. Albert Jenkins, Dr. Eli Banks."

William bowed. The other gentlemen bobbed briefly. William advanced into the room and, directed grandly by Mr. Bassett, took his seat at the banker's right hand.

The other gentlemen seated themselves. A heavy and oppressive silence fell on the company. The smoke of cigars rose from half a dozen receptacles; the spring sunlight mingled with it; in the stillness street-sounds became loud. Mr. Bassett glowed, but the glow was becoming embarrassed. Even the banker's aplomb took on a static and uneasy quality.

Mr. Bassett cleared his throat. "I have told you a great deal, gentlemen. Suppose we now allow Mr. Prescott to outline his plans for us."

He inclined his head graciously towards William, who was not in the least ill-at-ease, but had been sitting and studying the other men with a hard candor which they found disconcerting.

He spoke at once: "Mr. Bassett, apparently, has outlined much to you. Let me make a brief résumé." He let his eyes wander quickly from face to face. "Mr. Bassett held notes in the amount of $40,000 or more, money borrowed from this bank by Mr. Arnold, who had hoped to expand the American Lumber Company." He smiled faintly. "Unfortunately," he continued, "Mr. Arnold's plans did not mature. Mr. Arnold had given as collateral for the money, his controlling stock in the American Lumber Company. The stock, as it now stands, is practically worthless. I intend to complete arrangements with the bank to take over that stock so that it may not suffer an irreparable blow. You know, of course, what such a loss would mean to the soundness of the bank! And to the community. I am paying, therefore, the par value of the stock, and a premium to compensate the bank for the interest due on the loan."

The cigars still smoked idly, and the air became charged with uncertainty and perplexity. No one spoke, for fear was in the room now, and excitement. Mr. Bassett, however, smiled, inclined his head, became rosier. He coughed. Unctuously, then, he said to all the watchful faces: "I had no choice. Moreover, I thought it amazingly good of Mr. Prescott. I agreed to sell the stock to him but, first, he asked that you gentlemen be called to a meeting of directors, to hold a new election for officers. Mr. Prescott, sir," and now he turned majestically to William, "I now offer you the stock, at your figure. You will hold a majority of the stock. I congratulate you, sir. Also, I congratulate these gentlemen, whose personal investments are now secure."

Mr. Chauncey Arnold was a huge fat gentleman, whose clothing always seemed about to burst under the pressure of his bulk. His great scarlet face had turned a pasty color; his tiny black eyes fixed themselves upon William with a look of virulent hatred and despair. He did not speak. Here was the man who had destroyed him, who was about to seize control of the American Lumber Company, which he, Mr. Arnold, had incorporated, had built up with his own hands, had established as a dignified and prosperous organization. It was almost more than he could endure. This thief and rascal! There he sat now, dressed to kill, smiling darkly and easily—this contemptible wretch who had worked as a humble clerk in Arnold's office, learning gratefully, applying himself energetically, and awaiting the day when he could cut his benefactor's throat and debase him before a whole city!

Mr. Arnold turned his suffused eyes towards Bassett, and their expression was hardly less murderous than when they had looked at William Prescott. Bassett, the pink fat slug, who had betrayed him like this! Some way could have been found; some way could have been contrived so that he, Chauncey Arnold, might not have been entirely ruined. At this point, Mr. Arnold's inflamed mind became a confusion of rage, desperation and abhorrence. He had lost all power of reason. He hated everyone, from Prescott to Bassett, from Bassett to all these others, his friends and neighbors, his directors and stockholders, who, less than six months ago, had fawned upon him, and had listened weightily whenever he spoke.

Those whom he now regarded with such loathing and wretchedness were actually smiling widely, and with relief, upon the man who had degraded and destroyed him. They were leaning towards William, and every eye sparkled eagerly. Mr. Jenkins, alone, had not recovered his color, and his thin face had become a wedge of venom. He, too, had his private thoughts.

Mr. Prescott began to speak, very quietly but clearly, almost with indifference, like a schoolmaster who speaks by rote: "You have heard that I have now organized the Prescott Lumber Company. As I shall have the controlling interest in the American Lumber Company, it is my plan, with your approval as officers and sole stockholders, to merge the American Lumber Company with my Company, to issue additional shares in the amount of the American Lumber Company stock outstanding, and exchange share for share. I am sure you will see the benefit of becoming shareholders in a strong and progressive company, instead of in one both stagnant, and," he paused for an instant, "practically defunct."

A few faces changed and darkened. It was bitter to look at this man, this pariah, this "outsider," and to feel so impotent. It was worse to avoid looking at Chauncey Arnold, who sat there more acute to their senses than he had ever been before, and to pretend that he felt nothing, and had nothing more at stake than themselves, and was still one of them.

As for William Prescott, he sat there quietly enough. "Gentlemen," he said, "you have no choice." He waited. No one spoke. He spoke louder now: "I do not intend that the Prescott Lumber Company remain a picayune local concern. I expect to have branches all over the country, and the Territories, too, where lumber is cheap and abundant. I have immense orders. I am being heavily financed by—a certain New York gentleman." He was silent, as if waiting. No one spoke; there were a few quiet and portentous nods. "America is expanding enormously. The day of agricultural dominance is declining. This is the day of the city. Lumber will be needed in unbelievable quantities for all industries, and for construction. I have already bought up options on immense forests, not only in the Western states but in the Territories. I am no tyro. I know lumber. I expect to go as far as South America, for mahogany and other fine woods. There is no limit to my plans. There is no limit to what the Prescott Lumber Company can do. Gentlemen," he concluded, "you either join me in an enterprise which will make all of us wealthy, or you retain your stock in the American Lumber Company and suffer tremendous losses."

No one spoke, even now. They knew they could do nothing, would do nothing. They had decided that at once. After all, quixotic sentimentality had no place in business, not even where a friend was concerned. Everything but "soundness" and money was nonsense. All at once the air was filled with an almost wild excitement and jubilation.

William felt this, and suddenly every hard strong bone in his face became prominent with cynical acknowledgment and disgust. Here they were, all those who had despised him in his youth, had bullied him in his young manhood whenever they had encountered him in the offices of Chauncey Arnold, had ignored his existence on the streets and in other public places. And now, here they were, bestowing the respect and homage upon him which they had never bestowed on any other creature, not even on their ministers, and certainly not on their God. And just for money! All at once, he was sick of them, sick of their avarice and their cupidity, sick of their mercilessness and their smallness, sick, not only of them, but of a whole world which would gladly, even passionately, destroy all decency, all friendship—just for money!

Yet, he thought, I, too, want money, am willing to do anything to get it. But not for the reasons for which they want it, not for the mere possession of it, or even for the power of it. I want it so that I can be independent of such men, of all men, so that at no time can they hurt or injure me again. I want to be free of the whole world, locked in an invulnerable fortress, where creatures like this can never successfully attack me—or my children. Dr. Cowlesbury was right: A sensible man makes it a point to gather together as much money as possible, as soon as possible, so that he can henceforth be safe from his own kind, and can live in peace. A lion has his claws and teeth, an elephant has his strength, a fox has his cunning—to defend himself. And man must have money.

William's thoughts had wandered back to that house in the woods, and it was some moments before he became aware that there was a change in the atmosphere, disturbed and tense. He looked up quickly. Chauncey Arnold had struggled to his feet, a vast and heavy lump of shaking flesh. He was leaning his clenched fists on the table; slowly, he swung the mighty bulk of his head from one of his erstwhile friends to another, his face a dark and swollen crimson. He was like a cornered bull in chains, still full of desperate fight and violent terror. His voice also was like a bull's, roaring and clamoring:

"You will let this—this man destroy me—me, your friend and neighbor for fifty years?" He shouted this, incredulously. "You will desert me in my extremity, which he brought about? You will connive with him—you, who only a few weeks ago told me you detested him, and that you would work with me to throw him back into the gutter where he belongs?"

His small black eyes, sunken in the folds of scarlet flesh, both glared and pleaded. "Judge Muehller! Senator Whiscomb! Leslie! Jenkins! Doc Banks! You would do this to me?"

No one answered him. The sunlit room became full of a shameful silence. Every head turned aside furtively. But William Prescott looked full at his former employer and smiled.

Mr. Arnold uttered a choking sound. He put a thick finger between his cravat and his neck. Now he had turned a frightening purple. He stammered: "Can't one of you answer me? Isn't there one among you with one decent impulse left? Look at me! Dare to look at me!"

William Prescott waited. He, too, looked about the table with his slow and piercing stare.

"Well, gentlemen," he said, "Mr. Arnold is waiting for your answer."

Still, no one spoke, no one looked at Mr. Arnold. Even Albert Jenkins, though his expression was tight and vicious, did not turn to his old friend.

"My God!" cried Mr. Arnold, and he sat down suddenly, pressed his face into his clenched fists.

"Now, now, Chauncey," said Mr. Bassett uneasily, after a long moment. He coughed. "One must accept things, Chauncey. You are making matters very hard for us. What can we do? Let us be reasonable."

"Reasonable!" groaned Mr. Arnold, rocking in his chair.

"Realistic," said Mr. Bassett, his pinkness fading. "What can we do? There are your notes for $40,000. Have you the money, Chauncey? Can you raise $40,000? If you can, then I swear that I will deliver the notes to you, and at once."

Mr. Arnold lifted his head. His huge face had crumpled. "You know I can't raise the money, Ezra. You know that I borrowed it to expand my company, on the strength of the orders from the railroads, which had been practically promised me, and on which I had counted. Until this villain robbed me of them, with his lies and his schemings. Robbed me! I—I expanded. Now, well, you know what my balance is——"

He beat his fists on the table. "But you can all help me out of this. You know my reputation. You know what I've been able to accomplish. You've had faith in me before. All of you. I can get out of this—if you'll help me. I had a good sound going concern, until I was robbed. There isn't one of you who can't lend me part of this money. The whole six of you—you can lend me the $40,000 between you." His breath appeared to be shut off, and he struggled to regain it. "You can help me. Why won't you help me?"

He waited. His despair was abject; he spread his hands out to each man in turn, and in turn, each man looked away. He turned deadly pale, and was silent.

Mr. Bassett spoke tremulously, for he was not immune to conscience: "Chauncey, suppose you let Mr. Prescott speak. Then you'll see that everything isn't lost." He looked at William. "Speak, Mr. Prescott. We are waiting."

"Gladly," said William. "Gentlemen, Mr. Bassett has said that I have called this meeting for an election of officers for my new company. We have had a long consultation a little while ago. I intend to be president of the Prescott Lumber Company. For vice-president, I suggest Mr. Leslie; for secretary, Judge Muehller; for treasurer, Senator Whiscomb. For my

board of directors, Mr. Bassett, Mr. Jenkins, Senator Whiscomb, Dr. Banks, Mr Leslie." He paused. Every man listened
breathlessly, suddenly alert and electrified. William went on:
"And Mr. Chauncey Arnold, for executive vice-president. At a
salary of three thousand dollars a year."

Again, there was a tense silence in the room. Then, all
at once, each man found his voice and shouted his enthusiastic
acclamation. Everyone stood up, full of excitement, except
Mr. Arnold, who sat in his chair and regarded William with
profound hatred and misery.

He watched them surround his former employee. He watched
them shake William's hand, throw their arms over his shoulder.
He saw them forgetting him, abandoning him, ignoring him,
thrusting his embarrassing presence from their awareness—that
presence which had foolishly attempted to recall them to honor
and the obligations of friendship. He was a gross man, and
he had forgotten, in his own climb to success, what little
honor and sense of obligation he had ever possessed.

William's part in this no longer seemed of much importance.
What was important was the desertion of those who had been
his friends, who could repudiate him for a mere adventurer
and thief and scoundrel—for the sake of money.

He had lost more than his company, his prestige and his
money. He had lost what had made his whole existence worth-
while. He had lost the warmth of his home, his sense of security,
his dignity as a man. To these men he was less than a stranger.
Because of money. Because money was more to them than
he was. More to them, he thought incoherently, as it would
have been more to me.

He stood up, trembling violently. The scraping of his chair,
the shuffle of his feet, finally drew their unwilling attention.
They surrounded William, but they looked at Chauncey Arnold,
or, rather, they looked in his general direction with mingled
defiance and sheepishness. Some faces expressed annoyance
with him because he still had the power to embarrass and shame
them.

He stared steadfastly at William Prescott, and William
Prescott stared as directly at him. He said: "Three thousand
dollars. You dare to offer me—anything, you rascal and liar
and blackguard. I can give you the only answer possible—no.
No, not even if I starve."

"Now, Chauncey," said Bassett, with discomfort.

But Chauncey Arnold did not look at the banker. He looked
only at William, who no longer smiled, and whose eyes were
narrowed and still.

"Swine," said Mr. Arnold, quietly.

He turned away. He looked about the room slowly, as if sudden disorientation had overpowered him. He shook his head from side to side in immense despair. Then, without another word, he shuffled slowly and ponderously from the room.

That night, while Mr. Bassett entertained the new officers and directors of the Prescott Lumber Company at his home, and the wine was poured again and again into Mrs. Bassett's best crystal glasses, and the sound of congratulation, genial laughter and warm voices filled the house, Mr. Arnold suffered a severe heart-attack. His wife did not call the old family physician and friend, Dr. Banks. She was compelled to call a comparative stranger. Dr. Banks was very busy that evening. He was one of the guests of Mr. Bassett, and he sat beside William Prescott and told the younger man some of his choicer jokes.

It was almost impossible for William to unbend to anyone, except, perhaps, to children, of whom he was not instinctively afraid. So, though he attempted to smile easily, his eyes remained wary and morose, suspicious and watchful. He tried to reply to sallies and congratulations with some graciousness, some offhand remark, but his throat felt hard and stiff, and his facial muscles ached with the fixed smile he had imposed upon them. Once he thought: I hate them. There was a time when I considered them superior to the cattle with whom I was forced to associate when a child. Now I know they are superior only in cunning and in greed and ruthlessness. Bassett is no different from Gruber, who cheated my mother and hoarded his wages; Jenkins is a Carmer who pretended to fall down our front stairs, and threatened my mother until she gave him twenty-five dollars. Banks, that suave, medical charlatan, is brother to the mean poverty-stricken rascal who sent my mother a huge bill after my father's last illness, knowing she partially owned the wretched house in which we lived, and in which my father had sunk a whole life's saving. This Senator Whiscomb is the twin of the political thief, termed "inspector," who forced my widowed mother to give him fifteen dollars, lest he report the "dangerous drains" in our house. Hazlitt Leslie is kin to the little murderous scoundrel who employed my father, and who paid my father nothing when he lost his arm in the saw-mill, and who let him die of the blood-poisoning. Oh yes, they have the law with them! They are all fine Christian gentlemen, these around this table! But they are one with the little liars and cheats and frauds who made our lives so fright-ful, when I was a child! Well, at least those hungry wretches had some justification, for they were half-starved also. These men here tonight have no excuse.

A huge hatred for the conniving, treacherous and cruel human race pervaded him, so that he felt sick and shaken. His hand clenched about the wine glass he held; his face darkened and became fierce and ugly. And then he thought of Ursula, so cool, so gentle, so sensible and so kind, and of Oliver, who was a child and could do him no harm! He relaxed; he could turn to Dr. Banks, and pretend to be amused at the particularly luscious joke (which he had not heard) which the doctor had been telling him.

Dr. Eli Banks was the typical "society doctor," urbane, soft-spoken, rich of tone and solicitous in manner. He was careful to carry out his typicalness in his very exterior, for he was not only a tall, broad man of forty-five, clad in discreet black broadcloth, and wearing a black silk cravat nicely finished with a pearl pin, but he wore a neat thick brown beard, and an expression of kind thoughtfulness excellently calculated to soothe the sensibilities of hysterical ladies who had recently discovered that their husbands were bored with them.

Judge Oscar Muehller (who had served only one term, for the obvious reason that he was a man without mercy or kind-ness or understanding) had the face of a saint and an ascetic, with a tall pure brow, a pair of sweet and pensive hazel eyes, and a reflectively tender mouth. He had a soft and meditative voice, and could never be inveigled into a malicious remark about another.

Mr. Hazlitt Leslie, owner of the Leslie Carriage Company, was also the owner of so ruddy and genial a face, so loud and merry a laugh, so gay an eye, and was so ready with a story, a fond remark to a friend, or a hearty handclasp, that no party of any consequence was considered complete without his twinkling presence. His fund of stories was held in even higher esteem than that of Dr. Banks. A big square man of forty-four, he was a delight to the ladies.

Former Senator Kenneth Whiscomb did not resemble a politician. At first glance, overlooking the expensive untidiness of his clothing, one would have thought him a grocer. He was hardly taller than the rosy Mr. Bassett, and he had a floury but vigorous look, and was all bustle, gruffness and "forth-right" opinions. He had not run for a second term, for the simple reason that he had not considered it expedient. His enemies had mentioned to him, discreetly, that there was a little matter of a contract for state roads, given to a friend, which roads had later been discovered to be constructed of very inferior materials.

William Prescott was not ignorant of the character of these, his new officers and directors. But they were of the "best families," and William Prescott had use for such families. They laughed and joked with him; they slapped him on the shoulder; they chided him affectionately as "a rare rascal," they stared at him admiringly, even the now-reconciled Mr. Jenkins. Yet, well he knew, they despised him while they respected him; they thought him a very clever fellow, and forgot the friend they had betrayed for the opportunity to make money with him.

They had raged at him among themselves, and they had cursed him—until today. They had delivered themselves of opinions about him—until today. They had been his indignant and loquacious enemies—until today. They wished, however, that, in appearance and manner, he were not quite such a "queer fellow." It would be easier to accept him, they reflected, had he more resembled themselves. There was an etiquette in finance; he had not learned that etiquette.

Moreover, he regarded them oddly and keenly when they spoke, and his smile was dim and unpleasant. He did not lean back negligently in his chair, or exchange jokes. He sat upright, and very rigidly, and listened. They were suspicious of men who talked little, listened much, and watched everything. All this was quite correct, of course, for a new captain of industry. But he ought not to be so obvious about it, was the general opinion.

At nine o'clock he stood up and announced abruptly that he must go. And he went, without another word, without glancing back once, without the formality of a hearty good-bye. He left them, and for a long time afterwards they only sat and smoked, and each man avoided his neighbor's eye.

CHAPTER X

MRS. TEMPLETON had gone to bed, claiming a severe headache. She had been very dignified with Ursula, these last few days, and very stately, because of Lucy and Oliver. She had pointedly refrained from giving orders or suggestions to the nursemaid; she had, except when momentarily alone with the baby, pretended he did not exist. If Lucy asked her for advice, Mrs. Templeton, slightly raising her thin voice, would reply that "Miss Wende, I am sure, is more competent to answer these questions than I, who have borne three children—though God, in His infinite wisdom, saw fit to take them from me." Under other circumstances, Ursula would have considered this amusing. But she was too racked with her own uncertainties and premonitions to be amused now.

Ursula had, during these days, carefully searched for evidences of the "spoiling" of Oliver. But the young child serenely displayed consistent good temper, cheerful obedience and the rudiments of a sense of humor. An average child, subjected to such lack of discipline, to such wild and doting lack of restraint, would end up as an animal, demanding, greedy and irresponsible. Hence Ursula's uneasiness and fear. Oliver was not like other children.

She thought of possible coming children with intensity, and at one time she hoped, with real fervor, that she would have none. She was not fond of them; she was indifferent to them. Nevertheless, if she should have them she would owe them a duty, and that duty consisted in bringing them up to be self-controlled, civilized and mature men and women, full of responsibility towards their fellow creatures, and well-trained to make as little nuisance of themselves as possible.

During the first day or two, Oliver talked of "Papa" somewhat uneasily, and searched for William. Later, he seemed to forget. This will never do, thought Ursula. So she spoke of William; a child forgot so quickly, and Ursula had no intention of letting William be forgotten by Oliver.

Lucy, in the meantime, had become Ursula's most devoted friend and admirer. The two young women found much pleasure in each other's company. Lucy had such common sense, such a blunt awareness of reality. She was in love with the coachman, John Shaeffer, who came of an Amish family. John was no longer Amish, but he retained, in his character and in his manners and sober conversation, much of the esteemed traits of his people. Each day, he brought the carriage around to give the three women, and Oliver, their airing. He and Lucy intended to be married in the late summer, as soon as Lucy had provided, from her wages, the minimum supply of linens. Ursula, investigating the big trunks and shelves, which her prudent German mother had filled with excellent sheets, towels, pillow-cases, and tablecloths to be bequeathed to children, grandchildren, and so on *ad infinitum*, discovered many articles which could be spared for Lucy.

Everything, therefore, appeared most propitious, and Ursula, when alone in the evenings, could have uninterrupted hours in which to think of William Prescott. Most of these hours could be, and were, very exciting. But many of them had their pain, their premonitions, their uncertainties, especially on a night like this, full of rushing rain, crying wind in the eaves, and closed shutters.

Half-past nine struck, tinkling softly against the background of vigorous spring wind and rain beating against windows. Except for Ursula, the whole house slept. The night was warm; there was no fire. The gracious little sitting-room was full of the scent of lilacs, freshly cut. The panelled walls gleamed in the lamplight; the portraits smiled down in friendly fashion on the young woman busy with her needlework near the cold fireplace. But, for Ursula, the night was full of voices. What would August think of the extraordinary man who was to marry his daughter? August's influence on his daughter had been an influence on manners, on one's approach to the outer world; he had never tampered with her emotions or opinions. If he had not agreed, he had merely shrugged his shoulders indolently, and had remarked that she had her own life to live, and that it was hers, alone. This, thought Ursula, with a touch of bitterness, was excellent in theory. But she suspected that August's attitude stemmed less from tolerance than from a desire not to be bothered.

There was a loud knock on her door, and Ursula started. The clock tinkled the three-quarters of an hour. Ursula listened for the stirring of Mrs. Templeton at this summons. But the house remained silent. It could be no one but William. Ursula set her mouth firmly and tightly, remembered that she was not to be a schoolmistress after all, let her lips relax, and went to the door.

It was indeed William, sparkling with moisture from the top of his hard black hat to his handsome black broadcloth coat. And smiling. He very seldom smiled unless he had first observed a smile on the faces of others. He said at once: "Good evening. Is it very late? I arrived home this morning."

"So I heard," replied Ursula, a little acidly. She opened the door wider, and let him in. She noticed at once that there was an air of dark exhilaration and grim excitement about him. He unbuttoned his coat, and she helped him remove it. Involuntarily, her hands touched his shoulders and lingered there, and a furious hot wave of something indescribable rushed over her.

He marched ahead of her into her parlor, and then, abruptly, he simply stood there, and looked around. He swung about to face Ursula, and his eyes fixed themselves upon her face. She had the momentary impression that not only did he see her body, and her features, but the thoughts that lay coiled disquietedly in her brain. He continued to stare at her, as he said, a little absently: "I had much business to do. That is why I didn't come before this."

He did not kiss me, thought Ursula. He has not even called me by my name. She stood before him, without speaking.

"It was important business," he said, and now it was as if she had challenged him.

"Of course," she murmured.

He was still vaguely suspicious, but when he saw how tranquil she was, he subsided. "I meant to bring you flowers," he said, a little lamely and impatiently.

"I have a garden full," she replied. Now she could not help smiling. "But thank you for the thought—William."

He rubbed his damp hands together. "But I did bring you a present from New York. From Cartier's." He glanced at her ring finger, and smiled again to see his extravagant emerald there. "My wedding gift. You shall have it on the day we are married."

"Thank you," she said.

He stared at her again. Then he said: "You look very tired and strained. Has Oliver been too much for you?" He glanced at the ceiling, then, not waiting for her reply, he exclaimed: "I must see Oliver at once!"

Ursula said: "He has been asleep since six o'clock."

"What does that matter?" he demanded. "I want to see him. I'll go upstairs," and he actually moved towards the door.

Ursula said clearly: "That would hardly be proper. This is a small house, and Lucy is sleeping in the same room."

He stopped on the threshold, swung upon her, and scowled at her. "That is wrong! I won't have a servant sleeping in the same room! How could you have allowed that? It is unhealthful for the child."

Ursula colored faintly. "I am sorry," she said, coldly. "I repeat, the house is small. I have three bedrooms. I occupy one, Mrs. Templeton another, and my father's room is big enough for Lucy and Oliver."

Her heart was beating angrily. She felt deprived. He was excited. "Lucy could have slept on a cot in the kitchen, or somewhere."

"No human being shall sleep in the kitchen in my house," said Ursula. Now her anger increased. He had not kissed her. He had not asked after her health. He had trodden over her, as if she were of no significance at all. He was glaring at her with the dull thick look she detested so heartily, and which made him appear insensate.

She had once believed him subtle. She saw, now, that she had not been wrong. He had a capacity for intuition. Suddenly he was smiling again, a changed smile. Very slowly, he came to her. He laid his hands on her shoulders. She waited, holding her breath. But he did not bend down his head and kiss her. With an odd little laugh, she raised her hands, took his face in them, and kissed him full upon the lips. He stood very still, and she felt his face stiffen, as if he wanted to reject her.

"William," she said softly.

The hands on her shoulders tightened. His lips had been hard and quiet under her own; now they suddenly became eager, almost ravenous. He pulled her to him. Then he thrust her away rudely. He went to the chair near the fire and sat down. He looked down at his wet boots. He said: "You look very pale." His voice was indifferent. But his face was heavily flushed.

"Wedding preparations are very tedious," she said. She felt curiously light-headed. She sat down near him. Out of the corner of his eyes he peeped at her, and in a less exigent man she would have thought the peep shyness.

"Wedding preparations," he repeated, disdainfully. But she knew he had not heard his own words. He bent down to remove an old leaf from his boots. He tossed it into the cold grate. "I want to see Oliver," he said, surlily. "You can't keep him from me."

"I don't intend to." She kept her voice calm and gentle.

"But I think the child ought not to be disturbed tonight." She added, cunningly: "It would be bad for his health."

After a moment, he nodded. "Yes."

There was silence in the room.

"I promised him he should see you tomorrow," said Ursula, mendaciously.

He looked up. His whole face was alight, sheepishly tender. "Has he missed me?"

"Very much. But he is a very understanding baby. And very patient. He never once believed you wouldn't return. I have heard that children believe they are forever deserted, when a parent goes away. Oliver did not believe that."

"He cried for me?"

Ursula's first emotion was impatience. Then she was compassionate. "Yes. But then I explained to him. He waits for you every night, and asks for you every morning."

"Then, I ought to see him now!"

"But he is asleep—William. It would be very upsetting for him to be awakened. He would be so excited that he might not sleep again, and become ill."

She sighed. "William, do you remember my name?"

"Eh?" He regarded her with astonishment.

"My name," she repeated, patiently. "I have a name. Have you forgotten it? You haven't mentioned it."

He still regarded her with astonishment. Then he began to laugh. "Ursula," he said. He stopped laughing. "Ursula," he repeated, more gently. He stood up, frowning again. "What foolishness."

She stood up, also. Her slight figure moved close to him. He turned his head quickly and, wary as always, tense and watchful, watched her come. She put her hand on his arm. "William," she said, "did it ever occur to you why I consented to marry you?"

He did not answer.

"I agreed to marry you because I love you." Her voice was very soft and low and pleading.

He still did not answer. Now he looked away from her.

"Do you understand what I have said, William?" she urged.

"I heard you." His words were almost inaudible.

"Do you believe it?"

He flung off her hand, went a few steps away from her. He rubbed his forehead with the back of his hand. "Love," he said. "There isn't any love, anywhere."

"That is not true," she said. "You love Oliver."

"Children are different."

For the first time, she was filled with a fierce jealousy. "No, they are not! I love you. You have never said you loved me. Why are you marrying me, William? I must know."

He turned to her. His face was very tired and haggard. He opened his mouth. Then he closed it again. "I can't believe in love between men and women," he said, finally, and with heaviness.

"You don't love me?"

He flung out his hands in exasperation. "Why do you keep harping on 'love'? I've asked you to marry me. I want to marry you. Isn't that enough?"

She studied him with great intensity. Her first impulse was to say: "No." Then she smiled. "Yes, I suppose it is," she said. She wanted to laugh, to kiss him again, to hold him protectingly in her arms. She said only: "Will you have some coffee?"

He was relieved at her change of mood. "No. I have had my dinner."

"I have some brandy. Would you like a glass?"

"I don't drink. There was wine tonight. I had half a glass. I didn't like it."

Ursula suddenly remembered a remark of her father's: "Beware of the man who never drinks, not even a little."

"It disagrees with you?" said Ursula, tentatively.

"No. It is just that I need all my wits about me."

"All my wits." He had set himself against the world, which he suspected would always try to outwit him. He had set himself against it because he feared it and could not trust it.

He sat down again, leaving her standing. "I had dinner at the home of our 'dear' friends, the Bassetts," he said. He laughed again, and the laugh was unpleasant. "There were other 'friends' there: Muehller, Banks, Leslie, Whiscomb. You know them?"

"Yes." She sat down, but at some distance.

Now he was excited again. He hardly seemed to see her. "I must tell you about it. About everything that happened today. You are a woman, and you will not understand all of it. But there is much that you will understand, for you are intelligent."

"Thank you," said Ursula, dryly.

His whole face became alive, thinner, darker, vital with power. He began to speak. His natural eloquence, released, painted for her the scene in the bank, at the Bassett dinner table. His voice, rising and falling, vivid, strident, sometimes vehement, sometimes full of detestation and loathing—but always triumphant—held her like mesmerism. Her hands lay quietly in her lap.

He hates them, she thought, though she was appalled at such malignance, such vindictiveness. He hates them because they are despicable and exigent and avaricious, because they would betray a friend, for money, because they would betray themselves, for money.

All at once she knew that he loved her; there was no longer the faintest reason to doubt it. Even more, he trusted her.

"Why are you smiling?" he asked, irascibly, halting in the very midst of the flow of his furious words.

"Smiling?" She had not been conscious of this. She stammered: "Was I smiling? Ought I not to be smiling?" She paused. "Should I be glowering?"

"But these are your friends."

"If you had thought them such friends of mine, would you be telling me this story?" she countered.

He gave a sudden shout of laughter. "Then, you hate them, too?"

She said, honestly: "No, I do not. I do not believe I hate anyone. No one has ever given me cause to hate him."

Again, his expression changed. "I have wondered whether you had the power to hate anyone. Or whether you were so egotistic that you did not consider anyone important enough for you to hate."

He had the ability to arouse more ire in her than she usually felt in the space of a whole year.

"You certainly have no flattering opinion of me, have you?"

He smiled derisively. "I think I ought to have remembered that 'nice' women are not supposed to have strong opinions about anything."

"You express yourself engagingly," she said. "But, pardon me: please go on with your interesting story."

He scrutinized her concentrated silence. Then he said in that dull tone of his, which could follow so quickly on violence: "That is all, I think."

He stood up. He began to walk up and down the room, restlessly, while she watched him with a good imitation of calm silence. She was startled when he halted abruptly, right in front of her. "You know so little about me," he said, looking down at her watchfully. "You know only what others have told you, and what I have seen fit to tell you. Have you never wanted to know more?"

I know all about you, my darling, she thought, her rage gone. She said: "It is true that I have not known you long."

He sat down once more, and he leaned towards her, speaking rapidly, as if throwing the words at her: "You might as well hear it all. My father worked in a little saw-mill down the river. He was badly injured; he died. I was very young, then. We had an old house, but a fairly large one, in a very poor section. My mother had always taken boarders. She continued to do so, after my father died. She worked hard; she worked herself to death. She was a very harsh woman, and she considered me a great responsibility. I don't think she ever thought of me in any way but as a burden."

"If she felt responsible for you, then she must have loved you," said Ursula, gently.

"No, you are wrong. She was an ignorant and religious woman. I was the millstone the Lord had thought fit to hang about her neck. So, she carried the millstone, grimly."

How tired she must have been, thought Ursula, with compassion. She said: "I imagine keeping boarders must have left her little time for anything else."

William ignored her crass remark. "I helped, as soon as I was able. Then I met Dr. Cowlesbury. I was in the woods one day."

He was silent for so long after he had said this that Ursula felt impelled to say: "Yes?"

He only said: "Dr. Cowlesbury was the only friend I have ever had."

He made an awkward but compelling gesture, as if denying a plea from her to hear more, or as if repudiating her sympathy. He said: "I really ought to see Oliver. Does he like you, still? He has not fretted?"

"It is almost eleven, William. It would be most unwise to disturb the baby. Yes, he likes me; very much, I think. After all, he is so young, and I am not exactly a brute. No, he has not fretted. He is too amiable and sensible."

"I hope you have not taught him to care for you more than for me." The words were childish, and he smiled. But it was a jealous and suspicious smile.

The clock tinkled eleven, and Ursula rose. "You will ruin my reputation if you remain a moment longer," she said. "Even though I have a chaperone."

Then she mentioned something of which she had been thinking these past few days: "I have thought, perhaps, if you have not planned a honeymoon, that we might spend the time before you have finished your own house in this one." She colored. William did not, apparently, find her remark in the least indelicate. In fact, he looked about him slowly and consideringly.

He studied every object in the room with great and thoughtful care. At last, he said: "It is a beautiful little house, I admit. But it is not so——"

"So magnificent as the Imperial Hotel?" she finished.

He did not apologize, or deny. "I don't like small houses very much," he added with candor. "This is a woman's house, also."

"My father lived here; my father furnished this house," said Ursula, provoked, "and my father was not in the least a woman."

"Who said he was?" asked William, absently. Again, he studied the room. "No, I think not. I should imagine myself poor again. Not that I do not realize that you have some treasures here. Still, smallness reminds me of poverty. I should stifle here."

"At least, you are frank," said Ursula. She was amused in spite of her vexation.

He was catching up his coat and hat and gloves and cane now, with those swift movements which so expressed his restless vitality. "You are right. It is very late, and I must go. I'll take Oliver off your hands tomorrow. The carriage will call for him in the morning."

He put on his coat. He went towards the vestibule. Then he turned about and looked at her. She went to him serenely, and held up her face. She waited. He did not move. She laughed a little. "You'll have to remember to kiss me occasionally," she said.

To her surprise, he colored. He brushed her cheek unwillingly with his lips. "Good-night," he said.

They looked at each other. He murmured, almost inaudibly: "Ursula." Then, with a kind of reluctant urgency: "Ursula. I have thought of you often, while I was away. You kept coming into my mind when I least expected it." He spoke accusingly.

"I am glad," she said, simply.

He repeated: "Good-night." He opened the door and closed it quickly behind him, and she heard him run down the stone steps outside.

Ursula went slowly back into the room, and sat down. It was wrong. Everything was wrong.

CHAPTER XI

THE NAIVE, EVEN those who called themselves friends of Chauncey Arnold, often wondered if and why his wife loved him, though they, themselves, were frequently as undeserving of the love of their wives and families. The men who, without the slightest hesitation, had betrayed him, knew him to be bullying, meanly expedient, sly and greedy. His father had owned a prosperous saw-mill, and had been famous for his ability to drive an excellent and ruthless bargain. But he had been content with the saw-mill. Chauncey Arnold had had larger ambitions. Before he was thirty, he had founded and organized the American Lumber Company. Before he was forty, he was a rich man. He had demonstrated the noblest virtue of all: He had a knack for making money. Moreover, he could be genial and expansive, had a loud laugh, a fund of stories, and a good table. His flaws of character were rarely if ever mentioned. Still, it was a wonder to everyone that his wife loved him. She had certainly not married him for his money, for at the time of their marriage he was only the manager of his father's saw-mill. Her own father had been a successful physician.

Had she been similar to him in personality, the question would never have arisen at all. But she was a gentlewoman, stately, full of personal integrity, kind and serene. Her manners were impeccable, her taste beyond question. In her youth, she had even been beautiful, a little austere, to be sure, but undeniably desirable. Sometimes he spoke rudely to her; she ignored it. It never occurred to anyone that she loved him because he loved her. There was a pleasant regard between herself and Ursula Wende, and they were always pleased to encounter each other. She visited Ursula occasionally, but always alone. No one needed to tell Alice that Ursula had an aversion for Chauncey Arnold. Had Alice been less intelligent, she would have resented this. But not only did Alice Arnold possess subtlety; she also possessed humor, tolerance and charity. Most of all, she had a strong pity for everyone, even the most fortunate, smug and complacent.

Alice loved her son, Eugene, as devotedly as she loved her

husband. But her pity for Eugene was, paradoxically, not so strong as her pity for Chauncey. With the inconsistency of human nature, she expected more of her son than she expected of her husband. After all, her father had been a man of high breeding, taste and great probity.

Observing the families of her friends, she had discerned that sons have a tendency to love their mothers more than they love their fathers. Sometimes, she found herself annoyed that Eugene, who did not respect his father, and who knew all about him, loved Chauncey more than he loved his mother. She was also aware that there was in Eugene a strong protective instinct towards Chauncey, and so she forgave her son and remained on excellent terms with him.

Eugene, at twelve, took an enormous interest in his father's affairs. Chauncey often said, with as much seriousness as chaff in his voice, that he never did anything of real importance without consulting his son. Certainly, Eugene was both intelligent and astute. He knew that some day a much cleverer man than Chauncey might possibly ruin him. Hence his protectiveness towards his father, which was also protectiveness towards himself as his father's heir.

When the first days of danger for Chauncey arrived, Eugene knew it. He acknowledged to himself that he had always expected these days. To him, it was no surprise, no shock, as it was to his father. It was simply inevitable. A man who thought himself secure was the most vulnerable. Even before the final dénouement, he listened for hours to Chauncey's incoherent and frantic denunciations of William Prescott. But Eugene did not hate William for it. William, unknowingly, possessed the respect of Chauncey Arnold's son.

William, however, had disliked Eugene from the time he had first seen the boy, which was when Eugene was about seven years old. The two had studied each other acutely, for only a few moments. For Eugene, the scrutiny had ended in admiration, but also in a faint disdain. By the time Eugene was twelve, he had recognized William's tremendous vitality and force of character; he knew also that here was a man of ambition and imagination, a man who could not be stopped. He had also recognized another trait in William, which only Ursula also knew, and that was a certain instability of emotion, and a certain fanaticism, a fanaticism which had nothing to do with the immense importance of making money. It was like a treacherous flaw in a glacial rock, which might at any moment expand in a great explosion and wreck the rock and all that surrounded it.

Eugene did not resemble his father very much. In appearance he was startlingly like his mother, very tall and thin and strongly angular, and of a curious pallor, almost a colorlessness. This lack of color in Alice added to her elegance. But in Eugene it was also formidable and arresting. He had his mother's pale, lustreless hair, straight and smooth, her pale, still eyes and bloodless lips, her regular, somewhat bony features, her wide, deep eye-sockets, her firm dimpled chin.

William had perhaps instinctively recognized the cold, child-like implacability of the boy, a quality which he unconsciously hated and feared as an adult quality. At any rate, after his scrutiny of Eugene, he had turned away. He never saw the boy after that without an increase in his aversion and disgust.

Their brief encounters left William with a feeling of uneasiness. In his mind, he rationalized this by telling himself that Eugene was like his father. Instinctively he knew it was not so, but he had no other explanation.

A month before the final collapse of the American Lumber Company, Eugene had listened more attentively to Chauncey's wild condemnation of William Prescott. He had made no comment, but, as he had a strange pity for his father—a pity he never felt for anyone else—he had touched his father's hand in consolation. Later, he said to his mother: "Papa just doesn't see that Mr. Prescott is a man who knows what he wants, and intends to have it. I can understand that. In his place, I'd do just what he is trying to do, but I'd do it without all that trumpeting."

Alice was more than a little shocked by her son's remarks. "But, my dear, Mr. Prescott appears to be a very unscrupulous man, and a bad one, because he is without honor and kindness." She paused. "What do you mean by 'trumpeting', Gene? Mr. Prescott impressed me as being a very quiet man."

"He trumpets inside," said the astute young Eugene, much to Alice's bafflement.

Eugene knew it was all inevitable. Yet when Chauncey returned home on that disastrous night, ill, raving, congested of face, in a state of collapse, the boy's imperturbability was temporarily shattered. He helped put his father to bed. At midnight when Alice tearfully begged him to go to bed also, he refused. He insisted upon sitting up with Chauncey, listening carefully to the weeping man's curses, his despairing cries of ruin. Even discounting the exaggerations of a man in his state, Eugene knew that the situation was alarming enough. He sat in the lamplight, while his father slept fitfully under the influence of sedatives, and moaned. He looked about the large rich bedroom. All this, of course, would have to go, probably by auction. It would interfere with everything, this débacle. He, Eugene, would no longer be respected at school, as the son of Andersburg's rich man. His pony would have to go; the three handsome carriages would have to be sold, and the servants dismissed. Temporarily, at least, the family would retire to ignominy and poverty. Eugene had no faith in the loyalty of his father's many friends. Friendship was too much a matter of success and bank accounts. Things would be very wretched, almost insupportable, because of the treachery and ambition of a ruthless man.

For a few moments Eugene allowed himself a natural and childlike emotion of hatred and bitterness towards William Prescott. Then he knew that this was foolish. From the moment William had become an employee of Chauncey Arnold it had been inevitable. Only a very silly person could have overlooked it. It had been so obvious to Eugene, so foreordained. His father had been a fool; he had lacked the capacity to understand, or even to see, what was right under his nose.

It was very silly of his father, Eugene meditated, to have refused the offer of a position in the Prescott Lumber Company, though Alice had tenderly applauded the "pride" of her husband. Three thousand dollars a year was a lot of money; the family needed that money. Even while Eugene gently held his father's hand, he felt an indulgent contempt for him. Once in the enemy's fortress, something might be accomplished. It was all very foolish, quixotic. Intelligent people did not do these things.

On the day that William Prescott married Ursula Wende, Chauncey Arnold died. Eugene did not cry. He stood by his father's coffin and looked down at him steadfastly. He did not cry at the funeral services, nor at the cemetery, where only a few furtive "friends" hurriedly appeared. He saw that his mother observed it all only too well, this small attendance, these averted faces, these awkward and uncomfortable notes in consoling voices. She did not seem bitter; her own grief was too intense, and she was too absorbed in it. Eugene, driving home with her to an empty house still haunted by the scent of funeral flowers, was silent and thoughtful, and there was a knot in the pale flesh between his light eyebrows.

At his own request, he slept on a couch in his mother's room that night. He did not fall asleep until morning, but pretended to do so, in order not to disturb Alice. He lay awake and listened to her helpless and half-stifled sobbing. He was still young, and he still loved his mother, and his hands gripped the quilts fiercely as he heard her subdued mourning. The dark house lay empty all about them. His father was gone. It was not until Eugene, himself, had cried a little that he could sleep.

Few friends called during the next days, and even these had a sheepish and embarrassed air. Eugene listened carefully to their vague offers of assistance, their attempts at sympathy. He smiled faintly and tightly. His mother listened in silence, but when the friends had gone, she would sometimes murmur: "How terrible. How very, very terrible."

This was folly. Eugene understood, with his intelligence, the whole meaning of what she murmured. Now, for the first time, he allowed himself to consider his mother a fool. In the past, her sentimental compassion had been only amusing; now, it was a source of danger.

After six days, he said calmly to Alice: "I suppose there is enough to see me through school?"

Alice responded vaguely in the affirmative. Her exhausted eyes quickened. "My poor, sweet darling," she said. "Of course, you must return to school, and on Monday." She paused, and sighed. "There was a little fund just for your schooling, dear. Papa laid that aside, separately, in your name, only two months ago. The Courts cannot take that away from us. As for myself, I still have my original money. It is not much, but it will keep us alive, until you are ready to make your own way in the world."

Two weeks later, a check for two thousand dollars arrived from William Prescott, accompanied by a stiff note of condolence. He had expressed his regret at the death of Chauncey Arnold; he "hoped" Mrs. Arnold would not hesitate to call upon him if she at any time needed assistance.

Alice read and reread the note. The check slipped to the floor. Suddenly, she began to sob again. "I ought to hate him," she said to Eugene. "But I cannot do it. The poor man."

Eugene looked at her without expression. Yes, his mother was a fool. He picked up the check. "This money?" he said. His fingers held it tightly.

"I must send it back at once, of course," she answered.

Eugene gave her the check. Once he had thought her a wise woman, in her somewhat befuddled way. But now, it was only too evident that she was a fool. He accepted the fact. One always had to accept facts.

CHAPTER XII

THE WEDDING WAS celebrated at the home of Mr. and Mrs. Bassett with as much pomp and lavishness as could be summoned up on such short notice. Mrs. Bassett did all she could. She was horrified when Ursula insisted upon being married in the "home-made" blue dress which Ursula had concocted, and which she had already worn. Ursula was obdurate. She had worn that dress on the night when William had proposed to her; she would wear it on her wedding-day. "Really, Ursula is becoming so stubborn," Mrs. Bassett tearfully confided to her husband. "But then, she is of German stock, and everyone knows that the Germans are obstinate people. However, she might have consented to a veil of sorts. A veil is absolutely necessary."

"Old maids," said Mr. Bassett, wisely, but not without rancor. He had intended this wedding to be quite an affair, entrenching himself as William Prescott's most important and influential friend. Ursula's guest-list did not please him. She had invited the most unlikely and insignificant people, including bearded old friends of August's, of whom nobody in the financial and business world had ever heard. They came, smelling mustily of moth-balls and snuff and tobacco; no one, except Ursula, noticed their intelligent and broodingly thoughtful eyes. They had written historical text-books, mathematical text-books, books of philosophy, books laden with heavy German poetry and quotations from Goethe and Schiller. Who cared for such people? Certainly not Mr. Bassett, who could not recall them as depositors of any substance.

William refused to invite Mr. Jay Regan, or any of his New York friends. This was a profound disappointment to Mr. Bassett. But Ursula, relenting, at last, allowed Mrs. Bassett, "her dearest friend," to fill out the guest-list with "prominent" people. She also relented to the extent of permitting her wide, yellow-straw hat to be engulfed in yards of blue veiling, which was to cover her face during the ceremony.

Mr. Prescott was the only "awkward" member of the party, if one discounted and ignored, as one did, the peculiar old men whom Ursula had invited. William was, as always, reticent, harsh, gloomy of smile. Nevertheless, to quote Mrs. Bassett, he carried things off very well indeed. Not once did he fumble. Moreover, he betrayed complete engrossment in his bride. Even after the ceremony (held in the Bassetts' drawing-room, appropriately banked with spring flowers, the organ properly played under the guidance of the minister's wife), he haunted his newly-wed wife as satisfactorily as any newly-hatched husband. He must already have been taught some manners by Ursula, for he seemed very interested in her father's old friends. Once, at least, he engaged in one or two heated arguments with a few of them; he thought Bismarck a very remarkable man; they disagreed with him with the courteous tenacity of the old and scholarly. He drank half a glass of champagne; he smoked nothing. Only Ursula knew he was embarrassed to the point of agony, though he had quite approved of so elaborate a wedding. He talked enough with his new directors and officers, but in such a short, arrogant and suspicious manner that she suffered for him.

She was also proud of him. In his long broadcloth cutaway and striped trousers and well folded black cravat and black pearls, he was easily the most impressive man present. But she saw that he made all near him uneasy by his very formidable manner.

She herself was so nervous and distraught that she had only passing, if poignant, impressions of these things. At the very last, before going downstairs on Mr. Bassett's arm, something had warned her: "This is impossible. This is a terrible thing I am about to do to myself."

Ursula thought of the long years ahead, and was afraid. Once, she fervently prayed she would have no children. She was sure she would not be able to manage William. There was a hard obduracy about him, which mature love could not reach. Also, he was immune to reason, especially where his emotions were concerned.

But she loved him. She stood beside him, straight and tall, her eyes sparkling behind the foolish blue veil, her pale face very tight and resolute, and made her vows clearly and strongly. She was committed; this was the thing she wished to do. If she was frightened, she would not now permit herself to acknowledge it.

Nothing mattered. She loved him. He loved her, even in his strange way. Yet she wished he were not quite so much the spectre at the feast. Once, hysterically, she thought how gay the wedding dinner would be if the bridegroom would eliminate himself! It was an absurd thought, but she could not rid herself of the conviction that everyone would have enjoyed himself so much more if the tall and stiff-legged figure of William Prescott had not been present. He had a dampening effect on laughter; voices died away when he approached; nervousness manifested itself when he spoke. He was not the only spectre there; Chauncey Arnold's ghost-face was in every shadow.

Ursula saw that everyone was afraid of William. The fools, did they not know that he most needed their pity and tenderness? Why could they not have a moment's intuition, perceive his loneliness, his insecurity, his uncertainty, as she perceived them?

Sometimes she glanced at William, as he stood beside her, and met his reluctant and saturnine smile. He stayed near her, for he trusted no one else. This both saddened her and made her happy. She tried to talk to him; to her consternation, she found she had nothing to say. Her throat was dry and tight. What did one say to one's bridegroom, whose wedding kiss was still strong on one's lips? Trivialities? One never could talk trivialities to William. Finally, to her dismay, she heard herself remarking: "I do hope little Oliver is well. We must take him a piece of the wedding-cake." Little Oliver! Of what importance was a small child now, at this moment, when one was married to a frightening stranger?

To her confused surprise, he replied spontaneously, and as if with pleasure: "Yes, we must not forget the cake. He would never forgive us."

It was ridiculous. William had spoken quite seriously, as if she had made an intelligent remark! She studied him to discover if he were joking; he was not. In fact, he was now selecting a special white box for the cake, and Mrs. Bassett was assisting him in choosing exactly the right size. "My son, Oliver, expects it," he was saying, and Mrs. Bassett beamed at him. Ursula was forgotten, she the bride, the woman, the presumably beloved. She pushed the blue veil farther away from her face with vexation.

Everything was disjointed, out of place, grotesque. All at once, she was very tired. Moreover, she was alarmed and afraid. It could not be explained. She looked at William's back steadily, tried to find strength for herself in his tall figure, his profile, the sound of his voice. Nothing came to her but a great loneliness.

It had been a warm and rainy day, ominous with a storm which never broke. At sunset, just when dinner was over, the

rain ceased. But the oppression remained. Ursula slipped
through the congested groups of friends, who were sluggish
with food and champagne. She found her way to a window
and, in this awful great loneliness, she stood and looked at
it, rather than through it.

She felt the immense silence of the darkening evening. The
sky appeared to press itself against the window, a dim but
intense blue, gem-tinted and flat, like the blue of the background of some illumination in a medieval missal. Across
it sloped the dark shape of a leafing bough and, beyond, the
darker mass of a more distant tree lifted itself. It was from
that sky that the stillness came; it had engulfed all sound on
earth, had absorbed it into the canvas of its blue but motionless
color. Not a bird cried nor a branch moved. For a few moments Ursula had the sensation that this sky had no depth,
that it was painted against the window-glass.

The windows had been shut against the cataracts of spring
rain. Now the house was very hot, the air heavy with perfumes,
the odors of food and wine and flowers. Ursula felt that she
must open the window to that pure turquoise blueness, that
fading light. But the catch resisted her efforts. She turned about
in exasperation, looking for assistance. It was then that
she saw Dr. Banks whisper something to William. Near William stood his new officers and directors, and Ursula's attention was immediately caught by their expressions, gloating,
mean, ugly, sheepish or hating. They were like a pack of
wolves around a larger wolf.

A change came over William. A servant had just finished
lighting the enormous chandelier over the table. Its glaring
light lay on William's face. It was that, of course, which suddenly made him appear ghastly.

The tableau was broken in a moment, even while Ursula
stared at it. It was nothing, nothing at all, only an effect of
gaslight suddenly flaring out into the evening shadow. Now
everyone was laughing again; fresh bottles of champagne
popped. But William was turning away. He was speaking to
Mrs. Bassett, and she was nodding archly. Though she could
not hear the words, Ursula knew he spoke with an old-fashioned
ceremoniousness. Whoever had taught William the formalities
of a gentleman had been old, had lacked the light touch. Dr.
Cowlesbury, naturally, thought Ursula.

Everyone knew there was to be no honeymoon at this time.
The bridal couple was to go immediately, and alone, to the
Imperial Hotel. Ursula, with a rush of almost hysterical thanks-
giving, heard the crunch of wheels on the gravel below the

window. In a few moments, she would be rid of all these people; she would go away with her husband. But her husband was a man she did not know.

Now a whole tide was rolling towards her, with laughter, with glasses upheld. She looked at them. She looked at William. Her first impression had been right; he was deadly pale, and his lips were fixed. She closed her eyes. Something was most terribly wrong.

Ursula's acquaintance with the Imperial Hotel was almost entirely hearsay. Once or twice, she had accompanied her father there to meet, in the lobby or large open dining-room, a colleague of his from Philadelphia, New York or Boston. Their conversations had had to do with the donkey-stupidity of students in general, the discussion of which had been, to them, a kind of catharsis enabling them to return to their classrooms refreshed and relieved, soothed by the knowledge that their own conviction that the whole human race was impervious to education was shared by unfortunate others.

The lobby was huge, paved with squares of black and white marble, ablaze with crystal chandeliers, crowded with gilt and red-plush, potted rubber-plants, masses of tables and close scatterings of rugs. An air of bustle pervaded the lobby. It pervaded the dining-room also, which glared even more than did the lobby, because of the reflection of gaslight on countless white tablecloths. Ursula had never seen the "suites" or bedrooms. She suspected, however, that the general scheme would be carried out there, also.

She was quite right, she saw with dismay, when she and William were ushered into William's suite attended by a coterie of curious and subservient employees in red uniforms heavily reinforced with brass. A hushed and ponderous silence also attended them. The servitors disappeared, happy in the possession of much silver; the manager, Mr. Ogden, remained for a few moments, obsequious and concerned with the comfort of the guests. Flowers were everywhere in the hot rooms. Red plush curtains had been drawn across every window. Ursula had never cared for red; now, no matter where she looked, this ubiquitous color assaulted her in all shades, ranging from bright pink to scarlet to crimson. There was no escaping the massive gilt, either.

Her two modest little trunks had been deposited in one of the bedrooms. She fled into this bedroom, while William conversed with awkward gravity with Mr. Ogden, who seemed in no particular hurry to leave. Perhaps William was detaining him, thought Ursula. If so, she was grateful. She saw her face in the glass; it was pale and tight. It was an old maid's face, more than a little censorious and drawn. The mirror also reflected the blue of her wedding-dress; the red of the room made this blue very intense and startling. She shuddered. Her first impulse was to remove it. She stopped with the initial hook; for the first time she was shy and nervous and embarrassed. She took off the yellow hat and tossed it upon the crimson counterpane. Again, she shuddered at the juxtaposition of the blue veil on the hat and the color of the bedspread. Feeling that she was rapidly losing control of herself, she caught up the hat and threw it into the great walnut wardrobe nearby, where she had hung her cloak, and her few dresses.

Now, near the dresser, she saw William's tall chiffonier. On it were his few brushes topped with silver, and a dispatch case. She approached them, and stood looking at them. All at once, though she did not know why, her eyes filled with tears. Perhaps it was because they were so lonely there, in all this gory magnificence. Now she was no longer afraid of William.

Mr. Ogden was still pleading with William in the "parlor," imploring that gentleman to tell him, the manager, if there was anything further he could do to increase the comfort of Mr. Prescott and his lady. William was denying this firmly. Ursula heard his voice, again a little hoarse and awkward. Why did he not dismiss the fool? Suddenly it came to Ursula that if she had been afraid of William he was equally, if not more, afraid of her. He was dreading the moment when he would be alone with her, his wife.

His wife. Ursula looked down upon the gleaming wedding-band upon her finger. Again, her heart ached. She kissed the ring. Then, with a bright smile, she went into the "parlor." The two men were suddenly silent. She wanted to laugh. Instead, she thanked Mr. Ogden graciously for the flowers and for his courtesy, and politely if inconspicuously dismissed him. He retired, bowing three times before the door finally closed upon him.

Ursula, carefully avoiding glancing at the sofa, sat down upon it. She looked at her husband, and again smiled brightly. The smile ached at the corners, but she maintained it. But William did not return the smile. He stood on the brilliant rug before the fireplace. He said, abruptly: "There is something I must tell you."

"Yes, William," she answered, with much quietness. But she felt a kind of dread.

William did not immediately enlighten her. He looked down at his hands, flexed and unflexed them. The signet ring on his left hand shone. He put his hands behind his back. Then he said: "Do you like this suite?" His voice was accusing, as it had so often been in the past, as if he were challenging her.

Ursula looked at him pleasantly, avoiding the pervading color. "It is very comfortable." Apparently this did not satisfy him. She tried again, though she knew he hardly heard her: "But then, everyone knows the Imperial Hotel is very luxurious."

William was silent. He turned away from her, and faced the fireplace. The mantelpiece was embellished by a cloisonné clock and two vases to match. He said, in a strange and muffled voice: "It never occurred to me that he would die. I never thought of it."

Ursula's hands tightened together. Now the whole immense and glittering room became full of horror and menace. She made her voice very calm and without inflection. "Who, William?"

"Chauncey Arnold." William paused. "He died just about the time we were—married."

Oh, my God! thought Ursula. She did not know what to say. But she knew she had to say something, and it must be at once. Her own voice, though still calm, in spite of its steadfastness had dwindled when she said: "Of course not. Of course, you did not know he would die. But everyone knew he had a bad heart; he ate so very much. Dr. Banks had warned him repeatedly. I knew that."

She had a sudden vision of Alice Arnold, and for a moment or two she closed her eyes tightly. The room was very quiet. Ursula opened her eyes; William's back was still turned towards her.

"I wanted him to be a vice-president. I offered him three thousand a year."

For an instant Ursula was incredulous and filled with a wild anger against William. What a dreadful cruelty he had perpetrated in that offer! Then, with that mysterious intuition which always came to her when dealing with William, she understood that it had not been cruelty.

"After all," William was saying, "it meant a livelihood for him."

Ursula could not speak. She had no words. Again, she saw Alice Arnold. She sat on the sofa, and her lips had no more color than her cheeks.

William turned to her and she saw his face. He was suffering.

"I thought you ought to know," he said, and his voice had a rush of brutality in it.

"Why?"

"Well, he was a friend of yours, wasn't he? You've known him for years, haven't you?"

Ursula's chest was tight and breathless. "I told you before, William, that I never liked him. I am sorry he is dead. But I never liked him. My father despised him."

"I heard, once, that his wife was a particular friend of yours."

Why did he speak so brutally, throwing the words at her like stones? Did he expect her to rise up and denounce him, perhaps walk out of this appalling place? Ursula frowned. "I never had any 'particular' friends, William. Probably I have been too self-centered. I don't know. I've liked Alice; I still like her. I am sorry for her. It is too bad that Chauncey has died. But it cannot be helped. Perhaps his—his loss— might have hastened the time of his death. That is something I can't tell. At any rate, if it had not been you, it would have been someone else. He was a fool of a man."

"Yes," said William, slowly. Then, more heavily: "Yes."

He stood there so stiffly on the hearth, and now he thrust his hands into his pockets. He regarded her with phlegmatic curiosity. "I thought it might change—might do something to you, when I told you."

"And if it had?"

He shrugged. That dull thick look she despised had settled on his face again.

"Did you actually expect I might become hysterical, might even leave you—I, your wife?" she asked incredulously.

Again, he shrugged. He was a tall and stolid peasant, when he stood like this, just looking down at her with a peasant's expressionless stare.

"I shall send her—Arnold's wife—some money," he said, still watching her.

"She will return it," answered Ursula.

"Then, she is as big a fool as her husband is—was." The voice, for all its heavy coarseness, was not a peasant's voice.

"She might have some pride," said Ursula, coldly.

"Why? She'll need the money, won't she? What has pride got to do with money?"

He means it, thought Ursula, with fresh incredulity. The

whole scene was taking on the quality of a nightmare. Again, this man was a stranger. She was not afraid of him. But she was coming perilously close to disliking him.

"Nevertheless," said Ursula, wearily, "Alice will return the money. Why should she take it from a stranger? Have you ever met her?"

"No."

Ursula smiled without mirth. Don't be a fool, she wanted to say. She repressed the natural and healthy impulse. "Alice has some money of her own, I believe. And there's probably enough for the boy, too."

This is my wedding-night, she thought, tiredly. And here we are, talking of tragedy, and my husband looks like a big and obstinate ditch-digger, and stares at me as if I am a disliked and suspected stranger. I am not saying what he thinks I should say, but if I said it, it would be all finished between us.

William was saying: "The boy. That boy of his, Eugene. He was always about. His father often brought him to board meetings, and had him lounging around the offices after school and on Saturdays, letting him hear what went on, as if it could possibly have interested a child of eight or ten or twelve! There the boy would sit, just staring; sometimes my attention would wander away from the business at hand, and I would sit there myself, trying to see if he ever blinked!" He was becoming heavily excited. Some deep resentment and contempt were stirring in him. "If the boy ever did blink, I never saw it. Sometimes Arnold would turn to him and ask his opinion. I'll say this for the kid: I never heard him say very much in return, which shows he had more sense than his father. They went down to the mills together, often."

He waited for Ursula's comment. She made none.

William made one of his powerful if uncouth gestures. "Oh, I suppose it was all right. I can see now that it wasn't that that annoyed me. It was a way the boy had of looking at me, even when one of the other men was speaking, or his father."

Ursula said: "Gene isn't stupid. He is extremely intelligent, in a somewhat formidable way, I am afraid. He is very like his mother, in appearance. But certainly not in character. Nor is he like his father."

She gazed at William with a curiosity of her own. He hated Eugene, he who professed to love all children.

"Eugene is only twelve," she said, with some malice in her voice.

"I don't care what his age is," said William. "Boys like that are never young."

Ursula lifted her eyebrows. "You are right, of course."

Now he actually smiled, his gloomy smile. "He isn't stupid, either. It is just that I don't like him. But I think his mother ought to accept money, for his sake. I know that if he were consulted he'd take any money that came along."

Ursula repeated: "Yes, you are right. But I am thinking of Alice." She added: "It is evident that you interested Eugene."

All at once, she was completely exhausted. She had just been married; she was alone with her husband. Perhaps it was selfish to think of herself just now, but distracted resentment took possession of her. Why did he need to tell her of Chauncey Arnold at this time, to discuss Alice and Eugene? What did it all matter, on her wedding-night? William had not kissed her; he had not spoken her name. He had been carrying on an insistent and disturbing conversation when he ought to be speaking to her with tenderness and desire, when she ought to be in his arms. All her body yearned for deep and passionate reassurance, for love and the drama of love. She sat there on that horrible rubicund sofa, in a vivid blue dress which she now hated and which she would never wear again, and her face appeared white and thin, and her russet hair had dimmed in contrast with all that effervescence of stormy and clashing color.

He must have sensed something of all this, for his face turned as red as everything about him and he looked down awkwardly at his feet.

"Why are we talking about these things?" he mumbled. He paused. "I had ordered a little dinner, and champagne for us, at ten. It is almost that, now."

She laughed, and the sound had a wild note. "I don't want anything to eat. There was so much at the Bassetts. And, frankly, I never liked champagne. Could you not cancel the order, William?"

He appeared relieved. He almost ran to the bell-rope. A boy appeared as if by magic. William cancelled the order. His voice was strong again, and reassured. He closed the door and returned to the spot in front of the fireplace. Now he began to stare fixedly at Ursula, and his face was redder than ever.

"My name," she said, smiling faintly, "is Ursula."

He frowned, then laughed. "You tell me that so often. Ursula," He paused. "It doesn't suit you. It is a rough name."

Such a weight was lifted from her now. She said: "What would you prefer?"

He shrugged. "I don't know."

"Nevertheless, it is my name. I really should like you to use it, William."

He was a strong and vital man. He ought to be wooing her. What was wrong with him? Then she saw that he was afraid, with that queer, dark fearfulness of his which underlined all that he ever said or did.

Suddenly all her conjectures and reflections vanished, blew away. She stood up, and lifted her arms towards him. She understood so much. This man had known nothing but bloody struggle all his life. He had never had any roots anywhere; this had been the impulse behind his dynamic insistence upon success at any price. It had also made him a dangerous man. Perhaps if he had roots, if he knew himself loved and established, firmly planted, it might still be well with him, and with her, Ursula, who had married him.

"William!" she cried.

She ran to him then, and threw her arms about him, holding him close, weeping on his shoulder, clutching him, torn with pity and compassion and a fierce tenderness. For several moments he did not respond; he stood unbending in the circle of her arms. She cried, as she was to cry after his death: "My dear, my dear, it doesn't matter! Nothing matters!"

His arms were about her, holding her so close to him that she could not move, could scarcely breathe. "Ursula," he said, his lips in her hair. "Ursula, Ursula."

CHAPTER XIII

URSULA WAS TO forget many things, as she had forgotten many before, but she never forgot that moment during her first night of marriage when William whispered against her ear: "Sweet. Sweet."

It was such a reluctant word, coming from him, as if hugely forced from some denial in himself. Ursula heard it with bliss and joy. She did not reply to it. No one had ever called her "sweet" before. She was glad of it. This was something she could hold to herself forever, forever remembering. Even in that moment she had a premonition that she would need this memory.

She could not sleep, even when it was early morning and William slept beside her. The most irrelevant ideas kept coming into her mind, but she was so orderly of thought that she was soon able to see that they were not so irrelevant after all. Once, she said to herself: If only he had a cantankerous father, or mother, with whom he had to deal, or a few worthless brothers always in difficulties, or a crowd of exigent sisters! These would give him stability, draw him away from a dangerous center of self.

At last, she slept fitfully. When she awoke, the place beside her was empty. She heard William in the garish "parlor" giving orders for breakfast. She rose and put on the rose-colored velvet peignoir she had made only two weeks ago. It was becoming. Nevertheless, there was so much red about that she hastily removed the garment, found another of white wool with black velvet ribbons. Calmly, without embarrassment, she went into the parlor. William, she discovered with some surprise, was completely dressed. He did not look at her directly; his mouth had a sullen expression. He said: "There will be breakfast in a few minutes."

Ursula sighed. She sat down on the crimson couch. She waited. He said nothing else. Someone had brought him the morning paper. He stood starkly in the center of the room and rustled the sheets all around him. Finally, he said, in a voice of satisfaction: "There is a prominent article, here, about our marriage."

"Is that important?" Ursula could not keep the acid from her words.

He dropped the paper a little to stare at her with stolid affront.

"Of course it is."

"Why?"

He opened his mouth to answer, then turned quite red.

"What do you care whether the papers in this town write about you or not?" she went on, wanting to hurt him as he was hurting her.

"If we are going to live here, it is important that our existence be noticed," he said, with sarcasm.

"I never particularly wanted to live here," said Ursula. She was weary of this childish battle of words. It was so foolish. She went to the window, pushed aside the crimson velvet draperies and looked down at the busy street below. She wished it were a street in New York. All at once, she felt deprived and injured. A few days more or less would not have mattered; there ought to have been a honeymoon. Vaguely, she noticed that it was raining again; the street had washed itself in gray and glimmering water; umbrellas moved below her. Carts and carriages and drays rattled by hastily. The gaslight was flaring behind her, for the day had begun in drabness and dimness. It was not May, after all. It was an ugly timelessness. Some new guests were coming into the hotel, the women scurrying, holding up their skirts, the gentlemen bobbing umbrellas about, the hotel men in their red uniforms dragging leather baggage from the hired carriages. It was only Andersburg, though this was the Imperial Hotel. Futility filled Ursula. Who had called her "Sweet" in the night? It had been a dream.

She turned back to the room. William was picking up the scattered newspaper sheets. She thought: He is embarrassed. He does not know what to say to me. I am a petulant fool.

She said, gayly: "What am I going to do, before Oliver and Lucy return here, while you are off most of the day, as you threatened you were going to be?"

His dark face had resumed its natural color. "I thought," he said, "that you might visit your friends."

"Good heavens, they certainly would not expect it of me!" She was amused.

"I don't intend to leave you today." Again, he was embarrassed. "I thought, if it cleared, we might go for a drive." He paused. He said: "I am sorry about not having a honey-

moon just now. I can see that it leaves you at odds and ends.
But perhaps you can read, or something, while I am away
a few hours during these next few days—"

It sounded very absurd to her. She laughed.

"We'll go out and see how the new house is coming along,"
he added. "I'd also like you to see the—I mean, my new saw-
mills."

Ursula became grave. She twisted a tassel of the draperies
in her hands. William's taste in everything was execrable.
She had to admit that. She must accept it.

She felt a rush of compassion for him. "I should like that,"
she said, simply. "Please don't be concerned about me. I
should have enjoyed a honeymoon. But it is only temporarily
delayed." She waited. He was moving a table to the center
of the room, very carefully. "I suppose we could call around
and see Oliver?"

To her grateful surprise, he replied at once: "No. Not for
a day or two, at least." The table was moved to his satisfaction now. He looked down at it. "I suppose Mrs. Templeton
told you I have asked her to be our housekeeper, when our
home is built?"

"No!" cried Ursula in sudden exasperation. "You never
told me, and she did not! Really, William, ought I not to
have been consulted?"

She waited for him to say something, but she did not wait
very long. She went on: "I am not fond of Mrs. Templeton.
She was only a temporary expedient, for appearances' sake.
I cannot imagine her in my house. Why should we have a
housekeeper?" continued the daughter of frugal Germans.
"I am quite competent, I assure you. I presume there will
be other servants besides Lucy, but I can manage them. A
housekeeper! How ridiculous!"

He sat down, heavily. "Ursula," he said, with deliberation,
"I don't think you understand. I intend to have a large establishment, the best and most formal in the city. There are
a few families here who have housekeepers. I am not thinking
only of them. There are the others who come here in the summer, and some who live on the hills most of the time. I know
some of them. They are not provincials, like many of your
friends. They have fine homes, conducted in the best style.
I do not intend that they shall surpass me."

Ursula considered this. She had a faint moment of pleasure
in contemplating the fact that William was richer than she
had supposed. But she was still annoyed at the thought of

Mrs. Templeton. She said: "Let us put aside for a little the discussion of future grandeur." Her voice was satirical. "Let us consider my regard for Mrs. Templeton. I have nothing against her of a serious nature, except that she annoys me. She is very petty and pretentious, in a tight sort of way. She and I would get very much on each other's nerves."

"I find her very capable. I noticed that she can manage servants." William's tone was obdurate again.

"You mean Lucy? Why, Lucy is a far better person than Mrs. Templeton. She is certainly more human. She understands children. She is much more intelligent than Mrs. Templeton."

There was a knock on the door, announcing breakfast. William rose with alacrity to greet the two waiters. He said, as the door opened: "Nevertheless, I want Mrs. Templeton to be our housekeeper."

Fuming, Ursula kept her peace while the breakfast was being arranged on the table. She watched William as he supervised the placing of the silver dishes. She could not help smiling to herself. What a child this was! A clumsy, dynamic and inarticulate child, for all his bigness and his enormous capacities! But she would not give up the argument about Mrs. Templeton, for whom she had suddenly conceived an intense dislike. However, William managed to retain one of the waiters to serve him and his wife. It was done deliberately, she saw, to avoid further controversy with her. This amused her still more. She would not be contentious before servants.

She decided, however, to be perverse, and not to be a lady, in order to vex him. He had not kissed her this morning; he had shown her no tenderness. He had arbitrarily thrust Mrs. Templeton upon her. She would punish him. She sat down at the table, allowed herself to be served, and then repeated: "Mrs. Templeton annoys me. I can't bear the woman. If we have to have a housekeeper, it must be someone else. Why this insistence upon Mrs. Templeton?" The waiter was impassive, but he was listening with keen enjoyment, she saw.

"Why discuss it just now?" asked William, giving his white napkin an irritable flip, but still not looking directly at her. "Is that bacon crisp enough?"

"Of course. But I want to discuss Mrs. Templeton. I have the deepest desire to discuss her."

He suddenly looked up at her, and she was startled. His eyes were flat and blazing. His rage was all out of proportion, she thought confusedly. Now she felt fear and repulsion. It was a violent face that confronted her, almost savage, as if he hated her.

"I said," and he spoke quietly, "that we shall have Mrs. Templeton."

Ursula turned very pale. She glanced at the waiter. "That will be all," she said, clearly. The man bowed, and removed himself.

There was silence in the room. William's face was still ugly, with an immense ugliness she had never encountered before in her life. He ate his breakfast, every movement deliberate. Ursula's breakfast cooled before her, as she watched her husband. The rain lashed the windows. The light outside became grayer and duller.

"William," said Ursula, gently.

He ignored her; then, very slowly, he put down his knife and fork. "Ursula," he said, and she thought there was something terrible in his voice, "I want you to know this now: When I make up my mind I don't intend to be disputed or opposed."

Fear, anger, affront, all tightened Ursula's heart. She spoke resolutely: "Don't talk to me like that, William. This is our first day of marriage. You have forgotten, I think. No matter. But this must be settled now. You mustn't talk to me as you have just talked. I won't have it."

All his features appeared to swell, to become congested. He said: "Don't provoke it, then. Ursula, you were brought up by a very womanish man, I have heard. You have always had your own way. You are a married woman now. You are my wife. I have no time, and I shall have no time, to engage in small domestic arguments with you. You must learn this. You must learn that I intend to have my way."

Ursula's fingertips pressed into the white tablecloth. She could not speak. Her throat had closed. She knew that what she felt in herself was horror and insult and outrage. No, while she felt this way she must not speak.

He was staring at her formidably. Then, while she watched him in a daze, his face changed again. She did not know that her own face startled him, had taken him aback, with its stern pallor and immobility, and that he was ashamed. He was not turned from his purpose but, still, he was ashamed.

"You are thinking that I am a vulgarian without manners, that I am disgusting," he said. "Perhaps I am." He paused. Her yellowish eyes did not move from his; they had brightened and dilated. Her mouth was only a pale carving in her face. He looked away from her. "I haven't forgotten this is our first morning together, Ursula. At least, I am remembering it now. Probably my manner to you has been unpardonable. Will you try to remember that I know it was?"

"Yes," she whispered at last, with difficulty. There was such a terror in her, such a repudiation.

"Shall we forget it?" he asked. There was no humility in his voice, but she knew he was ashamed.

"Yes," she repeated.

He smiled. "Well, then, won't you eat your breakfast?"

She took up her fork. Her hand was very cold.

He tried for a lighter note. "I'm sorry you don't like Mrs. Templeton. I'm afraid that it's too late for any other arrangement. I asked her, the other day."

"I don't care about Mrs. Templeton," said Ursula, speaking through the pain that would not leave her throat.

"Well, then, it is settled." He tried to sound relieved. But he was enormously uneasy. "There is another thing: Could you arrange for flowers to be sent to Mrs. Arnold, in both our names?"

"No," she said. "I shall send no flowers."

Very carefully, he poured coffee for her.

"It would be bad taste, you think?" he said.

"It would be the most horrible bad taste." She tried to drink the coffee. Her only desire was to rise and leave this room, to go away into quietness, and not to remember. Her head began to pound heavily, and to swim.

"I shall always defer to you in matters of taste, Ursula," he said, seriously.

He was trying to apologize, she saw. If the offense had been less, if she had not seen what she had seen in his face, if he had not looked at her as he had done less than ten minutes ago, she could have forgotten, she could have forgiven, she could even have felt tenderness and compassion for him. She might feel all this later; but as yet the shock was too great.

He was so intuitive that he guessed much of the turmoil of sick emotion in her, and he was freshly ashamed.

"Ursula, you are not forgetting, are you?" he said.

She lifted the cup to her lips. She put it down. "I am trying," she answered.

She wanted to cry, suddenly and wildly. "It was all so trivial," she stammered.

He got up, slowly and awkwardly. He came to her, and put his hand on her head. "Ursula," he said. She sat there, her head bent, not moving. "Believe me," he went on, "it won't happen again."

Oh, yes, she thought. It will happen again. It will happen over and over, all our lives together. You will look at me like that many times, and each time I shall be shocked almost to death. I shall never become accustomed to it.

She reached up, touched his hand gently, then removed it. "It was all so trivial," she repeated.

A shaft of pale sunlight struck into the room, bringing with it a lighting up of all the dreadful redness. "We shall have our drive after all," said Ursula.

CHAPTER XIV

IT HAD BEEN ONE of Ursula's private axioms that one should, as much as practical, avoid too earnest an introspection about unpleasant things, and live as much as possible on the surface of life, especially with regard to any disagreeableness which might affect one's personal serenity and detached point of view. The art of living, August had once drily observed, was not to involve oneself in living to the extent of experiencing any strong or upsetting emotions. "Leave the passions to the poets and the statesmen and the saints and the busybodies," he had told Ursula. "Ordinary mortals must, for the sake of their very existence, pretend, even to themselves, that God is working for the Good, twenty-four hours a day, and that all's well that ends well. Clichés? Well, then thank God for clichés! They keep the majority of us from madness."

Now in the early days of her marriage, Ursula turned thankfully to clichés. Of course, it would only be temporary, she assured herself. A woman must certainly not let herself be engaged too intensely in the study of her new husband, especially not during the first months or so. One must accept, be as serene as possible, and watch and wait. Dull clichés, but she suspected that many a marriage reached ripeness and calmness because of this early attitude on the part of a wife.

Love, before marriage, had brought to her hours of exaltation, when her mingling of passion and pity and tenderness had been like a great and sudden light on the once-shadowy landscape of her spirit. It had revealed to her depths of feeling of which she had always believed herself incapable; she had learned suffering and, through that suffering, joy.

She had been married hardly forty-eight hours when she knew that for a time, at least, she must withdraw from too much feeling, from too much ecstasy and abandon. And especially from too much expectation. Her love for her husband was an immense flood which must be held back by the dam of that old serene acceptance which had held her a prisoner of complacency and resignation. She could permit herself to love William, and to feel for him that immense charity

which is the essence of the deepest love. But it must be a love
which did not analyze, did not demand, did not look beyond
the hour, the day, the surface. She very early saw that there
would never be any companionship between herself and her
husband, such as there had been between herself and her father.
William feared what was weak in himself.

What shall we talk about, we two, when we are alone? she
thought in moments of despair. The men he knew were known
to her, but they did not have her interest. She and William had
no mutual background; their attitudes of mind were completely
antagonistic. William, too, was a man without humor, and
while he was subtle, it was a subtlety without lightness or
wit. It operated only in an atmosphere of suspicion and dis-
quiet, or pain.

It was late May now, and in May it was not possible to
be desperate every moment. William, on the second day, and
on the third, and on the fourth and fifth, was gone every morning till noon. She felt some comfort in being lazy, even amid
the florid atmosphere of the suite which was to be her home
until her house had been built. She breakfasted alone, and
late. She read, and planned the furnishings of the house.
When William returned for luncheon, and to spend the rest
of the day with her, she greeted him with warmth and calm
and tenderness, and with no suggestion in her manner of
any passion there might have been in the night. Then, in the
afternoon, they would go for a drive through the country,
return and have dinner alone. It was the hours after dinner
and before retiring that were the worst. She began to be glad
that, after the first few nights, William would open his dispatch case and go over thick sheafs of paper. Then she could
read or think, but not too strenuously, and watch him furtively
over the top of her book, while only street noises could be
heard and the rustle of the papers.

William had given Ursula the architect's general outline
of the plans for the new house. She had studied them with
mingled amazement and misgiving. The house was too formidable. It would be quite the most imposing and enormous
structure in Andersburg or its wealthy suburbs. She could not
quite conceive of it standing on that desolate tract of land
which William had purchased from her, even when he impatiently reiterated over and over that the whole area would
shortly be very fashionable, and much desired.

Ursula repeated to herself that her husband was wealthy,

and that he would most probably become even wealthier. But she had not come of a German strain to whom a "Schloss" was a familiar thing, and one to be accepted as natural. She came of a burgher strain, prudent and careful. One spent a certain proportion, to live in comfort and even in a sort of solid and suety richness. But only if one could afford it. Even then, one thought of the future, and a sensible man had no particular trust in the future. Was it possible that William trusted the future, or, more probably, trusted himself?

She said, one night: "William, this house! Why such a huge house? Now, please don't think that I prefer 'littleness'," she added, as William began to scowl at her over his papers. "It is just that all this seems—seems redundant," she went on, helplessly. She glanced at the plans on her knee. "A ballroom! None of our acquaintances have ballrooms. Yes, I have heard there are ballrooms, perhaps one or two, in the houses on the hills. So absurd, really. Our friends simply remove most of the furniture from the drawing-room, where they *have* a drawing-room, turn over the rugs, and dance. Besides, Andersburg is not exactly a dancing city; most of us feel that dancing is either too 'grand' or slightly immoral.

"And two drawing-rooms, each one tremendous! Andersburg is not a great city, and even if we have guests from other cities two drawing-rooms would be too much. A music room! A library! A billiard room!

"Look at this reception hall. Does it have to be almost as large as one of these drawing-rooms? Oh, please do not frown. I am only joking, but really, the dining-room is too large. It would seat at least thirty people, with much space to spare."

She hastened to another page of the plans, which covered the second floor. William was ominously silent. His own papers no longer rustled. The blazing chandeliers flared down. But Ursula was desperate and determined.

"The bedrooms. Fourteen of them, eight with dressing-rooms. Who will fill all of them?" She colored slightly, then compressed her lips and went on: "A conservatory to grow enough flowers for half a dozen houses and a funeral establishment or two. Stables for about five carriages, with rooms above, for grooms and stable-boys, I presume, and gardeners."

She put down the plans on the red sofa beside her. "William," she said, seriously, "have you really decided upon such an enormous household? Have you counted the cost? And, even if you have, why do we need it?"

His dark face tightened. "I told you before that I expect to have the finest house in this part of the country. Have you forgotten? As for the cost, I was under the impression that it was a man's place to consider that, and not his wife's. I assure you, I am well aware of what I am doing."

"Such a house would be very bad taste in Andersburg," said Ursula. "You said you would defer to my taste, William."

"I intend to, if it is at all sensible." His voice rose, and she heard anger in it, and impatience. "You are not being sensible now."

William's face changed, became almost pleasant. He said: "I forgot to tell you. The stone for the house arrived late today. Tomorrow, we'll go out and look at it."

He returned to his papers. Ursula sat and stared at him fixedly. She thought for a few hopeful moments that he was only pretending to forget her, and then she saw that he had indeed forgotten her.

She sighed. It was too ridiculous. She had a vision of an enormous pile on the lonely land he had bought; it would tower over the whole landscape, ludicrous and too impressive, for all the grounds above it. She said despondently: "The stone? White-gray, I hope? Surely not brick?" She shuddered slightly, contemplating such a house of brick. Even covering it with ivy would not be enough.

He looked up from his papers irascibly. "Brick? Don't be a fool, Ursula. Brick! No, not white-gray stone, either. But why speak of it now? You'll see the stone tomorrow."

"Not brown?" said Ursula, faintly. "I loathe brown stone."

It is probably brown, she thought with consternation, when he regarded her blackly. He said: "What is wrong with brown? The best houses here are of brown stone. Why are you so insistent? I haven't said it was brown, have I?" However, he was uncomfortable. "Have you no patience at all? You'll see it tomorrow."

Ursula had another frightful thought. "William, the furniture! When is it to be bought? When am I to help choose it?"

He did not reply. He frowned at a paper or two, wrote several lines, put some sheets aside with the swift and certain movements she had always admired in him. He said absently: "The furniture has already been chosen. I chose it a month ago, in New York. Also, all the chandeliers, the marbles, the rugs." He did not look at her.

Oh, no! she protested to herself. She cried, with spirit: "But William, am I not to be consulted at all? Let us be reasonable; I am to live in that house. A woman's tastes are usually considered."

He did not answer her.

"You have chosen everything, for every room?" murmured Ursula, aghast.

"Everything."

Ursula rubbed her forehead. It was too much. Now she, too, was angered. "I think that is very inconsiderate of you! You know my own tastes. I had thought of moving the best from my own house to our new one. How can I visualize it there if I have not seen the furniture you have already bought?"

He folded his hands together strongly on the papers. His eyes sparkled at her inimically across the room.

"I do not intend that you shall bring any of that furniture to my house," he said, in a cold, neutral voice.

"But why? You once said it was beautiful! Besides, it was my parents' furniture, and they had taste!"

"Why do you harp on 'taste'? Do you think I lack it entirely?" His voice was becoming ugly.

Yes! she said inwardly. But aloud, she only protested: "I have my own taste, also."

"It is not mine," he replied. He glanced at the clock on the mantelpiece. "It is almost eleven. I am tired. I must get up early."

He put the papers away, quickly and neatly, and rose. Without glancing back at her, he left the room.

Ursula did not follow him. She sat for a long time alone. It was not until half an hour had passed that she reminded herself that clichés served an excellent purpose. "Things are not usually nearly so bad as one imagines beforehand," she said aloud.

CHAPTER XV

FIRMLY DETERMINED to hold to every cliché she knew, Ursula accompanied her husband to the site of the new house on Schiller Road.

William was as amiable as it was possible for him to be, but Ursula detected an uneasiness under all that solicitude for her comfort in the rich and sparkling carriage, under his attempt to infuse her with his own delight in the house he was building. Looking at him with the large and tender charity of her love, she replied gently, pretended to a girlish enthusiasm and anticipation. Very carefully, she avoided any comment upon the hugeness of the building, and studiedly kept the fatal word "taste" from every remark.

The late May weather assisted her. It was not hard to be gay and optimistic amid all this great foam of green and lilac and white and blue and gold. They passed through streets where every window glittered in a brilliant sun, and every newly-leafed tree swung in a soft sweet wind against the blue-green skies. A shining sprightliness moved in the air, a reassurance from the earth. The cobbled streets sparkled; even ugly vistas had acquired a mellowing beauty. The lavender hills above the city lay overlapping each other, in folds of velvet. Ursula had a glimpse of the golden river, full of barges and flat-boats. Down there lay her husband's saw-mills; he had promised to take her there soon. She was in no particular hurry for this "pleasure," for she had very early come to the conclusion that the less she knew of her husband's affairs the less friction there would be between them, and the less apprehension she would suffer. "If ignorance is bliss, 'tis folly to be wise," Ursula said to herself, grateful for another remembered cliché.

William had never appeared to her so impressive as he did today, and she was proud of him, in spite of the unfamiliar sadness which had come to her in these days, even in the face of a premonition that this sadness would never again entirely leave her. There was no doubt that he made her nervous, for, tactful though she was, she never knew when she would offend him by the most innocent remark and cause his capricious rage to explode against her.

She became aware that there had been silence between
her and her husband for several minutes, when he spoke awkwardly: "You look so well today, Ursula. That—that bonnet
is very becoming, and the cloak also."

Ursula was surprised and pleased. She could not, at the
moment, recall ever hearing him make any comment on her
dress. She remembered that she had indeed appeared very
fashionable in her mirror, even chic, in these garments she
had carefully made or chosen for her trousseau. After a mental
survey of herself, she looked up to see William smiling at
her uncertainly. His hand touched hers for a brief instant,
and then he looked away stolidly.

He had a roll of paper at his side. He unrolled it slowly.
"I never showed you the architect's drawing of the exterior,"
he said. He avoided her eyes. She took the roll from him ap-
prehensively.

She had need of all her natural self-control, when she saw
the drawing. In that moment, she could hardly restrain a
cry of pure dismay. It was much worse than she had feared.
All those turrets, those towers, those rounded windows, those
swelling bays! The great stone piazza which encircled two-
thirds of the house! Even set in the midst of beguiling trees
and gardens and flowering borders and walks, the house was
a monstrosity. It was of stone, and the stone was a swart, almost
blackish, brown.

It was no worse, in many ways, than many of the wealthier
homes in Andersburg and its suburbs, except that its enormous
size made all its ugliness and architectural faults more overpowering. Gone, forever then, was her dream of a chaste
and noble Georgian house of whitish stone, with a fanlight
over the door, and fine casement windows. This was the house
where she was to live, where she would spend so many years,
and where she would doubtless die. She could not bear it.

"Well?" said William, impatiently.

She rerolled the paper with great care. "It is certainly—magnificent," she murmured.

He almost snatched the paper from her. "You do not like
it!" he said, accusingly.

"I did not say so, William. It is just that I—that I have never
imagined I might live in such a house." Her voice was very
calm.

"That is a very ambiguous remark," he said, wrathfully.

She did not know what to say in answer. She had tried so
hard, and now he was enraged again.

"You have always lived such a bloodless life," he said, with sneering condescension. "You have never really known anything except a little house with pale furniture and dim walls and shuttered windows and tiny fireplaces. A woman's house. This is a man's house."

Then she saw that he was deeply hurt, even greatly pained. This was the dream of his life, this dreadful house. He had planned it and loved it, had smiled over it and cherished it, even before he had bought her land. She detested herself for wounding him so. Quickly, she placed her hand over his and held it tightly, and looked at him with eyes bright with tears.

"Dear William!" she cried. "I am sorry I am so stupid. You are right; I haven't really appreciated such a wonderful house. What do I know of houses? Nothing! But this is not really a house; it is a mansion, and you deserve it, and I have no doubt that when it is completed we'll both have reason to be proud of it."

He stared at her with fierce and almost childlike intensity. She looked at him, her eyes still wet, her mouth smiling and trembling. For once, his subtlety deserted him. He did not remove his hand.

"You are not—not deceiving me?" he asked.

"Oh, no. How can you think that, William? I mean every word of it, I assure you."

He smiled at her then. Once or twice, in the past week or so, she had caught a flash of tenderness for her in his eyes. Now that tenderness was alive again, deeper than she had ever seen it before.

"Even if the house might seem too big to you?" he insisted.

She made herself laugh a little. "Indeed, it is big. I am afraid that is why I was frightened last night, and even just now. I have never lived in a big house before, William. I never expected I should live in one."

She had pleased him. He patted her hand with affectionate patronage. "I understood from the beginning," he said.

She smiled at him meekly. Nothing mattered, except his peace and happiness. She would live in a worse house than this, gladly, if it gave him pleasure. She would live anywhere, if she could help alleviate the chronic tensions and torments that tortured him.

They had reached the large desolate plot of land which had once been hers. Here May had briefly triumphed. The shacks on the borders of the land, already cleared by William of their former inhabitants, were almost hidden in flowering trees. More workmen were on hand. Ursula saw the stone.

Her last hope fled. The color was even worse than in the drawing. Each hewn stone gilttered in an ugly chocolate brown on its high surfaces, with ridges and curving valleys of blackish brown in the hollows and depressions. The workmen had been very busy. The framework of the house was already up, raw and yellow in the bright sunlight. A few stones had been mortared, and it took very little imagination to see the whole edifice towering to the sky, and spreading out in a massive pile. Fifteen acres of land would surround it or, rather, would be overpowered by it.

"I am breathless!" cried Ursula. "I cannot wait until we live here!"

A few days later, Lucy and Oliver came to the red suite. Mrs. Templeton returned to her own home, on salary, until the house on Schiller Road should be completed. Ursula welcomed Lucy and Oliver with an almost hysterical pleasure and relief. Now the days would not be so empty, the after-dinner hours not so taut and filled with apprehension. She had never thought to be glad to see a child, but she embraced Oliver with such vehemence that she came close to frightening him. She beamed upon Lucy, who was watching her with blue-eyed gravity and strange understanding.

Dear Lucy! thought Ursula. What a comfort this girl would be in the coming days and years! Her blunt intelligence, her wisdom and strength, would be urgently needed by her mistress. Lucy was a friend, and all at once Ursula understood that she had never really possessed a friend before.

CHAPTER XVI

SO IT WAS THAT Ursula struggled with herself to forget the growing house as much as possible. She did, however, have a few rebellious and secret thoughts. Elegance, she reflected, remembering William's condemnation of it as "bloodlessness," does not necessarily mean effeminacy. Refinement is not austerity or bareness. Greek architecture, the very essence of noble simplicity, was not inferior to Byzantine over-ornamentation and confusion and lavish heedlessness of color. Bright gilt and plush and vivid damask do not excel muted grace, cleanness of line and quiet panelled walls.

In late June and July, William was compelled to go on business journeys to Ohio and Michigan and Illinois, and even to other states. Sometimes he was gone for ten days or more, returning with an air of victory and satisfaction. She would listen with eager attention, exclaim admiringly at the proper intervals, and look at him with love. But, for her, the lumber business remained always a complete mystery which she had no desire to penetrate and understand. Apparently, William was becoming wealthier, for not only was he triumphant, but his directors and other officers showed every sign of elation. The ladies of Andersburg displayed towards Ursula an affection and solicitude and tenderness whose origin was very evident. Again, she took refuge in clichés, and tried to suppress a growing cynicism.

In August, the red suite began to oppress Ursula unbearably. The weather had become intolerably humid and hot. With a passion that approached desperation, she longed for her garden. The house, with its contents, was up for sale. More than once, Ursula went to visit her house, to sit in the quiet rooms, whose walls flickered with the shadow of leaves, to lie down upon her old bed, or to wander like a lost soul in the gardens, there to pluck away a yellowing leaf or a blown flower. There was comfort in the house, though it was beginning to have a faint, old and musty smell. It was filled with ghosts. Once Ursula found herself weeping uncontrollably in the small and charming parlor. She was shocked at her own

tears, and reproached herself sternly. It then occurred to
her that she was pregnant.

She visited Dr. Banks, who heartily assured her that her
suspicions were correct, and that she might make plans for
"a fine heir" the latter part of March. She returned to the
suite, somberly considering her condition. She felt no real
happiness, but, instead, a sudden upsurge of fear. William was
away in Michigan, and it was to Lucy, and to Lucy alone, that
Ursula confided what she knew should be regarded in the
light of great good news.

Lucy regarded her pale mistress seriously. Oliver had just
had his afternoon nap, and was sitting on Lucy's knee while
she brushed his damp hair. All the crimson draperies were
pushed back to admit what breeze might be hovering through
the street. The hot sunlight splashed the red damask walls,
the fiery red carpet. Ursula closed her eyes on a swell of nausea.

"Well, ma'am," said Lucy, in her sound and sturdy voice.
"Mr. Prescott'll be very happy to hear it."

Ursula whispered, her eyes still closed: "All this red! It
makes me quite ill."

Lucy set Oliver on his feet. The child sensed something
wrong. He stared at Ursula soberly, his underlip thrust out
as if he were contemplating a few tears. Lucy said: "Let me
help you undress, ma'am. You should lie down. I'll make you
a cool drink with lemons."

Ursula opened her eyes; they had a slightly wild expression.
"Lucy! Do you know there'll be endless acres of red in the
new house, too?"

Lucy did not reply to this. She assisted Ursula into the bedroom, removed her thin batiste frock and wide straw hat and
gloves and boots. Ursula lay down on the smooth white sheets
and let Lucy slip a pillow under her head. Then she remarked
with a sick smile: "I am hysterical. It is so hot."

Lucy brought cool water and bathed Ursula's face, brushed
her hair and neatly braided it. Oliver crept uncertainly into
the room. Ursula's tired eyes touched him; they brightened,
and she held out her hand to him. Immediately, and with
relief, he ran to her and kissed her. "Mama," he said, and then
patted her hand gently.

"He knows. He always knows when someone feels bad,"
said Lucy, with a fond glance at the child. "He's got a heart.
Haven't you, dear?" she asked, stooping to kiss him.

"Yes," he replied gravely. This broke the tension, and both
Lucy and Ursula laughed together. After a bewildered moment,

Oliver joined them, clapping his hands together in prideful glee that he could evoke such abandoned merriment.

Later, Ursula said: "If only we could be spending this time in my own little house, Lucy, where it is quiet and cool and peaceful. There is more room there than in this suite. But Mr. Prescott does not care for the house."

Lucy replied: "Well, then. At least, ma'am, when you go there, you must use the carriage."

Ursula regarded her with surprise. "You knew, then, I went home occasionally?"

"Oh, yes, ma'am. It was only natural," said Lucy, quietly.

She, herself, was to be married to John Shaeffer in October. Both she and John were to remain in William's employ. That was understood, tacitly. William liked neither of them, but then, he would never like any servant except Mrs. Templeton, who had somehow ingratiated herself with him. Ursula knew that both Lucy and John remained for her sake and Oliver's.

It had been Ursula's intention to tell William immediately of her new prospects, when he returned to Andersburg. But he entered the suite looking so stern and abstracted that she decided to delay the telling for a while. When he was in this mood nothing could distract his attention from his own affairs for very long. She could not understand her relief at her decision not to tell him just yet. She wondered what was engaging all his concentration this time, but the wonder was brief and indifferent.

Ursula, remembering the whispered and oblique stories of married friends, expected to be ill during this period. To her surprise, she remained conspicuously well. After that initial loss of self-control, she recovered her equanimity, and when William, a day or so later, suggested that she could visit his saw-mills if she wished, she consented at once. They drove away together, with John driving them. William's abstraction had disappeared, and Ursula felt his restrained elation and high confidence. He remarked that she appeared rather pale, accepted her murmur about the heat, advised that she rest as much as possible, then told her briefly of his new triumph, which had at first threatened to be a defeat. It had something to do with an option on an especially fine pine forest. Ursula listened attentively, and nodded her head. He said once more: "But you are pale."

Ursula had a quick reply to this: "The hotel is so hot, William, I cannot wait until we have our own home, among gardens." She was touched by this unusual solicitude.

He was highly pleased, and for the moment forgot her paleness. "It ought not to be too long, now. I expect to spend our first Christmas in the new house. Yes, the hotel is hot. But you have the carriage; you ought to go for frequent drives."

Ursula contemplated Christmas in the new house, and felt a great weariness. She smiled with every appearance of anticipation.

Once before, some four years ago, she had accompanied Alice Arnold on a visit to these mills, which had then been the property of Alice's husband. The mills had appeared large and sturdy. Now, as the carriage approached the river, and Ursula saw the mills again, she was astonished. The original buildings had become only the small nucleus of a newer and more imposing aggregation, all, apparently, having been built during the past few months. Some of them were still unpainted, others were in this process, still others had been finished.

Full of pride, William told John to halt the carriage a little distance away, and then sat back to wait for Ursula's astounded comments.

The late August day had turned fearfully oppressive, the heat sultry with an ominous threat of storm. The earlier blue of the sky had been replaced by a ponderously moving mass of dim lavender clouds, streaked with brassy gold. Under this lay the river, plum-colored water flowing into eddies and little tides of burnished yellow. The trees along the river banks hung dark and weighted, smelling of dust. The opposite shore lay, a dull irregular streak, beyond restless water. When the sun could force its light through the clouds, it was in the form of straight coppery beams, which suddenly, and until the sun was obscured again, lit up the river and land with a strong and eerie light, rendering everything unnatural and foreboding.

Ursula's attention was drawn to all this, away from the mills, and she felt again the nameless threat which hung over her marriage. A heavy despondency took hold of her, and a new fear. She forgot what she had come to see. She could look only at the sky and the river.

William said, growing impatient because of her prolonged silence: "Well, what do you think of it all?"

Ursula brought back her attention forcibly. She regarded the mills with concentration, and now she saw that the piers along the river were lined with flat-boats and barges, some of them being filled with sawed lumber by busy workmen, and some still waiting for cargoes. She became aware, for the first time, of smoke pouring from chimneys, and the deep throbbing of the steam-driven saws within the mills. The air was pungent with the smell of sap and resin. Near the mills stood huge piles of raw yellow sawdust.

"Astounding," she murmured.

William was apparently disappointed at this vague comment, so Ursula tried again: "How much you have accomplished in such a short time, dear William. It is hard to believe. Why, when I first saw these mills, they were so small and insignificant —in comparison." Her tongue felt dull and ponderous in her mouth, and she moved it with an actual physical effort.

"I think I have made considerable progress," admitted William, smiling again. He looked with satisfaction at the huge lettering on the buildings: "The Prescott Lumber Company."

Now something else caught Ursula's attention. One of the small buildings was in process of being repainted. Scaffolding stood along its side. A painter was just beginning to attack the faded words: "The American Lumber Company." This was in preparation for the new name. Just below the painter stood a tall thin boy, leaning against a pile of newly-sawn lumber.

Letter by letter, the old name began to be washed away in paint. Above the older building, a newer one rose wide and stark. The wild and terrible sun suddenly struck the words on the face of it: "The Prescott Lumber Company." The smaller building, with its old lettering, now being obliterated, sank into its shadow.

William had not as yet noticed the boy who was watching the disappearing of the name which had once sparkled so brightly on the smaller building. Somewhere, in the distance, Ursula heard William's strong voice speaking on and on. She saw only the boy as he gazed upward at the painter. He continued to lean against the cut lumber, his attitude almost nonchalant. But Ursula knew this was not nonchalance at all. Her first impulse of pity, her first look of concern at that colorless, lean face, turned to a keener insight, a sharper watchfulness. She had begun to think: "Poor Eugene! How frightful it must be for him to watch the name of his father's company disappearing before his eyes!" But the thought fell away, dwindled and faded. For there was no anger, no regret, no sadness, in that hard, clear profile.

Ursula, determined to feel only pity and pain, tried also to forget that she had never liked Eugene. His manners had always been grave and impeccable, his voice polite; he had always bowed to her with ceremony, and had invariably inquired after her health. Thereafter, thankfully, and not in the manner of other children, he had removed himself. Once she had even thought: "I should feel easier if he were about!" There was no explaining, even to herself, why she thought this, but Eugene present was less ominous than Eugene absent.

Now, as she looked at him acutely, she forgot him and remembered his mother. Her face grew troubled. No one ever spoke to her of Alice Arnold. In her presence, that name was carefully withheld. No one ever mentioned having seen the widow of the man whom William had ruined. Her friends had simply decided not to be aware of Alice any longer, nor to speak of her. She had lost prestige in Andersburg; she no longer existed for those who had still retained their importance or were striving madly for it.

I must see Alice, thought Ursula, wretchedly. But what could William Prescott's wife do for the widow of Chauncey Arnold, which Alice would accept?

"Ursula!" William's voice was loud and vexed in her ear. "You haven't been listening to me."

Ursula started. She tried to think of some remark to placate her husband. But none came. She touched his arm swiftly, then said in a low and anxious tone: "Look over there, William. That boy. Eugene Arnold."

William's eyes followed her quick gesture. His dark face flushed uncomfortably. For a few moments he watched the unaware Eugene, then he said: "Let us drive on."

It was then that Eugene stood upright, carefully dusted off the hands which had lain along the lumber, turned, and saw them. He stared at the carriage for what seemed to Ursula a miserably long time. He did not move, or seem in the least embarrassed. His pale fine hair lifted in the slight breeze from the river. Standing there, regarding the man and the woman in the carriage, he had a fine distinction, an attitude of dignity and poise. Ursula saw his face clearly, that face so like Alice's, with its marks of breeding, and yet so unlike in its expression.

Ursula wished herself a thousand miles away. She could not look at her husband. Fervently, she willed Eugene to walk off quietly. To her acute misery, she saw that the boy was beginning to move towards the carriage. His tall young figure did not appear defenseless against the purple and yellow of sky and water. Rather, it had strength and a kind of power.

"What shall we say to him?" whispered Ursula to William, in distress.

He did not answer. He watched Eugene come. His flush was deeper than ever.

Eugene did not hurry. He came to them, and there was something about his quiet manner, his straightforward look, which gave Ursula the impression that he was entirely aware of their embarrassment, and disdainful of it. Now he was standing but five feet away.

"Good afternoon," he said, and bowed a little.

"Eugene," murmured Ursula. She paused. "How is your mother, Eugene?"

"Very well, thank you," replied the boy.

Ursula's hands were damp. "Please tell her I asked about her. I—I have been very much engaged lately, Gene. I mean to call upon her soon." She stopped a moment. "I am sure your mother will understand."

"Oh, yes," said Eugene quietly. He looked at Ursula directly, and she saw a flicker in his almost colorless eyes. "Mother always understands." Was his tone ironical?

William sat stiff and bulky beside Ursula. Ursula could feel his angry unhappiness. She felt, rather than saw, his awkward gesture. She knew it was a prelude to an even more unfortunate remark, and she wished she knew how to forestall it. He said, too loudly: "How do you like the new mills, Eugene?"

Eugene regarded him thoughtfully. "I've been watching them being built for a long time. They are wonderful."

William studied the mills with an elaborate attention which Ursula suspected was to cover his overpowering discomfiture. "Yes," he said, heavily. "A lot of work has gone into this expansion." He added, lamely: "Thank you, Eugene."

"Do give your mother my love," said Ursula, helplessly.

Eugene said, very politely: "Of course, Mrs. Prescott."

He turned to William then, with an air of expectation, and now there was something about the boy which made Ursula's lips tighten and her eyes narrow with trouble. But her chief concern was with William, and with his dreadful tactlessness. He had not intended the brutality of his question to Eugene. It had been only a lack of taste, and however deplorable that lack it had still not implied any meanness. William, Ursula thought, had not had any formal or consistent education, and this had narrowed his life, had prevented him from acquiring a fixed point of reference; hence his want of taste, his inability to understand his fellowmen, his vulnerability when confronted by delicate situations, and his capriciousness.

Eugene still waited, with that air of polite expectation. Why does he wait? thought Ursula. It only prolongs the discomfort of both William and myself. And then, with incredulity, it came to her that this was exactly Eugene's intention. She regarded the boy sharply. She had not been mistaken. With more abruptness than was common with her, she said: "Eugene, please tell your mother that I hope to call upon her within a few days."

"Yes," muttered William, and lifted his hand to John, who had been watching with deep interest.

Eugene bowed again. He was smiling almost imperceptibly. "Good-bye, Mrs. Prescott. And Mr. Prescott." His voice was smooth and courteous.

The carriage turned about. Ursula did not glance back, for she was positive that she would see Eugene still standing there, smiling inscrutably. It was a most repugnant idea.

William said, after several long minutes had passed: "I am sorry for the boy. It is too bad he had such a father. Still, I can't like him, even if he is young. In fact," and he laughed shortly, "I don't think he ever was young."

"No," said Ursula, "he was never young."

The lavender clouds had deepened to purple. Now the sky was disturbed by a surge of distant thunder, and then a flash, and a louder surge. The horses quickened their pace, and there was a restless movement to their heads. Just as the carriage approached the Imperial Hotel, Ursula told William that she was expecting a child.

CHAPTER XVII

URSULA, FIVE days later, was still anxiously contriving a graceful, warm letter to Alice Arnold, a letter to be as smooth as glass yet transparent as genuine friendship. Just as she had finally become satisfied with the last draft, a note came to her from Alice, herself. Alice had written:

"Dear Ursula: Eugene has given me your very kind message, which gave me great pleasure. He also told me that you wished to call upon me, a very delightful prospect. Would Sunday afternoon, about four, be convenient for you? There is a matter I should like to discuss with you which is of importance to me. But I prefer to come to the Imperial. If Sunday is not feasible, please send me a message. Yours, with affection, Alice."

The short note was implicit with Alice's gentleness and tact. Ursula read it with sadness. She endeavored to surmise what might be of such importance to Alice as to bring her to this violent suite, at an hour when the streets would be filled with carriages and walkers. Ursula's anxiety made her throat tighten. Alice no longer had a carriage. The auctioning of her property had begun. Daily, her house was filled with the curious and greedy and shamefaced. To spare her former friends any embarrassment, Alice would invariably retire to the servants' quarters on the third floor of her house, while her cherished plate and china, rugs and cabinets, Chippendale chairs, Queen Anne sofas, lace curtains and draperies, glassware and ornaments, were being auctioned and fingered and appraised.

Fortunately, William had again gone to Michigan. Alice probably knew this, for surely she would not ask to call upon Ursula with William present. But, remembering her friend, Ursula was not too sure. There was such a pellucid serenity about Alice, such a noble simplicity and majesty, that not even the thought of meeting William could have disturbed her.

Ursula wrote: "Instead of coming to this hotel, dear Alice, I think I should prefer to see you in my home, which I visit regularly. William is not in the city, and I intend to go there this Sunday, as the prospective buyer for the property has asked me to choose what I wish to take with me to my new home. Four o'clock, then."

Sunday dawned, sultry and molten. Perhaps it was concern for her friend, and the anticipation of pain at meeting her again, which made Ursula feel quite ill all through the morning, and even far into the afternoon.

The street on which Ursula's house stood was very quiet in the still blankness of the heat. Every blind was drawn; every shutter was closed against the blast from the shimmering cobblestones. Not even a child strolled languidly before fenced gardens, or sat on a doorstep. Ursula's hand trembled as she inserted the key in the old lock; she heard the loud click echo back from the sleeping faces of the sun-drenched houses. She closed the door behind her. Now the drowsy odors of potpourri and lavender and old leather drifted in the silent air. Here, too, the shutters were closed. The silent rooms lay in bluish shadow, cool and restful and welcoming, the polished furniture and walls shining faintly in the dusk, the portraits masked and dim in their ancient gold frames.

Ursula went into the kitchen. She lit a fire in the black stove, worked the pump until the rusted water disappeared and sparkling fresh water replaced it. She filled the kettle and put it on the stove. She opened the parcels she had brought; one of them was a small packet of tea; she had also brought a lemon, some sugar, and a box of fresh biscuits. She brought out her best lace and linen traycloth, placed it on a round silver tray, and laid upon it her priceless old egg-shell teacups and saucers of ivory and pale rose. Her silver, wrapped in flannel, was not yet tarnished; the thin silver bowls of the spoons glimmered in the tree-shaded quiet of the kitchen, as did her silver teapot, hot-water jug and sugar bowl. She found a fluted plate for the rich biscuits. All of this she carried into the parlor and laid upon a table.

At four o'clock, precisely, she poured boiling water onto the tea in the teapot. She had left the front door ajar, so that no clamor of the knocker would awake the curious neighborhood. As she had expected, she heard quick light footfalls on the street outside as she made the tea, a rustle of stiff silk, and then a soft knock on the door. Alice Arnold entered the parlor, tall and very thin in her heavy widow's weeds, a black veil hanging over her face from the brim of her small black bonnet.

"Alice," said Ursula, faintly.

Alice drew back the veil, and advanced to greet her hostess, holding out her hand. Even in that shuttered dusk Ursula could see the clear, colorless shining of her tender eyes, so candid, so wise and so gentle. She had no need of beauty or ringlets or jewels. She had a dignity which quietly denied that she was a woman open to any expression of sympathy. A single smooth strand of light hair passed across her high forehead under the bonnet. There was a seed-pearl brooch at her throat, and for an instant the broad gold band of her wedding-ring gleamed in the shadowy room.

"Dear Ursula," she said, softly. Very simply she kissed Ursula on the cheek. There was no hint in her manner of any embarrassment, only a mild kindliness. Ursula gave a sigh of relief. She ought to have remembered Alice more clearly. They had not been very intimate friends, yet all at once Ursula felt an overpowering need for Alice's friendship and understanding.

"It was so kind of you to see me today," said Alice, as she sat down near the tea-table and smiled gratefully at it. "I do hope it was no inconvenience."

"On the contrary, Alice," murmured Ursula, "it was very good of you to come." The words sounded fatuous in her own ears. She sat down near Alice, and poured the tea.

Alice went on, as she took a biscuit: "How cool it. is in this sweet room, Ursula. It always was so charming. I have always loved your house."

She glanced about the room, smiling faintly, her eyes lingering on every object. She sighed, the merest breath of a sigh.

"Yes," said Ursula. Her glance followed that of her guest's. She added, politely, "How is Eugene, Alice?"

"Eugene is quite well," replied the other woman. "I am thankful he can still attend his school." Her voice was quietly impersonal. "He does so well there. He had honors again this year."

"Eugene is a very remarkable boy," said Ursula, already tired of Eugene. Her poise was very ragged. This was painful beyond her previous imagining.

Alice was so delicately subtle that she sensed at once Ursula's misery and lack of interest in Eugene. She said: "Please forgive me that I did not ask you before how you are, Ursula."

"I am very well," replied Ursula, mechanically. "And you, Alice?"

"I am always well," answered Alice, with almost her old light cheerfulness. "Not even the heat can disconcert me."

Ursula thought of the dismantling of the beautiful Arnold home, of the constant rumbling of strangers' footsteps in the large rooms, of the endless mutter of alien voices in the halls. Her fingers tightened about her teacup handle.

Alice said, in a tranquil voice: "It was really very rude of me to ask you to meet me here today, Ursula. After all, we all of us have our duties. I am being very selfish, and you must forgive me. I must make my visit as brief as possible, and my request." She paused. "You said you had a buyer for this house, I believe."

"There is a gentleman who is interested," stammered Ursula.

"But you have not sold the house as yet?"

"No." Ursula could glance up now. Her face was very pale, and even in the cool of this room it was damp and beaded.

Alice sighed. Then she laughed a little. "I have been wondering, Ursula, if you would rent this house to me, with its contents. As I said before, I have always loved it."

Ursula put down her cup. "Rent the house to you?" she repeated in a dull and stupid tone.

"Yes." Then added Alice, quickly: "But perhaps you would prefer to discuss this with your husband first. That would be only right, of course."

Ursula looked at her cup. "The house," she said, without inflection, "is mine. It belonged to my father. No one else dares presume——" She went on: "You may rent it, Alice, if it pleases you."

But Alice did not speak immediately. A strong deep solicitude shone in her eyes, illuminated her face like a beam. Almost abstractedly, she murmured: "Do not make an immediate decision, dear Ursula, for I cannot pay you more than twenty-five dollars a month." There was nothing of self-pity in her words or inflection, just a quiet statement of fact.

There was a silence between the two women, while Ursula fought down the mortifying desire to cry out to Alice: "Take the house! I ask nothing for it!" Then Alice said, gently and slowly: "It was most kind of Mr. Prescott to send me that check, Ursula. But, of course, it was not possible for me to accept it. I do hope he did not think I misunderstood his gesture. I am truly grateful."

"William sent you money?" asked Ursula, in a stifled voice. Bitter color ran up her cheeks.

Almost playfully, Alice said at once: "Yes. It was so very kind! I was extremely touched. But, I am so sorry! You did not know, Ursula?"

Ursula could only move her head in negation, and numbly.

"Please, then, do not tell him. I pray you."

Ursula was still speechless. She clasped her hands on her knees. She thought of William and his stupid action. Had she not, only a moment or two ago, had her own impulse to offer Alice charity, she would have experienced anger against her husband, and humiliation for herself.

"It was so very kind," urged Alice, as if pleading for William.

"Yes," whispered Ursula.

Now the two women regarded each other with somber gravity.

Then Ursula heard herself saying, still in that whispering voice: "Alice, I am going to have a baby."

"Ah," murmured Alice. Her worn face smiled at Ursula, but her eyes remained grave.

Ursula stood up quickly, as if distracted. "I am afraid!" she said, almost inaudibly.

Alice did not even pretend to misunderstand. She watched Ursula, and the gravity in her eyes became more intense.

She said: "Do not be afraid. It will not help."

Ursula suddenly pressed her hands to her face, and again there was silence in the room. It was only after some time that Ursula dropped her hands and gazed at Alice despairingly. "You always understood everything, Alice. I think, after all, that was the reason I never saw you more than two or three times a year. I avoided you, deliberately. I did not know it then, but I know it now. I was always a complacent woman; I was afraid you might see what there was to see."

Alice did not answer. Compassion was tender about her mouth, and a great sadness.

Ursula gave a short sick laugh. "Don't look at me like that, Alice. You see too much."

"Do not be afraid," repeated Alice.

Ursula interlaced her fingers tightly, and looked down at them. "When I told William, he was beside himself with joy. It is no use telling me not to be afraid, Alice."

"I know," said Alice gently. "I was very afraid before Eugene was born. I conquered that. Now I am afraid again."

Ursula glanced up at her quickly. Alice nodded simply. "I love my boy with all my heart. But now I am terribly afraid. I look at him, and I see a stranger. He thinks I do not see; he thinks I am a fool. I stare at other mothers, and I wonder whether they have this pain in their hearts, that I have. They seem so—contented, as if all were well with them. Do they see, I ask myself, or do they refuse to see? I cannot know. And no mother will ever honestly tell anyone else, not even her own God!"

She sighed. "I know it never helps to cherish fear. A mother can only hope a little, or pray a little. Beyond that, she is powerless. There is a Hindu saying, I believe, that it is an evil thing to love any creature too much, or to fasten one's hopes too strongly on another."

She lifted her hands, dropped them on her thin knees, where they lay in an attitude of utter resignation.

"What else is there for any woman, but love? Somewhere I read that God forgives mothers almost any sin. If so, I think it is because of their suffering, which they will never admit to anyone, but which lives with them to the day of their death. No one can help them, not even God, because they have asked so little—the affection of their children—in return for so much more, so terribly much more. But even that is almost always denied them."

Ursula gazed fixedly at Alice, and momentarily forgot her own pain in the contemplation of Alice's. "Oh, Alice," she murmured.

Alice did not speak. Ursula came closer to the other woman and stood beside her. She cried: "I am not afraid of that! With me, it is something else. I don't want children, Alice. I never liked them, or desired them. I had hoped I might not ever have them. I have seen what they can do to their parents; I don't want to endure that. I don't want to waste my life."

"I wonder," said Alice, meditatively, her head slightly averted, "if our own parents thought of us as we now think of our children."

Ursula was silent. She remembered her father. It was not possible that he had been lonely when with her, had waited for her to say the words which would have told him that she cherished him. But, had she really loved and cherished him?

"Oh, William!" she cried, and did not know that she had said this aloud.

She sat down abruptly. Suddenly she gave Alice a white smile. "I wish you were a sentimental woman, Alice. I wish you were a cozy liar. Then you could have said: 'How delightful, Ursula! A dear little baby! I am so glad for you!'"

Alice did not smile in answer. She leaned forward and took Ursula's hand strongly, and held it. "Ursula, again I say: Try not to be afraid. Try to remember that even if you are to be a mother you will remain a human being, that you have your own life, and what you do with that life is the most important thing of all. Love, yes. But not too much, not ever too much."

"I do not expect to love my children to such self-destruction," said Ursula.

Alice pressed her hand, then released it.

"We can really help no one but ourselves," she said. "Sometimes, if we are blessed, we can console and comfort. Not always. Only very rarely. We can just stand by and pray that a little of what we have to give will be accepted."

She stood up, tall and emaciated, and her black skirts rustled about her. Now she hesitated, looking down at Ursula. She opened her mouth to speak, then closed it helplessly.

"I wish," said Ursula, brokenly, "that I had known you better. I wish I might have had you for a friend."

"But I am your friend," said Alice, gently.

Ursula shook her head wearily. Then she, too, stood up. "It will make me happy, knowing you are in this house, Alice. I hope you will let me visit you sometimes. It is my home; nothing else will ever be home to me."

She sat for a long time alone, when Alice had gone. She did not have the strength to move.

PART TWO

"These are my dearly beloved children."
CORNELIA

CHAPTER XVIII

ON DECEMBER fifteenth the Prescotts took possession of their new home.

Ursula knew man's anthropomorphic tendency to find, in the movement of the stars, and in universal phenomena outside his own tiny orbit, omens meant for his little self. It had always seemed to her a most silly if almost insane egotism. Nevertheless, she could not help feeling that the very elements were conspiring to force her to sense a certain ominousness in the day on which she entered the great house.

There had been no snow, or even rain, for the eight days before the fifteenth. But on that morning the bleak skies, palely lit by a wan sun, steadily darkened. By noon, fold upon fold of dull-purplish and heavy gray clouds stood crowded and massed from horizon to horizon. Against them, the mountains dissolved, merged into their substance, so that it was impossible to discern any line of demarcation. A grayish-lavender light lowered over the city, too dim to cast shadows, and throwing an atmosphere of desolation down the vistas of every street. It blotted out, or absorbed, most of the usual sounds of the city, so that carriages or wagons passing over cobbled streets gave out a hollow sound, bodiless and unreal. It distorted perspective; houses, churches and other buildings took on a curious flatness and lack of depth.

Shortly after noon, dry sandlike particles of snow began to fall, accompanied by a hard and whining wind. It was hardly a storm, for though white ridges appeared in the fields and in gardens and upon lawns, the wind roughly abrased most surfaces and exposed their stony brownness. The cold pierced the warmest furs and cloaks and coats. It was impossible to keep it out.

The enormous house waited for the family. On every marble hearth in every room a fire blazed. But it could not dispel the gloom outside and the oppressiveness within. Ursula resolutely refused to look at the grounds surrounding the house, lonely and desolate and, as yet, without landscaping. She was conscious, however, of the presence of the mountains beyond the gray and purple clouds. She consoled herself with

149

the promise that in the spring these broken and empty grounds
would be planted, graded, green and full of flowering trees.
In the meantime, it was best to ignore it all, just as she had
carefully refrained from visiting this house more than two
or three times during the process of its construction. Everything
was now complete, even to the last of the six servants, whom
she had never met, since William had delegated Mrs. Templeton to the task of securing them.

Nothing had been spared, Ursula saw, to make this a magnificent house. She had not proceeded through two rooms
before her dismay had become horrified awe and fear. She
did not know the extent of her husband's new fortune; she
was shrewdly certain that he still owed much money for this
house and these crushing furnishings. He would without doubt
be able eventually to pay for it all; in the meantime there must
be an astronomical debt hanging over his head. After a little,
even her fear and awe were swallowed up in her realization
of the pathological vanity, egotism and hidden terror which
had built the house and had filled it with these overpowering
treasures and baroque decorations.

The reception hall, so vast that the fire at one end, blazing
on a black marble hearth, could hardly lift the winter cold
to an endurable temperature, was breath-taking enough. The
floor was paved in black-and-white marble squares. Black-and-
white marble panelling covered the walls. The shadowy ceiling
had been decorated with a muted mural, a garden scene. The
clusters of gaslights, flickering in dim golden globes, did not
give out enough illumination for Ursula to see the details
of the painting. Yellow-glass candelabra, circled with many
pendent prisms, stood on the mantelpiece. A tremendous grandfather clock, of intricately carved ebony, stood against one
wall, its ancient gilded face glimmering in the winter dusk.
As Ursula entered the hall, the clock boomed out the stroke
of two with so deep and sonorous a note that mournful vibra-
tions echoed back for some moments after the ceasing of
the actual strokes.

Ursula and her husband entered the first, and the largest,
of the tremendous drawing-rooms. Here there was a sudden
change from the black and white and gilt of the reception hall,
but the effect was no less oppressive. It had been furnished
predominantly in various shades of red, ranging from pale
delicate pink to a strong crimson, with flashes, here and there,
of turquoise and emerald, of black and white and gold. The
walls had been hung with a faint rose satin damask, inter-
spersed occasionally by a plaster-bas-relief of a tall Ionian

pillar reaching to the ceiling. The incredibly high ceiling had
been painted to resemble white marble with black veins. Never,
not even in the Imperial Hotel, had Ursula seen such mammoth
furniture, such gigantic fireplaces. Throne-chairs, covered with
rose damask, stood against the walls. Chairs of turquoise or
emerald were grouped around mighty circular tables of mahogany. Sofas, in scarlet or green or determined pink, broke
up the vastness of the room. High carved marble pedestals
held priceless oxblood porcelain or marble or Chinese lamps.
The floor had been covered with an unbelievably huge rug
in dull green. Along the walls were gaslights in spun glass,
and from the ceiling hung a chandelier like a glittering sta-
lactite of crystal. There was a fireplace at each end of the
room, in rosy marble surmounted by Venetian mirrors of
a very ornate design. Again, the fires could not entirely banish
the cold.

"Glorious," murmured Ursula, faintly, her frugal German
heart sinking abysmally. She looked at the crimson damask
curtains looped at every arched window, and closed her eyes.

The second drawing-room was, by comparison with the
first, almost a relief, for here sanity had vaguely prevailed.
There was a renaissance quality about it. Ivory and gold pre-
dominated in the furniture, which, by contrast, appeared delicate and even restrained. But again, there was no escaping
the general florid tint, for wine-red velvet portieres and draperies hung at the windows and in the archways, and there were
a few rosy chairs mingling with the paler sofas, and ivory and
gilt and silver lamps. The fireplaces had been constructed of
a creamy marble, possibly, thought the despairing Ursula,
because the builder had run out of pink marble. It probably
broke his heart, her venomous reflections continued.

The gold satin and antique white of the music room lifted
her spirits for a moment. Here there was not even a hint of
red. Yet the ivory piano, and the organ (who is going to play
the latter? thought Ursula), with its gold-leaf pipes and cream-
colored console, managed to give a florid air to what otherwise
might have passed as elegance and restraint. Here, too, a
fire burned on a yellow marble hearth, but the shadows in
the corners of the room were ghostly.

Ursula was, by this time, completely oppressed. It was hard
to maintain a happy smile, and to keep up a constant bubble
of admiring and awed remarks. William stalked beside her,
weighing every word and exclamation she uttered.

Now she entered the dining-room, also huge. The dark
walnut walls, the subdued chandeliers, the fire lurking on

a brown marble hearth, filled her with despondency. Here furniture, monolithic and ponderous, petit-point chairs in dull shades, a round table which even without leaves would seat twelve people comfortably, a buffet at least ten feet long and surmounted by a mirror reflecting an enormous collection of silver, two cabinets glimmering with endless dozens of glasses and china pieces, completely overwhelmed her.

Thereafter, the inspection of the house acquired a nightmare quality. The morning room, in red and blue, only vaguely disturbed her. She must inspect a mighty kitchen, and allow the cook and two housemaids to be introduced. She smiled at them with a glassy graciousness, her face gray with exhaustion and misery. She did not remember their names. Nor did she remember, that day, the visit to the attached conservatory, the gleaming ballroom, the walking through a labyrinth of halls. Fires and flickering chandeliers merged in one mass before her. Slowly and heavily, she mounted the giant black-and-white marble staircase which rose from the reception hall to the upper regions. She must have visited the many guest-rooms and the dressing-rooms, all furnished with a crass magnificence. She did not remember. She discovered that William was to have his own bedroom and dressing-room, and she, also. This stirred nothing in her. She did look at her apartments with a last flicker of interest, for here she would sleep every night, in this bed she would have her children, and here she would die.

Then, she was aroused to pity and love again. William, probably remembering her own muted tastes, had insisted that the ornate decorations of the other rooms should here be more subdued. The walls had been covered with pale yellow satin, in which a soft gray design had been woven. The curtains were of Cluny lace, the draperies of silver brocade. A white marble fireplace had been installed, and here was the most comfortable fire of all. Two French girandoles embellished the mantelpiece, while from the ceiling hung a chandelier of yellow crystal. A fine Aubusson covered the floor. The canopied bed dripped with delicate Brussels lace. The furniture was not mammoth; rather, it was somewhat small and happily sparse, painted old white and tipped with gold. A beautiful Venetian mirror hung over the dresser, and a chaise-longue in soft blue stood near a window. Ursula caught a glimpse of a small and dainty desk, a cabinet of objets d'art, a bookcase waiting for her own books.

"Dear William!" she exclaimed, "it is so beautiful, so lovely!"

She caught his hand and held it tightly. "It is the most delight-ful room in the whole house!"

William had begun to smile; his fingers had closed upon hers. Then, as he grasped the import of her last words, he removed his hand and glowered down at her. "You have no high opinion of the others?"

A tremendous weariness flowed over Ursula. She said: "You do not understand. This is my room, my bedroom, my very own. I shall spend much time here. Besides, I can see that you thought it all out so carefully; you chose what you believed, and knew, I would like."

He was pacified. He beamed about the room, rocking back on his heels. "Everything in the house is priceless," he said. "Almost everything is imported from France or Italy. There is a fortune in this house," he added, dropping his voice to the timbre of reverence.

Ursula, tired and now completely disoriented, had a series of wild and incoherent thoughts. Yes, there was a fortune in this house. Was it a mortgaged fortune? She had no way of knowing, and she dared not ask. After all, she thought hysteri-cally, I can always be a schoolmistress if necessary. There is always my own house! At least, there is no mortgage on that, and all the furniture is paid for! And I still have my ten thousand dollars!

As if in a dream, she saw Mrs. Templeton lurking in the doorway, a pious smile of pride and servility on her long dun-colored face. Mrs. Templeton suddenly loomed beside her. She and William were holding her. She heard their voices from a far distance. She did not remember much after that, but when she opened her eyes again she was in bed, the golden bed with the Brussels lace and the silken quilts.

CHAPTER XIX

BY THE END OF January, Dr. Banks was reluctantly forced to consider twins. Nothing else could explain Ursula's condition. William, when discreetly informed of this, was incredulous though delighted.

The end of February found Ursula lethargic and ill. Not even little Oliver, with his affectionate face, wise eyes and sprightly manner, could draw her long from an apathetic seclusion. When Oliver slept during the day, Lucy sat beside her bed, sturdily knitting or sewing or embroidering. She was routed only when Mrs. Templeton came down from her afternoon nap. But, after dinner, Mrs. Templeton was not permitted to return to Ursula's bedroom.

"I don't know what you have against the woman," William complained gloomily. "I can't be with you every night," he went on, trying to hide his secret pleasure when Ursula cried that in the evenings she wanted to see him and him only. "I have to be away, a few days at a time. I don't like to leave you alone."

"The bell-rope is right at my hand," pleaded Ursula. She wanted him so desperately, these painful sick days. They could hold no conversation which interested either. His world and hers lay inexorably apart. Yet she loved him, and never so intensely as she did now. It was comfort and strength to have him beside her, while she lay lapped in the cold wavelets of fear and dread.

There was no doubt in William's mind that the children would be boys. Girls were not to be considered in the least. Girls might come later. These children would be male. So determined, so sure, was he, that Ursula also came to accept the coming babies as of the masculine sex. They discussed names.

"I want them to have the names of Dr. Cowlesbury," said William. "Matthew and Thomas Cowlesbury Prescott. Your father's name? August—good God! It is not an American name. I won't consider it for a moment."

Ursula had no objection to Matthew and Thomas. Now she developed a habit of awakening alone in the night to fresh terror and apprehension. Sometimes she could not return to sleep. She would rise and wrap herself in a velvet peignoir and sit by the window, watching the moon pour down its white desolation on the broken land which lay about the house. She knew loneliness as she had never known loneliness before.

On the 29th of March, while the last snows of the year swirled around the great dark pile of the house, the children were born. They arrived with surprising celerity and with the briefest of suffering for their mother.

As William had always predicted, they were boys. They were fraternal, but not identical, twins. This was obvious even from the first day. The one to be christened Matthew was long and delicately formed, with a light fluff of hair and a slender face. Thomas was of a sturdier frame, and shorter, with streaks of reddish hair and a square little face. Both were fine and healthy, and exceptionally large for twins.

William's pride reached a peak of stern frenzy, and Ursula, from her pillows, smiled weakly at him. She had begun to love her children. Now began for her, for a few weeks, a time of real happiness and sense of achievement. William approved of her enormously. The children were good, Lucy reported. They were lovely children.

The christening was an important event in the city. Gifts heaped the tables everywhere. The soft April sun slowly turned the new lawns about the house green. Soft April rains rustled at the windows. The world flowered again. Ursula was happy.

It was not until July that she suddenly became aware that William was not displaying his former interest in Oliver, and that he sometimes admonished the child harshly for playing too noisily in the hall outside the nursery where his sons lay. On these occasions, Oliver would become completely silent, looking up at William with a strange expression in his eyes, and following his foster father with a long slow glance as William would walk away.

The knowledge came to Ursula with the sickening force of a savage blow. At first, she could not accept it. She began to observe William and Oliver acutely. When she was finally obliged to acknowledge the truth her grief was terrible. It was no use thinking of telling William that he was being both cruel and obtuse, that he owed a duty to this child as much as he owed it to his own sons. William would not believe that he had changed.

Yet he had changed. His interest in Oliver as a person was declining surely if slowly. At times, he displayed an irrational irritation with the child, and called for Lucy to take him away when the babies were being nursed. There were days he did not even inquire about him, or ask to see him.

Now the old terror and dread returned to Ursula in stronger measure than ever before. She and Lucy knew so much which they could not discuss. Lucy had married her John in October, and they occupied two rooms on the third floor. There Oliver would play, and even sleep. The exile was becoming complete. Mrs. Templeton began to discern it. Her treatment of Oliver, formerly overly saccharine and sentimental, took on an overtone of thin impatience when the child showed himself.

CHAPTER XX

JOHN OPENED THE carriage door for Ursula and Oliver a street or two away from her old home. "Meet me here in about an hour, John," said Ursula. The young man nodded. It was an old formula now, this monthly visit, on a Sunday afternoon. Did William know of it? Ursula had become certain he did, and that, in his obscure and twisted way of thinking, it pleased him.

This Sunday, the last Sunday of October, was brilliant and cool. The copper and brown and scarlet and gold of the earth, the intense purple of the mountains against the gem-like aquamarine of the blazing sky, combined in an incredible medley of color. About every tree or building the shadows stood vivid, carved of shining jet. Strong scents of burning wood, of apples, of drying grass and spicy leaves, filled the cold sharp air. Ursula's cloak blew about her; she had to bend her head against the skirling wind.

Oliver, at six, considered himself almost a man, and sworn to protection of his mother. He held her elbow firmly; he was a tall boy, reaching almost to her shoulder. He walked with light grace and surety, guiding Ursula across rough or broken cobblestones as if she, and not himself, were the child. Solicitously, he watched every movement of her heavy body. Ursula, who, as usual, lacked all female "delicacy," had already informed him that within another four months or so he would have a fourth brother or sister, besides Thomas and Matthew, and Julia. Oliver had accepted this with his customary gentle gravity, and had made no comment. He knew that Thomas and Matthew did not know of this as yet. After all, they were only four, while he was approaching seven. As for Julia, or Julie, she was hardly more than a baby, still toddling about in the imperious bad-temper of her twenty-four months of life. He, Oliver, was a man. He had already learned that men not only were informed of secrets, but that a man must learn to bear slights, injustices, heart-burnings, bewilderments and sadness with silence and fortitude, whether these things were inflicted upon him by his parents, servants or governesses.

It was Ursula, and Ursula alone, and Lucy and John, like

himself also outside the family, who loved him now. It was not enough for Oliver, but no one but Ursula guessed this.

The trees along the street were painted with light, just as they had been in all the autumns of Ursula's youth. She looked at them, and they were not joy to her, but only mournfulness. She glanced down at Oliver, and said: "Is it not a lovely day, dear? And this street is always the same; it was like this when I was as young as you, and when I was a girl, with my father, and when I was a woman, and left it forever."

Oliver looked at the trees and the sky, and all the bright ghosts of the dying year. He said: "Yes, Mama," and pressed her arm. Strangely, Ursula was comforted. It was no use for her common-sense to say: "He is only a child, and he can't understand what autumn can mean when you are sad or wretched, how all its color is no comfort, but only a reminder that life is brightest when it is about to go, and that there is nothing anywhere, nothing at all."

Ursula paused a moment before her house, and looked up at its gray broad quiet and green shutters and shining windows. It gazed tranquilly, in its old wisdom, at the house opposite. She said: "Yes, it's my home."

Alice Arnold, in her neat black bombazine, a trifle rusty at the seams, but always elegant, opened the door for them, and said in her gentle, playful fashion: "I have been watching for you, and hoping you would come." She drew them into the tiny hall, bent, and kissed Ursula's cheek. As always, she gave Ursula a quick if surreptitious glance, and then smiled tenderly at Oliver. "How is your throat, Oliver? I do hope it is better."

"Yes, Aunt Alice," he replied, gravely, but smiling at her. "It is quite well now."

Alice took Ursula's cloak, while Oliver unbuttoned and removed his coat. "I have made your favorite tarts, Ursula," she said, "and Oliver's. With new plums, just picked yesterday, from your own tree. Such delicious ones. I think they are the best ever."

Ursula, as always, drew in a deep breath in the parlor, detecting, with sad delight, the old odors of lavender, potpourri, wax, soap, hot fresh tea, newly baked pastry, sunshine on ancient leather and carpets, and burning firewood. The tenseness in her tired body relaxed, leaving a hardly perceptible aching behind. Oliver smiled about him happily. It was as if this were home to him, too. He helped Ursula to a chair, sat down near her on a footstool. He looked with pleasure at the shining tea-things glimmering in the firelight, and at the tray of tarts.

"It is the nursemaid's Sunday off, and the twins were a little obstreperous," said Ursula, removing her gloves. "At least, Tommy was. Such a rowdy child."

Once or twice, during the past year, Ursula had brought her boys to this house. The last occasion had not been a pleasant one. Matthew had sat solemnly in a corner of the sofa, and had whimpered a little, drearily. Thomas had raced wildly about, climbing on furniture, demanding bric-a-brac out of his reach, shouting, behaving abominably, like the spoiled and demanding child he was.

"How are the dear babies?" asked Alice, settling herself with a rustle behind Ursula's cherished silver, and beginning to pour.

"They are very well," said Ursula, listlessly. "They are always well." This was not quite true. Thomas and Julia usually burst with red health, but Matthew was less robust. He was too thin and pale, too quiet and solitary. She added: "Matthew has been a little feverish with a cold. He is better now, however." A weariness, as of intense boredom, filled her. She asked: "And how are you, dear Alice? And Eugene?"

"I am always well," answered Alice, looking at her friend with her radiant pale eyes, and smiling. There was considerable gray weaving its way now through her fine light hair, and she was more slender than ever. She was worn as an old silver teaspoon is worn, thin and fragile, but pure to the last delicate edge. Nothing could obliterate that shining, that colorless but valiant lustre. "As for Eugene, he is the same. His schoolmasters are quite lyrical about him, and constantly assure me of his remarkable mind." She smiled; it was not the smug smile of gratified motherhood. It was, for Alice, almost a wry smile. "He is working at his lessons today, though I have urged him to go out into this wonderful weather. He is quite relentless about his school work."

"But Eugene never cared about playing games with the other boys," said Ursula, heavy with her boredom.

Alice laughed again. "I would rather he were not quite so grim," she said, giving Ursula one of the latter's own teacups filled with steaming and fragrant tea. "Sometimes he almost frightens me, he is so coldly intense about his school work. I don't think he really enjoys it; I think he regards it as a means to an end." She paused. "He will be down shortly. He always enjoys seeing you, dear Ursula."

I doubt it, I seriously doubt it, thought Ursula. But she smiled falsely. Eugene filled her with uneasiness; he disconcerted her by his very presence. Yet, always, he was politeness and grace itself.

"He finishes with his school in the spring, does he not?" asked Ursula, disturbed as always when Eugene was mentioned. "Will he then go on to a university?" Immediately, she accused herself of tactlessness. She did not know the extent of Alice's small private fortune, but she suspected it was very small.

Alice gave Oliver a glass of milk, and, as if he were an adult, she proffered him the tarts. She waited until the child had accepted both before she said quietly: "I have discussed a university with him. He says he prefers not to go. He has other plans. I don't know what they are. But I know this is not just a childish whim."

She lifted her eyes to Ursula. She said nothing else. Ursula did not continue the subject. They never went beyond these superficial personalities. When she returned home, Ursula could never quite remember what conversation had passed between her and her friend. There was nothing much ever said. Quite often Ursula would leave this house, namelessly desolated, filled with nostalgia for she knew not what, still hungry, still unsatisfied.

But there were other times when Ursula felt that the things they never discussed were really discussed between them, wordlessly, that there were matters they dared not speak of, and that under the friendly casualness of their meetings there pulsed a tragic meaning not to be expressed.

Nor did they speak of those who had formerly been friends of Alice's. She did not ask about them. If Ursula inadvertently spoke of them, Alice was silent. She conveyed, most gently, that she no longer was part of the old life, that she had completely discarded it, that it interested her no more. There was about Alice a kind of high and serene isolation, a disembodiment, a withdrawal, such as lives about the memory of the dead.

The idle, agreeable conversation went on now between them. All at once, Ursula was again embittered, weighed down with weariness and yearning. But still she could not break through the kind and compassionate indifference which surrounded Alice.

She glanced up, to see Alice watching her steadfastly. Alice's expression, for all her slight and gentle smile, was moved and sad.

Alice turned to Oliver with her tender air. "You are becoming so grown-up, dear," she said. "I hardly know you when I see you."

Ursula turned too, and the women regarded Oliver with affection. He smiled at Alice fondly. Ursula felt a rush of pride for him. He was her love, her delight, her consolation, as her own children were not. She no longer pitied him that he did not know his parents, or his origin. There was no compassion in her attachment. It was something else and, again, it was something beyond words. As she had done a thousand times before, she speculated on his mother and father. Who had given him his tall, slender, well-knit young body, his cleanness of line, his graciously natural manners, his look of maturity? Had his mother had that dark brightness of skin, those tilted dark eyes, that sleek fine mass of black hair?

My dear Oliver, thought Ursula. My darling.

Why did she not feel this urge towards her own children, flesh of her flesh? Why were they strange and incomprehensible to her? Why did they weary and fatigue her? Why was it not possible to understand them, try as she unceasingly did? She had, in her desperate efforts to be a real mother, certainly given more attention to them than she had ever given Oliver.

Alice stretched out her hand and softly brushed her fingers over Oliver's hair. There was infinite sweetness in her eyes as she did so. "Would you like to see the garden, dear?" she asked. "It is so beautiful just now. Tomorrow, it might all be gone."

He went at once to Ursula, to help her rise. He was only a child, but he had the air of a solicitous man. Ursula could not help smiling; yet it was delightful to be cherished. They went through Ursula's shining kitchen. Ursula looked about her with homesickness, longing for her house, for her kitchen. They stepped out into the garden, and her heart was heavy.

She had hardly believed it when Alice had assured her, years ago, that Eugene was a devoted gardener. But she had been convinced. Never, even in her most industrious days, had her garden looked so beautiful, though it was somewhat too precise for her own taste. Everything was so disciplined, so implacably tidy. Not a weed marred the still-green smoothness of the grass; it was the time of falling leaves, yet hardly a leaf cluttered the hedge or the flagged walk.

There, beyond, lay the hills, not purple, as they were from the windows of the great house on Schiller Road, but closer, and the color of bronze, burning here and there with a scarlet maple or a splash of gold. Clumps of dark-green evergreens

stood out against the coppery background; in this clarified
light, tiny white houses glimmered in the late sunshine on
the sides of the mighty hills. At the end of the garden, the
old gray wall had almost entirely disappeared under climbing
ivy, brilliant as red fire.

The ancient and mighty elms in the center of the garden
were thin bright ghosts of their summery selves, yellow and
tattered. A bed of zinnias and asters, cannas and salvias, flamed
against the green grass; the old apple tree near the wall was
rich with crimson fruit. There, near the bird-bath, empty now
of the colorful creatures who swarmed about it in July
and August, was the sundial, still marking the hours. Someone
had taken away the swing of her childhood, which she had
sentimentally allowed to remain. The plum trees which had
sheltered it hung with purple globes. A late bee or two hummed
through the air, which had warmed a trifle, and a few white
butterflies hovered languidly over a clump of golden calendulas. Here, in a corner, pansies had not yet died; their tiny
pert faces looked up at Ursula inquisitively. Between the stones
of the flagged path the moss was the color of verdigris. A
breeze blew through the garden, languorous with late sun and
spice and the smell of burning leaves.

The garden was haunted by a hundred Ursulas. So many
summers she had sat on that white stone bench under the elms;
she had filled that bird-bath thousands of times. From her
earliest days she had seen this clear autumn light on the trees;
she had looked at these hills from the window of her room.
Again she thought: Home. This is my home.

She did not know, lost as she was in her dreams and her
sadnesses and longing, that both Alice and Oliver were watching her. For all her rich clothing and the sparkling rings on
her fingers and the fashionable expensiveness of her dark-blue
velvet bonnet, there was a still weariness in her posture, a
mournful loneliness. She stood apart, and to the woman and
the child who watched her she appeared abandoned and inconsolable.

A door opened and closed quietly in the Sunday quiet.
Eugene entered the garden. Ursula and the others watched
him come. He was almost a man now, just seventeen, tall,
moving quickly yet without an appearance of haste, his straight
hair falling across his forehead. It was Alice's face under
that hair, but a face become masculine, impenetrable and
alertly still. He had Alice's lean elegance, but it was a hard
elegance. He might be thin and angular, like his mother, but
his shoulders were broad under the black Sunday broadcloth,

the outline of his legs and arms firm as stone, and as inflexible.
And his eyes, though he smiled politely at the guests, expressed
nothing at all. They were pale and shining, but without depth
or warmth or any shared human feeling. He greeted Ursula
with dignity; for an instant, she thought she saw in his eyes
a gleam inimicable and contemptuous. But it was gone immediately, if it had ever been there, which she now doubted.

He stood at ease and, after he had glanced briefly at Oliver,
politely inquired about Ursula's health. She answered him
stiffly. Again, as always, she was uneasy in his presence; she
was filled with discomfort and dislike. Why did she detest
him so? Was it some quality of implacability in him, a mercilessness? What did he think, this young man, at whom his
mother gazed with such tranquil affection? For what was he
waiting?

She wanted to go away. She could not endure Eugene. She
took Oliver's little hand; it was warm, and had a reassuring
strength of its own. He, too, was looking at Eugene. His very
young face was intent and absorbed and rather stern. It
was ridiculous, certainly, but Ursula drew closer to Oliver,
not to protect him, but to be protected. The movement was
instinctive.

"I hear the most excellent reports about you, Gene," stammered Ursula, speaking exactly as she always spoke to him,
and in the same words.

"You are very kind, Mrs. Prescott," he said.

"You are going to the university?" she asked, moving towards the side path.

"I have not yet made up my mind," he answered. His voice
was as expressionless as his face.

"I am sure you ought to. You would distinguish yourself,"
she faltered, wishing only to be away from this garden which
he had despoiled with his presence.

"You are very kind," he repeated.

They walked along the path towards the street. All at once,
Ursula could not bear the idea of him walking near her. She
told herself that her emotions were irrational. Still, she could
not bear it. Once or twice, he had even insisted upon accom-
panying her to her carriage. She contemplated the idea with
a horror out of all proportion. So, as she reached the street,
she hastily held out a trembling hand to Alice, and exclaimed:
"I really must go! It is getting quite late, dear Alice."

Alice took her hand, bent and kissed her cheek. "Eugene
will go with you, my dear," she said.

"No! No! Not at all! Oliver will take care of me, won't

you, dear?" Ursula looked down at the child, who was holding her arm tightly.

Ursula hurried away, not looking back. Alice watched her go. When she turned to speak to Eugene, he was gone. She went back into the garden. He was snapping off the heads of a few faded calendulas. She stood and watched him. His long hands, like hers, were delicate and fine. He said, bent over the flowers: "What is wrong with that woman? She has everything she wishes. Yet, she is miserable." He crushed the flower-heads in his fingers, for he would not toss them untidily on the ground.

Alice said, and now her face was sad: "Yes, poor Ursula is miserable."

Eugene contemplated her contemptuously. "Why? She is a fool, of course."

"Dear Eugene! You are most uncharitable. Ursula is anything but a fool. If she were a fool, she would be happy. I take exception to your language."

Eugene laughed. It was a light but ugly laugh.

"I have often wondered how Prescott can stand her. But, of course, he is a fool, too."

Alice spoke with as much anger as it was possible for her to feel: "Ursula is a woman of great character. I don't think she ever particularly wanted a lot of money. Her husband is very rich; that does not make her happy, it seems."

"Because neither she nor her husband knows how to use money," said Eugene.

"You are talking nonsense, Gene. Mr. Prescott uses his money to make more. He is extremely ambitious."

"Money will never be enough for him, nor the power that money brings."

Alice was silent.

She said: "I think that is proof of both Ursula's and Mr. Prescott's intelligence."

Eugene laughed. "Only fools strive for what they do not really want—or people who are afraid. They are both terrified. That is what is so amusing."

"Gene. I do not understand you."

The young man shrugged. " 'Take what you want, says God, but pay for it.' They don't want what they have taken, and they don't want to pay for it." He looked smilingly at the mountains. "Now, I want money. I am willing to pay for it. I shall have it. I am a very simple person, Mother. You ought to be glad of that."

Alice spoke very softly and slowly: "No, Gene, I am not

glad. And you are not a simple young man. Sometimes I think you are a very bad one."

He stopped smiling. He turned to her quickly. She did not look away.

Then, she went quietly and without hurry towards the kitchen door. He watched her go. There was a deep pucker between his eyes. He had always thought his mother a fool, ever since his father had died. But he had been fond of her. Now, he was not sure she was a fool. Moreover, for the first time, he disliked her.

CHAPTER XXI

HAD URSULA HEARD the conversation between Alice and Eugene, she would have wretchedly agreed with the latter.

Most of the people she had known all her life had been of the "respectable" and smugly religious great middle-class which had arisen after the Protestant Reformation. They had given a certain stability to the world, had brought about the industrial revolution, and had bestowed upon modern life a kind of unimaginative probity. They had conferred righteousness and moral approbation upon the making of money, implying, from pulpit and press, that he whom God hath blessed will undoubtedly succeed in business and get the better of his associates. All this, admittedly, expanded man's ambition and worldly horizon, thus replacing an agricultural society with a society of immense stony cities and fuming factory chimneys, and creating a vast market for goods.

Yet, reflected Ursula, was all this more desirable than the colorful, light-hearted and brilliant society preceding the Reformation, which, however raffish and irresponsible it might have been, lacking in sober realism and an eye for profits, had endowed life with a mystical adventurousness and exciting gaiety? Was man born to laugh, or was he born solely for the purpose of spending most of his life in a factory in order to supply other men, including himself, with goods?

The majority of business men whom Ursula knew believed that it was immoral not to succeed, and they believed this piously and thoroughly. They had stern anger and contempt for those who failed, or who remained poor. They were men without imagination, the fat burghers of the common-place, the laymen in the temple of mediocrity, the heirs of the Puritan doctrine that religion and respectability resulted in possessions.

William Prescott had become rich; he was successful. Accordingly, he ought to have been admitted to the sacred communion of those upon whom God had smiled. Yet Ursula knew, and she suspected others also knew, that he had been received under false pretenses. William was not truly one of the elect. There was something wrong with him. He was not respectable,

166

for in his heart he did not truly believe that possessions were holy and that money automatically admitted a man to the company of the seraphim.

He had not only to struggle against the stifled but powerful tensions within himself, but with the less subtle yet even more powerful suspicions and enmities of his associates, who were instinctively impelled to destroy him if they could. Though he never spoke of these things to Ursula, she knew that he knew them. Nothing else could explain his almost constant somberness and gloom, his desperate ambition, his feverish drive toward expansion, his amassing of the outward evidences of his triumph in a materialistic and malignantly acquisitive world.

How wealthy was William? Had he enough now, or was he precariously situated? It was impossible for Ursula to know. If he had enough, yet must go on making more, then his situation was tragic. If he did not have enough, and must drive himself relentlessly to keep what he had, then his situation was terrifying. Ursula, who, despite herself, was also heir to the Puritan middle-class tradition, was stricken with fear.

She leaned back in her luxurious carriage, pulled the sable robe over her knees. She dreaded returning to her great mansion, to her servants, her children, the husband she loved so intemperately and so unreasonably. Until these past few years, she had always thought she understood herself. Her father had substituted for Socrates: "Know thyself," the dictum: "Analyze thyself." She had been fond of this mental exercise and occupation, and had complacently believed that self-analysis had become an art with her. That, she told herself today, had been only an indication of her stupidity.

An immense weariness washed over her. Usually, on these excursions, she chatted fondly with Oliver, for his intelligence delighted her and she was invariably pleased by the freshness and originality of his young mind. But now she was silent. She did not know that the boy was watching her anxiously, and that he was coming to some quite acute conclusions of his own.

He said at last: "Mama, please don't take me with you when you go to see Aunt Alice again."

Ursula brought her vague but disturbed attention to him: "But why, my darling? I thought you were fond of Aunt Alice."

"I am, Mama. But I don't like Gene."

Ursula became interested. "Well, neither do I, Oliver. I

don't know why. Perhaps I am uncharitable." Her interest quickened. She even smiled mischievously. "Is it because he never speaks to you, pet? Maybe it is because he thinks you are too young."

Oliver was grave. "No, Mama. I don't mind Gene not talking to me. I shouldn't like it if he did. I wouldn't know what to say to him." He hesitated, regarded her seriously. "I love your house, Mama. But Gene hates it."

Being "sensible" had always been one of Ursula's virtues; now she was beginning to doubt it. However, she said: "I can understand why Gene might not like my house, Oliver. After all, he was born in a much handsomer one, and lived for twelve years in the midst of considerable luxury and wealth."

Oliver shook his head. "No, Mama. It is not that. I don't think Gene minds being poor now. He hates your house because of something else."

Ursula became very thoughtful. She looked with sober pleasure at Oliver. It was very odd that a child his age could be so subtle. "How can you know?" she asked, in her "reasonable" voice, which she knew Oliver disliked. Yet it was often necessary to be "reasonable" with Oliver. He had a habit of being disconcerting.

Oliver did not answer immediately, and then he said in a quiet and determined voice: "Gene doesn't think of his papa. And he does think Aunt Alice is very silly. I think the house makes Gene hate it."

Ursula was about to make a sturdily rational comment on this, and then was silent. Oliver, she marvelled, was quite right. Why had she not seen this before? Was Gene another William? Did he prefer opulence and extravagant ostentation?

No, Gene did not want opulence and ostentation. Ursula knew that, suddenly. There was, she reluctantly admitted, a certain elegant austerity in him, a fineness. He might long for grandeur, but it would have to be an immense and majestic grandeur, clean and bare and hard, like marble.

My imagination is running away with me, thought Ursula, severely. But Eugene's face rose before her vividly. There was something barren about him, and barren men were sinister.

Ursula shook her head impatiently. "Of course, Oliver, if you do not wish to visit Aunt Alice, I shall not insist that you do so. But she is fond of you. She will wonder."

Oliver said quietly: "No, Aunt Alice isn't fond of me. She isn't fond of you either, Mama. She is just sorry for you, and for me, too, and perhaps for everybody. Except that maybe she isn't sorry for Gene. I think she is afraid of him."

In spite of her common-sense, Ursula was startled. "Oliver! How can you say such foolish things? You are only a child. What an imagination you have!" She waited. Oliver did not appear sheepish at her reproach. He only gazed at John's back.

She was so perturbed, so humanly hurt, that she did not realize, immediately, that Oliver had taken her gloved hand and that he was pressing it. His voice was a child's voice, simple and eager: "But I love you, Mama. And so does Papa."

"Thank you, dear," said Ursula. The silly tears were in her eyes.

She became aware of his silence, and looked down at him. Now she felt real pain. He was so quiet, so grave, so still. She wanted to comfort him. There were so many reasons why she ought to comfort him: she saw the enormous house in which she and Oliver lived, she saw William's face.

Ursula had been brought up in the well-bred tradition that unpleasant things were best "ignored." In all these years, though keenly aware of Oliver's changed status in the Prescott household, most deeply aware of William's indifference, his passionate concentration on his own children to the detriment of Oliver's needs, and always conscious of the malice of the servants toward Oliver, Ursula had maintained before the child and before everyone an attitude of serenity implying that all was well, that nothing had changed in the least. She had hoped that matters would adjust themselves. They had not.

I have been so hopelessly middle-class, she thought with bitterness. There is no fire, no real indignation in me, nothing strong or assertive. I have always considered these things "ill-bred," the attributes of those who were still uncivilized. Or perhaps, in common with my class, I have just been afraid of disturbing the stolid surface of things.

Ursula sighed heavily. Oliver looked up at her. He could not know her thoughts, but perhaps he felt their sadness and disgust. Ursula put her arm about his shoulder, and throwing common-sense away in one impetuous gesture, she said: "Oliver, my darling. You are such a dear child. You understand so much, and you never complain or protest. I think you are wiser than I am. You maintain your integrity." She paused. "What I am saying is beyond you, isn't it? But I have to say something, and I am saying it to myself. Oliver, do you know about Papa? Do you know how strange he is? And that no one understands him at all, except you and me?"

Her words sounded incoherent even to herself. She awaited

a perplexed smile from Oliver. But he was not smiling. He said: "Yes, Mama."

"He doesn't even understand himself, my darling, and that is why he is so unhappy. You know he is unhappy?"

"Yes, Mama."

"Dearest, I love you as much as I do my own children—or more. You know that, too?"

"Oh, yes, I know, Mama." He smiled now, and leaned against her.

Ursula felt weak and undone, but she went on resolutely: "You must know that Papa doesn't really love or like children in general. He says he does. He always says that children are the most important people in the world. He doesn't really believe it. What he means is that his own children, who are part of himself, are more important than anything else in the world. Just because they are his. Oliver, do you understand even a little of what I am saying?"

Oliver drew the sable rug over Ursula's knees again, for it had slipped. Then, in a low voice, he answered: "Yes, Mama, I think I do. That's why I don't ever get angry with Papa, or feel badly when he doesn't notice me."

Again, Ursula sighed. "I am sure he loves us," she said, almost pleadingly.

Oliver nodded gravely.

John, on his high seat, smiled a little grimly. He had been listening with hard sympathy and comprehension to this hushed conversation.

"I'm awfully sorry," said Oliver. Ursula tried to understand this remark. She told herself that the boy could not possibly have as much understanding as his words might suggest. Then she wondered if she were wrong.

"I love you so much, my dearest," she said, faintly. "I love you much more than I do my own children. Sometimes I don't even like them. Tom is so obstreperous and selfish; Matthew doesn't notice or care for anybody. Julie is a little greedy minx. Oh, I ought not to be saying this! I do love my children!"

She wanted to cry, her misery was so unbearable. Oliver regarded her deeply. He said nothing.

"I am afraid I am a bad mother," said Ursula, wretchedly. "I can't dote on my children. But I think that I like them better, most of the time, than Papa does. At least, I am very sorry for them."

Yes, she was sorry for them, these children to whom nothing was ever denied, these children who had never experienced frustration, who had never been disciplined or defeated in the smallest thing, who were surrounded by love, devotion, solicitude and kindness. Because of this, they were in the most desperate danger, but only she, Ursula, understood this. The fear that lived with her constantly made her faint and sick.

The carriage was now rolling down Schiller Road. It was amazing how this lonely and barren stretch had taken on beauty and richness during the past few years. William had been right: This section was considered the most desirable and fashionable in the whole Andersburg area. William had made his profits from this land. There still were woody spots, unbuilt as yet, but the land was already sold. What had been desolation and forlorn stretches, dotted with hovels and ruined barns, had taken on dignity and opulence. In the midst of it stood the Prescott mansion. The raw ground had become a small fifteen-acre park, filled with flourishing young shade-trees, evergreens, gardens and grottos. The stone wall that surrounded it was not too high to permit a vision of long green lawns, arbors, summerhouses, hedges and ponds. Nothing, however, could add real and classical loveliness to the mighty swart pile of the house, not even the ivy which had been trained to climb over it, the evergreens which surrounded it. It might be impressive but, to Ursula's eyes at least, it was hideous.

The gates opened. The gravel paths had been newly raked. The carriage wheels grated over them, approached the porte-cochère. The great bronze doors of the house opened promptly; John leapt down to assist his mistress from the carriage.

Ursula, now in the tremendous reception hall, asked if there had been visitors this afternoon. She was courteously informed that Mr. Jenkins and his lady had dropped in for tea, Dr. and Mrs. Banks, and Mr. and Mrs. Bassett. Ursula was relieved that she had missed them; she disliked them all, quite unreasonably, as they always showed her the greatest affection. Mr. Jenkins had married the elder Miss Bassett, who had been one of Ursula's bridesmaids. Ursula could not even think of the young lady without a frown, Mrs. Jenkins was so proper, so primly well-bred, so very careful in speech and demure in manner. As for Dr. and Mrs. Banks, Ursula disliked them with vigor; the Bassetts were intolerable to her. At least, thought Ursula, as the butler assisted her with her cloak, my mind has not yet become flaccid. I can hate quite heartily, much more than I did in the old days.

The great marble drawing-room was empty. In spite of the fires on every hearth, and the quiet flare of gaslights, the vast house lay in a mist of Sunday gloom. This meant that all the children were in the nursery. But where was William? Ursula inquired, then sighed at the answer. It was to be expected that he was in the nursery. He was probably indulging in his favorite and conscientious Sunday amusement: he was being a "companion" to his children.

"Oh, my God," murmured Ursula, who had learned in these years to swear fervently.

CHAPTER XXII

THREE OF THE larger rooms had been thrown together to make the nursery. Ursula had objected to this. The Prescotts had frequent and important visitors; they deserved the best, the lightest and most impressive rooms. When Mr. Jay Regan of New York had visited this house, William had relinquished his own room rather than disturb the children. Ah, nothing must disturb the precious children! Mr. Regan had had much difficulty in concealing his ennui when the children had been brought frequently into his presence. But William, selfishly, did not see this.

Ursula never quite recovered from the mortification she suffered during Mr. Regan's visit. Mr. Regan was a genial and brilliant man, shrewd and witty, an entrepreneur on a grand scale, a familiar of presidents and kings. Such a man, at home anywhere in the world, was certainly not a man to be enchanted by childish babble, or by having his hours of business and pleasure interrupted by petulant childish demands. He had grand-children of his own; he did not afflict hosts or guests with tales of their intelligence or escapades. He had been a fond father, but he had confined his fondness to the nursery.

On the second evening of his visit to the Prescott home, Ursula and William gave a magnificent dinner in his honor. A carefully selected guest-list had been prepared, in order that Mr. Regan might not be bored by inferior minds and mediocre conversation. This selection had caused Ursula many anxious hours, but finally she was satisfied. Though rarely interfering in the affairs of the household, she had, herself, prepared the menu, had superintended the setting of the dining-table for twenty-eight people. She knew the importance, to William, of this visit. Pridefully, too, she was determined that Mr. Regan should be convinced that insular life was not barbaric, and that the social amenities, and culture, were not confined to New York and Europe. She had met Mr. Regan before, had admired him greatly, and had known that he, in turn, had admired her.

The dinner began very auspiciously. Ursula had warned

the nursemaids and Mrs. Templeton and Lucy that everything must be so conducted that no adult guest would ever suspect that children lived in the house. To her, this was so elementary that it irritated her that servants must be reminded of the fact.

The food was excellent, and beautifully served. William knew nothing of wines, so Ursula had studiously selected them. Mr. Regan gave every sign of enjoyment, and his full booming laugh was heard frequently. Ursula, drawn taut for hours, began to relax and enjoy herself. Dessert was brought in, a mousse made by Ursula under the amazed nose of her cook. In a few moments, she thought, the ladies would "retire," and the gentlemen would have their cigars and brandy alone. The dinner had gone off splendidly; nothing could have been more perfect.

All at once, while Mr. Regan was in the very midst of telling a joke, there came a roaring screech from outside the dining-room, and little Thomas, followed by his even smaller sister, Julia, and a scuttling battery composed of nursemaids, Miss Andrews, and Mrs. Templeton, exploded into the room. Instantly, it was as if a menagerie had poured itself pell-mell upon the company. Thomas and Julia were robust and agile children; they tore about the table snatching nimbly at nuts and wafers and glasses, stuffing their mouths, eluding their guardians deftly, and emitting screams when a distraught hand tried to catch them. Round and round the table rushed the children and the servants, while glasses toppled on the damask and ladies cried out and shrank in their chairs and gentlemen looked on in cold disgust.

Ursula, in horror, clutched the edge of the table and tried to make herself heard in the uproar. Then, incredulously, she heard someone laughing. She looked at Mr. Regan. But Mr. Regan was not amused; he was busy removing plate and silver and glasses from the small hands that reached for them. No one was amused. Except William. It was from William that the laughter came, the fond and doting laughter of a man who could find something entrancing in this wild mêlée of children and servants.

He held out his arm and caught Thomas, on the third round. He caught Julia as she tumbled after her brother. He lifted both children upon his knee, and they climbed over him, not affectionately, as he imagined, but like swarming animals. Ursula saw their wide restless eyes; she saw them grasping morsels from their father's plate; she heard their incoherent cries. She turned her head aside in complete demoralization and shame.

William looked at Mr. Regan through a tangle of arms, and lovingly bobbed his head about between two smaller and much more vehement heads. Behind him, the servants gathered breathlessly, avoiding the eye of their mistress.

William said, indulgently: "They're furious, the rascals. They didn't want to be shut out of things, and I don't blame them! After all, they like excitement, too."

Mr. Regan did not reply. He looked at his sleeve; there was a large red wine stain on his immaculate linen. Some had also splashed on the bosom of his shirt. All at once everyone sat very still, heads averted. There was no sound in the room but the meaningless jabber of the scrambling children, their insistent, infantile voices.

Then Ursula, white and trembling, said to the servants: "Take the children away, please. At once."

William stared at her down the length of the table. He held the children to him tightly. "What do you mean?" he asked, roughly. "They have a right here. They're only enjoying themselves. Perhaps," he added, with weighty sarcasm, "our guests don't have the aversion for children you have."

He looked at his guests, inviting them to smile in agreement. But no one returned his glance.

Oh, it isn't possible he is such a fool! thought Ursula, desperately. She tried to smile at Mr. Regan. It was a painful smile.

"Our children are very—active," she murmured. She dropped her eyes helplessly to Mr. Regan's sleeve and bosom. "But perhaps you know, Mr. Regan, how active children are."

Mr. Regan said quietly: "My children, my dear Ursula, are grown up. Thank God." Then, seeing her misery, he added kindly: "They grow up very very fast. Fortunately. It doesn't matter in the least," he continued. "Don't be disturbed, Ursula."

Ursula rose, and all rose with her. "We'll leave the gentlemen alone," she murmured, and led the ladies out of the room. Once in the drawing-room, every woman tactfully tried to help her regain her poise. No one mentioned the children. Ursula smiled and chatted and hardly remembered what she said.

She learned, later, that William had not sent the children away. He had allowed them to remain while he and Mr. Regan and the other gentlemen had tried to discuss some very serious financial matters. They had not succeeded. The guests, finally reduced to silence, had been compelled to sit there, while William had conducted a laughing conversation with his children, and had carefully translated their screaming babble for the edification of his friends. Only when the men stood up to join the ladies did William reluctantly carry his son and daughter upstairs to the nursery. He did not return for at least half an hour.

After that, the children were permitted at the table during the stay of Mr. Regan. Ursula shuddered for months at the memory of dinners disrupted by overturned milk-glasses, shriekings, roars for attention from servants busy about the table, cries and weepings, attempts at pacification by Miss Andrews, who ought not to have been present at all, but who had been assigned a conspicuous place near William where she and the master could devote at least half their time to Thomas and Matthew and Julia.

Mr. Regan cut short his stay, on the plea of some unexpected business which demanded his presence in New York. During his visit, Ursula had contained herself, but when she was alone with William she embarked on a serious quarrel with him. She was both hysterical and distracted as she recalled to her husband her embarrassment and shame of the past week.

"I suppose it never occurred to you, William, that Mr. Regan left when he did because of Tom's misbehavior and Julie's constant roaring? Doubtless you thought Mr. Regan found Miss Andrews' company fascinating! It is my opinion that Mr. Regan considers this a madhouse, as indeed it is! Why he continued negotiations with you is beyond me."

William flushed darkly at this, and gave Ursula a savage look. He said: "You do not seem to understand that children are more important than their elders."

"Mr. Regan does not think so!" cried Ursula. "Neither does anyone else with any sense at all."

It had ended in nothing, as it always ended in nothing except hostility and bitterness between husband and wife. Ursula tried to entertain as little as possible. When she and William were alone she kept the conversation on a superficial level, where it was safe.

It was a terrible thing for her to see that William's children, young as they were, were beginning to have for him a certain ugly contempt, and that they displayed towards their mother a sullen resentment because of her attempts to discipline them when their father was absent.

These children, who ought to have been the delight and happiness of a well-managed and disciplined household, had made of this magnificent if garish house a place of quarrelings and unhappiness and tension. They had appeared between their parents like a deadly enemy, creating hostility where there should have been devotion, alienation where there ought to have been companionship and communion.

Ursula, as a sensible woman, had attempted to salvage what she could from the fiasco of her marriage. She proposed small journeys for herself and her husband. Very rarely, he agreed to them. But when they were alone together in some luxurious hotel in Washington, Chicago, New York or Pittsburgh, she was aware of his restlessness. They had nothing to say to each other. There were moments, however, when he looked at her and his small hard eyes softened involuntarily. These moments were few. But she cherished them. She determinedly remembered them when he informed her, usually on the second or third day, that he was lonely for the children and wished to return home. She kept the memory of them before her during the long weeks of estrangement, during William's absences.

Sometimes, when she believed happily that the children were in bed and asleep, she attempted to talk to William, using a soft and loving voice, trying to arouse his interest in matters which were important to her. It was not often that he gave her his complete attention but, when he did, these moments were almost invariably interrupted by the sudden boisterous appearance of Thomas in his nightshirt, or of the wailing angry Julia in the arms of her current and harassed nurse. Then they were finished, these quiet hours before the fireplace or in the garden together. William would forget his wife; he would take the child in his arms and go off, or settle the weeper upon his knee and speak to him in a voice which he never used towards Ursula, so rich and deep was it, so moved and tender.

A less intelligent woman would have come to resent or hate the children who had deprived her of her husband, who had ruined her marriage and created chaos about her. But Ursula was too intelligent for such unrestrained, if natural emotions. If William was destroying the happiness of his wife, he was destroying his children also.

CHAPTER XXIII

ON SUNDAY AFTERNOONS, when William performed his fatherly rites in the nursery, Ursula had need of all the patience and calmness she could command. When she was well, it was not too hard. When she was pregnant and weary, as she was today, it was almost more than she could bear. She longed for personal tenderness; she longed to lie down and have William hold her hand and speak gently to her. These were longings not to be satisfied. She must play the devoted mother, if she was to get the slightest attention from him, the merest smile. Sighing, and accompanied by Oliver, she entered the nursery.

Yes, everything was as absurd and boring as usual on Sunday afternoons. The large and beautiful play-room was dusky, full of firelight. Near the hearth sat William; Julia upon his knee; Thomas at his feet, surlily tearing apart some toy. Thomas had a penchant for wanton destruction. Matthew sat by the darkening window; it was impossible to tell if he were listening to William, who was reading some fairy-tale by the flickering light of the fire. A nursemaid was laying a Sunday supper for the children, on a distant table, for Ursula, upon one explosive occasion a year ago, had insisted that she dine alone with her husband on Sunday evenings. This had been her only victory; she had clung to it, for all William's ugly silences on these occasions, his somber and repellent glances at his wife. Nearby, behind, and to the side of William, sat Miss Andrews and Mrs. Templeton, meek and adoring neophytes in this temple of child-worship.

Ursula smiled sweetly and impersonally at everyone, sweeping the room with a deceptively tranquil eye. No joyful cries from her children greeted her; William, in his abnormal possessiveness, his loud defenses of his children in his wife's presence, had succeeded excellently in alienating the two boys and the little girl from their mother. Thomas regarded her in rude silence; Matthew turned his small and apathetic face towards her for an instant, then resumed his blank staring at, rather than through, the window. Julia wriggled impatiently on her father's knee, and peremptorily demanded a sweet from the table. The nursemaid, who had stayed in this household the incredible period of six months, immediately brought a small cake, which Julia devoured with a kind of angry sullenness. William gave Ursula an abstracted glance, smoothed the little girl's long auburn hair with a tender hand.

In a voice falsely cheerful, Ursula exclaimed: "Dear me, how dark it is in here! Nancy, please light a lamp or two. How are you, William? Dear Tommy, look what you are doing to your lovely jack-in-the-box, and Papa only just brought it for you. Matthew, are you quite well? Why are you sitting alone at the window?" She did not wait for a reply, but increased the cheer in her voice: "Oliver and I have just returned from visiting Alice. A delightful day for driving."

"You are late," said William. But his tone was not accusing; it even had a slight satisfaction in it. "I decided to have a cold supper about an hour ago." He looked at Ursula without expression; his face was set and impervious.

So, we are not to dine together tonight, thought Ursula. Her smile remained fixed. "I am so sorry. I did not realize it was late. I can have a tray in my room."

But William was staring at Oliver. It invariably gave Ursula the strangest feeling when she saw her husband looking at the boy. His expression was not always harsh or rejecting; sometimes, as now, it was thoughtful or perplexed. Did he still have some affection for the child he had adopted and had adored so ridiculously only a few short years ago? Ursula had once thought that Oliver disturbed his father in a way impossible for any onlooker to understand.

Oliver went to William without hurry or hesitation or fear. He kissed William's hard cheek. "Good evening, Papa," he said. He smiled at William, and touched his father's shoulder lightly with his hand.

"Good evening," replied William, shortly. He continued to stare at the boy. "I gave you a fine gold watch for your birthday, Oliver. Surely you could have taken note of the time. You and your mother are nearly an hour late. You ought to have reminded her."

Ursula sat down. She said: "It was my fault, William. We went into the garden with Alice, and talked too long. Do not blame Oliver."

She gave Oliver a kindly look of apology. But Oliver only stood by William's side, as if protecting him. At this moment, Julia kicked furiously at Oliver's knee. "Go 'way!" she screamed. Ursula's attention was suddenly caught and transfixed. She had not been mistaken. Julia, though only a baby, had felt Oliver's protectiveness toward her father. Thomas knew it; he scowled up from his father's feet and made an ugly face at Oliver. Matthew, still at the window, turned and fixed his light-blue eyes intently upon his adopted brother.

"Hush, dear," said William tenderly, to his little daughter, and he stroked her head again with his big lean hand. "You must not talk that way to your brother." Julia screamed again, writhed on her father's knee; she turned her small pretty head and bit his hand.

Ursula sprang to her feet, forgetting all the self-control of years. "Julie! You dreadful child! Nancy, take Julie away immediately." As quickly as her heavy body would permit, she ran to William and caught at his hand. The teeth-marks were deep and reddened on it, and one or two were beginning to bleed. Apparently William was astounded; he, too, looked at the marks. Julia screamed louder, slipped from her father's knee, and ran, howling, to Mrs. Templeton. Mrs. Templeton did not know what to do. She stood helplessly, while Julia tugged ferociously at her skirts.

William snatched his hand from Ursula. His face, so deeply lined though he was not yet forty, flushed an unpleasant crimson. He regarded Ursula inimically. "Why do you make such a fuss? Please sit down. Julie is only a baby. She does not understand."

Ursula, seeing only the torn and bleeding skin on that beloved hand, was not to be quelled. She turned about. She reached Julia in a single moment, and slapped the child strongly upon the cheek. "You nasty little beast!" she cried. Her anger was a gust of strong and relentless wind. "Nancy," she said in a loud, breathless voice, "take Julie at once and put her to bed!"

Everyone stared at Ursula's aroused face, and shrank. Thomas no longer smiled; he glared at his mother. Matthew blinked his eyes. Oliver did not move. Nancy, with hesitation, and carefully avoiding looking at William, picked up Julia, who screamed and struggled, and held out her arms to her father, her baby features distorted with amazement and fury. Her sturdy feet flung themselves out spasmodically and vindictively at Ursula. Ursula caught one of them, and administered another sound slap on the child's thigh. Julia suddenly subsided, was silent a moment, then burst into sobs.

"Take her away, Nancy!" Ursula's voice was strong and firm. She saw William rising slowly and implacably. Nancy was already scuttling from the room. The door closed behind her and the squalling child.

"Ursula!"

Ursula swung on her husband, her heart beating heavily. "William," she replied. Their eyes met. William could not speak; his cheek twitched. He was remembering that Ursula was pregnant; he held back his own rage. After a moment, he said hoarsely: "How dare you strike that child, that baby! You know it is against my orders."

"Your orders!" exclaimed Ursula. Feigning distress, she put her hand suddenly to her side. William saw the gesture. His rage was still high, but he was frightened. "Ursula, I command you to sit down at once. You are making a most disgraceful scene." He caught her arm; his fingers might be rough, but she felt his fear in them. He forced her into a chair. He stood over her, his eyes gleaming but watchful. Over his shoulder, he called to the housekeeper: "Mrs. Templeton, a cup of tea for Mrs. Prescott at once."

So, thought Ursula, there is a way to control things. But she rejected the idea at once. That way was the way of weak women, without principle or resolution. She accepted the cup of tea hastily brought her by Mrs. Templeton. She could not stop the trembling of her hands. To her amazement, William awkwardly stirred the tea for her. She looked at him, and her eyes filled with tears.

"William," she whispered, "let us go away, into my room. Anywhere."

"Drink your tea," said William, sternly. But there was a kind of helplessness in the gesture with which he touched his temple. The firelight flared up a moment; Ursula, with a pang, saw again the patches of white in his thick black hair. "Drink your tea," he repeated.

Ursula drank the tea, slowly. She was not really hysterical, nor had her sudden loss of self-control been more than a flare. All her stern calmness returned to her. She looked at young Thomas, still crouched at his father's feet. He had retained the square promise of his babyhood; everything about him, from healthily flushed face to shoulders and body and legs, had a rude bluntness without refinement of line or hint of grace.

Ursula turned from Thomas to Matthew, for whom she had originally had a kind of sympathy. She had believed he would be her favorite. Now she knew she would never be able to understand him. He did not have the bold truculence of his brother. There was an elusive quality about him. As tall as Thomas, he appeared of a finer strain, and so gave an impression of slightness. He had a triangular face, a sensitive thin mouth, a good sharp nose. His blue eyes were set deeply, yet they were large and had a remote awareness. The light fluff of his babyhood had brightened to a definite gold molded caplike on his long and narrow head. There was nothing feminine about the child, but there was nothing that expressed great strength.

Ursula turned away from her sons, mournfully. As clearly as if Julia were now in the room, Ursula saw the little pert face, impudent and without shyness. A pretty face, yes; Julia had inherited Ursula's own eyes, though her long fine hair was inclined to wave nicely about the temples and at the ends. Julia had something of Matthew's delicacy of feature, but none of his reticence.

Ursula sighed. She was desperately sorry that she had struck the baby. It was not all Julia's fault; her ruin and spoiling had been received from William. For all her pretty wiles, her warm plump little body, and her bent for humor, she was well on the way to becoming detestable.

Ursula tried to stiffen herself against her own despair and sadness. She had seen the malevolence of Julia's little face when the child had looked at her father. It was a malevolence that could spring only from hatred and contempt.

Ursula's awareness returned to the room. She looked at Oliver, passing, with a shiver, over her own two sons. He smiled at her reassuringly.

She stood up. She said to her husband quietly but with determination: "William, I am going to my room. I want to talk to you. It is very important."

CHAPTER XXIV

WHEN IN HER OWN apartments, Ursula excused herself and went into her dressing-room, where she removed the heavy gown and corsets which encased her, and threw a light silk robe of a lavender color over her aching body.

From her window she had a view of the mountains. They were not the strong and quiet mountains that stood behind her little house. Here they had retreated, become immense and distant and cold. She could see the dark purple of them now against the lighter purple of the darkened sky. Above them, the evening star glittered restlessly. All at once, Ursula was overcome with melancholy. The sky, streaked with a whitish scarf, had a dull and remote look, as if a sun had never burned there in warmth and brilliance. She could hear no sound; the house was so very still. Had William remained in her room, as she had requested? She listened intently. She heard the slow and ponderous pacing to and fro of his feet. It, too, sounded tired, as tired as she was tired. All at once, she wanted to cry. She sat down, leaned her elbow on her dressing-table, and rested her forehead in her palm. She must go out to him. But what could one ever say to William? In these past several years, she had attempted to approach him, to become part of him, to touch him warmly with her hand. It had all been impossible. They were not stupid people. What was it stood between them, invisible but implacable, striking them into silence?

She was more sure than ever that he loved her. Yet, she could not speak with William, and he, in turn, could not speak with her. Once or twice she had thought: He is afraid and I am afraid of his fear, whatever it is.

She stood up, applied firm palms to her wings of russet hair, made herself as calm as possible, then went into her bedroom. William was standing at the window, looking down at the parkland which surrounded his house. He had not heard her reenter. His broad shoulders sagged a little, his head was bent.

William, too, was thinking. He did not see the land below

183

him, the distant gaslights which now ran, flickering, along Schiller Road, the outlines of other big houses which had chosen to be his neighbors. He was saying to himself, with angry gloom and somberness: There is no way to talk to Ursula. It is impossible ever to speak, to tell her what I think. But there never was anyone but Dr. Cowlesbury. Why have I told her so little about him? I promised to take her to his house, yet I never did. Why?

There is one thing I do know, his exhausted thoughts continued. I know she hates the people I hate. It is an easy hatred, a smiling kind of hatred, as if she despised them. I cannot hate them like that; I can only hate them with fury and rage. Why? Is it because Ursula feels equal to them that she can despise them pleasantly and serenely, while I do not despise them in that fashion because I cannot convince myself, even now, that I am equal to them—those sanctimonious fools, those bigoted wretches, those pious swine without honor or decency or mercy?

"William," said Ursula behind him, quietly.

He turned about, and immediately his expression became sullen and wary, in the soft light of the lamps. He stood there in the center of the big and lovely room, which she had subtly altered during her occupancy. She had "faded" the room, he had once thought accusingly. It had been muted enough to begin with; now, all color had been gently drained from it, leaving only a ghost of color behind, the merest suggestion.

"Please sit down, William," she said, almost impersonally. Already he was freshly angered against her; it was his defense against the sick and powerful yearning he had for her, his unremitting desire to speak to her and tell her of the dark and chronic rage which lived in him. But it was not possible to talk to Ursula of this; she was too cool, too balanced, too composed.

He did not accept her invitation immediately. They stood and looked at each other in silence, and the thing that always sprang up between them sprang up again, armed and watchful, dividing them. He sat down heavily in a finely carved chair covered with a faint rose damask, and she sat opposite him, crossing her ankles neatly, folding her hands in her lap.

Her voice was restrained but clear: "William, I think we should have a little talk about a number of things. I think we should speak honestly to each other."

Honestly! he thought.

"You never tell me anything. But I suspect there is something wrong." She paused. "In your affairs," she continued resolutely. "I think I have the right to know."

He had been prepared for a quarrel about the children, another of the many quarrels between them. She had not spoken about the children. Yet he had an intuition that she was approaching the subject obliquely. This exasperated him.

"What do you mean?" he demanded.

She lifted her hands slowly in a gesture of hopelessness, then let them fall again upon her silken knee. "William. You know what I mean."

"My 'affairs'!" he exclaimed, with an insulting intonation. "What can you know of my 'affairs'?" He waited for her to speak. She did not; she only gazed at him, waiting. He stood up, towered over her. "What is it that you want? Is there something you need, which I have denied you? Have I ordered the dismissal of servants?" Then he was really enraged. "What do you mean?" he asked again, and his voice became hoarse with his fury.

Still not looking away from him, Ursula was silent a moment. She said: "Perhaps I have no reason for my uneasiness. But our way of living is becoming even more opulent than before. People gossip; hints come to me that even the wealthy summer visitors from Philadelphia and Pittsburgh and New York and Boston discuss you."

"What are these wonderful 'hints'?" he asked, with what he considered savage humor.

Slowly, she said: "Perhaps I have spoken of this because thrift is a habit with me. I had been brought up to despise waste and extravagance. I do not know whether all this," and she gestured briefly, "is 'waste' or 'extravagance.' I never knew anyone who lived as we do but, then, perhaps Andersburg is a very conservative city. I often wonder whether we need so many servants. Why a nursemaid, when we have Lucy? She is capable of taking care of Julie, and Tom and Matthew, without assistance."

During all this, William had not spoken; his face had darkened. He waited until she had finished, then he said: "This is miserliness. You wish to count every penny. I have told you, over and over, that I can afford what we have. Why do you persist in wishing us to live like beggars?"

Ursula could not help smiling sardonically. It was these smiles of hers, cool and superior and half-suppressed, which he could not endure. "Even with the staff cut down, we'd hardly be living like beggars," she said indulgently.

"You must let me be judge of that," he said, trying to control his temper. The old sick panic returned to him, and he almost hated his wife. His voice rose: "You don't know what you do to me when you talk like this! I won't have it!"

She studied him earnestly. "Do to you, William? What is it I do to you when I suggest a little sensible economy?"

As if he could not endure looking at her, he moved to the window.

Ursula said, very gently: "It would not disturb me to have less than we have, to have fewer servants. Sometimes I find it all more than a little oppressive. I do not think ostentation more important than my husband's peace of mind."

"No," he said, "you would be quite content to crowd all of us into your miserable little house! I know that. You have no real appreciation for good living. The piling up of a useless and untouched fortune would be much more to your liking. You would prefer that to living as we ought to live." His irascible temper flared. "A man must have evidence about him that he is a success. But that is something you'd never understand."

I see, thought Ursula, with aching pity. She tried to speak serenely, in order to calm the fear she felt in him: "I have told you before that my father and I lived very modestly. I respect money; I had to learn to respect it. So that, while I know that you can afford all this, and perhaps even more, I still do not believe in wasting money when it is not necessary to waste it."

He said, violently: "You try to undermine me at every step! You try to make me lose faith in myself!"

How childish, how piteous, thought Ursula. She sighed. "Well, then, if I have offended you, I can only ask you to forgive me. After all, I cannot rid myself of the habits of a lifetime."

Whenever she apologized like this, it only excited him the more. He exclaimed: "You resent our children having the best I can give them. You'd prefer them to suffer privation, no doubt for the good of their characters!"

Goaded, in spite of herself, Ursula replied: "Something ought to be done for their characters, God knows!"

"Oh, I understand! If it were left to you, they'd live on bread and water and live in a garret; to 'strengthen' them, I suppose, to teach them to love money, as you love it! It has never occurred to you that we owe our children everything. They did not ask to be born. We forced them into existence——"

Ursula interrupted quietly: "William, you are not talking

sensibly. You and I did not ask to be born either; we, too, were 'forced' into existence. That is a silly argument. Our children should be grateful to us for having been born, just as we ought to be grateful to our own parents, because they caused us to be born. It is good to live. It is the highest, and, in fact, the only good."

Ursula went on: "It has been my observation that those who hate life are potential murderers. Every tyrant must have hated life, his own and the lives of others."

William asked furiously: "You say you are grateful to your parents that you were born? Born into such a world?"

Ursula said wearily: "I do not find it 'such a world', as you imply. I find it interesting, fascinating, full of excitement, even when I suffer, and therefore I can endure my suffering. Yes, I am grateful to my parents for my life."

"Sentimentalism!" he cried. "Only one who has never lived can speak of living with so much fatuousness. What do you know of living? Nothing! But I have noticed that those who do not know what it is to have lived are always the most enthusiastic about the very idea, and can even get lyrical about it."

She lifted her head in a quick movement of offense. He saw this, and his disgust and tiredness became too huge for expression. He could only look at her pale fine features and think how alien they were to him, as if she were of a different species.

He thought: What do they know of the violences, the passions, the terrible stresses and strains, anxieties and drives, that motivate men like me? These pallid, restrained little people, whose dull eyes have never seen lightning, who have never, because of incapacity or circumstance, been confronted with the necessity for desperate decisions and struggles! It is easy for them to smile, in their detestable superior manner, to call another man rampageous or brutal or frantic or extravagant or over-vivid, and despise him with one of their tight little smiles. Their meagre lives have never presented them with enormous problems or aroused them to gigantic rages.

He recalled what she had said earlier, and he exclaimed: " 'Never tell you anything'! Why, I couldn't tell you 'anything'! You wouldn't understand. It would be unintelligible to you!"

He watched her while she bent her head silently and studied her clasped hands. Her composure charged him with fresh anger.

"Yes, life is 'ill-bred'," he said, bitterly. "It hasn't any manners. It doesn't know anything about 'form', the thing you are always talking about. It's explosive; it's terrible. And that is why I am trying to save my children from as much of its dangerousness as possible. You wouldn't understand that, either. But I'll save them in spite of you."

"You mean," she said, "that you want them to be secure? Secure from living?"

"Yes, you can put it that way," he answered with contempt.

Ursula thought of what her father had once said: "Man constantly craves security, and I am afraid a time will come when a supine and truckling government might try to create security by fiat. That will be the end of American power and zest and inventiveness." She said: "What you are really saying is that you want to keep the children from living, to shelter them so that they'll never know what life is like. You are not very consistent."

She looked at him for a long and thoughtful moment: "I'd much rather that they live, even if it gives them pain. You don't want them to have pain; but there is no living without pain."

He laughed caustically. "When one hasn't known pain, that is easy to say."

She sighed, and rose. She went to a lamp and turned up the flame. She stood and looked down at it in the deepest depression. She ran her finger over the crystal shade, and said quietly, almost sternly: "We shall never, I understand now, agree about our children. But I want you to know, William, that my children are less important to me than you are."

He was involuntarily touched, and then his natural combativeness sprang up against her as it always did when she spoke of the children.

"They aren't important to you because you are cold to them, and they are cold to you because you don't understand them. You resort to discipline because you have no imagination."

"Oh, William. Look at our children. Julia is an arrogant little animal, vicious and mean, and it is your fault." Ursula tried to keep her voice calm, but it shook. "You made her so. And you've made Tom into a quarrelsome little beast, too, without the slightest consideration for anyone but himself, and without any manners. And by indulging Matthew in everything, you have robbed him of interest in anything. You are ruining my children, William."

William's eyes glittered with an angry defensiveness. "You accuse the children of everything rotten because you don't like them. You don't know children at all."

"I don't 'adore' children in a silly, maudlin fashion—no,"

said Ursula. In spite of her understanding and pity, her own temper was rising. She had to persist for her husband's sake. "I am not blinded by sentimentality. Children are not a special species apart from the human race. They are only people, and if people refuse discipline, if they are not taught form and manners and civilized conduct, then chaos and nihilism inevitably result. My children's lives are chaotic. And you are the cause of it all."

Before William could speak again, and she knew that what he would say would be both offensive and abusive, she went on: "For instance, the boys ought to be in Sunday school. They are going on five. But they know no more of God than does an insensate rock. Oh, I know your argument—that religion is superstition! How do we know there is nothing in religion? How can we judge? At any rate, we have no right to deny the children the contact with a civilizing influence, which may, at some later time, give them consolation and hope, and help them in some crucial situation of temptation or agony."

"Form!" cried William. Now all his hatred and rage against restraint of any kind rushed out to meet her cold reason. "I am not going to have my children's minds polluted by superstition. They are going to be free individuals, in spite of you and your friends, who have such an adoration for 'manners', and who spend half your time in the ancestor-worship you call tradition——"

Ursula interrupted. Her temper was under control now. She dropped her voice, so that it sounded more emphatic against the vibrating background William's loud voice had left in the atmosphere. "I am afraid I haven't made myself very clear. I don't admire form and tradition as things in themselves. I admire them because they are civilizing influences. Convention and form are the patterns of civilized behavior and culture. Out of them comes a code of ethics which enables man to live in masses, in cities, without murdering his neighbor. And without form, there can be no graciousness in living."

In spite of himself, William listened, as he always listened when Ursula spoke in this cold and remote fashion. He listened, though he liked her less when she spoke like this than at any other time. He tried to keep his voice down as he said: "I want my children to be natural. Anything else is hypocrisy, and dangerous. Freedom is more valuable than mincing manners."

Ursula laughed wearily. "Naturalness and freedom, the

social sense, cannot exist save in a society of civilized people. You don't want the children to be barbarians, do you? Discipline, too, is one of the aspects of 'form'. The undisciplined man, who is free to express his natural brutality, coarseness and 'honesty', cannot live in a civilized society without becoming its enemy, and being rejected by it.

"By evolving form and ceremony, and even ritual, we have, over the centuries, acquired a little civilization, and what is called 'grace'. 'Grace' is the difference between man and the other animals."

William looked at her in silence and, again, he almost hated her. He hated what he thought she represented: people who had phlegm in their veins instead of blood. His biased mind had fixed upon her as the archetype of those who both disconcerted and infuriated him.

Ursula, for once losing her subtlety, believed that he was listening to her. She went on: "There never was a society distinguished for refinement and polish which lacked reticence and self-restraint. Form, then, is man's civilized substitute for the innocence he never possessed, an innocence which, in an animal, is a stern code of instinctive behavior."

He said, with malignance: "You shall not make weaklings of my children, with your 'form' and your discipline."

Ursula sighed. "It is not I who am making our children weak. It is you. You are not preparing them for life. When they encounter it, it will destroy them, for they will be too weak to fight."

She thought: He does not hear me at all. It is not that he deliberately refuses to listen. It is just that he is on the defensive all the time.

She was sure she was right, for he did not reply to her last words. Instead, his voice loud again, he said: "You dislike our children. You care for none of them, except Oliver."

She turned to him incredulously. "How can you say that? I love them! That is why I am afraid for them. Oliver? Yes, I love Oliver, too. William, why are you so antagonistic to Oliver?" She knew, but she wanted to hear it from him. It was too much to expect, she realized, when he said, "I, antagonistic? You must be out of your mind. Though Oliver is not really my son, I treat him as if he were. Can you deny that? Can you honestly say he is deprived of anything, or ill-treated, or neglected?"

"Neglected, yes," she answered, very softly. "He worships you. You hardly give him a word. Why, William? You used to adore him."

Again, he was furiously excited. "I have never distinguished between him and my own sons. But I have noticed that he avoids me. Young as he is, he is ungrateful. He is indifferent. You are the cause of that, Ursula. You have turned him against me, and mine."

The accusation was so absurd that Ursula could not answer it. She sat down in her chair and closed her eyes wearily. It was no use.

She heard her bedroom door bang behind her husband; she did not open her eyes. Depression weighed her down. She was not given to crying, but now the tears ran down her cheeks, silently.

They were not for her children, nor even for Oliver. They were for William.

CHAPTER XXV

WILLIAM PRESCOTT, in his office, glanced somberly at his watch. In two hours, his Board of Directors would meet in the Board Room. He put away his watch; he tapped the dully shining surface of his desk. He stared through the large windows of his office at the brilliant snow outside. The office was very quiet. The small mahogany clock on the stone mantelpiece ticked loudly; the fire-irons twinkled in the strong red blaze of the fire, and now and then the burning wood crackled, threw up a miniature storm of sparks behind the screen. It was a large and pleasant room; he had made it so. Once it had been Chauncey Arnold's office, gloomy and cluttered. Now a row of books stood against one panelled wall; chairs in red and green leather were scattered about, and a sofa in crimson leather stood against another wall. There were some who discreetly suggested that he had an unbridled and untidy mind. The large quiet order of his office disproved this, in business matters at least.

He liked the portrait of Dr. Cowlesbury, which hung over the mantelpiece, and often, during conferences, or in the midst of lonely work, he would glance at the portrait, or would regard it steadily. Though it had been painted from an old daguerreotype, it was an excellent piece of work. Dr. Cowlesbury had given it to the younger William, mockingly, because William had insisted. The thin but ruddy, bearded face, the intense narrow eyes, the fine long head, had been wonderfully reproduced by the artist. The background was of a deep but neutral green, suggesting the woods in which the old man had lived. William, tapping his fingers on his desk more and more restlessly, looked up at the portrait. The fingers slowed, and finally his hand was still. Suddenly William remembered a conversation he had had with Ursula when she had first seen this portrait. "There is a man who has always known what he wanted," she had said.

This, for some reason, had irritated William. But Ursula frequently irritated him, without conscious reason. "Well, then, he and I are alike," he had replied, "and he taught me very well. I, too, have always known what I wanted."

Ursula had only said: "No." And she had turned away from the portrait and had begun to talk of something else.

His clerk, Ben Watson, came in with a small sheaf of papers. "This is the report on the cypress wood, sir," he said. He laid the sheaf on the desk. William frowned at it, then looked up at the clerk. Ben Watson was a man of his own age, a bald neat man with a large crooked nose and an efficient manner. His air was always respectful to his employer; he rarely made mistakes. He was, in all ways, impeccable. Ben Watson, like all his other employees, might show the greatest respect to the man who owned this huge company, might at all times display the utmost alacrity and willingness. Yet, in some subtle and undeniable way, William knew that his employees hated him and derided him among themselves with slight smiles, slighter gestures, a word or two murmured under the breath. Why was this? He paid them almost extravagantly. He never overworked them. If any of them were ill for short periods, he did not deduct money from their salaries. He had established something revolutionary in his dealings with them, something so startling that his associates were staggered and indignant: he had put aside a fund for his employees from which they could draw for medical bills, or other catastrophes. Yet they hated him, and despised him.

"Thanks," he said to Ben Watson, and the clerk withdrew, walking on quiet feet. Was that contempt in the discreet closing of the door? William, as he had done a thousand times before, tried to tell himself it was his imagination. Yet something assured him he had not imagined it. There was Bassett, for instance, the banker, and his employees. Bassett might be genial to equals, but he was remorseless and hard with employees and others dependent upon him. He treated them brusquely; he spoke to them as little as possible. He made it plain that they were of an inferior species. In his presence, they cringed; they showed every evidence of servility. If they had tails, thought William bitterly, they would probably wag them!

He said to himself: I'll discharge that damn Watson. But he knew he would not. Watson had a family of five children. His salary was large, almost twice as large as anyone else would pay him. Damn them! Is it impossible to trust anyone whom you treat decently? Must you hound a dependent like a swine, and abuse him, in order to get his respect? Do they think generosity weakness, and is it in the nature of man to attempt to destroy weakness, to despise it? Am I weak?

A subtle but powerful anger started up in him. He began

to get to his feet when the door opened again, and Ben Watson reentered. He said, in his quiet and respectful voice: "There is a young man to see you, sir. Eugene Arnold. I have told him you are not to be disturbed, but he begs you to see him. He won't go away."

"Eugene Arnold!" William's dark face colored.

Ben Watson was silent, waiting attentively. The answer to many things, had William been able to see it, was in that clerk's attitude—the oddly watchful speculation, the concealed and furtive derision, the elaborate deference. Ben Watson knew that another man, in William's position, would not have colored, would not have betrayed that tight uneasiness. He would have said, indifferently: "Eugene Arnold? Send him away."

Ben still waited. There was no pride in working for a man who had twinges and uneasinesses and insecurities, who was no better than those working for him. Ben felt the stirring of his secret ridicule, which he shared with his fellow-workers. He looked down at his boots, afraid that this might be seen by William, yet not quite afraid.

"Eugene Arnold," repeated William. Moments went by. "What does he want, Ben?"

"He wouldn't say, sir. But he stands there, and short of throwing him out bodily, there is nothing we can do."

William picked up a paper-weight, set it down heavily. He felt Ben's contempt.

"Did you tell him I am busy? Well, then, why does he stay?"

"He wouldn't say, sir," repeated Ben, imperturbably.

"The Board meets in little more than an hour. You ought not to have annoyed me with this, Ben. Go tell Arnold that I cannot see him now."

"I shall tell him to return later, sir?" Nothing could have been suaver than Ben Watson's voice. William looked somberly at his clerk.

"I didn't say that, Ben." He kept his voice quiet.

Ben was surprised. He glanced up, swiftly, with disbelief. Then he bowed again, walked slowly towards the door. He might be wrong—they might all be wrong. Now he heard William's voice, rising irritably: "Never mind! Send him in. but warn him that I can give him only a few minutes."

Ben went out, smiling contemptuously. He left the door ajar, a piece of impudence which made William start to his feet. And so it was that when Eugene entered, William was standing behind his desk, as if expecting and awaiting an honored visitor, and not a young man who was little more than a beggar, the son of a dead and bankrupt father.

"Good afternoon, Mr. Prescott," said Eugene. His hat was in his hand. He held it with negligent dignity.

William sat down. He looked at Eugene over his desk. His old dislike for Eugene returned violently, but with it was a kind of discomfort. He saw that, for all the elegance of Eugene's manner and dress, his clothing was shabby. The boots might be polished, but they were cracked, wet with snow. He noticed all these things before he noticed Eugene's light expressionless eyes, pale and colorless face, and smooth, pale hair. In consequence, he did not sense Eugene's assurance, composure and air of self-confidence and authority.

"What is it, Arnold?" asked William, abruptly. "I think you have been told I am very busy." He paused. "Sit down," he added, even more abruptly.

Eugene smiled to himself. But he was far more intelligent than Ben Watson and his kind. He felt no contempt for William. He knew the flaw he had suspected long ago was as deep and as wide as ever, capable of cracking asunder. But it would take much to crack it; perhaps it could never be cracked.

"Thank you, sir," he said, and sat down. He paused. "I am sorry to disturb you. I know you are very busy. I came to ask you if you could find a place for me, here."

"You want to work for me?" William's voice was cold and incredulous. "Why?"

"Because I wish to learn the lumber business. And I wish to learn it from you."

William stared at Eugene, his eyes narrowing. He had come to Chauncey Arnold like this, many years ago, a young man like this. He had come with a purpose. Had Eugene come with the same purpose? William smiled grimly.

"There are other lumber companies," he said.

"Not in Andersburg. And none as large or important as this." Nothing could have been more dignified than Eugene's tone. William continued to look at him intently. He could not read beyond Eugene's face. Beyond those eyes that told nothing at all.

"This might be tactless," said William, with deliberate slowness, "but I shouldn't have thought you'd have wanted to come—here."

"If you are thinking of my father, Mr. Prescott, I can assure you *I* am not," said Eugene. He added: "I am thinking of myself. I have always been interested in this business. I have some knowledge of it. I must do what is best for myself, and for my mother, and for my future. Nothing else attracts me."

William again picked up the paper-weight, and set it down. He studied it. "You sound like a sensible young man." He hesitated. He knew what another man in his position would have done, even if he had been fool enough to have allowed this interview to take place at all. But he could not do it. This made him irascible.

"But what can you do here? Do you want to work in the mills? After all, you have had an education. Or, was it your idea to ask for work in these offices?"

Eugene heard the tone. It had iron in it. He must be very careful. It was dangerous to underestimate this man.

"I want to work in the offices," said Eugene, calmly. He crossed one long leg gracefully over the other. "As you have said, sir, I have had an education. And I know there is no better place than this company in which to work."

"You could go to another city," said William. He was contemplating Eugene with a hard expression in his eyes.

"Perhaps. But I prefer to remain here."

William leaned back in his chair. His hands were no longer restless. In a long silence, he studied Eugene. I was right, thought Eugene. Only a fool would underestimate him.

William's unshakable dislike for Eugene was increasing. He remembered the young man as a child, standing near his father, sitting by his father's side, always watching, always waiting. Waiting for what?

Eugene said: "I have my way to make, sir. And I am being as realistic as possible."

He is another of those I detest, thought William. Again, he studied Eugene, and Eugene returned that look with quiet respect. Still, William could not conquer his dislike and aversion. He did not want Eugene near him. He did not want to see him. It had nothing in the slightest to do with Chauncey Arnold. Then, involuntarily, William thought of Ben Watson. He touched the bell on his desk, leaned back in his chair, and waited.

Ben entered almost immediately. William spoke to him, but kept his eyes on Eugene: "Ben, Mr. Arnold has asked for a position here, as a clerk. I understand you need an assistant."

Ben was nonplussed. He looked at William, then at Eugene. Eugene did not rise, as a young man ought to rise in the presence of a potential superior. In fact, he appeared unaware of Ben.

William smiled. "Arnold, this is Mr. Watson, my chief clerk, and secretary."

It was then, and then only, that Eugene stood up. He looked directly at Ben Watson, whose expression had become flustered and uncertain. "Good-afternoon," he said. He was taller than the other man; authority was implicit in his bearing and his voice.

"Good-afternoon," he replied sullenly. He turned to his employer. "Mr. Prescott, I don't need an assistant. I have never asked for one."

"You have one now," said William. Ben was silent. He had made a mistake, a bad mistake. He saw it now; he saw it in William's eyes, which were staring at him fixedly.

"Ben, suppose you take Mr. Arnold out now, and begin to explain his new duties to him," said William.

Eugene turned to him. "Thank you, sir. I shall do my best." Nothing could have been more courteous or more formal than his manner and his voice.

William did not answer. He watched the other two. Eugene bowed, then went to the door. Ben Watson followed him more slowly. At the door, Ben hesitated. He turned quickly, but before he could speak, William said: "I am not to be disturbed again today, Ben."

Ben closed the door very softly behind him. His own office adjoined that of William. It was smaller, but very comfortable. Ben went to his desk, sat down, picked up his pen. Eugene watched him. He began to smile. Ben threw down his pen. He opened his mouth to speak, to express some of the rage he felt, but Eugene said, very quietly: "My duties, Mr. Watson?"

He put down his hat and coat on a chair; then, seeing a clothes-hanger, he carried his coat and hat to it, and hung them up. He said, as if speaking aloud to himself: "Only a fool thinks others are fools."

CHAPTER XXVI

MR. WATSON DID not like Eugene Arnold. A minor source of the dislike had been the forcing upon him of the young man as his assistant, an assistant he had not requested. But more than this was the acute apprehension which Mr. Watson was now suffering. The fact that the apprehension was the result of his own under-estimation of his employer, and that he, himself, was at fault in this, did not occur to Mr. Watson. Instead, he felt greatly abused and viciously resentful.

Under Mr. Watson's reluctant tutelage, Eugene at once displayed great intelligence and understanding. His politeness and dignity never failed for a moment, in spite of Mr. Watson's surly manner and sneering comments. His grasp of the subject matter amazed, and frightened, Mr. Watson. He suspected that William had known of this, and that a plot was beginning to reveal itself in all its sinister outlines.

Mr. Watson was very curious, as well as mean-spirited. During a lull, he leaned back in his chair and scrutinized Eugene slyly.

"Your dad once owned this firm, didn't he, Arnold?"

"He did," replied Eugene, coolly. He examined a paper intently. "Cypress wood," he remarked. He quoted from the report: " 'Though buried for nearly one hundred years, cypress retained its indestructible strength, in spite of water and the natural decaying action of earth and minerals. Ought to be important as a source of coffins.' I suppose this is to be presented at the meeting of the Directors?"

"Yes," said Mr. Watson, impatiently. He continued, with a leer: "Must feel funny coming here as a clerk, after your dad got thrown out."

Eugene appeared slightly bewildered. "No. Why should it? Fortunes of war, to quote a fine old aphorism."

"Good Christian charity," said Mr. Watson, sarcastically. "I shouldn't have thought you'd feel like that."

Eugene smiled. "Why not? Resentment, if I ever felt it, which I did not, is only a waste of time. I greatly value time. It is all any of us have, really. And I don't want to attach myself to any minor lumber company. I want to work here.

Emotions, of any sort, have nothing to do with it. I have no time for emotions. They are the luxury of the very rich, or of the very poor."

"Dear, dear," replied Mr. Watson, mincingly. "Well, I'm not a scholar. I don't know much about these 'emotions'. But then, I'm not educated—like you."

Eugene placed his long pale hand over the papers, and smiled again.

That smile infuriated Mr. Watson. Superior young hound! he thought. I'll take him down a peg. There's some place I can hit him—hard.

Mr. Watson shook his head regretfully. "Education is wasted here, Arnold. You won't find no Greek or Roman grammars around, and no poetry. That'll be bad for you, eh?"

"Not at all, Mr. Watson. It is true I have some education in Greek and Latin, and that I like poetry. But I hardly expected to find them here. This is a lumber business, isn't it?"

Mr. Watson studied him narrowly. His instincts were not unsound. In spite of Eugene's blandness, he felt something intangible. He could not think what it was. But he knew it was there.

"Still," he insisted, "it must be funny, you coming here, Christian sentiments and all, and no 'emotion', as you say. Don't see the ghost of your dad around, do you?"

There was no change in Eugene's expression as he regarded Mr. Watson with a long contemplativeness. Yet the older man had the sensation that something had subtly changed. It was too tenuous for a man like Mr. Watson to perceive in its completeness; he could not be aware of what it meant. He knew only that the change had come, that in a moment it had already gone, and that Eugene had not stirred.

Eugene said, almost gently: "I don't believe in ghosts, Mr. Watson."

Mr. Watson studied him with a curious uneasiness, but why he should have felt this uneasiness he did not know. The change, if there had been any at all, was in the atmosphere.

Mr. Watson rubbed an ink-stained finger along the side of his big crooked nose, his eyes closed almost to slits. His bald head glimmered in the reflected light of the snow, which came through the windows. He said, slowly: "You're only a young shaver. You're just out of school. I've heard about you. My cousin's janitor at the school you went to. He said you've got the reputation of being bad medicine."

Smooth and indulgent surprise made Eugene's face almost boyish. "In what way, Mr. Watson?" His tone was very polite and interested, but something in it made Mr. Watson's seamed face turn a dull crimson.

"Impudent," he remarked, in an ugly voice. "Look here, boy, there's no room for impudence in this office. I won't have it. I'm chief clerk here, and you're only my assistant. I hope you won't forget it." He added, more loudly: "And no tricks. You are a natural trickster; and I've lived long enough to recognize a trickster when I see one. Understand? There'll be no tricks here, from you."

Eugene laid down his pen. He did not smile, yet Mr. Watson felt that he was smiling. "Mr. Watson, you wound me. Frankly, I am afraid I do not understand. I need to work; I like this business. I am prepared to do my tasks well—under your intelligent direction. All I ask is that I please you—and Mr. Prescott."

Again, there was that change in the atmosphere, but now it was stronger. Mr. Watson stared at Eugene with open vindictiveness, in which there was a touch of unconscious fear.

Eugene was "quality." Ben feared and distrusted gentlefolk. They were "tricky." They had manners and desires and aspirations beyond his comprehension. As these were not to be comprehended, they could, Ben sensed, be very dangerous, and very potent. They rose from an obscure kind of thought and code, and they had an easy and ominous power.

Suddenly Ben was exhilarated. All his life he had dreamed of humiliating Eugene's class, of having power over them. It would be a revenge upon one of those whom nothing could openly disconcert, one who could smile with assurance in the face of disaster, who had the gallantry to regard events, however fearful, as impotent to disturb some inner and invulnerable security.

"I know you," said Ben, with slow deliberateness. "I wasn't born this morning. There's just one thing to remember: I'm your superior, and I'll be watching you. Any tricks, and out you'll go. I've worked for Mr. Prescott a long time; my word about the other clerks in this office goes with him."

"And why should it not?" asked Eugene, suavely. "It would be surprising if it were otherwise." He paused. "Mr. Watson, I can only promise to do my best. I hope it may please you."

"It'd better," said Ben Watson, threateningly.

The door opened and William Prescott appeared on the threshold. Eugene rose at once, in one angular movement, and with a look of polite expectancy. It was not Ben's custom to rise at the appearance of his employer. Eugene had risen;

Ben could do no less, but as he did so he flashed at the youth a glance of intense hatred.

William regarded Eugene in silence. "Oh, Arnold," he finally said. He turned to Ben. "Ben, I'm on my way to the Directors' Room. You'll take the minutes, as usual. And, Ben, please bring Arnold with you." He studied Ben Watson almost pleasantly. "We must teach him to take the minutes, mustn't we? Then, after he has learned, he can relieve you of the job entirely. That ought to be a relief, eh?"

Fear struck at Mr. Watson. He had never been afraid of William before; he was afraid now. "But, Mr. Prescott," he faltered, "I've always taken the minutes. I don't mind it at all. In fact I—I like to do it. And it's confidential, and—"

"And?" said William, agreeably.

Ben was silent. Out of the corner of his eye he thought he saw Eugene make the slightest of movements.

"Arnold, I am sure, realizes that minutes are confidential," said William. Never had Ben heard him speak so heartily. "You do realize that, Arnold?" he continued, turning to the young man.

"Indeed, sir, I do," said Eugene.

"Well, then, come along with Mr. Watson. It ought to be very educational, Arnold. I don't think you have forgotten that your father permitted you to attend such meetings? I thought not. I was chief clerk myself, then, wasn't I?"

Ben looked furtively from William to Eugene. There was a quality they both shared, and this quality, too, could be felt but not comprehended by Mr. Watson.

"You were, sir," said Eugene.

"It is the same room," said William. "Nothing has been changed. It will be familiar to you."

Something tight and fearful in Ben Watson relaxed. He almost grinned.

"I have never forgotten," said Eugene. Now he was apart from William and Mr. Watson, in his inaccessibility, and Ben knew that William hated and distrusted it as much as he did.

"Good," said William. Nothing about him was pleasant now. He walked abruptly to the opposite door. "In five minutes, Watson," he said, without looking back.

Eugene stood and looked at the door which had slammed shut behind William. Ben sat down, and chuckled to himself. But Eugene continued to look at the door. Was he smiling faintly? Ben leaned forward the better to see. If it had been a smile, it was no longer there.

CHAPTER XXVII

NO MATTER HOW often William Prescott saw his Directors assembled together, either here in the Board Room or in private, he felt for them the same aversion and disgust he had felt at first acquaintance, and, though he did not know it himself, the same wary fear.

Once, when he had been a child, his mother had found the ten cents necessary for him to visit a wild animal show as it passed through Andersburg from its spring engagement in Pittsburgh. There, with fascinated eyes, he had watched a tamer, armed only with a flimsy whip, enter a cage of tigers. The tigers had sat on their stools, tawny and sleek and indifferent, only their slit-like eyes revealing their innate savagery. "Ain't they the perfect gentlemen?" a woman within William's hearing had asked of her escort with admiration.

The "perfect gentlemen" had watched the entrance and approach of their tamer with superb poise. They regarded him with courtesy and polite detachment. But William was enthralled by the eyes of the tigers, sleepily but unremittingly regarding the man. He wondered if the tamer saw that look, was aware of it, and understood it.

He wondered no longer. He knew. He was now the tamer, and the "perfect gentlemen" who surrounded him might conceal their sentiments under smiles, proper gestures, and sleekness; he knew, nevertheless, that these sentiments were hatred, contempt, and a relentless waiting to destroy him. Let them wait, he thought, grimly.

There were "bears" in what William privately called his menagerie. He was not too wary of them, for they were so obvious. The "bears" were Albert Jenkins, the lawyer, former suitor of Ursula, present husband of Rose Jenkins (née Bassett), ex-Senator David Whiscomb, and Mr. Hazlitt Leslie, owner of the Leslie Carriage Company. They might be dangerous and cunning, but they lumbered, though they had acquired the "gentlemanliness" of the "tigers" who were their associates: Ezra Bassett, the banker; Judge Oscar Muehller; and Dr. Eli Banks. He, William Prescott, dared never be careless in their presence. He was not of them, he never had been of them.

The Directors were waiting for him, and greeted him in their "bear-like" or "tigerish" individual fashion. Jenkins, Whiscomb and Leslie figuratively hugged him in their excess of friendly cordiality. Bassett, Muehller and Banks smiled upon him with urbane suavity. Their handclasps were like soft fur, laid gently across the palms. The "bears" wrung his hand. He did not know which he detested more. But he did know that if he had any respect for any of them at all, it was not for the "bears."

The past five years had not dimmed Ezra Bassett's rosy round geniality. He asked after William's fourth child, Barbara, born three months ago. Barbara was Bassett's goddaughter. He beamed upon the father of Barbara, earnestly inquired after Ursula's health, which, he confessed, was still causing him and Jemima some secret anxiety. Dr. Banks, with his usual rich urbanity, reassured both godfather and father. The lady was recovering nicely, though, of course, it was sad that there would be no more children. "However, my dear Prescott," said Dr. Banks, touching his thick brown beard with dainty fingertips, "four children are a good family. Five, one might say, with Oliver." He paused, and twinkled. "Of course, Oliver is not really your own child but, as I was remarking to Mrs. Banks recently, the lad is evidently of good blood, and that is reassuring. Astonishing if one remembers that he was an abandoned orphan, before you rescued him."

William glanced at the doctor sharply. "Wonderful manners," murmured Dr. Banks. "Native good manners."

Did he mean that William's own children did not have "native good manners"? Dr. Banks met William's glance with a deep unctuousness.

"Ah, yes, remarkable," said Judge Oscar Muehller. "I commented upon it myself, when we saw him at the Christmas party at the church. His behavior is perfect. And his superior intelligence was quite obvious."

Thomas and Matthew had been at that party also. No one mentioned them. Were these men twitting him, William? Was this one of their delicate tiger scratches? He stared at them somberly. They smiled back at him with ease. Their manner suggested that they had gratified him. William was silent. He turned from them abruptly.

The Directors still used Chauncey Arnold's Directors' Room, but William had changed it. It was no longer plain, bare, and somewhat dusty. The wooden fireplace had been replaced by one of white marble. A thick brown rug lay upon

the floor. The chairs were of red leather, the long table of
dark polished wood. It was a room for discussion, relaxation
and smoky pleasure. William had had the three narrow windows
thrown into one, so that a view of the wide river might rest
and fascinate the eye. Today the river ran like liquid steel
under the brilliant winter sky; flat-boats, loaded with lumber,
or waiting, stood at long neat docks. The whir and hum of
the great saw-mills could be heard in the clarified air.

The "tigers" were too polite to sit down before their president
did. The "bears" had no such breeding. They were of the mentality of Ben Watson. They sat back in their deep leather chairs
and puffed contentedly upon their cigars. William sat down
at the head of the table, his back to the blazing sun and water.
They could not see his face clearly, but he could see every
other face as if it were illuminated.

In a few moments, Ben Watson and Eugene Arnold would
arrive. William looked slowly from one man to another. He
sat at the table, big, bulky, indomitable. His hands never lay
at ease on the table; no one could remember seeing them except tensed. As usual, he gave the impression of surly fierceness and power.

"Before the meeting is called," he said, in the loud neutral
voice so distasteful to three of the men in the room, "I wish
to mention a small matter. I have, today, hired an assistant
to Ben Watson, my chief clerk. He will accompany Ben into
this room in a few moments, to learn how to take down the
minutes."

Again, his deep-set eyes passed from man to man, more
quickly now. "Eugene Arnold," he said, and his voice was
louder than before.

The low creaks, murmurs and movements in the room suddenly subsided. Dr. Banks, Mr. Bassett and Judge Muehller
became very still; a deep paralysis fell upon them. Across
their faces slid a kind of inexpressive smoothness, which
washed away anything that might betray what they thought.
Dr. Banks slowly lifted his cigar to his mouth, removed it,
gently blew out the smoke he had inhaled. His black silk
cravat glimmered in a shaft of sunshine; a kind of contemplative thoughtfulness still lay about his eyes, which had become
bland. Mr. Bassett's rosiness did not deepen; no uneasiness
marred his faint and amiable smile. Judge Muehller, more
than ever, resembled a fine and ascetic saint. Pensively, his
mild hazel eyes gazed at William, as if expecting him to add
something to his remark.

It was the others, who had no advantages of breeding

to assist them, and no fundamental training to help them suppress normal emotions, who became obviously furtive and disturbed. Mr. Jenkins, his sharp features becoming even sharper, Mr. Leslie, turning ruddy with angry embarrassment, and former Senator Whiscomb, resembling a floury grocer in his uncouthness, could not completely hide their awkward confusion and umbrage. For an instant or two they glared belligerently at William. Then, as if called by some secret signal, they all of them looked at their three other colleagues.

Dr. Banks thought: What taste! He said, urbanely: "Eugene Arnold? Has he come back to Andersburg, with his mother?"

A gloomy smile appeared on William's face. "The boy has never been away," he said, with indifferent disgust. He shifted his hands on the table. "You know he has not, Banks."

"I really did not know," murmured Dr. Banks apologetically. With rich deliberateness, he turned to the banker. "Did you know, Ezra, or you, Oscar?"

"No, indeed," said Mr. Bassett. He was all roseate friendliness. "I did not know," said the judge, in his melodious voice.

Liars, thought William contemptuously. He said: "Of course you knew, all of you. That schoolmaster, Landsdowne, is your friend. He couldn't have failed, in all these years, to have mentioned Arnold."

As usual, reflected Dr. Banks, the boor never takes advantage of a discreet opening. Or, does he voluntarily refuse to take advantage of it?

The doctor said amiably: "Now, William, that is unfair. I don't happen to discuss Landsdowne's pupils with him. I am not interested in the younger male generation, possibly because I have been—blessed—with daughters rather than with sons. Moreover, Landsdowne is not a man to talk about the boys in his school, unless perhaps to their parents. I think the same is true of you, Ezra? Two daughters, young ladies—"

"As for me," the judge laughed softly, "my sons are at Harvard."

The circle was closed. Mr. Jenkins, Mr. Leslie and Senator Whiscomb scurried about the glassy contour of that circle, seeking to enter it, to hide within it. But on disagreeable occasions, such as this, the circle remained impervious. Mr. Jenkins looked with hard but shifting eyes upon William.

"Why employ him, Bill? It is embarrassing, to say the least."

"Very," said the senator, sullenly.

"I don't know why you should," grunted Mr. Leslie.

William could deal with these three. He regarded them in

a silence he purposely allowed to become almost untenable. He then said: "Why shouldn't I employ him? You all know him to have a considerable amount of intelligence. Besides, he needs to make a living, and he has told me he prefers to make that living in a lumber business." He dropped his hands from the table. He leaned far back in his chair. He began to enjoy himself a little. "Why should you all be so concerned? And you *are* concerned, you know," he added, looking now at the doctor, the judge, and the banker. "You might pretend not to mind in the least, some of you. But you do mind. After all, Chauncey Arnold was your—friend, wasn't he? You were associated with him, weren't you? You couldn't have forgotten him."

Openly and ruthlessly attacked like this, Mr. Bassett came to the rescue of his friends. He pretended to deep hurt, and to shame for William's coarseness.

"Let us be frank, dear William. Not for a moment would I suggest whom you should employ. That is not in my province. It is true we remember Chauncey. There were many—associations—between him and all of us. Perhaps we feel for his son more than we might wish to reveal. It is a delicate matter. Surely you must realize that it might cause young Arnold some distress to be here——"

"Nonsense," said William. "The fellow came to me a short time ago and asked me for employment. He was frank. He wants to work here. I might add that he seemed curiously devoid of sentimentality. I never liked him as a boy," continued William. "I don't particularly like him now. But he needs the work, he tells me. He wants to learn the business. I saw no reason why I should not take him on."

The judge sighed, and nodded his head. "Very exemplary. Very—kind. One understands, of course, that you were motivated by the kindest of sentiments. But think of young Arnold's feelings, when he enters this room, for instance, where his father sat where you now sit, William."

The tiger scratch did not touch William. It amused him. He allowed the judge to see his amusement. These men might have an inaccessibility he hated and secretly respected, but he had his own distorted inaccessibility. What could be touched by them they had not touched.

"It is kind of you, too, Oscar, to be concerned with the 'sentiments' of young Arnold," said William. "But then, we all know how charitable you are."

He went on: "I don't think young Arnold will shrink, inwardly, when he sees me in this chair." He looked slowly from one man to another, as if taken by an interesting thought. "It has come to me that he always expected to see me here. From the very beginning I think he always expected to see me here. From the very beginning I think he knew his father was a fool."

No one spoke. William waited. Dr. Banks continued to puff thoughtfully at his cigar. Mr. Bassett turned a pen in his small pink fingers. The judge sat in stately silence. The other three stared grimly at the table.

William moved in his chair with so much vigor that it creaked loudly. The sound was derisive. "I thought I ought to tell you," he said. "I didn't want to surprise you too much."

"But it has been years," murmured Dr. Banks. "I don't think we'd have recognized the boy. Would you have, Ezra, or you, Oscar?"

"No, indeed," they answered with simple gravity. The others did not speak.

"Good," said William. "Then young Arnold won't be—embarrassed. We must never cause anyone embarrassment, must we?"

He touched a bell on the table. "And now to work," he said.

The door opened. Ben Watson, surly and resentful, appeared, followed by Eugene Arnold. William did not glance at either of them. He watched his directors and officers. Mr. Jenkins, Mr. Leslie and the senator did not look up. The other three blandly nodded to Mr. Watson, let their eyes glide without recognition over the youth behind him. They relegated Eugene to anonymity.

Then William looked at Eugene. For an instant, the young man stood on the threshold. His face remained impenetrable. He sat down where Ben Watson abruptly indicated. His very lack of emphasis was the refinement of supreme emphasis.

Perhaps only a few moments passed, while Ben Watson prepared his pen and laid out his notebooks and drew up his chair to the table. It was during those few moments that William, through intuition and not through any thoughtful perceptiveness, suddenly became aware that three others in the room, for all their bland ignoring of the young man, were as suddenly and acutely conscious of Eugene Arnold as he himself was.

Eugene sat beside Ben Watson at the foot of the table and gave all his attention to the small business of preparing the waiting notebook. With every precise movement and careful adjustment of the pages, Ben Watson rejected him.

The officers and directors, well inured to William during the past year, suspected that he called this meeting in order to reveal another one of his disturbing plans. The fact that his plans invariably were enormously successful did not detract from the uneasiness of the gentlemen. It was not possible, according to the inexorable law of averages, that all future plans should be successful, also. A time would come when disaster might strike. Hence their constant watchfulness, their perturbation at any hint of another of William's unorthodox ideas.

Each had a neat little sheaf of personal notes before him. Ben Watson lifted his pen, and looked at William. The others awaited an opening. William gave it to them, for he knew what they were about and, as usual, he preferred to attack directly.

"Let us get to small matters first," he said, glancing quickly about the table. He smiled ironically. "I request an increase in the annual salary of your president from twenty thousand dollars a year to thirty-five thousand." He waited a moment; they stared at him, stupefied. He waved his hand with his familiar awkward but potent gesture. "A small thing, yes, I agree. The truth of the matter, gentlemen, is that I need the money."

Dr. Banks was the first to recover. He said, in a voice of calm and reasonable restraint: "Not a 'small thing' at all, William. I appreciate your desire for an increase of fifteen thousand dollars a year. I should like to have that increase, myself." He spoke pleasantly now, and with humor. "But, regrettably, we must face facts. Can the company stand any increase at all in salaries?"

The opening had been accepted. Dr. Banks turned with agreeable ceremony to his colleagues. "Any comments, gentlemen?"

It was Mr. Albert Jenkins who made the first real gesture of revolt. He glowered at William. He leaned forward in his chair, his color higher than ever, his prominent blue eyes glittering. "I want to go into a little history, Bill," he said. "Just a little history. I hope it won't bore you."

"Not at all," said William, readily. His hands were again on the table, tensed. His eyes measured Mr. Jenkins with open contempt. "Go on. I like history."

Mr. Jenkins felt the solidarity behind him, and he did not look away from William. He spoke slowly and deliberately:

"When we first consented to the merger of the American Lumber Company with the Prescott Lumber Company, and elected you president, we had two reasons. First, we believed our capital would not only be safe, but that our stock would appreciate in value. Second, we expected that the company

would make profits, and that from these profits we should receive adequate dividends on our investment." He paused, leaned
even closer to William. A kind of furious excitement, born
of hatred, took possession of him. "We have been in this
business together for some years now, and so far we have not
received any part of the alleged earnings. We get reports that
the profits we have turned back into the business have been
used to buy larger tracts of lumber in different States."

"The reports are correct," said William.

Large knotted veins appeared at Mr. Jenkins' temples.
"I am not disputing the validity of the reports," he said, "and
you know that, Bill." He was the only one who had ever used
this nickname, and even he used it seldom, and only when he
felt he had the support of his colleagues. He had guessed that
William, for some obscure reason, detested it. It was his one
small weapon against the other man, to be used like a wasp's
sting to goad him.

"Under your direction—Bill—we have expanded into various related fields of the lumber industry, which I, personally,
have felt was dangerous. Over-expansion, and entering into
irrelevant, if related, fields, is always precarious. Now, I'm
a comfortable sort of a fella, and I'm content with modest
profits based on sound business," he smiled indulgently at
himself. William did not return the smile. Dr. Banks, Judge
Muehller and Mr. Bassett exchanged mild glances.

Mr. Jenkins' smile disappeared, and sharp constrictions
of avarice dug small white pits about his nostrils.

William said, gently: "Yes, we have expanded. Once the
company merely cut the lumber, sawed it, and delivered it
to related industries. But, as you say, under my direction and
with your approval, we went into the manufacturing of various
wood products, doors, windows, platforms, housings, railroad
ties and frames for railroad cars. We have built factories
in conjunction with saw-mills, in Pennsylvania, Michigan,
Illinois, Wisconsin, and Ohio. You see, I know my history,
too."

Mr. Jenkins nodded. "Very good. But very—expanded.
I don't think, and I never have thought, that it was necessary
to go into the manufacturing field, too. But we'll let that pass
for a moment, though I have always felt that the manufacturing
field ought to have been left to old established manufacturers.
And now, before we go any further, I'd like to suggest that
we first ask for an accounting, and see if there is any cash
to vote a dividend to stockholders of record for the past three
months." He glanced humorously at his colleagues. "Then we'll

consider the validity of our president's application for a raise in his salary."

Judge Muehller coughed softly. "And while we are considering all this, we'll also discuss the fact that this company seems very interested in railroading, perhaps too much so."

William was silent. Eugene, apparently engaged in a fascinating study of Ben Watson's notes, watched William out of the corner of his eye. He saw the large predatory profile against a shaft of brilliant winter sunshine; he saw William's huge scorn of the fat and careful men about the table.

Eugene thought: He's a buccaneer, and these cosy little creatures are afraid of him, and afraid for their miserable investments. But he has to work with them; he has to struggle against them. Very unfortunate. They don't realize that, without the adventurer, America would be forever doomed to a small and narrowing provincialism, which would, in the end, decay.

William was speaking now, as if musing aloud to himself: "America will never be built on the cautious desire of small men for a safe bank account."

"Nevertheless," said Dr. Banks, with indulgent affection, "there is much to be said in favor of sound bank accounts. I have a weakness for them. Moreover, none of us is particularly young, and so, and I apologize when I say this, dear William, we are not particularly interested in the 'building' of America. We could leave that phase to our children."

"There'll be no America for our chiildren, unless we make it for them," commented William.

Dr. Banks made a genteel and deprecating gesture. "I have faith in the younger generation. They'll always find a way. The courage of youth, you know."

William smiled, and the smile was unpleasant. He did not answer. He sat there, waiting for further remarks, but he was not on the defensive. Eugene could feel his waiting, and his potential power. Whatever these fearful little men, these unctuous and careful little men, might say, do, want, insist upon, William would have his way.

Mr. Hazlitt Leslie, the carriage-maker, spoke in his deep voice, which was now without its hearty good-humor. "As Judge Muehller has just said, we are invested heavily in railroads. I don't know why, but we are."

William's hand increased the tempo of its tapping. "Yes, and fortunately so. Soon, the whole West will be available for lumber exploitation. Maine is practically finished as a source of lumber, more particularly of white pine. White pine is what our customers want, in large proportion. The Middle

Atlantic States will soon no longer be an adequate source of it. Saginaw is our largest source now. At the rate white pine is being cut there, not to speak of other lumber, Saginaw will soon be through. At present, as you probably know, our saw-mills at Saginaw and Bay City are cutting a large share of the more than one thousand million feet of lumber being cut this year. Again, though Saginaw today stands as chief lumber-maker to the world, she'll soon be interred under mountains of white-pine sawdust. And don't tell me about the wonderful possibilities of bringing logs from Canada, after that, for cutting in Saginaw. The forests up there are too far from the mills.

"The West will be necessary, beyond Wisconsin, where we are doing splendidly—at the present time. But we eat up lumber, gentlemen, we eat up lumber. To reach other sources, we need a big network of railroads, all over the West. We are invested in the future of railroads, not only as a source of income, but as a necessity. Ox-carts and sleighs won't be adequate.

"Our own State of Pennsylvania once led the whole country in lumber production. I don't have to tell you that Michigan is now cutting more lumber than ever did Maine and Pennsylvania combined, at their peak of production. But Michigan will soon be practically exhausted, for some time to come. Until the second growth is ready. No, gentlemen, we must not neglect the future. And so, the railroads. There is an almost boundless supply of yellow and white pine waiting for us in Idaho, Oregon and Washington."

"We shan't be alive to profit by that," said Senator Whiscomb, glumly. "And, frankly, I'm not interested in what might happen after I'm dead."

"I deny that you, and we, won't profit," said William. "And, again, that is why we are invested in railroads. The sooner the railroads expand, the sooner we profit. Railroads are the circulatory system of a nation."

Mr. Jenkins said stubbornly: "Railroads! You can't tell me, Bill, that we are anywhere near exhausting the Lake states as a source of lumber."

William shrugged. "We'll soon be. Lumber doesn't miraculously replace itself, immediately it is cut. It takes time. And, once more, our customers are mainly interested in white pine, in yellow too. It is getting scarce. Owners of the land now want a dollar and seventy-five cents an acre, whereas only two years ago we paid a dollar twenty-five. In the meantime, we've got to move very fast. Yesler has already built his first mill at Seattle, Washington. Unless we hurry, he'll have all the lumber. And there're Pope and Talbot's lumber men, moving in from Maine to the Pacific Coast." He paused, said idly: "I've taken large options on lumber in Idaho, Oregon and Washington. That's why I called this meeting: to tell you."

They stared at him, aghast. He went on: "And I have the plans for building saw-mills at Cosmopolis and Port Ludlow, Washington. The Northwest, gentlemen, the Northwest!"

"My God!" exclaimed the Senator, horrified. The others added their exclamations. Oddly, Mr. Bassett remained silent. The pencil twirled a little faster in his rosy fingers.

"Yes, 'My God'," repeated William, as if reflectively. His inner rage against these tidy and fearful little men showed in his eloquent face. "Others are moving in. We are moving in, also. I have all the papers here. One dollar and twenty-five cents an acre."

"Really, William!" exclaimed Judge Muehller, in his melodious voice. "Ought we not to have been consulted, first?"

"There was no time," said William. "No time for endless directors' meetings, palavering, discussion, speculating. This was a time for immediate action. I took that action. Another reason for this meeting. I thought you ought to know."

"After the fact," remarked Leslie, with bitterness.

"Yes," said William.

The others looked at one another. Dr. Banks said smoothly: "I often wonder, William, whether you ever stop to consider that you really do have officers and a Board of Directors. We exist, you know."

William allowed his glance to travel slowly about the table. "Yes," he admitted at last, and in a drawling and insulting tone. "You do exist."

Eugene, studiously watching the movements of Ben Watson's rapid pen, smiled to himself.

Only Dr. Banks, the judge and Mr. Bassett heard the note in William's voice.

"Well, I'm glad to admit that we have a part in all this," said Mr. Jenkins, sardonically. "It was kind of you to remember—Bill. And we'll be kind enough to remark, in passing only, of course, that we think your conduct high-handed." He paused. "Perhaps even illegal."

"That is something we shall discuss, privately," said Mr. Leslie, with an ominous frown.

"I haven't forgotten my law," suggested the senator, sourly. "And I'm treasurer of this damned company."

Dr. Banks, the judge and Mr. Bassett smiled faintly.

William rested his chin on a clenched hand. "I might as well go on and tell you about another of my—illegal—acts. I have invested money in forest conservation in Pennsylvania, and in the Lake states."

"Conservation!" exclaimed several voices together, in stupefaction.

"Yes." William was deceptively at ease. "You see, I do think of America, and of our children. After all, the forests won't last forever. In a generation or two, perhaps, the forests might all be gone. What then? I've been doing some interesting reading, lately. It is the belief of certain scientists that the great desert regions of the world were once forested and fertile lands. You know they are barren, eroded, lost forever to cultivation. Because there were no roots to hold the land to the subsoil. No trees to conserve moisture, or help bring it down again in the form of rain. Do we want that to happen to America? Do we want America to have no future lumber resources? So—lumber conservation, reforestation. I invested in that. I invested in the future of America. Good sound business sense, in a way, though only our descendants will profit from it."

He regarded them with brutal affability, mocking them.

"So, I did this: Timber is a crop, like any other crop. Most of us lumbermen, however, have been too content, and too greedy, to do anything else but harvest the great crops we found, doing nothing to replace them. We were careful of our investments, you see. Too careful to safeguard them for the future. Cut-out-get-out. That was our idea. Liquidation of the treasures of America. Permanent liquidation. Good for immediate profits. But not good for America.

"I thought it all out. I began to suspect the whole policy of the lumberman. Robbers, operating openly, taking away the treasures of the country, inducing bankruptcy. The first thing that occurred to me was that there was no real profit in making lumber out of weak little trees. Why not, then, I thought, take away only the big trees, and let the little ones grow up into fine lumber for the future? Good profitable idea. I began to put it into operation everywhere we cut timber. In the meantime, I went ahead giving out contracts on timber in the deep South. For, I had discovered, you see, that there is more than 300 billion board feet of saw timber down there, in pine. All this, in addition to the Northwest."

The others could not speak.

"As you know, I made a long visit to the deep South. Farmers down there, on the timber acreage I had bought, were willing to sell us all the timber on their land for very little an acre. I arranged with the farmers in the South, and in other regions where we cut timber, to leave the little trees alone, and to sell us the big trees. You will appreciate the simile, gentlemen, when I say I regard this as a kind of banking. You see that, eh, Bassett?"

For the first time, the banker nodded. His roseate smile widened.

"We take out the interest. We leave the principal," said William.

"Waste of money!" cried Mr. Jenkins, enraged. "When it could all be exploited——"

William let the remark lie before them all, in its nakedness.

William then said, breaking into the uncomfortable hush which had followed Mr. Jenkins' revealing remark: "I am afraid, Albert, that you would never be a good banker. No appreciation of the sound plan of living on interest only. Never touch principal, Albert. It is a bad policy. Bassett, here, could tell you so. Bassett could tell you that living on principal invariably leads to poverty and bankruptcy. Eh, Bassett?"

Mr. Bassett was struggling with some sort of hidden mirth. He cleared his throat. "A very bad policy: living on principal," he murmured. "I always discourage it among my depositors."

He winked at Dr. Banks and Judge Muehller. They were a solid bloc, now, against the vulgarians, Albert Jenkins, Leslie and the Senator.

William gently slapped his hand on the table. "I love sound advice. I always take it. Bassett's advice is invariably sound."

He paused, and appeared to be studying them seriously.

"And now back to my request for an increase in salary, and to the discussion of my—shall we say—precipitate action in buying those contracts in the Northwest and in the deep South? Perhaps I have been a little hasty.

"Shall we consider it this way: Instead of your granting me an increase in salary, suppose I borrow enough money from Mr. Regan to pay back into the company the money I have expended on these contracts? Mr. Regan has more than indicated that he will be glad to lend me this money. I shall transfer the contracts to my own name, leaving the company unencumbered. Frankly, gentlemen, I gave this matter considerable thought before proceeding as I did. After all, I am a loyal man," and he smiled at them amiably. "I thought all of you ought to participate in the profits. I see you do not want to do so."

All of them, even the urbane gentlemen, were horribly disturbed at this. Greed, caution, avarice, confusion and doubt struggled in their faces. Eugene watched them with impassive enjoyment.

Then Dr. Banks, actually stammering, said: "But William, you must give us time to consider—the salary increase—everything else. We can't decide things in an instant."

"Why not? I do," answered William. He seemed overcome with boredom. He took his watch from his pocket. "Mr. Regan is waiting for my reply. I am to telegraph him almost immediately."

"He is waiting?" asked the judge.

"Yes, I said so, didn't I?" William folded his arms on the table, and gazed at them somberly. "Frankly, and though I am betraying a confidence when I tell you this, Mr. Regan advised me not to buy the contracts through the company. But I have a sentimental concern for the company—my company."

He sat back. "Well, gentlemen?"

Slowly, they began to look at one another. Mr. Bassett was more pale than anyone had ever seen him before. Mr. Jenkins muttered: "We ought to have time——" No one listened to him.

Then Mr. Bassett stood up. It was as if at a signal from the others. He gathered all eyes together, and spoke to his associates quietly:

"Let us admit, gentlemen, from the very beginning, that we are not accustomed to do business, make decisions, so abruptly. Nor, from what I know, are other companies so accustomed. Everything is considered, weighed, discussed. That is the safe way, and, in many situations, the only sound and prudent way. Everything else is—extraordinary."

They listened to him with profound attention.

"But over the years, since our association with this company, we have been—er—persuaded that the somewhat arbitrary methods of William have had their basis in good sound reasoning and amazing ability. Almost prophetic ability, I may say. Occasions have arisen when we have—protested—against William's methods and decisions. Revolutionary, we have thought. Dangerous. Not done. But, fortunately for all of us, he has been right. That he will always be right, I am not prepared to say. That is another matter, and it seems we have no time to consider that aspect." He looked inquiringly at William.

"No time," agreed William, nodding his head.

Mr. Bassett sighed.

"Let us go back a little. It is true that we haven't received the dividends we had expected. They all went back into the expansion of the company. We agreed to that. To speak honestly, we have all been glad of it. The stock has appreciated enormously in value. Doubled or more, in equity. No one, and I think I speak for all of us, is prepared to sell his stock. Or, am I wrong?"

There was no answer. Mr. Bassett nodded, and smiled. "There it is. None of us needs money at this time. We all have our other—affairs. So, I am in favor of not selling any stock. I, at least, shall not sell mine," and he laughed tenderly.

"We all know what our president has accomplished for the company. I might remark that he has built it up from a modest firm to one engaged in national and international trade. It is one of the largest companies in America, and enjoys the highest esteem of competitors and customers. Its methods might seem, at times, slightly—unorthodox," and Mr. Bassett coughed deprecatingly, "but then, conservatism is not to be too highly valued in the opinion of those who are progressive, and have no objection to profits. The conservative," continued Mr. Bassett with pious unction, "are frequently an impediment in business. Though, of course," he added, a trifle hastily, "banking is quite another matter, quite. In banking, one has to consider one's depositors. It is a sacred trust."

He paused impressively. William said, gravely: "Money is always a sacred trust."

"Quite true, quite true, my dear William," said Mr. Bassett, with a slight bow in the direction of the president. Dr. Banks and Judge Muehller exchanged gentle glances.

"The matter of an increase of fifteen thousand dollars a year in the salary of our president ought to be a matter for long and serious discussion. Under ordinary circumstances," said Mr. Bassett, "we might be justified in demanding time for that discussion. However, I think, all things considered, and in view of our president's past remarkable record and the promise for the future, that we ought to show him our gratitude by not demanding time for consideration, but grant him the increase immediately as a gesture of our confidence. And, I think we should grant it unanimously, and spontaneously, without further discussion."

He sat down. He looked with pink expectancy about the table.

Dr. Banks stroked his beard. Judge Muehller played delicately with his watch-chain. Mr. Jenkins sullenly stared at his signet ring; Senator Whiscomb pursed up his lips, like a grocer watching the scales; Mr. Leslie's face, creased from his customary large and rollicking smile, was surly.

Dr. Banks sighed: "I second the motion, of course," he said.

One by one, then, the ayes came in. William watched each individual struggle before consent was given. He watched, and it was with open and massive derision.

Immediately the fact was recorded, the constraint, hostility and suspicion appeared to lighten. Each man insisted upon shaking hands with William. He stood up to receive these gestures of approval and good-will. He smiled, but his face had become dull and blunt.

They all seated themselves in a bright atmosphere of good-will, somewhat forced, however, on the part of Mr. Jenkins and his friends. Judge Muehller said graciously: "There's just a little matter we'd like to mention, William, and it's off the record," he added to Ben Watson with a condescending wave of his fine hand. "That is the matter of the increase in wages you contemplate giving the workers in our mills in Andersburg. Frankly, I can't see the necessity. They are paid more than other workers in this city."

"Yes," said William. He regarded the judge broodingly. "That is so. They are paid more. Accordingly, they can afford meat eight times a month instead of once a month."

"Well," prompted the judge good-temperedly.

"That isn't enough," said William. "Moreover, they are getting restless. Do we want a strike?" To himself, he said: Have you ever been hungry, you bastards? Have you ever been cold and homeless and desperate? Do you know what it is to be afraid?

Dr. Banks waved his hand indulgently. "A strike," he said. "I hardly think we need strikes." He laughed richly. "The Governor can always send us troops, if necessary, as he did in 1872. That was when Chauncey was president. Perhaps you remember."

"I remember," replied William. There was something pent in his voice. "Violence. Bloodshed."

"The strikers did threaten to burn the mills," suggested Dr. Banks. "Protection was needed."

"If they had burnt the mills, it would have been Arnold's fault," said William. He glanced at Eugene. The young man was staring expressionlessly at his crossed knees.

"Good heavens!" murmured Mr. Bassett. "That is very nihilistic, coming from you, William. I was under the impression you had no particular love for the workers."

William slapped the table with a hard flat sound. "I don't. That has nothing to do with it."

"Perhaps not," said the judge. "But you will remember that the ministers of our churches declared that strikes were acts against God. The people haven't forgotten."

"No, they haven't forgotten," said William. "Perhaps that is why the churches are so empty these days, empty of people who would ordinarily depend upon religion for a little excitement in their lives."

"Very nihilistic," repeated Mr. Bassett. "William, you aren't afraid of the Knights of Labor, are you? Troublemakers, I admit. But, as Banks says, we can always call upon the troops in time of trouble. I think that fact alone would deter the hotheads."

"You miss my point, deliberately," said William with contempt. "I am going to raise wages voluntarily, because I prefer to know that the men can eat meat twice a week."

"Very Christian, very charitable," said the judge. "I am the last to urge you to be reckless of the comfort of others. But I assure you that the men would be the last to appreciate it. They would only demand more. They would consider it a mark of weakness on the part of the company."

"Nevertheless, they are going to get the raise," said William.

Without a backward look, without a word of polite leave-taking, he walked out of the room. Ben Watson rose uncertainly, then followed his employer. Eugene walked behind him, abstractedly.

The large room was silent for a long time after he had gone. Dr. Banks and the others smoked reflectively. They looked at each other. Mr. Bassett spoke to Dr. Banks and the judge.

"It seems," he said with a smile, "that we have been led by a ring in the nose—as usual."

"But a golden ring," said Dr. Banks, with his comfortable physician's smile.

Again, they smoked reflectively. "Do you know," mused Dr. Banks, "I think he has a conscience, and I think it hurts him."

"A conscience!" exploded Mr. Leslie, moving his bulk in his chair.

Dr. Banks, the judge and Mr. Bassett looked at one another and smiled gently. "Young Arnold," murmured the doctor. Now they laughed ever so softly.

"A conscience," offered the judge, "can be very—dangerous —sometimes. For the man who has it."

CHAPTER XXVIII

IT WAS NOT ALWAYS that Eugene Arnold believed his mother to be a fool. She had, in spite of her ridiculous tendency to compassion, a disconcerting way of impressing him with a quiet remark which betrayed a deep insight.

So, when he arrived home from his first day of employment at the Prescott Lumber Company, he was quite ready to accept her as an audience for his remarks. She had objected to his applying for a position with William Prescott; she had told him, with chill disdain, that he was diplaying "bad taste." "In a parvenu," she had said, "bad taste can be forgiven. He knows no better. But you have been reared to regard bad taste as unpardonable and common. Why do you insist upon it?" She added, after a moment's concerned scrutiny of her son, in which aversion was mingled: "Eugene, what is it you want?"

He had merely smiled and said: "Want? We all have a number of 'wants'. I have mine. I have a certain idea. I may be wrong. I want to find out if that is so. If I am right, then I know what it is I must do—to get what I want."

She had hoped, but without reason to hope, that William would not employ her son. She knew William, even though they had hardly met. There was something strange about William, she mused. He was a paradox. She remembered the money he had sent her, and which she had returned. It was more than possible that he would employ Eugene. What if she wrote him and begged him not to do so? She suspected her request would have little weight. Besides, she was very tired. She was tired of living.

She had vaguely expected that Eugene would return within an hour or two. When he did not, she knew he had got what he wanted. Hour after hour passed; with their passing, a kind of lethargic indifference overcame her. It was settled; the inevitable had happened.

Eugene came in, this night, in his usual fashion, which was practically noiseless.

He never entered the kitchen. Alice, at the stove, removed her apron, went into the bright little parlor, where the last rays of the sun, scarlet and long, mingled with the firelight.

Eugene stood on the hearth, waiting for her. He drew out the chair by the fire, and Alice sat down, folding her worn hands on her knees. "Well, Eugene?" she asked.

Eugene gave her one of his faint smiles. "I am now," he announced, "assistant to one Ben Watson, chief clerk to Mr. William Prescott."

"Oh, Eugene," sighed Alice. Her dim tired face turned to the fire.

"I find it very interesting," said Eugene. He pushed a fallen coal with his foot. "I find Mr. Prescott extremely interesting. I must have been a very bright little boy. I understood him then. I wasn't imagining, after all. He is even more than I expected."

In spite of herself, Alice was intrigued. "Indeed," she murmured.

Eugene seemed absorbed. He sat very still. He might have forgotten her. He said: "Of course, he is unprincipled. But his power is tremendous. Rascals are even more necessary than good men—and by 'good' I mean what is accepted as 'virtuous'—because they can carry out huge plans and ideas without compunction. They have a singleness of purpose; that is why they are powerful. But, and perhaps this is a law of nature, by carrying out for themselves their own enormous plans they populate wildernesses and create civilizations."

"I can see that Mr. Prescott has impressed you," said Alice.

"Why not? He is a great man."

"I suppose, then, Eugene, that you are quite content to be his clerk?"

Eugene laughed lightly. "More than content, Mother. I'm grateful. Of course, I never doubted for a moment that he would employ me."

"I had my own private doubts, I am sure," said Alice, with weariness. She waited. Eugene did not answer. She said, "Why didn't you, yourself, doubt, under the circumstances, Gene?"

"Because," he replied, "I remembered that there was a flaw in him, somewhere. I didn't know what it was. I am only now beginning to understand what that flaw is. Mr. Prescott feels; he does not think."

"Yet, you have just said that he is a great man. I don't understand you."

Eugene regarded her with cold impatience. "Mother, you aren't as dull as you sometimes pretend to be. Men of feeling are usually very potent, if occasionally disastrous. Let me put it this way: William Prescott is incapable of abstract thinking and reasoning. Everything he does is colored or dominated by what he feels at the moment of doing. He is completely capricious. He is the real refutation of the stupid idea that man is a reasonable animal."

Alice was silent. She was thinking of the money William had sent her. A "reasonable" man would not have done this. Only a man of feeling was capable of so impulsive and spontaneous a gesture. Alice felt a deep, sad stir of pity for William.

Eugene inclined his head slightly. "You see, you do understand. And you are sorry for Mr. Prescott."

Alice flushed. "Eugene, you are so cold-blooded. And you are so young. You speak as if you despised Mr. Prescott——"

Eugene lifted his hand. "Mother, I did not say that," he interrupted, annoyed. "I'll even say that men of feeling ought not to be despised, but admired. The more intense their capacity to feel, the more intelligent they are. But intelligence should not be confused with reason, which is a different thing entirely."

Suddenly, Eugene laughed. "He hates pain. I found that out today. He hates the kind of people from which he came, but even more, he hates to have them suffer. You think this is a paradox?"

"I did not say so, Eugene." Alice's voice was cold.

"Good," said Eugene. "I didn't really think you thought that. You see, Mr. Prescott has a long memory. He remembers what he suffered, himself, and he hates hunger and poverty and homelessness. Who was it who said that altruism is the supreme cowardice?"

"You, possibly," answered Alice.

"Perhaps," he admitted. "At any rate, it is a sound epigram."

"I don't suppose it has ever occurred to you," said Alice, "that Mr. Prescott might be a good man, for all that he has done, and is doing?"

"You mean, the diamond in the rough, the heart of gold under the brutal exterior?" asked Eugene, with gentle derision. "Mother, that is sentimental. There are no good men. There are only men who are afraid. For themselves."

Alice considered this. She said: "Eugene, there is a flaw in your reasoning. It is a perilous flaw. What you say strikes at everything that is noble in humanity, everything the philosophers and the priests have taught us, everything that is decent and self-sacrificing and heroic. You don't think men are ever heroic, do you?"

"Certainly not," replied Eugene.

Alice stood up, abruptly. Her son rose also. Alice turned to him, and her light eyes flashed. "You do not consider yourself egotistic, I suppose, Eugene."

He seemed surprised. "Indeed I do not. Do you think so, Mother?" -

She opened her pale lips to affirm this with a kind of vehemence unusual with her. Then she did not speak at all. Finally, after several long moments, she said in a drained voice: "No, Gene. You are not egotistic. I only wish you were."

She turned away. "Dinner is ready," she said. She went to the door. She said: "It is useless to try to persuade you not to go back to that place?"

"Quite useless." Again, he seemed surprised. "I have a living to make, Mother. And I am not interested in law, or in anything but the lumber business."

"Oh, Eugene," she sighed, and left the room.

She returned to her kitchen and looked about her listlessly. Fatigue was heavy upon her, a fatigue of the heart and of the spirit. She leaned against a table, and so terrible was her despondency that for a few seconds she believed she was dying. And then she knew that she was terrified, and that all her life had been a useless thing, and that there was never a reason, not ever, for living.

PART THREE

"There are many loving parents in the world, but no loving children."

CHINESE PROVERB

CHAPTER XXIX

MRS. EZRA BASSETT alighted from the carriage at the door of the Prescott house, and paused, as usual, to give it a furtive but approving glance. Ursula, and a few others of taste, might detest the house, but many, like Jemima Bassett, thought that a home ought to be as magnificent as possible. A house of restraint and of small proportions inspired in her the suspicion that the owner could probably afford no better.

The grounds were really splendid. The trees had gained enormously in height and girth, and the formal flower-beds and grounds, this delightful July day, testified to the skill and lavish tendencies of the Prescott gardeners. Ivy now covered two-thirds of the great swart house, throwing its tendrils about the tall high windows, draping the turrets and false towers and bays in a rippling robe of green. Some of the casements stood open to the warm and flowing breeze, and the glass shone and sparkled in the brilliant light. Stone walls and trees hid most of the neighboring houses, except for a distant chimney here and there, a glimpse of part of a brick or stone wall, the glitter of a far window. This section, once so desolate and despised, was now so exclusive that Schiller Road was banally called "Millionaires' Row." The mountains behind it, today luminous in violet light, were no longer clothed with virgin wood, and primeval. Studded with great houses, like those below on Schiller Road, they boasted private parks, winding roadways, and enormous estates. Toylike though they appeared from the Prescott house, one could realize the stately magnitude of their proportions. But none, either on Schiller Road, or on the mountainsides, could approach the Prescott house for grandeur, or, in Ursula's opinion, awesome and majestic ugliness.

The day was hot and intensely still. The trees stood, pillars of shining green, held in afternoon sleep. The grounds had recently been watered; Mrs. Bassett was charmed by the scents of earth and grass and flowers. A robin or two pranced on the lawns, seeking worms, or fluttered over bird-baths. Nothing else moved. From a far distance came the muted and sleepy clamor of electric street-cars. Then, as this was late July, almost

August, locusts suddenly broke into the silence with a long and singing cry of life.

The children were, apparently, spending the hotter hours of the day indoors, for Mrs. Bassett heard no shouts or calls or laughter. As she lifted the knocker on the door, a faint cloud appeared on Mrs. Bassett's face. Children were children; she did not dislike them in the least. After all, she had two dear girls of her own, and the elder, now Mrs. Jenkins, had presented her mother with a grandson some six years ago. No, indeed, Mrs. Bassett really "loved" children, and "understood" them thoroughly, as she was fond of saying. But children could be very trying. The Prescott children could be more than trying.

John Shaeffer was no longer coachman to the Prescotts. He had been elevated to the position of butler. Grave, dignified and stern as ever, he led Mrs. Bassett into the house. She paused for a moment before a mirror in the hall to adjust her new wide hat, heavily weighted with pink velvet flowers and plumes, which gave her plump short figure a broad and squat appearance. But it was an elegant hat, and she admired it. She wore also her best summer suit, of dark-blue broadcloth, the skirt deeply folded, the bottom of the jacket flaring above it. Ruffles of lace appeared to hold up one of her two pink chins. She was a rosy matron, prosperous and respected, uncontested as the city's arbitress of manners, deportment, proper behavior and modes. She was also still the only reliable source of gossip and discreet scandal.

Satisfied that every gray-blonde wave and curl was in place, and that nothing was disheveled in either her manner or appearance, Mrs. Bassett allowed herself to be conducted into the immense marble-walled parlor where her hostess awaited her. Mrs. Bassett, surprisingly enough, admired the florid ruby and green room, the gilt tables and obviously expensive draperies.

One swift glance told her, happily, that the deplorable Prescott children were not present. The rich room was very quiet. Ursula, sitting and embroidering near a large arched window, rose to greet her guest. Before even a word passed between the two ladies, Mrs. Bassett had inspected, and approved, Ursula's green silk skirt and delicately embroidered white lawn shirtwaist with the high neck of lace, stiffly held upright by whalebone and fastened in the front by a small "sunburst" diamond brooch. Then a ripple of disapproval passed over Mrs. Bassett's eyes. Ursula was not wearing the jacket of her suit. Certainly, the day was hot, but formalities ought to be observed in the presence of even one visitor.

"Dear Jemima," said Ursula, coming forward and extending her hand. "How are you today?"

Mrs. Bassett's words were colored by her thoughts. "Dear Ursula," she murmured formally. She removed her glove; she took Ursula's hand; the two ladies kissed. Mrs. Bassett allowed herself to be conducted to a chair near her hostess. The tea things were already arranged. The summer wind, soft as satin, blew in through the opened window. Slightly beyond, massed trees to some degree mitigated the heat. A long ripple of white ran over them as the wind passed. The room was full of light, too much light. It will fade all this lovely color, thought Mrs. Bassett. Ursula sat down and smiled upon her guest. Mrs. Bassett studied her acutely, but in such a proper manner that her glance appeared only casual. Ursula was really beginning to show her age, commented Mrs. Bassett to herself, pleasantly. Of course, she had been an old maid when she had married, over ten years ago. She was nearly forty now. Certainly, after four children, she had kept her figure in the most amazing way. It was not the slenderness of youth, however. Rather, so ran Mrs. Bassett's thoughts, it was the thinness of a woman who was chronically tired. And, no wonder, indeed, with such children!

During these reflections by Mrs. Bassett, the two ladies had been maintaining an agreeable flow of conversation concerning members of their families, their mutual friends, and the weather. They sipped hot tea in the vast hot room, ate daintily of the fine little wafers. Ursula would have preferred cold lemonade and an ice, but she knew that, despite the seasons, Mrs. Bassett clung grimly to the ritual of afternoon tea. If one succumbed more and more to casual innovations, then civilized deportment would soon be a thing of the past and barbarism would rush in upon one.

The windy sun invaded the room in shafts of blowing light; the trees tilted gently from side to side; the clock in the hall struck a decorous five. Ursula swallowed a yawn, smiled brightly, and asked an amiable question quite automatically. She thought, with longing, of the wooden swing under the trees in the garden, and the quite "impossible" novel by Marie Corelli. But she controlled her thoughts. After all, Jemima visited her for tea only once a month, as she did all her other friends. Some called it her "excursions in news-gathering." It might well be so, Ursula thought. And why should I deny her this pleasure? Heaven knows, she garners no news from me.

Ursula was quite mistaken in this. Mrs. Bassett, of the keen eye and the quick, seeking mind, never left the Prescott house without new enormities to report, mostly about the children. She liked her tea in peace. Later, she welcomed the children, though not for the reasons normally expected.

Yes, Ursula was very thin. Her figure was good, yes. But then, there was a cascade of lawn and lace ruffles down what Mrs. Bassett circumspectly called Ursula's "front." Her color had always been very slight, but in her youth it had had a certain luminousness. Now she was wan. Her russet hair was still thick, and had kept its color, though still unfrizzed, and without the new pompadour now rapidly coming into fashion. All color had faded from her lips, which were slightly puckered, the corners somewhat tight in spite of her smiles.

Mrs. Bassett put her cup aside sedately on the table beside her, refused more tea. She said: "Ezra tells me that William is quite taken with that young person, Eugene Arnold. How remarkable that he should have—have been able so to win dear William's confidence! Chief clerk! How charitable of William, and how very fortunate for young Mr. Arnold!"

Ursula winced at the old-fashioned phraseology of her friend. She said, with more pointedness in her voice than was customary: "Ezra—is quite right. Ezra was speaking of it only last week, when he came to have luncheon with William." She paused. Her irritation subsided agreeably when she saw Mrs. Bassett's eyebrows quirk.

Ursula went on: "And Eugene isn't so very young anymore. How time passes! Weren't you his godmother, Jemima? I seem to remember you were."

Mrs. Bassett had turned a red to match the reddest sofa in the drawing-room. She said, stiffly: "Under the circumstances, dear Ursula, I felt relieved of my duties as godmother."

Ursula smiled. She, too, put aside her cup. "Well, at any rate, you'll be happy to know that William considers Eugene to be invaluable. He gives him a very large salary, and trusts him implicitly. Eugene is a very brilliant young man, and William has high hopes for him."

"How very kind of William!" cried Mrs. Bassett, pressing the palms of her plump hands together. Her round face was still red.

"William is hardly 'kind' in the way you imply, Jemima," said Ursula, consideringly. "Gene deserves William's approval, you can be sure."

"I trust so, indeed I do," replied Mrs. Bassett. "After all, one must remember the——the father, my dear."

Only the heat could have made Ursula's vexation break through her usual poise. "Remember Chauncey? Why should one remember him? And, anyway, Jemima, Chauncey did not exactly rob a bank or murder anyone, or embezzle funds. His only crime was overconfidence in himself, and if that is indeed a crime then most of us are guilty of it."

She paused. Mrs. Bassett stared at her, slowly blinking her eyes. She was truly shocked. Why, the man had failed, he had become a bankrupt, he had lost his house and his properties, he had lost his money! It was outrageous of Ursula to pretend that this was nothing.

"Of course, I know you are not serious, Ursula," she said, gravely.

"Of course I am serious." Ursula's tired body crawled with irritation. "But it does not matter. Chauncey has been dead a long time. Eugene is alive. There is nothing of his father about him."

"One should be grateful for that," remarked Mrs. Bassett with significance. Ursula's brows drew down. She did not reply. It was ridiculous that she should be defending Eugene Arnold, whom she disliked even more than before, though she received him politely whenever William brought him home to dinner, as a prelude to continued work in the library.

She said finally, looking at Mrs. Bassett with directness: "Eugene is very like his mother. You remember Alice, Jemima? She comes of one of the finest old families in Andersburg. My father used to say: 'How Alice can endure the fat fools of Andersburg is beyond my understanding.' But then, Papa had a high respect for race and tradition. One of his grandfathers had taught at Heidelberg. Literature, I believe. Papa was very proud of him."

Mrs. Bassett smiled with innocent sweetness. "Really, dear? How very exciting. But weren't your mother's parents nice, good, sturdy farm-folk, and didn't your papa's father once own a butcher shop?"

Touché, thought Ursula. She could not help laughing, and now her anger was gone. She said: "That is quite right. But, as I said, one of my great-grandfathers taught literature at Heidelberg. I should have said that Papa and I were both proud of it, farm-folk and butcher shop nonetheless."

Mrs. Bassett felt that she had scored. "This is a new country, my dear, and one ought not to be too intolerant," she said, with a pious air. "One cannot always pick one's ancestors, though one can always do one's best in one's personal life."

Ursula did not answer. She fanned herself with a palm-leaf fan. The clock struck half-past five. In a few moments, please God, Jemima would be gone.

Mrs. Bassett heard the clock strike, also. Where were those intolerable children? The house was very quiet. Perhaps they had gone for a drive. Mrs. Bassett was disappointed. Her eyes wandered about, vaguely. Then she noticed that something was missing. Between two great high arched windows there had once stood a tall and slender column of marble on which a small and exquisite Psyche had been poised in an attitude of imminent flight. William and Ursula had purchased it in Italy, only three years ago, when they had gone abroad for Ursula's health. It was a treasure; it had cost a fortune. Even Mrs. Bassett, who could not look at its nakedness without blushing, knew that it was priceless.

"Dear me," she said. "Have you taken the Psyche away, Ursula? Of course, it was lovely, but so very, very—frank, if I may say so without offending you. And children in the house, too——"

Ursula looked quickly at the vacant spot, and a desolate expression tightened her mouth. The statue, itself, had been only eighteen inches high, but had been chiselled so beautifully, and with so much detail, even to the tiny marble veins on the marvelous little hands, that it caught the eye and entranced it. Though it was there no longer, Ursula could see the flowing and delicate glory of the small white body, nude and airy, the carved, outspread wings that almost seemed to flutter, the flow of lifted hair, the eager and radiant smile on the translucent face, the outspread, welcoming arms. When she had first seen it, she had been moved to tears, for she knew that innocence had been caught here in all its shining grandeur.

"There was an accident—the other day," she said, and her voice was muffled as if with grief.

"An accident? How unfortunate, dear Ursula! It was so delightful." Mrs. Bassett paused. "A stupid servant, of course," she suggested, sympathetically.

"No, it was me!" said a loud boastful voice almost at her elbow. "And it was a silly old thing, and I don't care, either. Matt was painting it, and he's a silly old thing, too, and I pushed him, and he fell into it, and there it was, all smashed to smithereens!"

The voice broke into a roar of laughter. Mrs. Bassett turned sharply, to see at her side the most intolerable of the Prescott children: Thomas.

CHAPTER XXX

URSULA JUMPED quickly to her feet, flushed, and grim of lip. But her voice was controlled when she said to her son: "Tommy, I did not give you permission to come in here today, when I have a guest. Go back to your rooms immediately, and stay there until dinner."

The boy spread his legs far apart, put his big square hands akimbo, and glared derisively at his mother. His narrow brown eyes squinted at Ursula, radiated hatred. "Pa said we can come down here any time we want to. He said, and you know he said it, that the whole house belongs to us, and that he built it for us, not for you or him. It's mine. It's ours. We can do what we want to, any time and you can't stop us. You and your old silly statue!"

Mrs. Bassett gasped with happy enjoyment, though she was careful to put a horrified expression on her features. She disliked, and with excellent reason, all the Prescott children, but she disliked Thomas the most. She always referred to him to her husband as "that loutish boy." Certainly, the adjective was not too unjust. Thomas was very tall now, much taller than other boys of nine. The massive thickness of his rough brown hair made him look even larger than he was. Moreover, because he was broad and muscular and active, he gave the appearance of a maturity beyond his years. Mrs. Bassett considered him very ugly. His features, though so blunt and broad, that thick and heavy mouth, were not in themselves ugly. It was their brutality, their arrogance, and his physical lack of grace, which made Thomas appear unattractive, even to those who did not dislike children. His ruddy cheeks, coarse and sown with freckles, testified to a natural boyish health.

He looked at his mother now, and laughed with crude insolence. He repeated goadingly: "Silly old statue. Anyway, I can stay if I want to." He looked at Mrs. Bassett with an evil glint in his eye. "That's an awful hat. Why do you wear such awful hats? That's a girl's hat, not an old lady's."

"Let them be honest and without hypocrisy," William had said. "Let them express their real convictions, without fear."

Ursula said in a quiet and level tone: "Thomas, apologize immediately to Mrs. Bassett." She stood near the boy. Her first flush had faded; she was very pale. He stared back at her, mockingly. Then, as she did not look aside, as she fixed him with her eyes, as she betrayed no shock and no uncertainty, he glanced away, thrust out his lower lip sullenly.

"You wouldn't dare tell me to do that if Pa was here," he said, in his loud, grating voice. "But Pa's in Michigan, and you think you can do what you want. I'll tell him when he gets back."

"Thomas," repeated Ursula, "we are waiting for your apology."

He lifted his great heavy boot and kicked viciously at the leg of a table. He looked at Mrs. Bassett with deep enmity. "All right, then, I apologize. But it don't mean nothing."

"It means that you were a boor and a young fool, without manners or decency," said Ursula. She turned to Mrs. Bassett. "I apologize for my son," she said. Her voice broke a little with her deep shame and wretchedness. "He knows no better. He is very young."

Mrs. Bassett's enjoyment had been considerably reduced by Thomas' reference to her hat and by his designation of her as an "old lady." Her cheeks were hot. She did not reply graciously to the boy's apology. She said to Ursula, with stateliness: "Yes, Ursula, I realize he knows no better."

"I do too!" cried Thomas, infuriated. "Only Pa says we can tell the truth any time we want to!"

Ursula gazed at him with intense bitterness. She knew Thomas for the liar he was. She said: "Go back to your playrooms, Tommy, with the others."

"I won't!" he cried. He clenched his fists, lowered at his mother. "This is our house. We can do what we want to here, and you can't stop us." Now his attention was taken by the salver of little cakes. He reached out a big meaty hand, seized several of the cakes, crammed them into his mouth. Over them, he regarded his mother with hating triumph. He crunched loudly.

No one heard a light step approaching, but Ursula, feeling a slight familiar movement in the air, saw that Oliver had entered. Her tense face softened. She put her hand on the shoulder of the very tall twelve-year-old boy who had reached her side. "Oliver, my dear," she murmured.

Oliver bowed to Mrs. Bassett. She inclined her head very slightly. The Prescott children were Prescotts, after all, no matter how odious. But this was a boy of ambiguous ancestry, an orphan, a nobody, lifted from a doorstep. Oliver turned to Ursula. He smiled gently. "I didn't know that Tommy had left upstairs," he said, with apology. "I was helping Matt with something." He said to Thomas, quietly: "Come on, Tommy. We're starting to build a bridge, and we need your help."

Thomas crunched unconcernedly, as if he had not heard. He helped himself to more cakes.

"Go with your brother, Tommy," said Ursula.

Thomas crunched with deliberate slowness. He said: "He isn't my brother. He's only an orphan. I don't have to mind him. He ought to be glad we let him live here."

Ursula's self-control was always commended in Andersburg. Now, reckless of Mrs. Bassett, and stung to the heart by her son's brutishness, she lifted her hand and boxed Thomas' ears soundly. "You dreadful boy!" she exclaimed, and struck him again.

"Please, Mama," begged Oliver.

His words were drowned by Thomas' sudden howl of rage and pain. He clenched his fists and rushed at his mother. Oliver held out a hand, caught him by the shoulder, and held him. "Tommy," he said.

The boy struggled to release himself. He was so big and so heavy that it seemed a simple thing for him to twist away from Oliver, who was so slender and without obvious muscle. But, miraculously, he could not free himself. He swung his fists impotently, his head lowered like that of a charging bull.

Really! thought Mrs. Bassett. How can Ursula allow that boy to treat her son like that, as if he had the right! Why, he's no better than a servant, and ought to know his place. She sniffed, turned about in her chair in order to see better.

"Tommy," repeated Oliver, while Thomas stopped his howling long enough to draw a more vigorous breath.

"I'll tell my pa," sobbed Thomas. "He isn't your pa. He'll do something to you, you see!"

Oliver removed his hand. He did not appear disturbed. He put his arm about Ursula's waist; he could feel her trembling. His arm tightened. "Tommy doesn't mean it," he said, consolingly.

Mrs. Bassett gazed at him with disfavor. She studied the young unruffled face with its dark clear skin, the shining dark eyes, the smooth black hair and kind mouth. Though Mrs. Bassett's expression was all disapproval, she was happy. The day had not been wasted after all.

There was a loud and thunderous clatter on the marble

stairs in the hall, and the rest of the Prescott children burst into the room in a very riot of noise and shouting. But the voices were feminine, the running legs were feminine, also. The boy who brought up the rear was silent, and he moved more slowly than the others.

"Tommy!" shouted eight-year-old Julia. "Why, there you are, you pig! When you promised to help us build the bridge! And here you are, stuffing yourself, you horrible thing!"

"Pig!" repeated little Barbara, six years old.

"You always run away if there is any work," said Thomas' twin, Matthew, accusingly. He had a low hesitant voice, but it could be as withering as a louder one.

The girls snatched at the rest of the cakes, pushed them into their mouths. They stared at Mrs. Bassett boldly, without even the rudest of greetings. Nor did Matthew greet her. He was looking with concentration at his mother, and at Oliver, who stood by her side. His still blue eyes contracted a trifle. Mrs. Bassett thought him "well-favored," though just a little "girlish." He always seemed to efface himself, not out of shyness but with a kind of deliberate aloofness as if he disdained present company.

Matthew continued to regard his mother and Oliver inscrutably. He did not speak. After several long moments, he turned away indifferently, wandered to the spot where the lovely statue had stood. For an instant, pain wrinkled his forehead. He went to a window, looked out silently, and did not move again. The room might have been empty, for all he seemed to care. He was rapt in some withdrawal, a thing which Ursula always felt was dangerous. Ignoring both her guest and her children, even Oliver, she started towards Matthew instinctively, exclaiming: "Matthew, my dear!"

He looked over his shoulder at her, and said politely: "Yes, Mama?"

She stopped at once. "Nothing," she murmured, confusedly.

Then she put a smile on her face, went back to the little girls. Julia glared at her defiantly, put another cake into a mouth already filled almost to capacity. "Julie, your manners," said Ursula sternly.

Julia mumbled something. Barbara shrilled: "She's taking all the cakes! Pig! Pig!" The child slapped her sister's grasping hand vigorously, pushed it aside, snatched at a cake, the last one. Thomas was not sobbing now. He had planted himself at a little distance. He scowled at his sisters, his brother, Oliver, Ursula, and Mrs. Bassett, in turn.

My children! thought Ursula. My dear children!

There were times when she felt that she hated her children.
It took all her common-sense, all her courage, to tell herself
that she was unfair, that they had been molded to this horrible
shape by her husband, that what they were was his doing.

Barbara, in conduct, was little better than her brothers
and sister; her manners were as disgusting, her rudeness as
open. But there were times when Barbara's little face had a
sober and considering expression, when she looked with young
disgust at the others. Moreover, she was fond of Oliver, at
least at intervals. Her mass of waving hair, which fell to her
waist, was almost as dark as his, and she had fine gray eyes,
the color of William's but much larger, and very clear and
radiant with intelligence. Her sister, Julia, was considered the
beauty of the family, with her curling auburn hair, her amber
eyes—the color of Ursula's—caught in a tangle of russet
lashes, her full mouth as brilliant as a rose. Julia, too, was tall
for her age, had a wonderful gracefulness of movement and
gesture, and her laugh was musical and impish.

With a weak smile, Ursula said to Mrs. Bassett: "They have
such high spirits." She was quoting William. Mrs. Bassett
moved her head significantly. "It is Julie's and Barbara's governess' day off, and Lucy is still nursing a broken arm,"
went on Ursula, apologetically, praying that her guest would
go at once. "And Nancy is getting their tea, and Mrs. Templeton had gone to town on an errand. So they have got a little out
of hand, I am afraid."

Julia flounced her frilled skirts. "I'm not out of hand!"
she shouted. "And Tommy and I can have all the cakes we
want. Papa says we can always have what we want. He says
it's bad for us not to. You know he said that, Mama." She
stared at Ursula with scornful accusation.

Why did not Jemima Bassett go? Why did she sit there,
though the clock had struck six some time ago? Desperately,
Ursula willed her to leave. But Mrs. Bassett was engrossed
with the children, Matthew staring listlessly through the windows; Thomas glaring at everybody in turn, his head bent;
Julia defying her mother; and Barbara thoughtfully licking
her fingers. Mrs. Bassett ignored Oliver, standing beside Ursula.

Julia's attention was attracted to the guest. She widened
her eyes impudently at Mrs. Bassett. "I don't like Jimmie,"
she announced disdainfully, referring to Mrs. Bassett's adored
grandson. "He cries all the time. When we visited him at
Mrs. Jenkins', he just sat on his mama's knee and cried. Just
like a baby."

Mrs. Bassett colored with outrage. Ursula said sharply: "Don't be rude, Julie. You are too old for that."

Thomas forgot his sullen rage to shout: "Yah, a baby! He wets. He wet all over Mrs. Jenkins' best sofa." He burst into raucous laughter. He was joined by Julia, who screamed with mirth. Thomas added derisively: "He's too old to wet. He's as old as Barbie." He turned to his younger sister, whom he disliked heartily. "Barbie, do you wet, like Jimmie?" Again he laughed. "Barbie wets! Yah, just like Jimmie Jenkins!"

Aghast at this libel, Barbara shrieked: "I do not! I'm not a baby like that silly Jimmie Jenkins. I hate you, Tom Prescott!" She ran at her brother, her hands outstretched to grasp him. But, shouting with fresh laughter, he evaded her. He leapt over a chair; he jumped high on a sofa; he rushed into a table, upon which a priceless oxblood lamp immediately began to rock dangerously. Barbara pursued him. Julia, screaming her delight, joined the chase. The children were now swarming all over the room, the girls' skirts flying, Thomas, in his navy-blue sailor suit, leaping a few paces ahead. Matthew still stood by the window; he did not turn at the sounds of clamor. But Oliver looked at the desperate Ursula. She nodded, briefly.

Oliver went into action. He ran swiftly after Thomas, caught and held him. He smiled down at the boy, who was again infuriated. "Come on, Tommy," he said, in his quiet voice. "It's time for our supper. And then we can finish the bridge."

Thomas struggled a moment, impotently. The girls rushed up, stopped. "He swore!" cried Barbara with delight. "Mama, Tommy said a bad word to Oliver. A real bad word."

"A real bad word," echoed Julia, with pride. She tossed back her auburn curls, and threw Ursula a malicious glance. Then her pretty face changed, and she tugged at Oliver's hands, which were restraining her brother. "You leave him alone, Oliver. You leave my brother alone. He isn't your brother. He's mine." She kicked Oliver in the right knee. He looked down at her sternly.

"Stop it, Julie," he said in a peremptory voice. Amazingly, she fell back. Barbara stood and looked at him. She began to play with the ruffles of her pinafore, but her eyes did not leave Oliver, who had again directed his attention to Thomas.

"Come on, Tommy," he urged. He took the boy's arm, and half-dragged, half-led, him towards the door. Julia followed him like an angry dog, protesting. Barbara followed also, still watching Oliver. The procession left the room, Tommy crying his defiance and threatening his adopted brother, Julia still expostulating. No one saw Matthew drift out by another entrance.

Mrs. Bassett had often seen quite a good deal in this house. But today the odious Prescott children had surpassed themselves. Replete, she smiled at Ursula affectionately. "As you said, my dear, they have such high spirits."

Ursula could say nothing. She was humiliated and ashamed and full of bitterness. She accompanied her guest to the door. Mrs. Bassett's carriage had been waiting for a considerable time.

"Next Tuesday, then," said Mrs. Bassett, referring to her monthly tea. "And in the meantime, dear, do rest yourself. You seem so tired."

CHAPTER XXXI

WILLIAM LISTENED in his usual dark and obdurate silence while Ursula recited the story of the children's recent mortifying conduct in the presence of Mrs. Bassett. He sat and stared into space with that dull and earthy expression of his which she had come to hate, because it told her that he was completely resistive, completely unconvinced, and had no intention of regarding her complaints seriously. But despair drove her to a full recital.

Even when she had finished, he said nothing. A heavy summer rain was falling. It drummed against the windows of Ursula's sitting-room. The sky lowered overhead, thick and gray and heavy. A spectral and insubstantial dimness filled the room. She had always disliked this enormous house; now she was beginning to hate it with a kind of illogical passion. From her chair she could see the drowned earth, the rushing wet trees, dark green against the somber clouds, and the crushed flower-beds. The air was hot, but Ursula was cold, with mingled rage and impotence.

She had submitted too much; she had allowed him almost entire control over the children. If they were ruined, now, she was not guiltless, she told herself bitterly. She could think no longer of just herself and William. Her hope of true union must be abandoned. The terrible destruction of her children must be halted, even at the expense of her own marriage.

He moved ponderously in his chair. The pale light glinted on the white at his temples; it exaggerated the weighty sullenness of his face.

"I don't understand you, Ursula," he said, in his loud, harsh voice. "But I do understand one thing. You don't like our children."

Ursula lifted her hands, let them drop back lifelessly into her lap. "Oh, William," she said. He did not answer. She tried to make her voice resolute again: "How can you say that? It is because I love them so dearly that I am terrified for them."

Again he moved, and this time it was a quicker movement. "You admit you struck Tommy. I have asked you again and again not to do that, Ursula. Brutality never helped to control a child. They have their rights. You are always talking about being 'civilized'. Is it civilized to strike a child and make it suffer bodily? After all, a child cannot strike back."

Oh, my God, thought Ursula hopelessly. She had no words.

William went on, triumphant because of her silence. "You struck him because he reminded Oliver that we are not his parents. That is true. Is a child to be injured because he tells the truth?"

Ursula was losing control of herself. "You choose to take a distorted view of the whole thing. Tommy was not just 'telling the truth'; he was trying to wound and shame Oliver. Besides, Tommy is no sturdy advocate of truth. You have caught him in lies, yourself."

"He has a very active imagination," said William. "All children lie, and the more imagination they have the more fantasies they indulge in. It is a vicious thing to injure a child because he uses his imagination a little too much."

"Tommy," said Ursula, in a shaking voice, "has no imagination at all, except for cruelty. From the very beginning he has been crafty and mean."

"No natural and loving mother would speak so of a child of hers!" cried William, furiously.

"I am a mother, but I am not blind, William. My love for my children will never blind me to their faults. With the right sort of teaching and discipline Tommy might have learned to suppress these traits of his." She paused. "You approve of him hurting Oliver like that?"

Again William moved, and this time he was uneasy. "Nonsense," he said. "Children do things which often outrage adults. They outgrow them. Give the boy time."

Ursula said nothing. William went on, with more and more confidence: "As for what Tommy said to Jemima Bassett, that is a trivial thing. Children are honest and open; they haven't learned to be hypocrites and to conceal their feelings. If Tommy found Jemima's hat ridiculous, he was only expressing his childish dislike of it, and nothing else."

"Again, you miss the point, William. Tommy has been taught, repeatedly, that he must be polite. He was not being 'honest', in his remarks about Jemima's hat. His intention was to humiliate Jemima."

William said accusingly: "You haven't forgiven him about that statue. That is the real thing behind what you say about the poor child."

"Oh, William," said Ursula, wearily.

"You object to them 'swarming' all over the house, as you say. I've told you before, Ursula, that I built this house for my children. It is theirs, and theirs only. I want them to be free in every corner of the house. Let them romp anywhere; let them do as they wish. If they are kept, like prisoners, in certain parts of the house, they will feel restrained, unwanted, unloved. What if they do break a few things? We can replace them easily enough. Besides, they are curious. How can they learn about things otherwise?" He looked at the pale and silent Ursula, and again he moved uneasily. "I'm sorry about the statue. I—liked it, too. But it was an accident, even if Tommy did push Matt into it deliberately. He did not have any intention of destroying the statue."

"Yes," said Ursula, quietly. "He did. He destroyed it in order to hurt me, because he hates me. And he hates me because I try to discipline and civilize him."

"What damned rot!" exclaimed William. He stood up. He was really infuriated now. "You know that is untrue. And, again, I accuse you of hating Tommy. Can you deny it?"

Ursula cried: "I hate what you are making of him!" She went on: "But we are getting nowhere. I deny that the children have the right to 'roam' freely all over the house, when the notion takes them. After all, we, as parents and human beings, have rights, too. We have the right to talk tranquilly with our guests, without interruption. William, people despise our children."

She added, quickly: "If our children are hated by our friends, it is not their fault, and it breaks my heart. It is your fault, because you refuse to allow them to be trained to behave properly."

He lowered over her wrathfully. "I don't care a damn what prim fools think of our children. You talk of our 'rights'. Only children have 'rights', because they are defenseless and weak and must be protected from the abuse of adults."

Ursula looked down at her clasped hands. It was no use, no use at all.

William threw himself into his chair. "I'll go over all the children with you, since you have given me such a long recital of their 'crimes'. Julie. You accuse her of being demanding, bad-tempered, artful. She is just a gay and lively little girl. All children are more or less selfish. That is natural. She'll get over it. And if she is 'artful', as you say, well, then I can only reply that it is a female trait." He smiled, with sudden fondness. "I don't mind her cajoling me. I find it lovable."

Ursula stared at him, her lips tight and drawn. "I find it ugly. No woman can be happy who thinks only of herself, and what she can snatch from the world. When she is no longer young and pretty and 'lovable', she will be abandoned, no matter how much money you leave her."

"You talk like a fool," said William, with hard emphasis. "Give the child time. She is full of affection."

Ursula opened her mouth to speak, then closed it. Her eyes were suddenly wet with a tearing despair and anguish for her husband.

William continued: "Matt. What about Matt? Hs is a quiet and thoughtful boy. He is a genius. That is why he 'withdraws', as you say. Do you deny, after what has been told you by competent artists, that Matthew is a potential artist, too?"

Ursula brought herself out of aching lethargy to speak with vigor. "But you are killing his potentialities, William. Do you remember how, a few years ago, he could not live away from the piano? You did not let him dream on for a while, content with what he was trying to learn by himself. No, you immediately swamped him with teachers. You gave him such tremendous 'opportunities', as you called them, that he lost interest. Don't you know that artists, like young trees in a forest, grow only by struggle for existence, that they become strong by resistance, that they triumph only by conquering difficulties? The budding artist should walk part of the way by himself. But Matthew gathered the impression that he had to do nothing by himself, that he was already perfect, that he had learned all that anyone could teach him. Why, then, continue?

"And now he is beginning to draw and paint. I admit he shows more than talent. Oh, William, I wish I had kept you from knowing. But it is too late. Now he has drawing lessons from the best teacher you could import. He is praised to the very skies for his most meagre effort. He is beginning to believe that this gift, too, is already perfect, that he need learn no more. He is losing interest in this, also."

"Indeed, is that so?" said William, with enraged sarcasm. "How much you know about art, Ursula! Have you never heard of art being crushed and lost by neglect and lack of opportunity?"

"That is foolishness, William. No real art is ever lost by neglect or 'lack of opportunity'. If it is lost, and never sees the light, then it is, in itself, lifeless and weak and unworthy. But art can be destroyed by too much pampering, too much care."

William compressed his lips. He glared down at his wife. But he could not seem to find words.

Ursula hurried to speak again: "I am not going to talk too much as yet about Matthew's potentialities as an artist. He is elusive, William; he is dangerously uninterested in others, in life. That is deadly for him, both as a person and as an artist. I am afraid for him, William. He is becoming barren and bodiless."

"An artist owes nothing to anyone or to anything, except his art."

Ursula shook her head. "You are wrong, William. An artist is first a human being. He cannot even develop as an artist unless he has contact with humanity."

"You would deprive him of his whole life!" said William. "You would keep all encouragement from him. Let him dream; let him believe the world is beautiful."

"He will become—nothing," said Ursula.

"You are a wonderful optimist," returned William, with contempt. He stared at Ursula with a kind of pent-up animosity. "What are you trying to do to my children? Are you trying to beat them into a faceless conformity? Are you trying to form them on the colorless or stupid patterns of other children?"

"William, that is silly and childish!" cried Ursula.

William felt he had triumphed. He even sat down again, and smiled at Ursula unpleasantly. "You haven't said much about Barbie, I think."

"Barbie? Barbie imitates the others. She has more character in her small body than all the rest of them have together. I have great hopes for Barbie. Yet I am afraid that she, too, will become just like the others. I am going to try, William, and you may as well know it now, to save Barbie, to save all my children."

"You'll not destroy them as long as I am alive," said William, as quietly as she.

They gazed at each other in a deep and dangerous silence. They did not move, yet both had the impression that there was a tremendous pressure in the dank air.

Then Ursula said: "I am not going to say much more, William. I only want to tell you that Miss Andrews has left us. Even she, in your pay, and dogging your footsteps as she did, agreeing with you in everything pertaining to the children, could endure them no longer. She has gone. Tommy blacked her eye one day, when she tried to make him study. I had to give her two hundred dollars to soothe her feelings."

William's face changed.

"As for Mrs. Templeton, she keeps away from the children as much as possible. She is a fool, but in this I think she is being very sensible. Julie kicked her last week. Even Mrs. Templeton, though she is even more servile than Miss Andrews was, will not stand much more. Moreover, I have had to hire another maid to replace Ruth, who helps Nancy. I had to increase Nancy's salary, in order to induce her to stay. I think, too, that the gardeners are going to be difficult. They want to see you tomorrow. They don't like the children tramping over the flower-beds and destroying shrubbery with what you consider 'lively spirits'."

William looked at the windows in somber gloom. Ursula waited. She waited a long time before he spoke again. He said: "Oliver goes to Landsdowne's school. Tommy and Matt will be ready for that school this fall. I have already entered them there. Only Julie and Barbie will be left—to trouble you." He sneered suddenly. "You will have the house all to yourself, most of the day. The children are growing up. Soon, they won't bother you so much."

He stood up. Ursula rose, also. "William, you don't know, of course, that what you are trying to do is to possess the children, body and soul. You can't do that. You are always talking about their being 'free'. You have imprisoned them in their own ugly faults, and they may never escape. You don't know anything about freedom; freedom imposes obligations to the world. The man who feels he has no obligations knows nothing about liberty. William, you are driving the children from you. They do not love you."

He was so completely enraged that he looked insane. Without speaking, and as if he dared not speak, he went out of the room and closed the door behind him.

She went to the closed door, her knees shaking. She listened. William was entering the children's playrooms. They greeted him with joyful shouts. She could even hear Matthew's low voice. The children were now directing at their father a stream of insistent demands. The voices became loud and imperious. William's voice answered, soothing and full of rough endearments, full of promises.

Ursula closed the door. She went to the windows and looked down at the thrashing trees and the wet earth and the rushing wind and rain. Faintly, she could hear the children's voices. She put her hands over her ears.

There should be, she thought despairingly, something inviolable between a man and his wife, something private and unshakeable, something nothing could breach or sunder. That something was sacred. No child should be allowed to touch it with his hand or, with his voice, cause it to tremble. There was a temple which should forever be closed to the rioting footsteps of children. There was a fire upon which children should never be permitted to breathe. To ignore this was to ravage forever not only marriage but the children of that marriage.

Whatever could once have been between William and his wife, Ursula, now could never be. It had been too late, in the very beginning.

CHAPTER XXXII

URSULA SAT ALONE in the morning room, embroidering and listening to the autumn wind. She heard the dry crackle of leaves blown across the driveways. The draperies at the windows stirred; the fire threw out a spray of sparks. The house was quiet, blessedly quiet. It would be a little while before the boys returned from school. The girls were still upstairs at their lessons.

It was pleasant to be alone. Only a mother of several children could understand that, thought Ursula. Loneliness was another thing. Loneliness was in her bones and in her heart. She would have to endure it. She had endured it so long, and there was no cure for it.

She glanced up at the sky, the color of old milk-glass. The long rains of the autumn would soon be here, washing the brownness of the earth, running over the gaunt fields, roaring down the brown mountains. It was a time for sadness. Ursula resolutely plied her needle. She deliberately turned her thoughts from melancholy, remembering that the mind could hold but one thought at a time. But it was useless.

William had been gone to Oklahoma Territory for several weeks now. She had heard from him but twice, and then only brief notes. He had inquired about the children. In a postscript, he had uninterestedly inquired about her own health.

The door opened softly and, with a dismay she could not help but feel, Ursula thought: Have they been dismissed earlier? It was Oliver who stood there, looking at her smilingly, Oliver now almost a man.

"Come in, dear," said Ursula, with real happiness in her voice. She hesitated a moment. "Are Tommy and Matthew home too?"

"No, Mama. I had a talk with Mr. Landsdowne this afternoon, and he suggested that I come home earlier and talk with you, also."

Ursula put aside her embroidery. "Is something wrong, Oliver?" Her eyes, chronically uneasy, searched his face.

"No, Mama, nothing is wrong." Oliver's voice, a man's
244

voice, answered her reassuringly. "It is just that I want your advice."

Ursula put her hands in her lap and prepared to give Oliver her complete attention.

"Sit down near me, dear," she said, motioning to a chair near the window. She never tired of looking at her adopted son, who had become closer to her than her own children.

"What is the matter, Mama?" asked Oliver, growing aware of Ursula's earnest scrutiny.

"Nothing," she replied. "Nothing at all, Oliver. But you said you wanted my advice, dear."

"Yes." He paused. He had a firm voice, deep and thoughtful. "You remember the time, a year ago, when Pa suggested I go to Harvard later and then enter the lumber business?"

"Yes, I remember." Ursula thought of the scene between William and Oliver then. For the first time in years, William had appeared to become acutely aware of Oliver, but only because Oliver had obtruded himself vigorously into William's awareness.

"But I told him I preferred to study law," said Oliver.

"I remember," repeated Ursula.

To Ursula's surprise, William's first reaction had been a kind of inexplicable relief. She did not at first know the reason, and when she did know it she was filled with anger and distress. William did not want Oliver with him. Oliver, said William, not looking at the boy, had a right to choose his own future. If the lumber business did not appeal to him, then he certainly would not be forced to enter it.

"Mr. Landsdowne agrees with me that I would make a good lawyer." Oliver's smile now was comforting, when Ursula made a concerned sound.

"But your father always expected that all his boys, or I should say, you and Tommy, would go into the business with him," said Ursula. "Matthew, of course, was never even considered."

Oliver said: "But, I don't think I want to go into the business, Mama. Father has Tommy. He also has Eugene Arnold."

The name lay before them, like something visible and evil.

"Gene," said Ursula.

"He is Father's assistant, and there is no doubt that he is more than competent, and that he will continue to serve Father very well indeed," said Oliver.

"I have never liked him," said Ursula. Oliver made no comment.

"As for Tom, though he is just sixteen, he is already deeply interested in the business," said Oliver at last. "I'm not really needed. And I'm afraid I'd be no good at it. It doesn't appeal to me. I want to study law."

Ursula clasped her hands on her knees. "I wish Alice and Eugene had left Andersburg!" she said, vehemently. "I wish we had never seen him again. I ought not to have let Eugene live in my house after his mother died!"

Oliver smiled at her indulgently. "That wouldn't have sent him away from Andersburg, Mama," he said. "He could always have found another place to live. Anyway, he takes good care of your house, and has a fine housekeeper."

"I can't bear to think of him living there, now that Alice is dead." Ursula knew she was speaking childishly, but again she was afraid.

Oliver took out his watch and turned it, unopened, in his hands.

"My head aches," Ursula murmured helplessly.

Oliver stood up. "Let me get you one of your powders," he suggested sympathetically.

But she stopped him, lifting her hand. "No, dear. I think it is more than my head that aches." She tried to smile. She sighed. "Well, Oliver, if you wish to study law, I shan't object."

Oliver tried to cheer her. He said, with humor: "Father employs very good lawyers, I know. Mr. Jenkins, and his partner. Just the same, it won't do any harm to have a lawyer in the family."

Ursula joined in his laughter, but without heart.

"It might be a very excellent idea," she said.

"And then, when Julie and Barbie marry, their husbands might also want to enter the business," said Oliver. "So Father will have enough of the family around him."

"Why, Julie isn't quite fifteen yet," said Ursula. "They won't be marrying for years. Dear me, how time flies," she added, banally, for her thoughts were very distressing. "Barbie is just thirteen. It will be years before they marry," she repeated.

"Not too many years. Julie is such a belle. She'll marry young, perhaps in two or three years. And Barbie." Oliver paused. He turned the watch over and over in his hands, looking down at it.

"Oh, Barbie," said Ursula, with impatience. "I hardly know Barbie any more. I had such hopes for her. She seemed, when she was younger, to have such common-sense. Now she is almost like Julie. I expected too much of her, I suppose."

"Barbie hasn't really changed much," said Oliver, very

quickly. "She is just imitating Julie now. I suppose girls always try to imitate their elder sisters. And Julie is a beauty; it is natural that Barbie should want to be like her. She'll get over it when she's older."

Ursula's eyes had darkened. "No," she said, in a dull voice. "I have lost all hope for Barbie. Her character has changed. Perhaps I was wrong from the very beginning——"

"No, Mama, you weren't," said Oliver. He seemed troubled. "Barbie is really a wonderful girl."

"Thank you, dear Oliver," said Ursula, mechanically. She knew he was trying to comfort her. She sighed; her drawn face became a little more weary. Her tawny eyes, by comparison, had gained in a kind of feverish brilliance so that they dominated all her other features. At forty-five, though there were long ribbons of white in her russet hair, she was still firmly slender and lithe.

After a short period of sad reflection, Ursula looked up swiftly at Oliver. "Oh, Oliver, how I shall miss you! You'll be away from home—it has just occurred to me. How am I going to get along without you, my dear?"

"I'll be home for all the holidays," he said. "And I'll write regularly."

"But," Ursula began. Then she stopped. There were light running footsteps in the hall outside the morning room. Two young girls appeared precipitately on the threshold. Julia in the bright flush of her girlhood, dimpled and vivid, her auburn hair tied back from her lovely face with a blue ribbon to match her light-blue wool frock, and Barbara, sensitive and quick and dark, her large gray eyes expressive and shining. Her red hair-ribbon was somewhat awry, and the white pinafore over her dark brown frock was stained with ink, as were her fingers.

Julia said at once, in her sweet hard voice: "Mama, Barbie is so stupid! Miss Vincent insists her French accent is wrong, but Barbie has become so arrogant because of that summer in Paris, where she says she learned to speak French properly." She had given Oliver only the briefest of glances, though he had risen at the entrance of his step-sisters. Now she turned imperatively to Barbara. "Now, just say in French: 'The gallery is filled with beautiful pictures,' and let Mama decide, you pert thing!"

Barbara was smiling quickly at Oliver. With a bored expression, she translated the sentence into exquisite French. "There!" cried Julia, in triumph, "you see! Her accent, her phrasing, are atrocious!"

"On the contrary," said Ursula, a little sharply, "it is perfect. I really must speak to Miss Vincent, if she insists that Barbie's French is not correct. I have always suspected that her own was provincial." She added: "Julie, Barbie, your manners."

Julie's beautiful amber eyes darkened. She looked at Oliver again: "Oh, hello," she muttered with disdain. Barbara said: "What are you doing home so early, Oliver?" Her young face, much more mature than her sister's, was touched with a momentary gentleness.

"I wanted to talk something over with Mama," he answered. Julia's full red mouth tightened, but she turned from Oliver as one turns from an upstart servant. "Mama," she said, "Miss Vincent is a teacher. You aren't. Surely Miss Vincent ought to know how French should be pronounced, and not you."

Ursula could never become accustomed to the rudeness of her daughters. She tried to control her voice: "I have visited France very often, Julie. Also, I had excellent teachers when I was a girl, such as your grandfather, who spoke French perfectly. Miss Vincent acquired her French in Andersburg, though she taught it in Philadelphia for six months."

Julia was mortified and resentful. "Well, we were in France, too, and Barbie's French doesn't sound right to me. Miss Vincent's does."

"Then I can't congratulate you on your ear," replied Ursula.

Oliver moved swiftly into the path of the approaching quarrel. "Julie, Miss Vincent has a voice without too much pitch, and so, I think, she finds French a little difficult."

"That's what I'm always telling her," said Barbara, smugly. She flipped her apron in mockery at her sister.

"Do you mean you are that rude to Miss Vincent?" asked Ursula.

Barbara laughed. "She is too silly to suspect rudeness, Mama. Besides, Papa always tells us we must tell the truth." Mockery was little pin-points of light in her eyes. She added: "I think Papa's wrong. You can do a lot of harm, always telling the truth."

Ursula was silent. "Stop flipping that dirty apron at me, you saucy thing!" cried Julia, with anger.

" 'No ink on the fingers, no words in the brain'," quoted Barbara, maddeningly. "Oh, go upstairs again, Julie, and console Miss Vincent for being wrong. You are her pet, you know. Maybe because neither of you knows how to speak French."

"Barbie," said Ursula. Julia, goaded, snatched at the long dark cataract of her sister's hair, but Babara, shrieking with laughter, swung out of the way. She danced back a step or two. "Oh, go upstairs!" she repeated. "Pat silly old Vincent's thick shoulder, and then sit down and moon a while about Eugene Arnold. That's all you're good for."

"Barbie!" cried Ursula. "How dare you say such a thing to Julie!" Her expression was shocked. Eugene Arnold! Was she never to be rid of him, never to hear the last of that name? She went on, her voice quick and trembling: "Julie is your sister, Barbie. She is only a little girl. How can you speak so to her, and especially in connection with Eugene Arnold, a man in his thirties!"

The very thought horrified her. She stood up, looking from one of her daughters to the other, and so appalled was her manner, so angry her face, that both girls were frightened. Julia, however, had turned a dark red.

"What do you mean, Barbie?" exclaimed Ursula. In her agitation, she caught Barbara by the shoulder. Barbara, with the deftness of long practice, wrenched herself away. She ran towards the door, stopped on the threshold, defiantly. "I was just teasing Julie," she said. "But she does moon about him, every time he comes here, though he just ignores her."

Oliver said in a low tone to Ursula, standing at her side: "Mama, young girls are just romantic. It doesn't mean anything."

For once, Ursula disregarded him. "I should think he would 'ignore' a chit her age! Really, Barbie. How vulgar you are. I think you, too, ought to go upstairs. And don't ever let your father hear such remarks from you."

"She's always saying ugly things," agreed Julia. She had recovered herself, and now she gave her sister a malicious glance. "Little children ought to be excused, I suppose. They don't know any better." She waved her hand airily and gracefully at Barbara. "Back to the nursery, pet," she added.

Barbara seemed to be thinking; she overlooked her sister's flippant gesture. Her eyes had narrowed. She looked slowly from Julia to Ursula. "Gene Arnold," she added, quietly, "is a rascal. Mama, I was wrong. He doesn't ignore her. He—he looks at her, even when he pretends not to, even if she is only fifteen. And she smirks at him, when she sees that."

"Barbie!" cried Ursula.

Julia laughed. "She is just making up things, because she is ugly and jealous." She tossed the bright heavy weight of her auburn hair. "Gene's an old man, and he doesn't think about anything but Papa's business——"

"And what to do about it," interrupted Barbara, still quietly.

Julia went on, as if her sister had not spoken, "He's an old man," she repeated. "I'm almost young enough to be his daughter." Her voice was loud, but quicker now. She regarded her mother with hard concentration. "I never heard anything so ridiculous. Gene just lives to help Papa. He hasn't another thought in his head."

"He has plenty of thoughts," said Barbara. She came back a step or two into the room.

She waited. Ursula sat down slowly and heavily, her fingers clenched together, her head bent. Barbara took another step towards her mother. Her voice was level and mature. "Mama, why does he come here? Oh, I know he works in the library with Papa some nights. But he comes here for another reason, too." She waited. No one spoke. "Gene is really bad, Mama. I wish he wouldn't come here anymore."

Ursula lifted her head. Before she could stop herself she had said bitterly: "I wish so, too."

Julia had been standing still the last few moments. "How can you talk so about Gene, either of you?" It was a woman's voice now, cold and contemptuous. "He is Papa's assistant. He does everything for Papa. Papa couldn't get along without Gene, and he trusts him, as he ought to."

It was that voice that aroused Ursula. She looked at her older daughter with a terror so great that she could hardly breathe. And Julia looked back at her, no longer childishly defiant, but impervious and flashing as a polished stone. "I like Gene," she said, as if in warning.

Holding her beautiful head very high, she went out of the room, passing her sister as if she did not see her.

Ursula could not speak. Oliver stood at her side. He exchanged a look with Barbara, and, as if he had commanded, the young girl approached her mother. "Mama," she said. "I'm sorry. I'm very sorry. Please don't be disturbed, about Julie or anything. I was wrong. Please forgive me."

It was seldom that Barbara was contrite and earnest. Had the occasion been less ominous, Ursula would have responded with affection and gratitude. Now she sat in her chair, motionless, staring before her. She was remembering Julia's voice.

She said, her own voice breaking: "Please, Barbie. Please go upstairs again."

Barbara went, silently, twisting her pinafore between her hands, moved but resolute.

Oliver put his hand on Ursula's shoulder. "Mama, remember

they are just little girls, both of them. They are always quarreling. You mustn't listen to them. They mean nothing."

Ursula lifted her own hand, removed Oliver's. She had never done this before, but it was as if she was distracted. "Oliver," she said, "I think I'd like to be alone, please."

CHAPTER XXXIII

IF URSULA HAD any influence upon her children at all, it was during William's absences. She lost this meagre influence just before his return, during the four or five days after he left, and, of course, during the time he was at home.

She had to admit that Thomas had improved to some extent. His years at Mr. Landsdowne's school had tamed him in a certain way. Mr. Landsdowne had inherited, some six years ago, from an old uncle he had long forgotten, a considerable sum, and this, combined with his intellectual independence and a certain integrity, had enabled him to be openly honest in his dealings with his students. Now, economically secure, he could exercise a probity which he had to suppress, bitterly, in the past. There is nothing like an inheritance, a good, sound, plump inheritance, to make men honor you, seek your company and buy your wares, whether intellectual or material, with gusto and gratitude, said Mr. Landsdowne, with a cynicism born of long-dealing with the human race.

He had not immediately accepted Thomas and Matthew Prescott. In fact, he had, in his mind, immediately rejected them, had sat down to write William of his rejection. But one of his friends, Dr. Banks, had good naturedly urged him to accept the boys. "After all," said Dr. Banks, "the rascals will inherit the business, and I am concerned with the business, too."

The reputation of William Prescott's sons had preceded them into the school. It was known that Thomas was "impossible," that Matthew was silent and mysterious and disinclined to study. Mr. Landsdowne contemplated Thomas' reputation even before the boy's arrival. It would give him pleasure, he thought, to "put the young scoundrel through his paces." Mr. Landsdowne believed firmly in the rod, judiciously applied. Mr. Landsdowne had a personal interview with William, and candidly expressed his views about the rod. "If this is distasteful to you, sir," he had said, coolly, "pray do not consider sending your sons here. I have my ways, and I shall not abdicate them for anyone."

Not to have gone to this school, not to have been admitted,

was a serious social detriment to young boys, and William knew this. He glared formidably at the schoolmaster. But Mr. Landsdowne had remained imperturbable, conscious of the inheritance.

"My sons are well-mannered, though Thomas is at times high-spirited. As for Matthew, it has never been necessary to punish him. I leave it all to your own good judgment."

Thomas was no fool. There was a sly intelligence behind those narrowed brown eyes. He knew immediately that complaints about Mr. Landsdowne would not be much heeded by his father, that they might even antagonize him. This did not prevent him, at first, from attempting to bully his classmates, from lying about them, from intimidating them or seeking to cause them trouble. A few excellent strokes of Mr. Landsdowne's switch eliminated manifestations like these, however, almost immediately.

It was enough for Mr. Landsdowne that Thomas caused him little trouble. He knew boys like Thomas. It was useless to attempt to teach them anything but what was in their textbooks. Being a philosopher, Mr. Landsdowne even became proud of Thomas' marks in mathematics, history and biology. People like him, he thought, have their place. We cannot all be educated.

Matthew was another matter entirely. Matthew's teachers might have hopes for him, but Mr. Landsdowne had none, and this saddened him for several reasons. Here was a potentially great mind, a mind capable of splendor. But whenever he attempted to stimulate him, he encountered a strange lassitude, a kind of quiet and indifferent arrogance and withdrawal. He eluded his teachers, became passive, cold, silent. There was no "drawing out" of Matthew. What lay in him could not be reached. It could not be expressed, because Matthew had no desire to express it. Therein lay the tragedy.

Before dinner, this evening, while the autumn light still lay in a quiet flood of lavender over the hills and the valley, Ursula went up to Matthew's room. Matthew no longer occupied a room with his twin; several years ago he had insisted, without emotion however, upon being alone. After the age of eight, he had never asked for anything but this: that he have a room to himself. Ursula had been pleased at this one pallid symptom of self-assertion; William had not been pleased at all. He had wanted the twins to be "close," to develop a brotherly comradeship.

Matthew's room was stark and austere, completely uncluttered, and somberly tidy. It was a big chamber, facing north. Along one wall stood a huge bookcase, filled with books personally selected by him. Those fatuously alleged by William to be "natural for boys, and bound to be of interest to them," had mysteriously disappeared. Matthew had one small petulance: he disliked anyone touching his books, he even disliked to have their titles read by a scanning eye. Ursula knew, however, what the books were. Few were fiction. There were the plays of Shakespeare, of Molière and Sheridan, and of many others. There were books on music, biographies of the great composers. The histories of the world's gigantic artists in paint and stone were there also. And, oddly, the more cynical books of Racine and Voltaire stood cheek-by-jowl with volumes of the world's noblest poetry. There was a magnificent Bible, too; Ursula had examined it curiously during Matthew's absence at school. Ursula had the uncomfortable conviction that piety had not induced the reading of the Bible, just as she was convinced that Matthew had not been inspired by the artists of the past to do anything creative himself.

Ursula found Matthew standing before an easel on which was propped a rather large canvas. Sometimes he painted, though it was with a distant lassitude which could not give his mother cause for hope. It was as if he painted because he had, at the moment, nothing better to do. Yet, his teachers, gone now these past three years, had seriously told Ursula that her son was "touched with genius, if he could only try." Some impelling force was absent in him.

Matthew glanced up briefly when his mother entered. He replied to her greeting. When he had been younger, she had put what is called "enthusiasm" into her voice, in an effort to arouse him. Now she no longer insulted either herself or her son with any foolish ardor; she had a respect for Matthew if not too deep a love.

Ursula walked over to the easel, and stood looking at the painting, which shone starkly in the last of the north light. Her sixteen-year-old son was taller than herself, his yellow head was slightly above hers. He stood beside her, completely indifferent to her response to his painting. Ursula studied it gravely. She became aware of a strange thumping of her heart. It had been a long time since she had seen any of Matthew's work. If he painted at all, and she was not even sure of this, he hid his canvases. He was letting her see this one now. Her first puzzlement disappeared before an incredulous awe and emotion.

Two years ago, she and the children, accompanied by Lucy

only, had visited Europe. Mrs. Templeton, who had striven
for years, as a good clergyman's widow, with the souls of
the Prescott children, had retired on the small but, to her,
substantial pension William had given her. It had been an
arduous journey, and Ursula had been exhausted by it. But,
so far as Ursula knew, Matthew had not been moved, not even
by Italy, that land of light and color, civilization and nobility,
life and passion. He had given up his art lessons some months
before. Ursula had hoped that Italy might inspire him, as
it had inspired so many who had passed through its almost
incredible beauty. He had gone through it all, aloof, silent,
mysterious as always, and had betrayed only a pale impatience
when the desperate Ursula had called anything to his attention.

Yet, he had seen. He must have seen! On a small table beside
his easel stood a great opened book, which Ursula remembered
having bought for him in Italy. And it stood open to a large
and excellent photograph of the "Pietá," the white and exquisite
marble high-lighted against a dark background. It was as
distinct as a fine cameo; it stood out from the page as if
possessed of a third dimension.

Matthew had been painting from that photograph. But
he had not painted it as marble. He had painted it in the
hues and lines of life. Against a fateful and Apocalyptic background of purple, faded gold and muted scarlet—like the twilight of a world dying forever—sat the Mother, with her cru-
cified Son across her knees and in her arms. The figures had
a spectral but luminous quality, dying, too, in the death of
a world, and they imparted to Ursula a sorrow and hopelessness
beyond the power of any word to express. Mary's resignation
was the tragedy of one who was beyond solace; her bent head
threw a shadow across her face so that the features could barely be discerned. Ursula felt the mute and inconsolable bewilderment of all the mothers of the world whose sons had been
done to death.

The figure across Mary's knees, subtly stronger in execution
than the marble, was the figure of a young man newly dead,
not weakly supine, not yet completely alienated from life,
but implying a human despair, a struggle against the death
which had been forced upon it. This young man was not the
Lord of Heaven, resting before rising in triumph; he was the
embodiment of all who had suffered and been fiercely defeated,
who had died irreconcilable, and with no hope.

How could one so young as Matthew create such a painting,
with such delicacy, with such a poignant intuition, with so
much perfection? Ursula marvelled. What lay in him, still

unfound, which had enabled him to conceive such ghostly power, such majesty?

And then her exultation died, and she saw all the terribleness of the picture. All its beauty, all its original artistry, was destroyed. It was a portrait of a deprived mother and her dead son; the resignation of Mary was frightful, and this death was a most awful thing, beyond redeeming, beyond understanding, with no future but oblivion. The background, itself, was less background than an agony—its flowing purples, its slashed golds and scarlets, were an agony made visible.

Ursula was silent. The evening sky, while she stood there, darkened more and more. The painting dimmed. Now it was unearthly. Without her knowledge, Matthew had moved away from her. He was standing at a distant window, as he always stood, lost and untouchable.

Ursula said quietly: "Matthew."

Slowly he turned from the window. In the gloom, she could not see his face or his blue eyes, but she knew he was watching her. He came back to the easel, and stood beside her, looking at what he had painted.

Ursula faltered: "It is not like the statue."

"No," said Matthew.

"It does not imply what the statue implies."

"No," he repeated.

He stretched out his long thin hand and turned the painting so that its raw back faced them, and the painting was gone.

If there had been something dramatic, something violent, in his gesture, Ursula would not have felt the enormous despondency that came to her. But there had been a finality about it, an ending.

It was her private tragedy that she could not speak to Matthew from her heart or her emotions. She had nothing but banalities to use. She said: "I think you have missed what the sculptor meant to imply. This was the beginning of life."

"It never is," said Matthew. His voice was low and indifferent.

"Perhaps not. But Michelangelo implied that."

Matthew said nothing.

"And Mary," continued Ursula, foolishly desperate, "knew that her Son would rise again. She was not hopeless."

"She should have been," said Matthew, in his usual lethargic tones. Again, Ursula felt him look at her. It was even darker in the room; his eye-sockets were without expression. "It might have been no use, but she should have tried to help him."

"How could she?" asked Ursula, trying to speak reasonably.

"It might have been no use, but she should have tried," repeated Matthew.

"Perhaps she did," said Ursula.

There was no sound or movement in the room.

"There are some things beyond the strength of any human being to change, or to help," said Ursula, thrusting against the void in the darkness.

She heard the scratch of a match. It tore the blackness with a thin flare of light. Then the gaslights went on. Matthew blew out the match.

He stood and looked at the charred stump in his fingers. So far as he was concerned, his mother might not have been in the room. He carefully deposited the stump in the china dish on the mantelpiece.

She stood up. "Fifteen minutes until dinner, dear," she said. Matthew did not turn. Ursula went out of the room. The gaslight was bright, but to her it was as if she walked through water, so misty were her eyes.

She closed the door behind her. There was no joy in her now that Matthew had painted, painted anything at all. There was only terror and foreboding. She repeated silently to herself: There are some things that are hopeless from the very beginning.

CHAPTER XXXIV

IT WAS QUEER, but Ursula, standing in the hall, felt a sudden sharp relief to see the commonplace light shining through Thomas' half-shut door. She pushed it open, smiled brightly, and said: "Tommy!"

Thomas' room was crowded with furniture, but it was warm and disheveled and human. He sat at his desk, his school-books untidily heaped about him, his head bent over his school papers. He lifted his rough brown head at his mother's entrance; he scowled briefly. He started to rise, as she had unremittingly taught him, rose half-way, and sank down again. "Hello, Ma," he added.

He stared at her, half smiled. His smile had its earlier goading quality, but at least it was a smile. "Come for the twilight confidences?" he asked.

At another time, Ursula might have been provoked. Now she actually laughed. She advanced with good humor into the room, sat down near the fire. She lifted her russet brows. "And so?" she said.

"It happens I've got the most stinking problem in trigonometry to work out," he replied.

"Let it wait," said Ursula.

Thomas shrugged his big and bulky shoulders. "Old Wilcox won't like that, Ma. There's nothing in the world half so important to old Wilcox as mathematics. He says mathematics are mystic, by God!"

"Tommy," rebuked Ursula, but mildly.

"They're only worth-while for figuring out feet of lumber." Thomas threw down his pen, frowned at the neat problems on his paper.

"You like the lumber business, don't you, Tommy?"

"Eh?" He stared at her, as though she had said something absurd. "Why, of course, I'm going into it, aren't I?" His expression became malign. "Or is our Oliver going to take over?"

Ursula controlled herself. She said: " 'Our' Oliver isn't going into the business at all, Tommy. He is going to study law, at Harvard."

"A lawyer!" He burst into a raucous laugh. "Pa had better watch out. Nothing like a lawyer to cheat the—the money out of you!"

Thomas' crudeness usually revolted and angered Ursula, so that almost all conversations between mother and son ended in caustic exchanges which left Ursula with a feeling of futility. Now she welcomed the crudeness. It was earthy. She studied Thomas in silence.

She had never discussed any child, in his absence, with any of the others. It was, according to her code, not only bad taste, but unfair. She had confined herself to a rebuke if any of them commented, unkindly, on a brother or sister who was not present. But now she said: "Tommy, you don't seem to get on well with anyone but Julie, and 'getting on' with others, and having some regard and kindness for them, is absolutely necessary to your own happiness."

Thomas smirked cynically. He leaned back in his chair, folded his big arms across his chest, as William did, and waited for further comments from his mother. She also waited. So he said, with impatience: "I am happy. I don't know what it means to be 'unhappy'. You are always talking about 'unhappiness', Ma, as if it were a kind of disease waiting around everywhere to be caught. Anyway, I don't think it's important to sit down and wonder if you are happy or unhappy. That's a disease in itself."

He has common-sense, thought Ursula, with a strange rush of gratitude. She found herself smiling. Thomas smiled back, and this time without nastiness, for he was very shrewd and understood his mother better than she knew.

"You are right, in many ways," she said, thinking that if she had more time, and that if William, when he was at home, did not always overthrow whatever influence over her children she had attained, she could reach a really sound rapport with all of them.

Thomas, himself, was also pleased. "Let's look at the family, and see if your accusation that they're hard to get on with is just," he said. "There's Julie. You don't understand Julie. She's just as entitled to be a minx as Matt has the right to go around in a big fuzzy cloud of thoughts." He paused, pleased again when his mother laughed, though he detected a note of hysteria in her laughter. "Julie's Julie, and you ought to get used to the fact," he continued. "When she was younger, she ought to have been thrashed a lot more. Yes, yes, I know," he said, when Ursula was about to interrupt. "Pa

didn't 'approve' of thrashing. Some kids need it. Julie did.
But there's a lot in Julie you don't see. She isn't a fool. She
knows what she wants, and she intends getting it. Maybe you
think that's not so good, not all of the time. I think it is.
Somebody's got to get things; most of the others are too stupid
to get them. Sure, she's selfish. So am I. Everyone is who
amounts to anything. Julie and I understand each other."

The dressing-bell sounded, but neither Ursula nor Thomas
cared. The boy was too earnest. For the first time in his life
he appeared to want his mother to comprehend him.

"In your code, Ma, getting something at the expense of
someone else, either of his 'happiness' or his money or his
own desires, is immoral. I don't think it is. There's just so
much of anything in the world, and not enough of everything
to go around, so that nobody has as much of everything as
he needs and wants."

"Go on," said Ursula, quietly.

"Your moral laws, Ma," said Thomas, speaking more rapidly
now, "if generally applied all over the world, would result
in nobody getting enough of anything. And, besides, the weak
would prosper, and, as they compose the majority of the
people in the world, they would soon crowd out the strong.
We'd all starve to death together."

"I think, Tommy, that your ideas are a sign of weakness,
and not of strength," protested Ursula.

"You don't think that at all, really," said Thomas, with
good-natured scorn. "You know, I'm beginning to like this
talk. You see, I've always known what you thought of me,
and maybe you're right. But you can't change my nature.
I, myself, like it."

Ursula, though she felt she ought not to, could not help
laughing.

"When Pa goes away," Thomas went on, shrewdly, "I
can almost hear you think: Now I'll have some influence over
the children, and I'll try to teach them the way they should
go." He watched the slow rise of his mother's flush, and nodded slyly. "You see, I am right. But you can't 'influence' us
much. We are the way we are. Perhaps Pa helped us to become
more so."

Ursula stared at the floor.

Thomas went on with even greater vigor: "Now, there's
Barbie. I don't like her. I never did. She wants things just
as much as Julie and I want them. But she has a 'code' and
it's a lot like yours. I don't like your code. I don't think it's

sensible, not the way the world is. Anyway, Barbie's strong, and that ought to please you."

Ursula said nothing.

"There's Matt," said Thomas. "I detest Matt. You think he doesn't want anything. You are wrong. He wants himself. He wants to sit in himself. He just loves himself. He can't find anything outside himself better than he is. Ma, I advise you to leave him alone."

"Thomas," murmured Ursula in distress, remembering the terrible picture she had seen only fifteen minutes ago.

"You think he is a genius," Thomas countered, relentlessly. "Maybe he is. He thinks so, too. That's enough for him. He doesn't want to do anything with it. It's enough for him to have it, God bless his little soul!"

"Oh, Thomas!" exclaimed Ursula.

Now Thomas pointed his big thick finger at his mother, and said, with emphasis: "See here, Ma. Remember when the depression started 'way back, and kept getting worse, though I guess most of it's over now? Pa used to talk gloomily at the table about things going to pot, and the lumber business and everything else going down. All of us were interested. You thought Matt wasn't. But he was! He was scared."

Ursula stared intently at her son.

"You remember he began to take a little more interest in his 'art' then? He began to paint again. He kept at it for all of six months, until Pa said things had got back on their feet. Then out went the teachers, and the dreadful idea of 'commercialism'. He could hug his 'art' right back into his arms again, and keep it from being 'profaned'. Oh, he never told anyone that, but I knew it all the time."

He is right, thought Ursula. But he is not completely right. He is incapable of the subtleties.

She saw that Thomas was watching her, and, if it were possible, his narrowed brown eyes had even become a little soft, as if he pitied her.

Suddenly the softness, if it had been there at all, went from Thomas' eyes. He thrust out his thick underlip. "There's Oliver. You think Oliver's just about perfect. So does Barbie. Maybe you're right. You like him because he's never caused you any trouble. I'd like to be able to say he's a prig, like Matt. He isn't; I'll be honest in that, anyway. In lots of ways, he's stronger than we are. He wants things too. He'll get a lot of what he wants, maybe more than we'll get."

"What does Oliver want, Tommy?"

"He wants not to be poor. But he wouldn't do anything he thinks is rotten to keep from being poor. Perhaps you think that is wonderful." Thomas paused, rubbed his forehead. "I'm going to try to keep him from getting what he wants."

Ursula said: "Tommy, that is vicious."

He laughed. "Maybe."

"And Oliver does have a 'right', too. Your father adopted him, and loved him. And I think he still loves him."

Thomas did not reply. He stared at his mother with a hateful half-smile. After some moments, he continued: "He's going to be a lawyer, you say. He'll try to stand in the way ——" He stopped abruptly.

"Of what, Tommy?"

Thomas did not answer. He stood up. "I heard the dinner-bell," he said.

It was singular that after this conversation, so much of which had been sensible and astute, Ursula felt a weight of misery and depression such as she had not felt even after her conversation with Matthew.

CHAPTER XXXV

BARBARA THOUGHT it a trifle precious of her mother to tiptoe softly into the school-room, some mornings, indicating by a bend of her head that she was not to be noticed but only to be permitted to listen for a few moments. She would watch Ursula seat herself at a distance, smiling somewhat faintly and uneasily, and pretending to a deep interest. She well understood that Ursula was seeking a close intimacy with her daughters, and that she believed it her duty to follow their lessons, and Barbara experienced compassion, discerning that Ursula felt only boredom and futility.

Perhaps all this was because Barbara was angered by her sister's own knowingness about these visits, and by Julia's smirk of contempt. Sometimes Barbara was so exasperated that she wished at one and the same time to slap Julia and call her mother a fool.

Miss Edna Vincent would give Ursula a quick sweetish smile, but she never paused, not even for a word of greeting. Ursula had indicated this was unnecessary. Miss Vincent was not perturbed by Ursula's presence. She was a woman whose tranquillity was rarely shaken. Her broad dim face peered peacefully at everyone beneath an untidy tangle of straw-colored braids, and her voice, a little thin and shrill, had a lilting quality which Ursula loathed.

This morning, when Ursula entered the school-room, was the first bright day of spring, following almost a month of cold and flailing rain. Barbara longed for her bicycle and the mountain roads. She was no sentimental gatherer of wildflowers in the hills and woods; rather, she preferred the high and windy solitudes where no "nonsensical" thing could intrude. She did not love solitude as her brother, Matthew, loved it. Solitude, for Barbara, meant freedom, a vigorous yet exalted freedom both of the senses and the body. Sometimes she would encounter Matthew, walking, his head bent. She would race sturdily past him, her strong legs churning at the pedals, though she knew he did not see her. Sometimes she would come upon Thomas, determinedly jogging along, elbows flexed, conditioning himself on the steep roads for baseball or basketball or football, and scornful of sisters, especially of Barbara. The girl would wonder which she detested most: Matthew's ghostly self-absorption in his sterile visions, or the animal exercise of Thomas. Barbara, like Ursula, was a born compromiser. Somewhere, between dreams and brute activity, lay the middle-road of satisfying and complete life.

Spring had always been to Barbara an eager and simple delight, for her nature, though at times discerning, was not complicated. But now there was for her, in the spring, a certain restlessness. She was afflicted by a loneliness and longing which she could not impale on the pin of common-sense.

Since very early childhood, Barbara had always been able to regard her family with entire detachment. She recognized her own similarity to her mother, and distrusted in Ursula what she distrusted in herself. She was more fond of Ursula than was any other member of her family and, though Ursula did not know this, Barbara alone, of all the children of her body, loved her. Barbara understood her father; she knew that he loved her, as one of his children, but that he did not like her.

Barbara thought Thomas a crafty animal, and her childhood dislike for him was becoming an intense aversion and disgust. His exploitation of his father infuriated her, but when he wounded Ursula the girl felt a desire to do violence upon him.

As for Matthew, Barbara rarely thought of him at all. In her opinion he was a hesitant-voiced shadow, strangely immovable, beyond the touch or reach of others. Sometimes she was afraid of him, afraid of what lay behind his silent presence.

Julia was a simpler matter, almost as simple as Thomas. Unlike Ursula, Barbara did not believe that Julia was empty-headed. Behind all that brilliant comeliness, there was a very good, if calculating mind. It might, one day, be a dangerous mind.

The trouble, Barbara would think, was that the normal hatreds and stresses in all families had in her own family neither been guarded against nor reckoned with. Ursula had known of them, but she had been powerless to control them or to render them ineffectual by discipline and training. As a result, among the children when they were together, there was always an atmosphere of impending violence, a lack of consideration for one another, an open hatred.

Only one stood outside the ring of invisible tensions which gripped the Prescott family, and this one was Oliver. Barbara, given to frowning whenever her mother appeared in the school-room, was so engrossed with thoughts of Oliver, and with the queer yearning and loneliness that thickened her throat, that she only stared momentarily at Ursula, and then bent her head over her books.

"Dear Barbara," said Miss Vincent mildly, with an indulgent smile at Ursula, "we were discussing the late—misunderstanding—between ourselves and Spain, and I am afraid that you haven't heard anything at all. Do tell me if I am prosey, and I'll try to correct it."

Barbara said: "I'm sorry, Miss Vincent. My attention wandered for a moment or two."

Julia jeered in her musical voice: "She was thinking how handsome Oliver looked—for two months—when he was in the Army, even though he didn't get to ride with the Rough Riders!"

Barbara's pale cheek flushed, but she said calmly: "No, I was thinking what a waste of life it is to be sitting here when I could be riding on the mountain roads on my bicycle."

Ursula, who rarely made any comment in the school-room, was irritated at Barbara's remark. It was strange that Barbara usually annoyed her more than did any of her other children, and in the annoyance lay a deep vein of disappointment. "What a silly thing to say, Barbie," she said. "The time for study, for the preparation for life, is in youth."

Barbara, ordinarily considerate of her mother, especially during the past year or two, answered with spirit: "I disagree. The time to live is when one is young, and the time to study, and remember, is when one is old."

"Except," interrupted Ursula, with cold sarcasm, "that all children are not so fortunate as to be supported until middle-age by wealthy parents, while they romp and have a gay and heedless time."

Julia cast up her lovely eyes towards the ceiling and murmured resignedly: "Lecture on the Subject of the Honor and Necessity of Duty will now be delivered by Mrs. William Prescott."

Ursula stared grimly at her elder daughter, then rose. "I am afraid I am interrupting, Miss Vincent," she said.

"Dear me, no," faltered Miss Vincent. "Not at all, Mrs. Prescott."

The girls were silent, but Julia smirked under the long fall of auburn curls which drooped across her cheek. Ursula left the room, closing the door silently behind her. Barbara, her gray eyes snapping, looked at her sister. "You are the

nastiest pig in the world," she said, quietly. "I've told you
that a dozen times or more. Do you have to talk to Mama like
that, you ill-mannered wretch?"

Julia laughed gaily. "Don't be a prig, Barbie. You get more
spinsterish all the time; you'll be a spinster to the end of your
life. Mama is so dull. She is so full of platitudes, just like
all her generation. And as futile, too. All old people are futile,
and now that it's a new century it will be the young people
who will teach their elders and correct their stupidities——"

"Oh, fiddlesticks," said the common-sense Barbara. "I don't
remember who it was who said it, but it's true: 'The young
generations blame their parents for evils for which parents
once blamed the grandparents, and for which the young generations, in their turn, will be blamed by their own children.'"

"Young ladies," murmured Miss Vincent helplessly.

But Barbara, aroused, jumped to her feet. She looked down
at her sister's beautiful face and at the patronizing smile that
curved Julia's full red mouth. However, before she could
speak, Julia said: "You talk about being 'weak', Barbie. You
are one of the weak ones in the family, because you have
what Mama calls 'common-sense'. Do you know what common-
sense is, Barbie? It is compromise. And when you compromise
all the time, it is because you can never take a stand for or
against anything, not even for or against yourself."

Again, she spoke before Barbara could speak in answer:
"Mama is weak, because she is 'sensible', and can always see
the other side, the other person's point of view. If she'd just
concentrate on her own point of view, sometimes, and insist
upon it, she might have a little personal satisfaction. She
might even have had some happiness with Papa, instead of
going around in an agonized fog all the time."

"Look who is talking about principles!" cried Barbara.
Her face was dark with a deep flush.

"I didn't mention principles at all," replied Julia, languidly.
"You've got 'principles' on the brain, just like Mama. I
was only talking about taking a stand for or against a thing,
and principles have nothing to do with that. Only getting
what you want."

Sick pain stood in Barbara's eyes. She said: "We have never
been denied anything——"

Julia nodded, smiling brightly. "Exactly what I mean, my
pet. None of us has an atom of love for Papa—because he
never took a stand against any of us, or denied us anything,
even when the biggest fool would know it was wrong. And
Mama was so concerned with trying to make Papa happy,

and keeping peace in the family, that she never fought it
out with him about us when we were little and she had at
least physical influence over us. Oh, she tried a few times,
but Papa got so stirred up, and she was so afraid he was being
hurt, that she gave up at precisely the moment when she could
have been victorious."

Barbara was silent. Julia's extraordinarily lovely face sparkled. " 'Blessed are the peacemakers, for they shall inherit
hell,' " she said.

"My dear Miss Julie!" cried Miss Vincent, aghast at this
blasphemy. "And what language for a young lady!"

Julia shrugged. "Somebody has to tell the truth around
here," she added.

"You dare to say you ever tell the truth!" said Barbara bitterly.

"Well, I do, sometimes," laughed Julia. "And you know
I am telling the truth, now, little Miss Spinster."

Barbara, though she knew that what she was about to
say was childish, could not help saying: "Being a spinster
is not half so bad as being in love with a dreadful old man."

She turned to Miss Vincent, who was much distressed
at these evidences of "dark disharmony", as she termed them.
"I am sorry, Miss Vincent, but I don't feel well. You'll have
to excuse me."

Accompanied by Julie's pretty laughter, she ran out of
the room, her dark mane flying.

CHAPTER XXXVI

THE COLD SPRING sunlight brightened upon the mountains, which were still dark and black against a brilliant blue sky. The piny ridges appeared almost black; no green promised that April was approaching. Barbara stood at the wide window of her room and stared somberly at the mountains that faced her. She saw the houses upon them very clearly, not yet hidden by summer foliage; she saw tiny red roofs, rising one above the other, or roofs of dull bluish slate, or the glisten of a white wall, or the flash of the sun on a far window. The house behind her was very still. It was not time yet for supper, when she and her sister would go down to the morning-room to meet her mother. There was still time for a swift bicycle ride on a mountain road, time for clean astringent air rushing against her face, for freedom and release.

How she hated this house! She hated the long gloomy corridors of the upper floors, the shut doors, the silences, the rich dim carpets, the opulence downstairs, the flare of color, the chill that lay in all the vast corners, the mighty circular staircase that rose, marble and cold and wide, to the roof. This was not a home, this house. She had been born here, but it was not a home for her. Perhaps there would never be a home.

If only I could get away, thought Barbara. If only I need never return here again. The silence of the great house lay behind her like a chasm. In a few hours, her father would be home, and he, and her mother and her sister and herself would gather in the shadowy and gigantic dining-room, and they would eat, and perhaps talk a little, tensely and warily, each fearing that a false word, an open word, would precipitate angers and fierce misunderstandings. If the meal survived without disruption, there would be nothing worse to carry into the evening than the memory of Ursula's drawn and haggard face, William's black silences, and the dreary reflections of servants tiptoeing across the mirror over the enormous buffet. After that, the preparation of lessons for the next day, a little needlework, a book; then bed, with the last fire glimmering on the hearth and the strong spring wind against the windows. But never, through it all, the sound of dear laughter, a gay joke, an eager rush of words, or the bantering voice of love that teased in order that it might not reveal itself too openly.

There would be no life or movement, no promise, until almost three months had passed, until Oliver returned from Harvard, Matthew from Princeton, and Thomas from Yale. Barbara gave a little short laugh of hard wretchedness. It was typical of this family that the young men in it should not want to be at any university together, that they had separated themselves from one another and that there was no question of their corresponding or inquiring about one another in letters to their parents. Only Oliver wrote her.

Well, thought Barbara, there is nothing anyone can do about us. Nothing at all. I must accept that, and not whine over it. She went to her wardrobe and brought out a small felt hat and a thick wool jacket and skirt. She must hurry, if she wished to have her ride. She stood before the mirror, a slender young girl, with none of Julia's beautiful charm, but with a firm straightness of figure much like her mother's. She saw the pale shadow of her face, her clear, wide gray eyes, her strong still mouth. No, she reflected, it was not a pretty face. It could not be called even a "wholesome" one. She shrugged, caught up her long dark hair and twisted it across the back of her head, where she fastened it with pins. She put on the rugged skirt and jacket, found a pair of gloves, and went out of the room.

She passed the shut door of her mother's apartments; she hesitated. Then, resolutely, she knocked on the door. Ursula's voice, weary and low, answered her, and Barbara entered. Ursula was sitting by the window, an unopened book on her knee. When she saw her daughter her lips tightened, her eyes became cold. "Well, Barbie," she said. "What is the matter? Why aren't you in the school-room?" She looked with deliberation at the watch on her shirtwaist.

Why can't we talk to each other? thought Barbara, with as much despair as a nature so firm and reasonable could feel. Why, when we are so much alike, isn't there any intimacy between Mama and me?

Ursula regarded her daughter with bleak expectancy. She had hoped so much for Barbara, but it had been useless, after all. She searched that young steadfast face, and saw there only self-sufficient hardness, without warmth, without tenderness. Barbara, so acute, understood what her mother was thinking, and she acknowledged that there was truth in Ursula's thoughts. But, was it not possible for Mama to see that she, Barbara, had changed?

"I thought a ride would do me more good today than lessons," said Barbara, trying to make her smile gay and succeeding only in making it appear superior.

"You are wrong, of course, Barbie," said Ursula, putting her hand on her book, and indicating that, as she had no control over her daughter, she had no desire for her presence. "However, you are old enough to know that you alone will suffer for a lack of education."

Barbara leaned against the door she had shut, and stared at the floor. She tried again: "Mama, we've talked about it so often. Julie and I are such big girls, now. We ought not to have a governess. We ought to be away somewhere, at school."

"Julie doesn't want to go away to school," said Ursula. Her hands dropped from the book, and her brows drew together in a wretched frown.

"That is quite true, Mama. But I want to go. Papa won't listen. I've tried to tell him that I'd like to go to college. I want to be independent. I have even thought I might like to teach in some school, afterwards. You promised to ask him——"

Ursula's pale dry mouth took on a distressed expression. "I have asked him, my dear. You know his usual answer: He doesn't approve of girls leaving home for school. You know what he calls girls who want to do so: 'Raucous, modern women, sexless and unattractive, repulsive to men.' Your father detests the 'new woman'. You made it no better, Barbie, by arguing that you thought women ought to have the franchise." Ursula could not help smiling, though it was a dull smile.

"His arguments are only an excuse!" cried Barbara. "You know the real reason. He just doesn't want to let any of us get away from him! Even I, for whom he doesn't care particularly. He wouldn't have let the boys get away, either, if there had been any universities near Andersburg."

Ursula sighed, put up her hands and pushed back the russet hair which was so heavily interwoven now with white and gray. Fatigue and abandon were in the gesture. She removed her spectacles, rubbed them abstractedly with her handkerchief.

Barbara was right. But Ursula would not admit this to her daughter. Her fanatic loyalty and devotion to William prevented her from allowing any criticism of him to be made by any of the children.

"It seems to me that you are speaking very treacherously of your father, Barbie, your father who has given you everything, denied you nothing——"

"Oh, I've heard that so often!" exclaimed Barbara. "Now it has become sickening. I'm not so stupid that I don't know what Papa has done and is always doing for us. But I don't want it any longer, Mama. I want my own life; I want to go to college. I want to be free."

"You mean, you want to leave this house, and everything and everyone in it," said Ursula, in an inflexible voice which rejected all that was Barbara.

Barbara again stared at the floor. Her head bent slowly. Very quietly, she said: "Yes."

She lifted her head again and fixed her eyes upon her mother. Ursula was silent. For an instant, she had the disloyal impulse to cry: "Barbie! I know, my dear. I know all about it. I wish I could help you. But I cannot. Your father comes first with me, and what he wants." She held back the impulse, made her face rigid.

"You are so ungrateful, Barbie," she said, with bitter dismissal. "You never think of anyone but yourself. Don't you think you owe your father something? Don't you think his desires should be considered, rather than yours?"

"Yes, perhaps I am ungrateful," admitted Barbara in a low tone. "Perhaps I am selfish, too——"

"There is no 'perhaps' about it, Barbie," interrupted Ursula.

Barbara went on steadfastly: "But I ought to be considered, too, and what I want, myself. I want to be a little happy. I know that happiness isn't something that comes easily; perhaps it doesn't come to any of us, ever. But it would give me some pleasure, some freedom, to plan my own life—and to go away."

Ursula wanted to say: "Why do you want to go away?" But before she could speak them the words were smothered in a kind of terror. She knew what the answer would be, and she could not bear to hear it. She lifted her hands again in an involuntary gesture, as if to cover her ears; then dropped them half-way. She said: "Young girls are so restless these days. They don't know what they really want, or what is good for them. They have lost their way."

Barbara drew herself up, standing straight against the door. "I don't want to lose my way, Mama. But I'm afraid I'll lose it, if I don't get out of this house and go away to school."

She waited for Ursula to speak, but her mother did not reply, did not look at her. She continued: "All of us have lost our way, because no way was ever shown us except the way of self-indulgence and self-gratification."

Ursula stood up, in panic. "Barbie! I won't listen to you any longer! You—you don't understand. You speak of going to college. You have made no allowance for marriage. You don't speak of marriage; yet, in two or three years, it will be expected of you that you'll marry."

"No, Mama," replied Barbara, calmly. "I'm not making any plans for marrying. I don't think I'm fit for anyone to marry—yet. I have so much to learn, and it's not in books. Mama, I've got to save myself."

"You talk like a silly romantic young fool!" cried Ursula, thrusting out her hands as if pushing away her daughter. "You are only quoting the words uttered by irresponsible spinsters and dissatisfied wives——"

Barbara opened the door. "If I don't hurry, I shan't have time for my ride," she said. There was no emotion in her voice, not even regret or anger. She closed the door after her, taking despair with her, leaving despair behind her.

She went out of the house to the stables. She found her bicycle, rolled expertly down the long winding road that uncoiled from the house through the parklike grounds. The harsh bright wind struck her face, but it gave her no delight. In her eyes there was the deepest and most desolate trouble. The gate-keeper opened the iron gates for her; if he spoke to her, she did not hear him. She rolled out upon Schiller Road, carefully avoided the carriage traffic which filled it, set out for the mountains. In a few minutes she was climbing; the resistance of the grade was a hard pleasure to her.

She was climbing rapidly. On a lonely mountainside, she rolled past the gates of the great estates which had grown up there during the past twenty years. Dogs barked at her fiercely. She climbed higher and higher. Everything about her was shining and lonely; stark and still were the empty trees tracing twisting branches against the intensely blue sky. Stone walls flowed past her; she crossed a little stone bridge, under which a brown brook, released from winter, chattered and foamed. She turned her wheel down a road which dipped and rose and curved, a road that ran with water and liquid mud. Now she had to get down and walk her bicycle; she could hear and feel the mud sucking at her heels. It was very early, as yet, for such an excursion. But there was in her a terrible need for solitude and flight.

She had left all houses behind. She was in a wood of fir trees, black and chill and motionless, though she could hear the rushing of the wind far above this sheltered place. Once or twice she saw a robin, newly returned. Sparrows chittered about her. Wings flashed through the illuminated air. A squirrel dashed across her path. Life was awakening. Barbara did not see it. Her hands and feet were cold, her cheeks roughened and reddened. The trouble was still deep in her eyes, so deep, indeed, that she did not detect the first faint sweetness of the stirring air, the clear fragrance of resin. She did not see, here and there, patches of old honeycombed snow, scabrous against the brown earth.

Now she emerged from the woods, reached her old favorite spot, unsheltered, open to the wind and the blue and brilliant air. There were the brown flat rocks, where she had sat so often in the summer. They were wet, dripping with moisture. Two snakes lay on them, folded together in a nuptial embrace. Barbara, who had no fear of these harmless serpents, decided not to disturb them. She leaned her bicycle against a tree, walked away from the stones, and stood on a narrow terrace. Far below her lay Andersburg, smoking, gray-and-brown, crowded, huddled and branching. Curving away from Andersburg lay the whitish-blue river. She could see the corroded floes of ice upon it. But river traffic was being resumed. She could almost hear the sound of the puffing tugs, towing flat-boats.

She could see the Prescott house clearly, a dusky toy house amid its grounds. There was an unreality about it. Barbara stood there and stared at her home for a long time. Even at that distance it had for her a quality sinister and threatening. She turned from it, found the gigantic saw-mills of her father, saw the smoke rising from them, the flat-boats at the docks. A spur of the railroad ran down to the mills now; she could see the tiny engine, gushing smoke, the flat cars covered with raw yellow lumber. Except for the birds cheeping in the bare trees and the wind on the higher levels, everything about her was silent.

The panorama of wide radiant sky, dark hills and jade river stretched before the girl, and—in the valley, and circling the river—the living city. She was free of the city, but she was not free of her thoughts, sadly rebellious and gloomy, too heavy for so young a creature. Only three months ago, on the eve of January, 1900, she had said to herself, hopefully: "It is a new century beginning! Everything will be new, for the world, for me." In spite of all the wild celebrations,

in spite of the predictions of oracles, nothing had become new
and promising, nothing had changed. Now, in spite of all
the late winter brightness lying beneath her, in spite of the
promise of spring in the rising excitement of the birds, in
spite of the sun and the wind, she felt in the air something
ominous, something baleful. She was not given to morbid
thoughts, so that these struck on her mind with fresh fear
and apprehension.

She was wrong, she thought. Something had changed, was
changing. She did not know what it was; but the premonition
persisted in her.

The sun lowered towards the opposite mountains, and
a sudden flush began to spread upwards above the folded
darkness of the hills. If she was to reach home before evening
came, she must hurry. But she could not make herself move.
She stood there, growing colder by the moment. Now the
air stung her eyes.

Oliver, she thought. Oh, Oliver, Oliver. Her hands were
numb in their gloves; the numbness crept up her arms, struck
at her heart.

CHAPTER XXXVII

THE ADMINISTRATIVE buildings of the Prescott Lumber Company had grown during the past ten years to almost twice their size. William Prescott's own offices were composed of his private inner office, much enlarged, and far more luxurious than before, the office of his chief clerk, once more Mr. Ben Watson, now that Eugene Arnold, some two years ago, had been promoted to the position of general manager of the mills, an office adjoining that of Mr. Watson's, filled with busy clerks and bookkeepers and stenographers, and a large room full of filing cabinets adjoining this office. There was also a waiting-room for salesmen, and a more gracious waiting-room for more important callers. Across the hall were Eugene Arnold's offices, much smaller, of course, but equally well furnished.

To William's massive and expansive furnishings had been added a heavy leather couch, with a folded afghan at the foot, for only six months ago William had suffered what Dr. Banks vaguely referred to as a "heart attack." The attack had not been serious, but orders had been given that William must have an hour's rest after his noonday meal, and must lie down whenever he felt "weak" or "faint." William acceded to the short afternoon nap; more than that he would not do. In fact, he was angered at the suggestion that he might need additional rest periods. But the seizure had been sufficiently painful to alarm him; he wanted no others. He remembered, only too clearly, the sensation of impending death which had accompanied the "attack," and the several weeks of miserable inanition in bed to which he had been forced to submit. It was all nonsense, of course; Banks was an "old woman." However, he usually lay down after his luncheon, and never confessed to anyone, not even to his physician, that he was grateful for the excuse.

Though Eugene Arnold was general manager of the mills, William had not deviated from his earlier determination to keep the most important part of the business to himself. The protests of his associates and officers, who more and more grumbled at his "high-handedness," had still no effect upon

275

him. The years of the nineties, with their economic and
financial upheavals, had been survived, with incredible profits,
while other businesses all over the country had succumbed.
William never failed to call the attention of his associates
to this amazing fact, yet their restiveness increased rather
than diminished. Upon leaving his offices, they would eye
the locked files hungrily. He would see the look, and smile
to himself. Not even Eugene Arnold had access to them.
Eugene knew only what it was absolutely necessary for him
to know, in connection with his management of the mills.

Accusations of "unorthodoxy," and of "single-handed authority," did not move William. They only amused him. The
most significant reports were made to himself alone. He
did not trust even Mr. Jay Regan, of New York. He asked
Mr. Regan's advice. Whether or not he followed this advice
Mr. Regan was not always certain.

William, always acutely intuitive, had noticed of late that
his officers and associates had become less impatient, less
demanding, that they appeared more placid, more complacent
and agreeable towards him. There were passing moments
when this caused him a vague thoughtful uneasiness.

In spite of all the responsibility which he had delegated
to the young man, he did not trust Eugene Arnold. Even now,
he did not like him. His attitude towards his subordinate was
paradoxical and capricious, moved by instinct rather than
by reason. He was grateful to have so intelligent and competent a manager, and his manner towards Eugene was sometimes paternal and affectionate. During his illness, Eugene
had carried on the business flawlessly and, again, William
was grateful. But still, it was not possible for him to trust
Eugene.

It was William's belief that any show of weakness, depend-
ency or trust inspired only scorn and suspicion in one's sub-
ordinates. So it was during the first acute weeks of his illness,
when Eugene visited him for orders, William invariably made
an exhausting effort to appear quite himself. Eugene, in
every word and gesture and enigmatic smile, betrayed an
admiration and respect which were entirely sincere. William
saw this. Again, he was grateful. He knew that Eugene was
not dissembling.

William knew that Ursula had a deep and instinctive hatred
for Eugene Arnold, which, though it had become somewhat
less vocal and more resigned, had not diminished in intensity
through the years. "You say he is honest in his admiration

for you, William," she would say, "and that he is devoted
to your interests. Perhaps you are right. But what else do
you know about him? What is he thinking? What, beyond what
I have named, is his feeling towards you?"

"Good God!" William would cry in answer. "What else
is there for him to 'feel'? He is paid for his services. There
is nothing else."

But he knew, or suspected, that there was something else.
He never watched Eugene approach, never spoke to him,
without staring at him piercingly, and trying to hear, with
an inner ear, what Eugene was thinking. He never succeeded.
He did not like people who had money (and Eugene must
have a good deal now) and did not spend it on the things which,
to William, made life tolerable.

During altercations at board meetings, at which, unknown
to himself, William was becoming more and more irascible
and impatient and overbearing, it was Eugene's quiet voice,
supporting him with facts and figures and impeccable reason,
which always quieted the angry voices of the others, which
had an almost magical effect upon them. They appeared to
trust Eugene, as they did not trust William. Eugene would
then efface himself. He had the ability to be physically present
yet unnoticeable, whenever he desired. This gratified William.
Had Eugene taken on an importance of his own, had he
asserted himself too openly, as a young man might have been
tempted to do, William would soon have found ways to
make him smart and to reduce his authority.

What Eugene did with his private time sometimes made
William speculate interestedly. Once or twice he had hinted
of his interest. Eugene, faintly smiling, would dexterously
fend off this curiosity. He read. He played Ursula's piano.
He had practically no friends. During his holidays he liked
to travel. He enjoyed his garden. He walked extensively.
No, he was not interested in marriage. "Why not?" William
would demand. "Don't you want children, Gene?"

"Not particularly, sir," Eugene would reply, with one of
his odd smiles.

"You aren't getting any younger," William had remarked
to the young man only recently. "You don't expect to spend
all the rest of your life in Mrs. Prescott's house?"

Eugene had shrugged his shoulders. "I am satisfied. And
I think Mrs. Prescott's house suits me perfectly."

"But to whom do you expect to leave your money, Gene?
You've asked me for advice on investments, and you've given

me to understand that you've profited neatly. I don't know just what money you have, but it must be very substantial. What do you intend to do with it?"

Eugene had smiled again. His pale eyes had rested on William inscrutably.

"One of these days, sir, I'll give it thought," he had replied.

He had left William then, and William had frowned to himself for several long moments, uneasily.

The same spring sun which was now lying on Barbara's head and shoulders on the mountain terrace struck her father's head and shoulders as he gathered up his papers in preparation for leaving his office.

He was unusually tired today. When this weariness came upon him he was ready with a dozen different excuses, all trivial, to explain it. It had been a "hard" day; he had not slept well; his luncheon had disagreed with him; some of his employees had demonstrated remarkable stupidity. He did not admit, even in the most unguarded moments, that his weariness might be part of a strengthening spiritual malaise, a terrible and still unrecognized hopelessness. He did not admit it, for he did not know it.

Two letters lay on his desk, one from his son, Thomas, one from his son, Matthew. Slowly he laid down the papers in his hands, and sat and stared at the letters. The exhaustion became an overpowering weight on his shoulders, so that he had to fold his arms upon his desk and lean heavily upon them, as if for support. His attitude was that of a man who is very ill and who, for a while, cannot fight against this illness, but must rest briefly.

Letters asking for money always came to the offices. Letters written jointly to both parents arrived at home. Ever since the twins had been away at school, these letters addressed only to William had begun to arrive, and he had smiled sheepishly and fondly, thinking how much his sons trusted him and how much they preferred not to have their mother know of their affairs. By writing only to their father, they excluded their mother. They reaffirmed their dependence upon him. Thomas, who understood his father's delusion, contributed to it craftily and deliberately. Matthew, who never had understood, nor cared to understand, any living being, knew only that Ursula would object to extra sums of money being sent him, over and above his already extravagant allowance. He wrote, therefore, to his father.

This sly leeching of money had gone on almost from the

beginning, when, two years ago, Thomas had entered Yale, and Matthew, Princeton. It was nothing new; it had given William the deepest pleasure. It was extraordinary, then, that as he now looked at those two letters on his desk he should feel so mortally tired, so undone.

The letters themselves were not at all extraordinary. In fact, they might have been mere copies of dozens of their predecessors. Thomas bluffly announced that "some of the fellows" were planning a "shindig" next week and every "fellow" was expected to pay his very large share. He had to confess that he needed at least two hundred dollars. Would Father send him a check "forthwith," and "thanks a million, kind sir," and, of course, he, Thomas, sent his love and hoped his father had completely recovered his health.

Matthew's note was as subdued and elusive as himself, but, coldly, more explicit than Thomas's. There was a sketch of Goya which he coveted, and which was for sale "very reasonably." Three hundred dollars, and warranted genuine.

William opened his desk with slow and deliberate movements, his fingers trembling. He found his check-book. He wrote out the checks. Thomas and Matthew would receive, not the two hundred or the three hundred requested, but at least one hundred more. It was very strange that William did not feel the old pleasure in writing these checks, only a queer sort of sickness.

In his tense small writing, in which the loops visibly trembled, he wrote a short note to each of his sons. The notes were full of his excessive love, his anxiety for his children, his hope that they would write again, very soon. He put the notes and checks in their envelopes, addressed them, stamped them. He would drop them in the post-office box in the general office. He put the letters aside for a moment, and said aloud, in a dwindled voice: "God, but I am tired!"

His thoughts returned inexorably to his sons. Thomas was popular at Yale; he excelled in sports; his marks were far above the average; he had made some very substantial friends, of whom William approved. Nothing more could be expected. William leaned his forehead on the back of his right hand and tried to subdue the sudden throbbing of his heart.

Matthew never spoke of friends. It was evident that he had made none, though he had developed a frail attachment for one of his instructors. His marks, as usual, were either phenomenally high or incredibly low, fluctuating without reason.

There was a light tapping, three times, upon his door.

He knew it was Eugene Arnold. He tried to call out, but his voice came only in a whisper. He gripped the edge of his desk, cleared his throat, and finally made himself heard. The door opened, and Eugene entered the room silently, and smiling. "Gene," said William, dully. He tried to smile. The letters to and from his sons lay on the desk before him. Eugene glanced at William's face, then glanced at what lay on the desk. William involuntarily put his hands over the letters, then turned them over so that the addresses could be seen. He did not know why he did this; he did not, in fact, know that he had done it.

"What is it, Gene?" asked William, impatiently. "I am about to leave for home."

"Nothing, really, sir," replied Eugene. "I just came to say good-night." He paused. He saw the sick pallor under William's dark skin.

But the smile did not change. "There is nothing else today, sir?"

"No. But there is a board meeting day after tomorrow, as you know."

"Yes, everything is ready."

There was a silence in the room. William's hand still covered the letters, as if defending them, as if hiding them. He looked at Eugene. The latter's earlier thinness had become a hard brittleness which yet curiously suggested enormous reserve strength. His narrow face, over these years, had attained a bleached dryness, so that though he was only thirty-three, sharp thin lines sprang out about his mouth and eyes when he smiled, and of late were etching themselves deeper. Even when he was not smiling, the lines remained, fainter, but incisive, as if drawn by a sharp knife. His fleshless hands, clean and without color, had a look of potency about them, and aseptic cruelty. His light hair had faded; in some lights it appeared almost gray.

William pushed himself to his feet, his hands on the desk. "I'll walk down to the gates with you," he said. For one moment, as if to escape those unreadable eyes, he glanced through the window at the shining river, the flat-boats, the tugs, and the distant mountains. Eugene deftly assisted his employer into his coat. His manner had just the slightest hint of thoughtful solicitude. "Thanks," said William, curtly. He slipped the letters into his pocket. He put on his hat. Eugene carried his until they both emerged into the cold and bitter air.

The carriage was waiting at the gates, and in the carriage

sat Julia, beautiful in her mink jacket, her wide, plume adorned hat, her red wool frock. Her gloved hands were cosily snuggled in a mink muff, and her knees were covered with a fur rug.

At the sight of his elder daughter the somber exhaustion on William's face lifted, was replaced by an expression of pleasure and delight. Julia often called for him lately, smiling at him with sweetest fondness and arch coquetry, so that gay sparks seemed to flash from her amber eyes and dimples indented themselves in her pink cheeks. No matter how dreary or vexatious the day had been, the ride home would raise William's spirits and Ursula would often hear the laughter of husband and daughter mingling as they entered the house.

Tonight, William hurried to the carriage as a frozen man hurries towards warmth and comfort. Eugene followed more slowly, again removing his hat. Julia's attention was concentrated on her father, whom she kissed affectionately, laying one gloved hand on his shoulder. It was only then that she apparently became aware of Eugene, who was waiting for recognition. She extended her other hand to him graciously. Their palms touched; Eugene felt, as he often had felt, the thin folded slip of paper in her hand. While he spoke to her pleasantly, and inquired about her health, he expertly closed two fingers over the note. It was all done so cleverly that William never suspected.

William's relief at what he believed the tender affection in the eyes of his daughter was so great that he turned almost excitedly to Eugene and said: "Will you join us for dinner tonight, Gene?"

Eugene said quietly: "Thank you, but no. I have these papers to go over tonight, in preparation for the board meeting," and he glanced down at the briefcase he carried.

Julia's lovely face darkened with disappointment. Eugene gave her a swift look. Her auburn brows relaxed, but some of the light went out of her eyes.

Masterfully happy and assured, William entered the carriage, and Julia covered his knees with the rug. Eugene bowed; Julia inclined her head in silence. The carriage drove away, its wheels twinkling in the thin and dying sunlight. Julia looked back over her shoulder for an instant. Eugene was still standing at the gates, watching the carriage. He lifted his hand briefly. She dared not reply.

He had not brought his buggy today. He turned from the gates, went towards the city. Now he was very thoughtful. He stopped for a moment to read Julia's note. It was brief but vehement. "I shall soon be eighteen. Don't ask me to

wait any longer, dear Eugene. I am sure you are wrong about
Papa; he will consent to anything which will make me happy.
Anything. I am afraid of this slipping out and meeting you.
Someone is bound to see us sooner or later. Then Papa really
will be angry. Shall we decide to tell him when I have passed
my eighteenth birthday?"

Very carefully, Eugene struck a match and burned the
note. He waited until the last frail wisp of it was carried away
on the cold astringent air. He pursed up his lips as if about
to whistle, but no sound came. Now he was frowning as
he swung up the grade leading to the nearest street. Julia,
he thought. He wanted Julia. He wanted her for many reasons,
and none of them, he believed, had to do with passion.

Yet, even when he had not wished to think of her, Julia
had a way of intruding into the most calculating of his thoughts.
After seeing her, he would hear her voice for a long time,
like an echo. He knew that she loved him as she had never
loved anyone before and as, most probably, she would never
love again.

He was approaching a quiet and almost deserted street.
He walked down it more slowly, for it came to him that
he had been hurrying and that he was short of breath, as
if he had been trying to run away from something that threatened. He began to glance about him, coolly wary, vigilant.
Nothing mattered, he thought, but what he wanted. If he
were guilty of a puerile emotion, that, in itself, would not
shake or change him.

He heard the quiet rattling of wheels on the cobblestones
of the streets. He did not look around, but he slowed his pace.
The carriage, undistinguished, passed him. It hesitated a
few steps down the street; he went towards it without hurry.
It was empty. The coachman muttered a greeting. Eugene
opened the door himself, got in, closed the door. He leaned
far back against the leather cushions, his hat tipped over
his eyes.

A half hour later the carriage stopped before the sheltered
brownstone house of Dr. Banks. Eugene left the carriage
swiftly. The large grilled door opened for him, and he entered
the warm and firelit hall. Dr. Banks, smoking a particularly
rich cigar, came into the hall and extended his fat moist hand.

"Well, Gene," he said, in the most urbane of voices.

"Well, Doctor," answered Eugene.

"Dinner is ready, I believe," said Dr. Banks, laying his
arm about Eugene's shoulder. "A pleasant day, wasn't it?"

CHAPTER XXXVIII

WILLIAM'S DELIGHT in Julia's company did not decrease as the carriage rolled towards Schiller Road. This gave him a sense of rejuvenation and well-being. Of all his children, Julia was his favorite, the dearest to him. He believed that she understood him; in this, he was quite correct, but he did not know that she understood him in a way that was both cruel and dangerous, and quite without illusion and love.

Because she was so precious to him he rarely, if ever, denied her anything. He was proud of her beauty, her wit and vivacity. He knew she had an excellent mind, and flattered himself that she had inherited this from him. Then, too, in these last few years, she had not been crudely exacting, but had extorted concessions from him in so gay and affectionate a way as to give him pleasure in granting her whatever she wished.

For the first time, he observed the signs of spring, and called Julia's attention to them. She leaned against his shoulder, and murmured assentingly. Her mind was busy, as it had been ceaselessly busy all this past year. It was time, she thought, that some hint be given her father of her restlessness and discontent; with the utmost artfulness, she would suggest to him that he must find the reason for her emotional state, and help her. It was a very uncertain situation. She knew that William had no strong liking for Eugene. She knew the family history. She knew that William admired Eugene and had relied, more and more, these months, upon Eugene's judgment. She knew also that William's distrust of his general manager always lay below the surface of his consciousness, and that it would take little to bring it to the surface.

She allowed herself to sigh, and because William was so attuned to all the moods of this beloved daughter, he heard the sigh and all his happiness was overcome by anxiety. He turned his head and looked at her. She was leaning back on the velours cushions now; her eyes were closed. There was a mournful expression on her lovely face.

"What is it, my darling?" he asked. He took her small gloved hand and held it tightly. Julia opened her eyes, gave him a gentle smile.

"Nothing, really, Papa," she said, as if with an effort. "But sometimes I am so worried about you. Did you have a hard day, today?" Her voice became sweetly concerned.

William was touched. He pressed her hand warmly. "Don't worry, dear. No, I didn't have a hard day." For this moment the letters he had just mailed had no power to hurt him. "I am getting better, Julie. And you are too young to be worrying over an old fogey like me."

"Papa, how can you talk so!" Julia sat up, regarded him indignantly. "But there, I admit I'm selfish. I sometimes think of all the terrible things that would happen to me if—if you went away." She could actually bring tears to her eyes, and William saw them, as she intended he should.

He laughed heartily. "I'm still in my early fifties, you silly child! I don't intend to die yet. I intend to see you married to someone worthy of you, and to enjoy myself at your wedding reception."

Julia sighed again, leaned against him. "But, Papa, I am almost eighteen, and who is there in Andersburg to marry? If I had gone away to school, I might have met the sisters of eligible young men, and have made friends of them."

William's expression darkened. He said, roughly: "Now, don't tell me you are just like Barbie, wanting to leave your home and go away to college, and become a 'new woman'. I couldn't stand that, Julie. I want my girls at home. It was bad enough that the boys had to go away." He paused. "Do you want to go away to school, Julie?" he asked, jealously.

"Oh, Papa, you misunderstand me," said Julia, with reproach. "I don't want to be a 'new woman' at all. I'm just a simple girl. But there are times, and I admit it, when I wonder what is to become of me, and whom I'll marry, if ever."

"Why, you have dozens of beaux," said William, soothed again, and indulgent. "The sons of all our friends. The house is full of young men, when they come home from college. Surely there is one among them, or even two, worth serious consideration."

"There are none like you, Papa," said Julia, in a low tone.

William straightened involuntarily. It ought to have been pathetic to Julia to see her father, so weary and pale, assume a debonair expression, smiling and pleased. He patted her shoulder. "Now, now, you are only flattering me, my darling. I'm nothing exceptional, nothing exceptional at all."

Julia sighed, laughed lightly. "There is no one, Papa, really. They are so boyish and irresponsible, the young men I know. I feel so old beside them. They have no minds." She paused. Now was the crucial moment. She laughed again, as if what she was about to say were very absurd. "Now, if Eugene Arnold were just a little younger, I might become interested in him!"

William's hand fell from her shoulder. It had never occurred to him for a moment that Julia might even have looked at Eugene Arnold. He said, coldly: "Even if Eugene were younger, I'd certainly never consider him fit for you, Julie. I never liked him. Yes, I know I've advanced him steadily through the years, and that he's worthy of his hire. But there was always something about him, and still is, which I feel I must watch."

Julia was silent. There was a sharp and bitter anger in her, and hatred for her father. She hated him for making her way so hard, for forcing her to the most exquisite tact and diplomacy. Of course, she and Eugene could elope, but Julia did not believe that William would forgive them. Eugene would be ruined. Worse, Eugene would not even consider running away with her. She was less to him than were his own ambitions.

She picked her way carefully when she answered her father: "You are so paradoxical, Papa. You do everything for Eugene, and acknowledge how valuable he is to you, yet you don't like him or trust him. Why?" she smiled at him ingenuously.

William stared before him. He felt somewhat ridiculous. He could not confess to his daughter: "I don't know why." There was too much emotion in him, and he knew it, and he felt it was a weakness which must never be revealed to Julia if he was to keep her respect.

He must answer her, sensibly. But where was there logic in his attitude towards Eugene? For the first time, it came to him that he was unreasonable, and this was precisely what Julia intended him to feel.

He said, shortly: "Whenever I see him, I think of his father, and I detested Chauncey Arnold. He was a boor, a fool and a scoundrel."

"But Eugene isn't, Papa, or you wouldn't have done so much for him?"

William did not answer. More and more, he was becoming sure that he was irrational, and this annoyed him.

"I don't know why I bother to defend Eugene to you," said Julia, obviously bored. "But it does sound sort of silly, you giving Eugene everything, yet not liking him or trusting him." She paused, while William glowered, confounded.

Again, William was silent. His annoyance with himself increased. He sat far back in the corner of the carriage, away from his daughter, while she watched him under her auburn lashes.

"I think, Papa, that you really do like Eugene," said Julia, fondly. "But you won't confess it, even to yourself. And he was so wonderful when you were ill. Do you remember saying that you didn't know what you'd have done without him? So, you must trust him, after all. And he admires you so much. I'm sure he'd be shocked to know that you don't like him or trust him."

Again, William was soothed and flattered. He smiled sheepishly. "My dear girl, I didn't say I actually disliked or distrusted young Arnold! If I did, I'd not have him within a mile of me. And I suppose it is a little stupid of me to keep thinking of his father. Yes, perhaps stupid," he added, half to himself. His instinct, usually so sure, was smothered. He even felt slightly ashamed of himself.

Julia was elated. It had been so easy, after all, to instil self-doubt into the mind of her father. Yes, he was stupid, as he himself had admitted. She leaned towards him and kissed him with apparent impulsiveness. "Oh, Papa, you are so precious!" she exclaimed tenderly.

She said nothing else. In these few minutes she had done excellent work. She must let the subject drop for a bit, until her artful suggestions had had time to seep fully into William's mind. She began to talk to him vivaciously, made him laugh at her little jokes. By the time the carriage had arrived home, William was again in high good-humor.

Ever since his illness, Ursula had listened with an almost terrible anxiety for the sound of William's voice. The tension in her would not relax until she was certain that his voice held no hint of pain or weakness; then she would tremble a little with relief. She always waited until she heard William and Julia go into the library before she would slip downstairs with a tranquil air and as pleasant a smile as she could summon. She knew it was not love which impelled Julia to call for her father; she knew that behind everything Julia did lay selfishness and self-seeking. Yet Julia gave William delight, even if the delight was a delusion, and she could make him laugh as could no one else. This was sufficient for Ursula, it helped her to endure her now chronic pain and fear.

Though they had long ago, as if by mutual consent, abandoned the home-coming kiss, her first and only glance was for William. If that piercing glance at him reassured Ursula that he did not appear more tired than usual, that he was not paler, she would sigh over and over, like one who permits himself to breathe after prolonged and frightened holding of the breath. Only then could she say, "Good evening, William," and smile.

Tonight, William's spirits were so high that his expression did not become as gloomy as it usually did on the appearance of Ursula. He even returned her smile, answered her questions about his health with less impatience than customary, and actually asked after hers. He held out a chair for her. Julia sat down too, and looked at the fire pensively. Ursula studied her sharply for a moment. She always knew when Julia was plotting.

The doctor had recommended a glass of whiskey before dinner for William, an order to which he had acceded with dislike. A glass of sherry was brought for Ursula.

What a cosy scene this is, with the three of us before the fire, and the lamps not yet lit, thought Ursula bitterly. Julia was absorbed in her thoughts; William sipped his whiskey and only grimaced once. Ursula put her sherry to her lips. She said: "Did you see Barbie, on your way home? It is getting dark. She went out on her bicycle."

"I detest women on bicycles," said William irritably. "Why does she have to have one? It's too mannish."

"It's a craze," said Ursula hurriedly, and in an apologetic tone. "All her friends have bicycles. In fact, almost every woman has one."

"I haven't," said Julia, sweetly. "And I'm sure, Mama, that I wouldn't ride one under any circumstances."

William gave her an approving glance. Ursula bit her lips in vexation but she held back a swift tart reply. Yes, Julia was plotting. Ursula changed the subject. "I was disappointed at not hearing from the boys today. This is the day we usually hear from them."

William said nothing. He put down his glass as one puts aside an obnoxious medicine. Ursula regarded him narrowly. He had heard from them, then. They had asked for money again.

"But there is a very nice letter from Oliver," she went on. "He is so concerned about you, William. And he has a very amusing story to tell about Judge Muehller's nephew."

William looked at the fire. It was as if he had not heard Ursula. Julia yawned delicately. "Dear Oliver," she murmured. There was the daintiest ridicule in her voice. It was then that to Ursula's astonishment William stirred and gave his daughter a cold, harsh look.

"Oliver," he said, "justified his education. I have only recently heard that he will graduate with honors."

Julia, too, was astonished by her father's strange defense of his adopted son. She stared at William, her golden eyes widening in the firelight. Ursula had the most absurd struggle against tears.

"Yes," she said, feebly. "It is something to make us proud. Proud," she repeated, and had to stop.

William became silent again. He sat in his chair near the hearth, and there was about him a dark and brooding quality which frightened Julia and renewed Ursula's anxiety.

They heard the distant crash of a door. Barbara had returned. Immediately following the crash, the dressing-bell sounded.

Another evening of tension and loneliness had begun, for William, Ursula and the younger girl. But Julia had her thoughts, and her plans.

PART FOUR

"Thy sons and thy daughters shall be given unto another people, and thine eyes shall look, and fail with longing for them all the day long: and there shall be no might in thine hand."

DEUT. 28:32

CHAPTER XXXIX

THEY ARE ALL old men, thought Eugene. And, above all, they are gentlemen. That is to say, not one of them would betray a friend or an associate for anything less than money. Their God, if they have one, is less substantial than their fortunes, and a word, however light, uttered against money is more of a blasphemy than the overturning of an altar.

Nothing of what Eugene thought showed on his quiet dry face. He sat in Dr. Banks' library, with the doctor's two closest friends and associates, Judge Oscar Muehller and Banker Ezra Bassett. Dr. Banks was a widower, now. His three daughters were married; they had done well in their marriages. He had six grandchildren. He loved them all dearly; he loved them almost as much as he loved his money. He was in his sixties, yet appeared much younger, so plump and ruddy was he, so interested and urbane of manner. Though he had learned nothing for twenty-five years, and smiled indulgently at the "germ theory," he was still the fashionable physician in Andersburg. His fat white hand gently stroked his white beard as he regarded Eugene intently.

Mr. Bassett was, as he would admit with a chuckle, "staring old age in the face." He, too, had no complaint to make of life. Still rosy, still radiant, still beaming with good-temper, he looked at Eugene with the friendliest of smiles.

Time had increased the saintliness of Judge Muehller; the years had refined even the original refinement, so that he was a silvery wisp of a tall old man.

A love for money, the possession of money, is a great preservative, thought Eugene, amused. All the original members of the board of directors, and all the officers of the Prescott Lumber Company, were still alive, and flourishing in bright autumn health, full of peace of mind, prosperity and zest, admired and honored by their neighbors, respected by their pastors. In short, they had attained that blissful state somewhat optimistically promised by religion to the pure in heart, the meek, and the merciful.

The firelight fluttered on the marble hearth of the library,

danced on the red and blue and brown and gold backs of
the morocco-bound books on the walls, joined with soft
lamplight to give the room richness, comfort and peace.
Dr. Banks' dinner had been excellent; later on, the two other
old gentlemen had joined the doctor and Eugene for brandy,
and for a very important discussion. The strong winds of
spring had been muffled by leaded windows and thick velvet
draperies. The sweet incense of cigar smoke rose tranquilly
in the warmth of the library. Eugene looked about the room.
His fleshless fingers tapped the briefcase on his knee.

He was one with these old men. He was, like themselves,
a gentleman. During the past five years, he had served them
well, and they knew he served them for his own purposes.
They approved of him heartily.

He had just finished outlining to them the national industrial and financial picture during the past five years. He
spoke quietly and dispassionately. They kept nodding.

"More and more," Eugene had just said, "and despite the
anti-Trust laws passed in the eighties, industrialization is
inexorably moving towards a concentration of ownership.
Laws can do nothing against the progress of industry and
finance; laws are impotent against a natural process. The
greatest five or six trusts in the country have now a capitiliza-
tion of nearly three billion dollars; they employ nearly three-
fourths of all the workers, and will soon produce at least
four-fifths of all commodities. Despite radical laws, centraliza-
tion is a fact. It is a natural and healthy process."

The three old heads nodded with sublime approval and
understanding. Eugene's voice continued, not stirring the
smoke-and-brandy-and-fire-scented air. His voice, if without
emphasis, was firm; it had authority. No business could exist
without amalgamating itself with other industries. William
Prescott at first had understood that fully. That is why the
Prescott Lumber Company had become so unbelievably prosperous. Later, William had lost courage, had attempted, with
more or less success, to make his company self-sufficient,
an island outside the trend towards increasing concentration.
In short, he was now doing what his associates had urged
him to do over twenty years ago. They had been wrong, and
they now realized it. He had been right, and was now wrong.
His fear was keeping profits down. He had lost that progres-
siveness which had enriched them all. The company was still
very prosperous, but it was steadily and inevitably coming
to a standstill. It would soon retrogress. As yet, his associates

and officers could do nothing. They could do nothing as long as he was president of the Prescott Lumber Company.

Eugene ceased speaking. The heads still nodded, but now with deep gravity. Eugene laughed faintly.

William was no longer investing, in the name of the company, in large corporations. He was frightened; his illness had frightened him even more. What investments he made, as in railroads, he made with his own money. He was speculating dangerously, recklessly. In railroads, especially, and railroads were a very volatile business. His family was a fabulous drain upon him. He lived as opulently as a prince, but his salary was not sufficient to meet the endless needs and demands of his children, for whom he was now spending his capital as well as his salary. There were signs that he was losing his head. At the present time, Mr. Regan was "carrying" him. So far, Mr. Regan held, as collateral, nearly twenty percent of William's fifty-one percent of the Prescott stock.

Dr. Banks interrupted: "You are certain of your facts, Gene?" Eugene looked down at his brief-case. "Certainly, Doctor," he replied, coldly. "I never speak without facts." Now he smiled at them. "You are thinking that I'm an excellent spy, though, of course, you were too gentlemanly to ask me for my sources of information."

"Oh, good Heavens!" exclaimed Judge Muehller. "Incredible of you to imply, Gene——"

"Incredible," murmured Dr. Banks.

"I cannot believe you are serious, Gene," said Mr. Bassett, much wounded.

"I have only the interest of the company at heart," suggested Eugene, piously.

"Certainly. Certainly! It's superfluous of you to mention that," said the judge.

Eugene nodded, seriously. "I beg your pardon," he said. He continued: "Prescott is trying to create independent fortunes and estates for his sons and his daughters. That is all that obsesses him now. He wants 'security' for them, he has told me. He has no liquid assets, to amount to anything; I know that, without mere speculation. Nevertheless, he continues to plunge. He will continue to put up his stock as collateral. And now for a prophecy, gentlemen. During the past ten years or so, we have survived several depressions. Prescott might not survive the next. I prophesy that by the fall of this year we shall have a really serious depression; short, perhaps, but devastating while it lasts. When that happens, friend or no friend, Regan will ask Prescott for more collateral." Eugene paused. "After all, Mr. Regan is a financier. He cannot be expected to carry even friends without substantial collateral. For I feel that the drop in the market this fall will be only a prelude to a prolonged depression some time within the next five or six years. This country has overexpanded in the manufacture of commodities. Our population—especially the flood of immigrants—is, as yet, unable to absorb all we manufacture. We are not strong enough—as yet—to battle England and Germany for new markets. So, before we can adjust ourselves, before we can absorb what we are manufacturing, before we can secure new markets, there are bound to be a number of serious depressions."

The others, remembering their own wide personal investments, became acutely uneasy. They frowned at Eugene, who smiled at them blandly.

"I hope your predictions are wrong," said the judge, briefly.

"No, I am afraid they are right," said Eugene. "However, gentlemen, I am certain that you, yourselves, need have no fear. I am certain your investments are sound. Your only worry need be about the Prescott Lumber Company. And yet, it need not be a worry. It may be a fine opportunity—to get rid of William Prescott, who is no longer an asset, or will no longer be an asset—to the company. Our time will come within five to seven years, perhaps sooner. We must be ready. We must be prepared to buy back, from Regan, the stock which Prescott has put up as collateral for his speculations."

Mr. Bassett, recovered from his fright, chuckled. "Mr. Regan is a banker, after all," he said, with brotherly fondness.

"It may not be possible to get rid of William Prescott immediately," remarked Eugene, almost idly. "He still has eighty percent of his stock. It depends upon how frightened he becomes, how desperately he needs money for his children, how much he loses his head. I doubt that he will attempt to cut down his lavish ways of living, or that he will deny his children anything."

"They always were worthless," said Judge Muehller.

"He intends to bring Thomas into the business," said Eugene, reflectively. "Now, Thomas! I think he will be an asset; in a minor capacity, of course. But definitely an asset. I think we can count on Tom Prescott, gentlemen."

Mr. Bassett nodded. "I talked to him at their Christmas party," he said. "A very sound mind, that young man has. No foolishnesses. Not capricious or unstable."

"And with excellent ideas about money," said Dr. Banks.

He laughed richly. "And no particular love for his dad, either. Shows he has a mind, and self-respect."

"As for Matthew Prescott, we need not consider him at all," suggested Eugene.

Mr. Bassett pursed his lips. He cleared his throat. "You wouldn't know, of course, Gene, what—er—provision he has made for Oliver? But, of course, it is foolish of me to ask."

"It isn't foolish at all, Mr. Bassett," replied Eugene. "A very pertinent question. It happens that I know. He has made a bequest to Oliver, in his will, of five thousand dollars. Nothing else."

The others were astonished.

Eugene nodded. "After all, Oliver is not his son. He has educated him. Oliver will be graduated from Harvard this spring. He is equipped to earn his living. Without doubt, Prescott will set him up in an office, and assist him for a while. And then, of course, there is that five thousand dollars, too."

He added: "There is a trust fund for Mrs. Prescott. But the major part of the estate, whatever it may be at the time of his death, is to be divided equally among his two daughters and two sons."

"At the rate he is going," laughed the banker, "there will be precious little left in the estate. Incidentally, Eli, what is the condition of William's health, at the present time?"

"Now that is a very hard thing for me to answer," said the doctor. He winked. "I presume you mean how long do I think he'll live? Frankly, I don't know. He may not have another attack for a long time, or ever. It all depends on how he controls his temper and his feelings."

"He has never been able to control his emotions," said Eugene. "He is like a man trying to drive a dozen wild horses all at once. They'll kill him, yet."

"I am afraid so," agreed Dr. Banks, very gravely. He sighed. "A very dangerous man to have at the head of a business."

The others looked intently at the fire. Eugene's eyes narrowed, as they studied each averted profile in turn.

Again, the doctor sighed; the others sighed with him. This was almost too much for Eugene. He had to clench his teeth to keep from laughing outright.

He said, almost softly, "You were friends of my father. He was your friend." He paused. He smiled a little. "We are all friends together. My father would have liked that. End of the circle, you might say."

Mr. Bassett moved his head so suddenly that the lamplight was like a flash of lightning on his rimless glasses.

"Eh? Ah, yes," said Dr. Banks. "Dear friends—of course, Gene. We always knew you had it in you."

"Thank you," said Eugene, with the utmost courtesy.

"We knew," said the saintly judge, "that nothing would ever be beyond you, Gene."

"Nothing ever will be," Eugene assured them.

Mr. Bassett was not certain he liked that smooth tone. He said: "In consideration—ah—of how we have all worked together for the good of the company, and in consideration of the invaluable services you have rendered the company, we believe, in the not too distant future, I hope——"

For the first time, he was inextricably wound up in the circumlocutions of his own banker's idiom, and he stumbled helplessly.

"Yes?" prompted Eugene, calmly.

By nature, and profession, Mr. Bassett could not be specific and decisive in speech. He looked eloquently at his friends. Judge Muehller resembled the statue of an old Roman senator, worn and refined by suffering in the service of his country. Naturally, such an old Roman could not be expected to speak of mundane affairs. He left that to Mr. Bassett and Dr. Banks. As for Dr. Banks, he managed to put his fingertips together benignly, and to look over them at Eugene.

"My boy," he said, sonorously, "what is it you have in mind? We must do justice to you, of course, though nothing, I am sure, could carry with it more responsibility—and salary —than the position of general manager of the mills. Some stock, perhaps——"

Eugene made no gesture of impatience; he did not stir. Yet Dr. Banks' voice faded into fluttering silence.

"Gentlemen," said Eugene, in the gentlest of tones, "I have a little over fifty thousand dollars, carefully and conservatively invested, and ten thousand in cash."

"Remarkable!" the banker could not help exclaiming, with respect. The others, too, showed their admiration.

"That isn't, however, a tremendous amount of money," said Eugene. "And so, gentlemen, in view of what I have done and shall do in the future I really expect to be voted the next president of the Prescott Lumber Company. I might point out to you that there is no question of my ability."

The others stared at him dumbfounded, unable to speak. Three pairs of old eyes regarded him incredulously, and with anger.

"You really have no one else," said Eugene, tranquilly. "Your sons, Judge Muehller? Your sons-in-law, Dr. Banks? Yours, Mr. Bassett?" Again, he coughed. "A hard question, this, but will any one of you gentlemen, in the future, be able to assume the responsibilities and rigors and work of the position I wish to have?"

They could not answer him. But each old head was craned towards him, every eye was grim.

"Have any of the younger men of whom you are thinking, gentlemen, the capabilities and the knowledge of the industry which I have? Or, do you think such a—relative—might act as a mere figurehead for you? No, no, gentlemen. That is something I couldn't, and shouldn't want to, believe. That is something I shouldn't—forgive me—permit."

"You—wouldn't permit?" faltered the doctor, hoarsely.

"Really, Eugene," said Mr. Bassett, deeply hurt.

The judge sighed. "Your language, sir," he said, and touched the long black ribbon that hung from his spectacles.

"I said—permit," repeated Eugene, indifferently. "But I'd rather not take advantage of you, gentlemen. I believe in being very frank. You see, I intend to marry Mr. Prescott's daughter, Julia."

The old men sat as still as wax models of themselves. The firelight was two silent pools on Mr. Bassett's glasses. The judge's hand stayed on the black ribbon; the doctor's fingertips were frozen together. Only the fire stirred.

"Your next question," said Eugene, softly, after several long moments had gone by, "is this: Does Mr. Prescott know it? My answer is: No. You see, I am very candid about my affairs. We have all been very candid, have we not? Once I was a clerk, and I kept the minutes. I have retained that somewhat superfluous habit, and I still keep minutes. In order, gentlemen, that we may, at a moment's notice, be able to refer to any past meeting of ours. So, when I arrive home, I'll write out the minutes of this meeting, as I have written out the minutes of all the others, and I'll put in your unspoken question, and I shall answer: 'No, Mr. Prescott has not yet been informed of my engagement to Miss Julia. When the time comes, he shall be so informed.' And should the need ever arise, he may read these minutes freely, as he may read all the others—should the need ever arise."

He stopped. The silence was not broken. Eugene looked absently at the fire, as if he were alone.

He said, almost inaudibly: "I have sixty thousand dollars. I also have some influence in New York. Mrs. Prescott has, I believe, personally saved nearly one hundred thousand dollars, neatly invested, upon good advice from a husband who did not use good advice himself. All in all, with what Mr. Prescott still has, we might go a long way towards redeeming considerable of his stock—I mean, if he ever wished to do so, or was assured that he must do so immediately for the sake of himself and of his children. For the sake of those children, if he saw their future even distantly threatened, he could be restrained from any madness, even speculation."

And now the old men knew that this was not just a brilliant younger man, one of themselves, of their own tradition, to be used and rewarded, generously, in their own way, but a man more terrible than William Prescott had ever been, a man far more ruthless and exigent, and utterly beyond appeal. They had not used him; he had used them.

Mr. Bassett made several attempts to speak, and could only half-whisper: "What if William refuses——"

"He won't," said Eugene, and smiled at them oddly.

"You are very sure of yourself, young man," said Dr. Banks, in a vicious tone which none of his fashionable patients had ever heard him use.

"I am, yes, Doctor. I have to be. And now, gentlemen, I wish to be frank again. It doesn't matter to me who helps me get what I want. It can be you; it can be Mr. Prescott. The decision is yours to make. Candidly, it would be easier for me to choose Mr. Prescott. He once told me that five percent of his Prescott stock will go to each of his daughters, upon her marriage. When I am married to Julia, and am a member of the family, it will be very easy to—assist—Mr. Prescott in every way."

It was the judge's cold legal mind which thrust out from the disorder of the thoughts of the others: "Then, why, my dear Gene, have you bothered with us, in the first place?"

"A good question," agreed Eugene, inclining his head courteously. "In the beginning, there was no thought of marrying Julia. Now there is Julia."

"You have plotted a long time," muttered Dr. Banks, breaking the silence that followed Eugene's words. None of them looked at Eugene now; every face, even the judge's, was unhealthily flushed.

"Not plotted—planned," said Eugene. He studied each old man in turn. He was very amused. "I'm not sentimental, gentlemen. But I love neatness."

He stood up. He was no longer a thin young man, their junior in scheming, their spy, their outpost, for whom they felt a paternal fondness and more than a little patronage. He was now their master. This man did not need them at all.

Eugene bowed to Dr. Banks, and thanked him for a delightful dinner. He bowed to each of the other old men. He did not expect them to extend their hands to him. In fact, his manner forbade them to do so.

"Good evening, gentlemen," he said, formally, and went out of the library.

For a long time the old men did not speak. With a hand that trembled Dr. Banks lit another cigar. The judge slowly pulled his glasses from his eyes. Mr. Bassett brooded at the fire.

He said, not turning to the others: "We've been had."

"Yes," said the judge, "and in a most thorough fashion. I might say, Ezra, and to you, Eli, that there is nothing we can do about it; no, nothing at all. We could not stop, even if we wished to do so. And I do not think we wish to do so?"

Dr. Banks said: "We ought to have known. We were fools. This is a bad man, this Eugene Arnold. It was always before our eyes."

CHAPTER XL

WITHIN A FEW DAYS, the boys, Thomas and Matthew, and Oliver, would be home. Barbara was not concerned with the return of her brothers. Her one obsession was Oliver. It was delightful now, as well as disturbing, to come to this high terrace above the city to think of Oliver. I am seventeen, she thought; I am not too young to think of Oliver, though he apparently is of that opinion. Or is it only that? Am I nothing to him? He calls me "sister." I am not his sister.

There had lately come to Barbara a sickening and most terrifying idea, and there was no one whom she could consult about it without betraying herself and Oliver.

Late May had thrown over the scene below her the most vivid curtain of green and silver and purple. No ripple or movement disturbed the river, so that it seemed carved of one great emerald cunningly cut to fit the contours of the twisted land along it which, in the shining air, was a confused mass of green, brown, white, black and yellow. The flat-boats and river steamers appeared not to move, but to be motionlessly super-imposed upon the water. Long plumes of smoke stood upright, did not drift, over the vessels, over the countless chimneys of Andersburg. The mountains in the distance were all amethyst and bright green, standing against purest blue. Whiffs of pine-scent, of wood violets, old leaves, sweet earth and grass, came to Barbara; the sun was warm on her shoulders, on her uncovered and blowing dark hair. It was not a girl's face, but a woman's, that stared down so somberly at the city and river below.

To ordinary ears, it might be quiet here on the mountain. But Barbara knew the voices of trees and grass and earth. Nevertheless, after a long time, she became aware that she had unconsciously been overhearing human voices also, the voices of people shut away from her by the curtain of pines behind her. Annoyed at this invasion of her privacy, she was about to get up and let the speakers see her, when she realized that the voices were familiar, that they were the voices of her sister, Julia, and Eugene Arnold.

"Dear Julie," said Eugene, in a very gentle voice, "all
299

that you say may be true, and it is true that Mr. Prescott has been very kind to me lately, kinder than usual. Yet I am still doubtful, and more than doubtful, how he will receive the news that you—that we—want to be married. Now, wait a minute, Julie. Let me talk a little. Let's be sensible. I've told you over and over that I'm not going to jeopardize my position by antagonizing your father—not even for you, and ——" Here he paused. He must have been looking at Julia intently, for there was a sharp silence. "Julie," he continued, in a different and rougher voice, "I want to be honest with you. I've always liked you, been fond of you. For a long time I've thought of marrying you. It's only lately that I've come to know that I love you. I don't know how it happened, but I do, and I'm not friendly to the idea. However, I want what I want even more; what I want is more important to me than you are."

"How can you be so horrible!" cried Julia, and it was evident from the break in her voice that she had been crying. "It seems to me that if you love someone that's the only important thing."

"You talk like a woman," said Eugene, impatiently. "What do you know about anything, Julie? What do you know about my life, before you were born, all the things I thought about, and wanted? They are there, and they always will be there. I'm not going to break the pattern, just because of you."

"What pattern?" demanded Julia. It was not her usual petulant tone, rebellious of anything denied, but an imploring one, heartbroken and desperate.

Again, there was a silence. After a long time, Eugene said: "I can't tell you, Julie." He must have turned away from her, for his voice was muffled.

Julia had apparently followed him, made him face her. "I know!" she exclaimed. "It's because of your father! Papa took away your father's business. You can't forgive him that! Oh, how silly you are, Eugene! It happened so long ago."

"You're wrong," he said. "My father deserved to lose his business. He wasn't the man your father is. I admire your father; I always did." He said, in a very peculiar voice: "You won't understand this, but to me it is the most important thing in life. Weak men deserve to lose what they have. Better men should have it."

"I don't know what you're talking about!" Julia was sobbing now. "You admit you don't resent Papa. Eugene, you are confused. You feel one thing, and say another."

"No." He was very quiet now. "It's impossible to tell

you, Julia, to make you understand. You see, Julie, I *must*
have what I've always wanted."

Julia was very still. She said, quietly: "You want what
Papa has. Yes, that's it, Eugene. And you can have it, by
marrying me. That was your original idea. And Papa will
be agreeable; if not just yet, very soon, I know. So why do
you torment me?"

"That's just it, Julie. I don't know. And until I'm sure,
I'm not going to speak, or allow you to speak. If you say
anything to your father, and he becomes enraged, that'll
be the end of me, even if I say nothing. And you'll never
see me again, Julie."

Again, there was no sound but the soft mournful wind
in the pines, the rustle of bird-wings and of the grass. Barbara
stood there, petrified.

Then Julia's voice, changed and torn and anguished, broke
the silence: "Oh, if he'd only die! If only he'd die!"

Oh! thought Barbara, sickened.

She heard Eugene laugh. "That, I admit, would solve a
number of problems. You don't know how many problems
that would solve, Julie. In the meantime, there's no getting
around our problem."

Hatred filled Barbara. She wanted to go and confront these
two, and denounce them. She had heard too much.

Cautiously, she approached the pine-curtain. She looked
through the furry and tangled boughs. Julia, agitated and
weeping, was standing a little distance from Eugene, in her
crimson wool suit and broad crimson velvet hat with the
cream-colored plumes. Her auburn pompadour sparkled with
golden threads in the vivid sun. Her delicate skin was flushed
with emotion and tears, and her trembling mouth, scarlet
and moist, was quivering. The sunlight had turned her wet
eyes to pure bright yellow. She was wringing her gloved hands.

Barbara saw Eugene clearly. He did not have his usual
courtly and sardonic air. He was resisting something, and
it took all his strength. He was resisting Julia.

"It means nothing to you that I love you!" sobbed Julia,
and even Barbara, involved in her own disgusted hatred, knew
that Julia was suffering unbearably.

"It means more than you'll ever know, you little fool,"
replied Eugene. He was not going to touch Julia if he could
help it.

"Oh, you are so clever!" said Julia, with tortured bitterness.
"You always have ideas. Have one now—for me. Gene, I
can't stand this."

"There is nothing I can do, Julie. You've done what you can. You've told me that your father admits he was wrong in distrusting me." Only Barbara heard the faintly vicious undertone in his voice, the ridicule. His voice, when he spoke again, was level, but he was watching Julia. "You've asked me to help you, Julie. Do you mean that?"

"Oh, Gene," she said, with utter weariness and misery.

"Well, then, Julie, just suppose something—incredible. Suppose it were possible for me to ruin your father—— Of course, it is all absurd, but perhaps I am testing you. Suppose I could take away from your father everything he has gained. Reduce him to nothing. Suppose, in so doing, it should be possible to tell him we were going to be married. Would you be willing for all this to happen, just so that you could marry me without losing anything, without my losing anything?"

Julia's hands parted; she dropped them to her side. Her eyes fixed themselves almost fiercely upon Eugene.

"You couldn't—do it—Gene," she stammered.

"And, if I could, Julie?" he said, softly.

She turned very white. She stood and stared at Eugene, her whole slender body as rigid as wood.

All at once, Eugene laughed. Even if it was indulgent, it was a very unpleasant sound. "Julie," he said, "if you had said 'yes', I'd have thought you a fool. And you'd have gone down in my estimation. You must have substance behind you; you must have money. I must have money, too, and something else."

Julia said nothing. She had not recovered her color. But she, in turn, was watching Eugene.

"It would not be so bad for you, naturally, if I were able, by fair means or foul, to take from your father what he has, provided it was not done before we were married," said Eugene, very lightly. "You wouldn't, then, be 'humiliated'. To do it before—well, you don't trust me, do you, Julie?"

Barbara never expected to hear Julia speak the truth, but she heard her sister speak truly when the older girl said: "No, Gene, I don't trust you. I don't suppose I ever did. I don't suppose I ever shall."

He was not offended. He came still closer to her. "I can return the compliment, Julia: I don't trust you, either." It was not possible to say that that dry face softened, but it became less unrelenting. "We can trust each other in the small things, say, like 'love', but not in the larger things, like money."

Julia pressed her gloved palms together, and looked down

at them. Her lovely face was pale and somber. "I trust that you really love me, Gene."

"Yes, Julie, you can believe that."

"But it isn't enough?"

"No, Julie."

Julia began to cry again, hopelessly. Gene did not move. He only looked at her. "Don't try to understand," he said at last. "You can't." He waited until she had wiped her eyes. She stared at him intently. A sort of flash passed over her face, and her mouth, usually so soft and full, became hard in spite of her sudden smile.

"I have an idea!" she cried. "I shan't tell you what it is, Gene. And it won't hurt you. I promise you that. I know if anything ever hurt you you'd never forgive me."

Eugene was silent. He took a cigarette from his pocket, struck a match and lit it. The smoke coiled slowly in the brilliant sunshine. He continued to smoke, while Julia's smile became fixed, brighter.

She said, at last: "How would it be if Papa suggested to you that he wouldn't mind your marrying me?"

"I can't conceive of anything more impossible," he replied, flatly.

She laughed, and the sound was sweet and amused. "I can, Gene. Please leave it to me."

She ran to him then and threw her arms about his neck. His arms remained at his side, even though she pressed herself against him. Barbara could see her face, moved, electrified, full of passion and love. Then Eugene, again as if against his will, lifted his arms and put them about the girl. She pressed her face into his shoulder and incoherent sounds came from her.

Barbara was very young. She realized how young she really was when she thought, marvelling: It is possible for such as these to love each other! Slowly, she dropped the branches of the pine tree, and retreated. She was filled with pity for Julia, and even for Eugene, while she despised and rejected them both.

She heard Eugene's voice, rough and tired: "Dear Julie. Darling Julie."

Barbara sat down on the warm flat rocks. She bent her head so that it touched her knees. Oliver, she thought. Dear Oliver.

The warm wind ran over her. The sun was hot on her bowed back. When she finally lifted her head, she knew that Eugene and Julia had gone.

CHAPTER XLI

THERE WAS SOMETHING about Matthew which hugely and acutely annoyed his twin, Thomas. Never, even in their earliest childhood, had there been that "closeness" which William had sentimentally believed ought to be active between twins, and which, even now, he sometimes tried to believe existed, and spoke of to Ursula.

William firmly believed that children, if only "adults would let them alone," had a natural affinity for one another. Ursula had often suggested to him that brothers might hate each other. This, even when it flourished openly before him, William had furiously refused to believe.

Thomas despised Matthew, not only because his twin was an enigma, but because of Matthew's negation of life. Thomas, cunning and exuberant, and very realistic, found Matthew's passivity and silences repulsive. Moreover, he hated what he could not fully understand.

Thomas enjoyed the Christmas holidays. He enjoyed the excitement; he particularly enjoyed the gifts, lavish from his father, prudent but adequate from his mother. He liked people about him, and parties, and gaiety and excitement; he was popular with his contemporaries, which emphasized the truth that it is not necessary to have love for one's fellows to be admired and sought after by them. If one thought well of oneself, one's gifts, however inexpensive, were treasured and had an aura of charm.

This year Matthew had actually brought himself to buy something for everyone in the family, even for Oliver. He had a most extraordinary imagination; the colorlessness of his gifts could be attributed only to his indifference. Thomas was not forgotten by his twin; Matthew gave him a rather good leather wallet, thriftily stuffed with tissue, much to Thomas' annoyance.

But Matthew, to the amazement of the family, gave Oliver a really astonishing gift. It was a miniature of Voltaire, exquisitely executed, old and authentic. No one was more astounded than was Oliver. He could not recall a single instance when

Matthew had spoken to him voluntarily, or given him a present, or shown the slightest interest in him.

The empty wallet, however, had greatly irritated Thomas. He knew that Matthew received an allowance as large as his own, and he suspected that additional money often found its way to him from the pathetic William, who tried to use money as a path to his silent son. There was no excuse, thought Thomas, for the tissue paper. A yellow note, at least, ought to have been included. It was with this in mind that he rudely, and without knocking, entered Matthew's austere room. Matthew was sitting by the window, looking out at the landscape, his elbow on the window sill. Snow was falling heavily; in the dusk the distant lamps on Schiller Road were blurs of indistinct gold. As it was the day after Christmas an apathy lay over the great dark house, a surfeit. Even the crackling fires on every hearth did not lift the gloom.

"Look," said Thomas, without any preliminaries, "I'm grateful for the wallet, but you might have included a little money. I'm broke. You aren't. You never are. You're a miser, but you might have remembered that I'm not."

Matthew slowly turned his head. His face, because the lamps had not been lit, was in darkness, but Thomas felt the queer aloofness of his brother's eyes, the rejection.

"What did you give me?" he asked, with indifference.

Thomas' large red face became even redder. "What can anyone give you?" he blustered. "You never seem to want anything. And you're so damn precious it would take too much time to think what you'd want. So I sent you a card."

Matthew was silent.

Thomas withdrew the wallet, regarded it with angry bitterness. He tossed it upon the table. "Keep it," he said, all his strong aversion for his brother in his loud rough voice. "You have money for it. You need it more than I do."

Still, Matthew did not speak. About the room, against the wall, canvases stood in ghostly array. Not one had been completed. The canvas on the easel bore a few slashes of color; they were dry and formless. Thomas glared at the wallet, then, with an ugly word, he picked it up again and put it back in his pocket. He stood there, big and hulking, his large round head thrust out like a bull's. "I'll keep it," he said ungraciously. "One of these days I might have a little money to put in it."

Matthew turned back to his contemplation of the white and lonely landscape. The spruces and pines bent under the snow. Thomas felt that he had been dismissed. He became enraged.

"Don't you think anyone ever becomes tired of your imitating a monk?" he demanded. "What a poseur you are!" Matthew did not answer. Thomas brought out some matches. He made considerable noise lighting the lamps, and he enjoyed seeing Matthew wince as, one by one, the lamps gushed into light.

Matthew blinked and shrank. His voice was always faint and distant; now there was a tremble in it. "I never bothered you," he said. "Why do you bother me? I never asked anything of anyone but to be let alone."

"Another of your poses! If Pa really did let you alone, and forgot your existence, which you pretend you want him to do, you'd soon be stirred up. What! No checks? No presents? No extra cash for your damned etchings and such? What a howl you'd raise!"

Thomas was really aroused. "I know all about you!" he railed. "You flunked this semester, didn't you? You and your 'genius'. Wait till Pa gets the happy news. But what do you care? You'll go back, and repeat your subjects, and fail again. You'll always fail. D'you know that?"

Matthew's dull face did not change. He merely looked down at the long white hands spread on the arms of the chair. "Yes," he said, almost inaudibly. "I know that. Yes, I know that."

Thomas was taken aback at this lifeless admission. "You don't care?" he taunted.

"Not particularly," replied Matthew. It came to Thomas then that this was the first real conversation he had ever had with his brother, and it excited him.

"Why don't you care?"

Matthew lifted his right hand, studied the back of it, then the palm. "Because I can't," he said. "It doesn't matter to me whatever happens. It never did."

"You'd care all right if you had to get out and earn your living," said Thomas. He thrust aside some books, sat on the table, swinging one of his big stout legs. He pulled out a box of cigarettes, struck a match loudly, and began to smoke. Matthew appeared to have forgotten his presence. Thomas let one large boot kick the leg of the table. "I have what they call intuition," he said, in a jeering voice. "I don't think Pa's doing so well. They call it 'hanging on the ropes'. Maybe I'm wrong; I hope, for my sake, that I am. But maybe I'm right. What'll you do then? Go on sitting in the twilight somewhere, in a garret, staring at the landscape? Even you, with your fancy ways, have to eat. What then?"

Matthew did not answer. Thomas said: "Ma's got a nice nest-egg tucked away. I found that out, too. But will she shell it out to us? You can bet not! Not Ma! She's known all about us for a long time. Ma's no fool. You can lally-dally around, and Ma'll say: 'Roll up your sleeves, Matt, and get to work.' Will you roll 'em up?"

"Will *you?*" Matthew's voice, for the first time, had quickened. He regarded his brother, not with his usual bemused expression, but with one faintly sharpened.

"Me?" said Thomas. He puffed out a huge cloud of smoke, stared at the ceiling. "Sure. I can roll up my sleeves. I'm not afraid of living. And there's always a way." He looked at his brother. "Ever think of Gene Arnold, feathering his nest? Julie's soft on him. I hate his guts, but if Julia gets him she's got somebody. And she's not going to forget Tom Prescott. Because nobody's ever going to forget me. I'm not going to let 'em. But she'll forget you. And good for her."

Matthew's eyes moved about the canvases stacked against the wall. Thomas watched him. "You and your paintings!" he exclaimed. "Think you can make a living at it? You never completed anything in your life, except maybe one or two daubs you've hidden away."

Matthew did not answer.

Thomas pointed the cigarette at him. "Know what I'm going to do? I'm not going back to Yale. I'm going into the lumber business. Pa will hear about it, in a day or two. He's going to shout, but that doesn't matter to me. I want the lumber business. And I'm going into the business so that I can get part of it from Gene Arnold, who's after it."

Matthew moved very slightly. "You talk like a fool, Tom. Arnold's only Father's general manager. What makes you think he can do anything?"

Thomas gloated. So, he had aroused that image, had he? "Just intuition," he replied, airily. "I'm not a fool. I've been watching that cut-throat for years. He's after something. And Pa trusts him. But then, Pa always was stupid. I found that out when I was a kid. Who gives a damn for him, except Ma and old Oliver? He thinks he is surrounded by a big and loving family. Let him have his delusions."

Matthew now appeared both bored and tired. "I don't believe you, Tom. Father isn't bankrupt. Look at this house. Look at the money he spends. Incidentally, now that we are exchanging confidences, I might as well tell you that I'm not going back to Princeton."

Thomas stared. "You aren't?" He burst out laughing. "Don't shock me. You aren't going to work, are you? In the lumber business?"

Distaste made fine wrinkles spring out about Matthew's eyes. "No. I want to go to Italy. I've never forgotten Italy. I can live cheaply there. I," and his voice became very dim, "can live there." He paused.

"Italy!" roared Thomas.

Matthew closed his eyes, leaned his head back against his chair. "Italy," he repeated, softly.

Thomas stood up. He threw his cigarette into the fire. "I'm going to enjoy this," he said. "We must have a fine education, Pa says. We must be educated like gentlemen, Pa says. After my education, I can go into the business. And you're going to Italy. That ought to gratify Pa no end. One of his darling children leaving him!"

Matthew turned his head aside. "I'm very tired," he murmured. "Would you mind leaving me, Tom?"

After Thomas had stamped away, Matthew resumed his slow and interrupted thoughts. He completely forgot his brother; he forgot what Thomas had said to him. He had this capacity to forget things. He could even forget himself, for to himself, he was a weariness, a great tiredness that filled not only his own mind but the whole universe.

What can anyone do, he thought, who has never had a reason for living? Someone who, from earliest childhood, had had all reason for living taken away from him? For what could one strive, when there was no incentive to strive? To have no motive, no urge for existence; that was life in death. There was such a thing as smothering in gratification. I am not reproaching my father too much but, by giving me whatever I wished, he flattened life for me, destroyed in me all desire. I was told I was perfect. I now know that I am not perfect, that I am no genius. My only hope is to acknowledge this, to go away and let my imperfections plague and torment me, arouse in me the impulse to live. I don't want to die. Or, do I? Is it possible that a man might kill himself because he had given him instantly all that he ever coveted or dreamed?

Matthew was now overcome by a real emotion of terror, but it was a terror he welcomed with a kind of exultation. The instinct of self-preservation had, then, not been entirely killed in him! He still wished to live. But if he was to live, he must go away, as soon as possible. He thought of Italy now as the land of his salvation. He might never paint there; his creative impulses might have been destroyed forever. He might be only a ghost in a land which teemed with creative spirits that had never really died. At least, in Italy he would see all his imperfections clearly, all his inferiorities, all his smallnesses.

He thought of what Thomas had told him. It did not matter. The collapse of the family fortune meant little to him; the misery of his family did not move him; he cared for no member of it. He wished only to survive, himself. It had become a desperation in him. To this had he been reduced by excessive love and indulgence.

He heard a soft knock upon his door. He sat very still. If he pretended to be asleep, or absent, whoever knocked would go away. But the door, after a second knocking, opened. Oliver stood there, smiling quietly. "Hello, Matt," he said.

Matthew did not reply. Oliver came in, shutting the door behind him. Oliver said: "I came to thank you for the miniature. How did you know I admired Voltaire so much?"

It was an effort to Matthew to reply, even indifferently: "I saw your books, years ago. I remembered."

Oliver sat down, quietly and easily. His dark eyes regarded Matthew with thoughtfulness. "It was a wonderful thing for you to remember, and I'm grateful."

Matthew lifted a hand in acknowledgment; it was a weary gesture. Abruptly, he said: "I am going away. To Italy."

Matthew was astounded at his own words. He was even more astounded that he could speak so to Oliver, for his foster brother had been even less to him than his own family. In enormous confusion, he tried to remember how he had come to buy that miniature for Oliver, for never before had he given him a gift.

"Italy," repeated Oliver, reflectively.

"You don't think the idea is stupid?" asked Matthew, with an effort.

"Stupid? No. Why should I think that?"

Matthew was silent. He studied the backs of his hands, the fingers and palms, in that familiar way of his. He waited for the tiredness to return to him, the tiredness that always came when a member of the family spoke to him. It did not come. He said, haltingly; "I must go to Italy." He looked at Oliver. "I may have some difficulty with my father. Mother is fond of you. Would you speak to her for me?" An expression of bitterness, entirely alien to him, touched his face.

"Mother," said Matthew, "always has such 'common-sense'. Why hasn't anyone told her that 'common-sense' is frequently just a lack of imagination?"

Oliver said calmly: "Of course, if you want me to, I'll speak to her. Though I think it might help if you did, too. I'm sorry, but I don't think Mother lacks imagination. Perhaps you've forgotten, Matt, that it was she who insisted on taking you to Italy again, three years ago."

"I had forgotten," muttered Matthew.

"I think she'll be glad," added Oliver. But all at once he did not believe it. If William objected strenuously to his son's leaving for an indefinite time, Ursula would immediately take William's side, despite any convictions she might have. She had long ago ceased to fight for her children. Her husband, alone, existed for her now. I must speak to her, thought Oliver, frowning.

Matthew's voice had always been dim and uninterested, and it surprised Oliver to hear a sudden desperate note in the younger man's voice: "You see, I've got to go. It doesn't matter who objects, though I hate scenes and noises. It's a matter of life and death to me. I don't know where I'll get the money to go but, if necessary, I'll sell everything I have."

Oliver was quiet for some moments, then he said: "That might not be necessary. I've never spent all of my allowance. I have saved about four thousand dollars. It's yours, Matt, if you want it."

Matthew stared at him, stupefied. He leaned forward toward Oliver. He stammered: "Thank—you. I don't know how to thank you." He looked at Oliver with a curious intentness, as if seeing him for the first time. "I—think you understand. Don't you?"

"Yes," said Oliver.

Matthew's hands moved restlessly. He stood up. He walked about the room. He lifted one canvas after another, dropped it back with a dull thud. He looked at the one on the easel. "I'll never paint again," he said.

"You might," said Oliver. "But even that doesn't matter, if you once learn how to live, or want to live."

He was startled when Matthew, who always moved so slowly, swung upon him, his light blue eyes astonishingly vivid. "I wasn't wrong!" he cried. "You do understand."

Oliver went on, as if Matthew had not spoken: "Even more important, you might possibly understand that others are living, too, that others have importance, also. In fact, I believe it's more necessary to understand that than it is to want to live, yourself. You can't affirm living without the affirmation of universal life, also."

Oliver stood up. "You're not alone, Matt. You may think you are, and that you live alone, and are interested only in living alone. An attitude like that is annihilation for you. But I know that you can't suddenly say to yourself, 'The whole world is part of me, and I am part of it.' Help for you must now come from outside yourself. It's too late for anything else. Perhaps that help may come to you in Italy." He paused: "You may deny it, but I think that unconsciously you want to be a part of all life, because you know that anything else is death."

"No," said Matthew. "No. You are wrong. I was never interested in anything at all. Except myself, perhaps, and even that is gone now."

He stood motionless, astonished. He waited for Oliver to speak, but Oliver merely gazed at him meditatively. He stammered: "You think that is ugly and self-centered of me, don't you? You think I ought to be ashamed?"

Oliver stood up. "I never condemn anyone," he answered. "No one can ever fully understand anyone else."

He went out of the room as quietly as he had entered it. For a long time Matthew stood, perfectly still, looking at the fire.

CHAPTER XLII

URSULA ALWAYS recognized Oliver's knock and, no matter what the time or the occasion, always welcomed it. When Oliver now entered her sitting-room, she greeted him with a genuine love and pleasure, which lighted up a worn face chronically drawn in an expression of sleepless anxiety.

"Dear Oliver," she said, holding out her hand to him, and looking at him fondly. "Where have you been, all this dreary day? Walking in this weather?" She glanced through the leaded windows, and shivered at the dark snow.

"No. Certainly not, Mother." Oliver smiled. "I was never an athlete. You know that. Frankly, I've been thinking."

"Very unprofitable," murmured Ursula, indicating a chair for Oliver. She spoke mechanically. The book that lay in her lap had already fallen shut. "How tedious it is, after the holidays! Christmas leaves a blankness after it. We ought to be thankful for New Year's. A sort of breathing-space of pleasure before we plunge into the miserable new year."

Oliver sat down. "How is Father?" he asked, tactfully.

"Well, he is lying down, until after tea-time," replied Ursula. "He balks at it. Calls it coddling. But he welcomes it, I know." She hesitated, and the anxiety made her face old and pinched. "That's what worries me. I'd rather he refused—but there it is."

"I thought he looked gay and happy yesterday," said Oliver.

Ursula's mouth became bitter. "He had his family all around him then, his children, to whom he has given his whole life. Oliver, is a delusion better than the truth?"

"If it brings happiness," he answered promptly. "What is the aim of life, anyway? Happiness, or at least the illusion of it. Anyway, I'd rather believe a lie that gave me pleasure than a truth that gave me a belly-, I mean, headache."

Ursula laughed a little. Oliver went on: "Do you remember what Charles Lamb once said? 'My theory is to enjoy life but the practice is against it.' What practice? Our own conviction that we must find 'truth' at any cost. Truth-seekers are usually masochists, and very tiresome folk, too."

312

"What unorthodox ideas for a lawyer! I thought law was the unrelenting pursuit of truth."

"A fallacy usually entertained by those who know nothing of law," said Oliver, smiling. "Why does a man consult a lawyer? In order to adjust himself and his affairs to an existing law? Nonsense. He wants a lawyer to show him how to get around a law. That's how precedents are made. Think how dangerous any law could become if it weren't frequently amended by precedents! Can you imagine how impossible the Constitution would be if we didn't continually add amendments? Amendments are signs that the Constitution is in a healthy state, and growing constantly. Whenever a man, or a nation, changes its opinions, or enlarges them, he, or it, hasn't as yet died."

The drawn lines on Ursula's face softened. "You talk like my father," she said. "He always had an argument. He once said that the Persian system of law collapsed, and the Persians with it, because they stood rigidly by outgrown laws. Oliver," she added, "I was so delighted when you told me, the other day, that Scott, Meredith and Owens had given you an increase in salary, voluntarily. And the strangest thing of all," she added, without thinking, "is that William, when I told him, was as proud as if——"

"——I were his own son," said Oliver, when Ursula, caught in an unusual breach of diplomacy, halted in confusion. "I'm happy to know that."

It was always easy to talk to Oliver; his asymmetrical eyes never lost their humorous twinkle. Ursula continued eagerly: "I told him just before we went to bed. He looked at me in the strangest way. But he only said: 'Lawyers are wily scoundrels. I suppose they are thinking they might get something from my own table. But you can be sure they won't; it's no use their trying to toady to me. I'm not interested.' But, Oliver, my dear, he knew they weren't trying to 'toady' to him. It's just William's way."

"Your fire is a little low," said Oliver. He stood up and threw coals upon the crimson embers. Again, as it had happened so many times before, Ursula was caught by some familiarity in Oliver's movements, and the old nagging wonder came to her. Whom did Oliver resemble so closely? Now he stood on the hearth, his hands clasped behind his back. Ursula leaned forward to watch him. His lean cheek, though clear and dark, was the cheek of someone else. Someone she hated.

Someone I hate! she cried to herself, with a revival of fear. The terror rushed out into words in her mind. Oliver bent and poked at the fire. There was a certain long movement of his arm, a certain bend of his shoulders, a certain elegance. She was not looking at Oliver. She struggled with a shifting image, trying to focus it clearly. Oliver turned, his back to the fire, and smiled down at her.

It was not Oliver smiling at her, but Eugene Arnold.

Eugene Arnold! Now a thousand corroborative likenesses came to her, likenesses which she had unconsciously suppressed in the past. Oliver, walking towards her down one of the garden paths; Oliver's faint laugh, when he was displeased; Oliver's quiet relentlessness, tempered though it always was by humor and tolerance and affection; certain gestures, certain intonations of voice, certain turns of the head, a certain immovable coldness, rare, to be sure, but evident when offended.

"What is the matter, Mother?" asked Oliver, quickly. She heard his tone with unbearable clarity. It was the echo of Eugene Arnold's voice.

Ursula's hands clutched the arms of her chair. But Eugene resembled his mother, Alice. It was impossible to think that Alice—and then, out of the past rushed the memory of the young Chauncey Arnold. In his later years he had become gross and clumsy and boorish, heavily shapeless. Suddenly Ursula remembered Chauncey as a young man, dark and slender and charmingly courteous, before some secret avarice and ugliness in his character had become dominant. Ursula suddenly put her hands over her face.

She felt Oliver beside her. Instinctively, she wanted to cry out, to push him away. I am going mad, she thought. I am seeing what is not there. For a few moments, at least, she dared not look up at a young man who might have been Chauncey Arnold as a youth.

"Are you ill, Mother?" asked Oliver. I must control myself, thought Ursula. I am imagining what does not exist. She dropped her hands. And then a cold and awful conviction came to her, a conviction which needed no affirmation.

"Please sit down, dear," she said, in a stifled voice. Oliver sat down, but he leaned towards her, his clasped hands between his knees. It was Eugene's old gesture. Because she had always hated Eugene, she had never recognized the resemblance before.

"The strangest thoughts come to one—in the twilight—sometimes," she stammered, trying to smile at her horror. She forced herself to go on. "Oliver, dear, have you ever thought who—who might be your real parents?"

She waited for him to give a laugh of indulgent dismissal. To her fright, he looked down at his clasped hands and his face changed. "Yes," he said, quietly. "For a reason of my own. It is very important to me."

She was terribly frightened. "Oliver!" she cried, and reached out and touched his hands so that they would lose their revealing pose. They did; he took her hand. "Oliver! tell me why you want to know. Don't look at me like that, my darling. You see, the—reason is very important to me, too."

He looked at her for a long time. "Mother," he said at last, with an effort. "You see, I can't go on this way——" He regarded her; he had become grim. "You won't mind, I'm sure. I love Barbie."

"Barbie," repeated Ursula, dazed. The objects in the firelit room began to move in long circles about her.

"Yes, Barbie," said Oliver, very quietly. "I love Barbie. But I can't tell her, because I know she loves me, too. She's young. If—if I should go away, she'd probably forget me, though Barbie is like you, Mother; she is tenacious." He tried to smile. "Yes, you'll hate me, Mother, when I tell you that I am trying to find out whether Barbie is my sister. If she is—then——" He lifted a hand, let it drop. Once again, it was Eugene's eloquent gesture.

Ursula could hardly make her voice audible. "Oliver, are you afraid that—that—William might be your real father?"

"Yes."

Ursula was silent. Too many thoughts, images, faces, were running through her mind. They confused and shocked her. She could not think of Barbara just yet. Ursula caught Oliver's arm, and said, vehemently: "Oliver! Don't be afraid of that. It isn't true. William——" And then she could not continue for a few moments. Her face was haggard with wretchedness; now it became stern. "Oliver," she said, "for many years something about you has plagued me. I put it out of my mind, because the very idea was loathsome. But it has just come to me, whom you resemble so—so terribly. And I'm convinced, now."

Oliver stood up; he moved to her side. She felt something threatening about him, something demanding. This, too, she recognized, and she shrank away from him. "Mother," said Oliver, "you must tell me. I have to know. It's the most important thing in life to me. I have to verify it. I must know what you mean. Whom do I resemble?"

She tried to draw away from him, but he put his hand upon her shoulder. "Don't, Oliver!" she cried. "I can't bear it! I can't bear even to suspect that you are like—him!"

"Who, Mother?" asked Oliver. "If you know anything, you've got to tell me. I can't go on this way. If you don't tell me, I'll leave this city forever. It's that bad."

She tried to escape him in false anger. "How could you think that of William? If you were his son, he'd not be afraid to acknowledge it. He loves his children. He'd never have treated you so——"

"Who, Mother?" repeated Oliver. She knew he did not quite believe her. She felt his terrible anxiety, held in control, but insistent. This was an Oliver she did not know.

She put her fingers to her lips. She looked over them at him. "Eugene Arnold," she whispered.

He dropped his hand from her shoulder. He stood very still beside her. The coals dropped loudly in the grate. Oliver stared at the darkening window. Moving slowly but steadily, he went to a lamp, lit it. He lifted it from its table. He carried it to the long pier mirror at the end of the room. He held it high and looked at himself, looked at his face from every angle, and then looked the full length of his figure. Ursula watched him, her fingers still covering her mouth.

Without speaking, he carried the lamp back to the table. He put it down. He walked back to his chair. He sat down and regarded the fire steadily. "Yes," he said.

"No, no!" cried Ursula. "It's just my imagination. You mustn't believe it, Oliver."

"It is not my imagination," said Oliver. The grimness had left his face. It remained dark and somber, but he was smiling a little. "I can see it. It may disgust you; but I'm glad. I'm glad for me and Barbie."

He looked at Ursula then. "I never told you, but I've been trying to find out for nearly two years. You see, I've always loved Barbie. But I knew it was impossible, if there were any chance that I was really her brother. You don't know what you've done for me, Mother."

She was incredulous. She could only stammer: "You don't care? You won't try to find out anything more?"

"I don't care, no. But I'll go on trying to find out. I'm a lawyer; there are ways."

"But—if you are convinced—and I'm sure we're talking nonsense—why should you try to find out?" implored Ursula.

For a few moments, he did not answer. He had never lied to Ursula. He had sometimes evaded, to spare her pain. But now he must lie to her, to assuage her frantic distress. He made himself smile lightly at her. "You're quite right, Mother. I'll drop the whole thing. I think we're just a little worked up."

She sighed deeply. If she made the effort, she thought, she might, in time, push the appalling thought from her mind. She might forget it. She might even convince herself that it was absurd.

Now I have even more incentive to find out the whole thing, and as soon as possible, said Oliver to himself. He knew all about Eugene Arnold; for a long time he had been looking for a weapon to use against him.

"He's been here so often," said Ursula, in a strained voice. "And children imitate. You've seen him for years. You have most likely imitated him, without knowing it."

"Of course," said Oliver, indulgently. He made himself sound amused. "There's nothing to it at all."

Now that she had chained this terror, at least for a time, Ursula had another thought. "Barbie," she said, incredulously. "You said you loved Barbie, Oliver. But Barbie——"

Oliver held up his hand. "You never really look at Barbie, Mother. I know what she is. Try 'looking' at her, dear. I love her, you see. And if she'll have me, I'll marry her."

His mind is at rest, thought Ursula. "I'll 'look' at Barbie, darling. I've always thought her a selfish and hard young thing." She paused. She was suddenly filled with joy and apprehension, joy that Oliver by this marriage would become more her son, and apprehension about William. "But Barbie's only seventeen."

"You mean that Father wouldn't have it," he said.

Ursula was silent. All the joy left her.

"Mother," said Oliver, "I know how it is with you, about Father. You'll do anything, now, even sacrifice your children, to save him pain, and possibly, as you think, to save his life. But I want Barbie. You've got to think about us, too. I'm not going to give up Barbie for anyone."

This was a new Oliver. The old Oliver had always retreated, abandoned his position, in order to spare others. This was an Oliver like Eugene Arnold.

"Wait," she begged.

"Of course. As you said, Mother, Barbie is only seventeen. When she is past eighteen, we must do something about it."

In a year, a thousand things could happen to save William this pain. Barbara wanted to go away to school. Perhaps it could be managed. The girl was still very young. If she went away, she might forget.

"You won't speak to Barbie, Oliver?" Ursula was too eager, too desperate. Oliver understood at once. He lied again: "Not if you don't want it."

She had always trusted him. She trusted him once more. William would never give his consent to a marriage between Barbara and Oliver. Something would happen to arrange things. In the meantime, William would be spared.

She said, trying to be casual and pleasant: "William asked not to be awakened for tea. Will you have it here with me? Just the two of us, near the fire?"

He was only too glad, he said. For the first time, he remembered Matthew. This was something else to be settled.

The tea was brought in on a tray. Ursula, with over half a century of tact and poise behind her, with a long training in the suppressing of open miseries and emotions, busied herself over the tray, remarked to the maid on the appetizing appearance of the cakes and the perfection of the tea, poured for herself and Oliver, and forced herself to be quite composed.

She was still shaken. Even while she talked calmly and affectionately to Oliver, she could not repress her fear and foreboding. But she had learned to control them, to refuse to think when thinking brought only anguish. By this method, she had salvaged at least a small part of her marriage. She had saved, not her children, as she had once promised herself she must do, but William, who was so infinitely more to her than any child.

Under cover of the pleasant tea-hour, Oliver watched Ursula with pity and complete awareness. He wondered how he could bring up the subject of Matthew. Ursula had had all the shocks she could bear today. But he had given a promise, and he was now beginning to see Matthew clearly again.

Oliver was not a devious man, but he saw he had to be devious now. He put down his tea-cup. He said, in an interested tone: "I went in to see Matt, just before I came here, to thank him for that wonderful miniature."

"Yes. It was chosen with such taste," said Ursula. Her poor haggard face lightened, its habitual mournfulness lifted by her smile.

Oliver leaned back in his chair and looked at the fire thoughtfully. "I wonder why he never went on with his painting? After we came back from Italy, three years ago, he began to paint furiously. Then it died away."

Ursula set her cup on the tray. She said nothing; she stared at the cup and the mournfulness was again on her lowered eyelids.

"He ought to go to Italy again," said Oliver, almost carelessly. "In fact, I suggested it to him."

"Perhaps next summer," murmured Ursula.

Oliver turned to her. She felt the movement, and glanced up at him. "I think," said Oliver resolutely, "that next summer will be too late. He ought to go now. At once."

"That is impossible, Oliver. What are you talking about? He returns to Princeton after the New Year. Oliver, dear, you talk very extravagantly, as if it were a matter of life and death."

"It is," said Oliver, seriously. "No, Mother, I'm not joking. I've talked to Matthew."

"But you had no right to suggest that he just pack up and go to Italy, now!" cried Ursula, with some temper. "You always had such good sense. I don't understand you, my dear."

Oliver saw that he had made an error. But he stood by it. He leaned towards Ursula, and again his clasped hands dropped between his knees. Ursula shrank, closed her eyes.

"Mother," he went on, "we've got to think of something much more important just now than his present studies. We've got to think of Matthew, himself. I am not talking extravagantly when I say that for him it is a matter of life and death. Haven't you noticed that his lassitude is worse than ever this Christmas, that he looks frightfully ill? I tried to arouse him. It was only when we spoke of Italy that he came briefly to life. Perhaps it won't work. But it is worth trying, for his sake."

Ursula's maternal instinct stirred vaguely and dimly. She remembered Matthew as he had appeared to her during the holiday. But then the thought of William intruded, and she shook her head, less in denial than in wretchedness.

"I still think you are extravagant," she said. "Even if you aren't, there's nothing I can do. His father wouldn't allow it, just now. Perhaps next summer. Yes, it will be all right next summer."

"Now," said Oliver. "And not for a few weeks or even months. For years, perhaps." He went on, more gently: "For years, if he wants. We can't move too fast to save him. Mother, you may be angry, but I've told him that I'll give him the money I've saved, if no one else will help him. But surely you won't refuse to help him?"

Oliver continued: "Robert Louis Stevenson has said: 'An aim in life is the only fortune worth the finding.' Perhaps

Matthew will never have an aim in life. It may be too late now. But it's worth trying. You know I'm telling you the truth."

"William will refuse, whatever I say," whispered Ursula. "Don't you know it's no use my ever talking to him about the children? He'll never let his children go; he'll hold them to him forever!" Now she spoke aloud, wildly. "He'll never let them go! And to try to take one from him would be to kill part of him. I can't let that happen. They have made him unhappy enough; they owe something to him, though he's never allowed them to believe it or know it. I'll fight any one of them who tries to hurt him; he's suffered enough!"

Oliver stood up. He went to the window and looked out at the darkness. "I understand," he said quietly. "I know how you feel, Mother. But there is something else for you to think of: Suppose Matthew—dies? Suppose he dies under the most awful circumstances? Will Father be happier then? Or won't he die also?"

Ursula sprang to her feet. She ran to Oliver, caught him by the arm and turned him to her. "Oh, Oliver, how dare you! Oliver, what do you mean? Why do you look at me so strangely! Oh, my God, what do you mean, Oliver?"

He put his hand very gently over the clutching hand on his arm. "Mother, I'm not going to try to soothe you with half-truths. I must tell you the whole truth. When I went into his room, Matthew was thinking. He was thinking of death. I know he was. It was in his face."

Ursula snatched her hand away from Oliver's. "You are torturing me," she said, and her voice was hardly audible.

"Mother, have you ever, for years, really looked at your children? I know that since Father was ill a year ago you haven't seen them at all. They don't exist for you. Yet they have an existence. In Matt's case it is dangerously threatened. And so, Father is threatened. I'm not talking foolishly. I know."

She went back to her chair, walking heavily, like an old woman. She fell into it. She huddled herself together, as if mortally cold. She stared into space. Oliver was right; she never saw the children any more. But now she saw Matthew. She shivered strongly.

Oliver came towards her. "I know you have very little influence upon Father," he said, compassionately. "If you talked to him about Matthew, he wouldn't listen to you. All I want from you is a promise to help Matthew, with money, with encouragement, with every impulse of affection you can muster up for him. Urge him to go, no matter what his father says."

"No one ever listens to me—ever," muttered Ursula, dully. "Matthew won't listen——"

"He will." Oliver was all pity. "Don't be too upset. Father will probably let Matt go at once, when Matt asks him. You'll probably have no need to do anything."

"He'll never let the children go. Never," repeated Ursula.

She thrust out her hands, as if to push Oliver off. The gesture was frantic. "Please go away. Please leave me alone," she pleaded. "I must think, Oliver. Forgive me, but you must go."

She was alone, and the room was dark. It was cold, despite the fire. The winter wind beat at the windows. She was alone. I have always been alone, she thought, I have four children, and I am alone. I have a husband whom I have never really had. I sacrificed my children for him, just as he has sacrificed himself for them. We have nothing. William, William, my darling, we have nothing, either of us, nothing at all.

CHAPTER XLIII

WILLIAM PRESCOTT sat alone in his great florid marble drawing-room, reading an accumulation of financial journals which had collected during the holiday and the two days before. At each end of the room the mighty fireplaces blazed with logs, but the center of the room was cold. There was no "happy gathering" of girls and young men about him. He knew that his daughters and his sons had no engagements tonight; he had hoped, as he had never ceased to hope through the years, that they would come to him, sit about him and laugh with him affectionately. This had never happened; but this did not prevent him from believing it would happen, on some future night. He had deceived himself to such an extent that he was actually convinced he had memories of such gatherings—in earlier years, or even recently.

Sometimes, when he sat there, Ursula would sit with him at a little distance, reading or embroidering by the light of an immense ox-blood lamp. He rarely spoke to her, or she to him. He would brood sullenly over his papers, while her eyeglasses caught the light. All at once, it came to him that she had not sat with him in this room for a long time. Irritated, feeling considerably abused, not by his children, but by his wife, he rattled his papers. He would not admit to his loneliness. He would never admit to himself that he had famished longings and sadnesses and heavy deep despairs. His children were perfect; they knew he was busy; they would not disturb him. He had only to reach out and pull the bell-rope to summon a servant who would call his children to him. He looked at the rope, but his chilly hand did not move.

The grandeur of the flaming room lay in vast silences about him; he could hear the far crackling of the fires. All the lamps were lit, casting shadows on the veined marble walls, the half-pillars, the green and red sofas, the brilliant rugs. The arched windows rattled very faintly under the assaults of the winter wind; the scarlet draperies stirred. There was no other sound. He might have been alone in the mighty house which he had built for the joy and pride of his children—and which was so empty.

Sometimes words or thoughts caught him unawares, like savage animals striking suddenly from the depths of a friendly forest. Empty! He sat upright in his chair. He was a fool. The house was not empty. It was filled with his children.

Yet the emptiness spread about him like a desert. It was silly of him to be selfish, to want his children just now. After all, he was getting old, and his children had their own pursuits. Nevertheless, he looked expectantly at the wide arching stairways. Lamplight glimmered on vacancies, untenanted, beyond them. Now his loneliness was like a tearing sickness in his flesh. Every lamp illuminated barrenness.

Empty, said the wind against the windows. He had known loneliness before, in his outraged and bitter childhood. He had thought it gone forever. It was here again with him, infinitely enlarged, infinitely more terrible.

Once more he looked at the bell-rope. But still he did not touch it. Now he said to himself: Why don't I reach for it? I've only to stretch out my hand. With a rattling sound the papers fell from his knees, and he jumped as if in great and sudden terror. My nerves, he said to himself. It is only my nerves. I have worked too hard. How can I be such a fool? I love my children; it is only natural that they should love me in return. I have given my whole life to them; if I ask it, they would give me a little of their time. But I have no right to ask it; their lives are their own.

He forced himself to remember how he had provided for his children, and now a brooding smile settled on his exhausted face. He had established large trust-funds for each of his sons and daughters. The money was safe; it could never be touched by anyone, not even by himself. It was, of course, not enough. He must devise ways of adding to these trust-funds. His whole life's effort had gone into them. He had little left for himself. It did not matter.

The whole world lay before him, a frightful and threatening world of ugliness, terror, hunger and darkness. This world could no longer threaten his beloved children; he had buttressed their dwelling with money. With money, he had bought them security. He had bought them friends and comforting fires and position and happiness—with the whole of his life. But still, it was not enough. There must be some way of augmenting those trust-funds.

Now he was filled with bitterness. His "great friend," Jay Regan, had treated him badly. When he had wanted to secure considerable railroad stock, a really substantial block,

Jay Regan had smiled at him in the friendliest fashion, but had asked: "With what, Will?" He had reminded William of what he already owed.

There was not the demand any longer for wooden cars. Steel had taken its place. But new and unique ways and uses for wood could be found. The slump which had occurred this fall would soon lift. Strikes were now less threatening. William thought of the strike-breakers he had used, and he shrank involuntarily. He thought of the blood-shed he had caused. He did not know why he shrank. He had his children to think of; nothing mattered but his children.

He was so tired. He had been tired ever since that stupid illness a year ago. His mind, of late, refused to sparkle, to contrive. Perhaps he needed a rest. A month, perhaps, in some quiet place, alone. After all, a man had only so much energy. If he rested a while, he could think of ways to make his children even more secure. Now he thought of the Prescott stock which Jay Regan held; he thought of the interest he must soon pay. He closed his eyes.

He heard a brisk step on the marble floor between the rugs. He looked up, eagerly. His furrowed face broke into a delighted smile. His son, Thomas, with his jaunty air, his jocose grin, was approaching him. Thomas swung his big body with speed, if with awkwardness. There was no grace about him, only a clumsy physical strength. Nevertheless, William regarded him fatuously. He said, fondly: "Hello, Tom. Finished your talk?"

Thomas was surprised. He threw himself down in a chair opposite his father, and stared. "Talk?" he said. "With whom?"

"Why, I suppose with Matt," he said, somewhat confused.

Thomas burst out into his usual raucous laughter. He understood. He allowed himself a few reflections of ridicule on this doddering old fool's illusions. "Oh, sure. We had our talk. Looking forward to tomorrow night."

A warm glow permeated William. "One hundred people, for dancing and a midnight supper. You children have a lot of friends, I'm pleased to see. You, Tom, especially, are very popular. And Julie." He paused. There had been something about Julia lately which had harassed him. He could not remember just what it was, except that the girl's lovely bloom had become somewhat dimmed. He said: "A six-piece orchestra from Philadelphia. I was told it was the best. I hope you will enjoy yourselves."

"Oh, sure," repeated Thomas. He looked at his father with

his narrow brown eyes; they glittered thoughtfully. "Look, Pa," he said, "I wanted to talk to you, tonight."

Immensely gratified, William exclaimed: "Why, of course!" It seemed to him that he had had many intimate conversations with Thomas. There had always been open fires, and confidences. He was certain of this. He settled himself comfortably in his chair. All his tiredness was gone. "You don't need money again, do you, Tom?" he asked, indulgently.

"Well, I always need that," laughed Thomas. He could use a hundred. But he decided to postpone the asking for a little while. William, however, was already taking out his wallet, pleasantly thick. He removed two one hundred dollar bills, and tossed them affectionately to his son. Thomas caught them deftly. "Why, thanks," he said, and grinned again. "You know how it is: all those presents for Christmas. And my other obligations."

William beamed. His face, unusually so somber and so brooding, shone with gratification. "I know, I know," he said, though he did not really know. He could not remember whether Thomas had made him a gift. But it was there, surely, amid the heap on his table in his dressing-room.

Thomas carefully tucked away the bills. He took out a pack of cigarettes. "Mind if I smoke, Pa?" he asked. Without waiting for permission, he lit the cigarette, leaned back, crossed his legs.

He stared up at the ceiling, "crawling," as he put it, with painted nymphs and cherubs. He did not look at his father when he said: "I've been thinking. You need help, Pa. You know how interested I am in the business. I've read all those books you sent me. I've read others. See—I'm over twenty-one. I'm wasting my time at Yale. Oh, I like it, and I have a lot of friends there, and I'm not saying I don't enjoy every minute. But," and his loud rough voice slowed, "I want to go into the business with you. Now. I don't want to go back to college. You need me, Pa. You really do."

William, listening to this, was torn between delight and dismay, between gratification and disappointment. He said: "But, Tom, I want you to complete your education. I'm not saying that I'm not—overcome by your offer to help me. You work every summer in the office, and in the mills. I can't tell you how that pleases me. After all, part of the business will be yours some day. But I want you to be a gentleman, too. I want you to have your education. You have only eighteen months more. It would be unfair to you to permit you to throw all that away."

Thomas puffed placidly on his cigarette. He was relieved. He had expected a categorical refusal, and considerable shouting. This was going well. He made his face assume deep seriousness. He leaned towards his father.

"Pa, you know how I appreciate everything you've done for me. You've done too much for all of us. You've given up your whole life. It's time now one of us did something for you. And I insist upon bearing my part of the obligation."

At this, William was so moved he could not speak.

Furtively, he took off his spectacles and rubbed them. Thomas saw that his father's hands were trembling. He grinned to himself, cunningly.

But it was not over yet. William clung stubbornly to his idea of what was best for his son.

He began to speak, a little hoarsely: "Tom, when you talk that way it does something to me. I can't tell you. But you're young. You don't know what is best. Not to graduate would be a lifelong liability for you. Only eighteen months."

In eighteen months it might be too late, thought Thomas, grimly.

"Pa, please consider what I want," he pleaded. That always made his father listen, intently. "I don't want to go back. I want to go into the business. You've been ill. Let me take some of the responsibility, in minor things, off your shoulders. I owe it to you. Now, please wait, Pa. You always say we owe you nothing. We do. But let's put that aside a minute, and just think of what I want, personally. I want to go into the business at once. You've said I do a good job in the summers. I can do a much better job, if I'm there all the time. That's what I want. I'll go back to Yale, if you insist, but I can tell you I'll be damned miserable. You don't want that, do you?"

"No," murmured William. Beyond that, he could not speak. His loneliness had gone; he was warm inside, as if new life had been given him. His son loved him, had observed his weariness, wished to spare him. He thought of Tom permanently beside him, in his office. He saw Tom slightly older, efficient and absorbed, a Tom he could trust. Emptiness had fled away; the immense room was full of light and comfort.

Thomas' big features expressed seriousness, and concern for his father. He reached over, patted his father's knee. The old boy could never resist that, thought Thomas with inner amusement. What a fool this was, weakly dependent upon the love of children.

"Only eighteen months," pleaded William. But he was weakening. And then he saw the face of Eugene Arnold. He said: "Tom, I'm a fool even to listen to you. But if that is what you want, I'll put my own disappointment aside. After the holidays, you can come into the business. As my secretary." He paused, then said recklessly, with a deep smile of pleasure and content: "At fifty dollars a week."

Now he was elated, full of excitement. Thomas pulled his chair closer. Again, he patted his father's knee, heartily.

"I'm getting old," said William. "I wouldn't tell it to anyone except you, Tom, but there're times when I'm infernally tired. You're a brilliant young feller. I could pass along a great deal to you."

"That's the ticket!" exclaimed Thomas. He stood up, strutted up and down, grinning at his father. "Look at these shoulders. They're big and willin'. They're for you, Pa. All for you."

William followed him with eyes that shone with emotion. He laughed richly.

"What a rascal you are, Tom!" he said.

A rascal. Thomas contemplated the word with cynical satisfaction. There was no pity in Thomas when he stopped before his father, leaned down and put his hand on William's shoulder, and pressed it vigorously.

"William Prescott and Son," he said.

Again, William was profoundly moved. But he said: "William Prescott and Sons. There's Matt, too, you know."

This so amused Thomas that it was all he could do to keep from laughing outright into his father's face. It was a struggle; to help overcome it, he drew out his watch. "Nine o'clock," he said, ruefully. "And I am due at Mary Blake's home in fifteen minutes. Wish I could call it off."

Mary Blake was the daughter of one of the richest "outsider" coal families. The Blakes always came for the holidays to their home on the mountain overlooking the city. William almost smirked with pleasure. The girl would inherit at least a million dollars. He expanded his chest, proud and smug. A pretty little baggage, too. He was about to say this to Thomas and then he wondered whether young men called girls "baggages" these days. He did not know. He contented himself with saying: "A very nice girl."

"And a million dollars isn't to be sneezed at," said Thomas, winking.

"It never was," laughed William.

When Thomas had gone, a warmth lingered about William, and he sat there alone, smiling, no longer hearing the wind at the windows, not feeling the bitter silence. He was still smiling when he glanced up to see Matthew before him, Matthew who moved with no more sound than a shadow.

"Matt!" said William.

"Father, I want to talk with you," said Matthew. His voice seemed to come from a long distance.

"Well, sit down, sit down, my boy," said William. The warmth in him increased. His children were remembering him; they were coming to him, as children ought always to come to their father, in affection and in search of understanding.

Understanding Matthew, however, was a trifle difficult. He was, by nature, "quiet." He was a "genius." One could not expect such as he to display Thomas' exuberance and vitality. William's illusions again rushed to help him. He seemed to recall that, as a child, Matthew had sat near his knee, silent, but depending upon his father for help and comfort.

Matthew sat down, stiff and straight, and looked at William with eyes that never appeared to see one. "I want to go away," he said, and it was as if he spoke in a dream. "I must go away. At once, Father."

CHAPTER XLIV

SLOWLY, THE WARMTH about William retreated. He could say nothing to Matthew. He could only look at his son, and then there was a confused clamoring in him, a rushing together of wordless thoughts against the very bones of his skull. He said to himself, putting the back of his hand against his forehead: I am ill, again. He thought of Dr. Banks, but the thought was lost, and he forgot the doctor.

He dropped his hand; it fell heavily to his knee. It was the gesture of an old sick man. The furrows in his face deepened; his shoulders bent forward; his mouth sagged in an expression of great and hopeless pain. He still could say nothing to Matthew. Matthew was regarding him without expression, and it was this, now, which seemed to William more dreadful than anything else.

He said, painfully, after a long time: "Why must you go away, Matt? What is it you want?" He waited. Matthew did not move. William drew a deep breath. "You have only to say what you want, Matt, and I'll—I'll get it for you, buy it for you——"

"I know," said Matthew. He turned his head aside. He repeated: "I know. And that's why I've got to go away."

"I don't understand you, son," said William, faintly.

Matthew was silent. Then, very slowly, he folded one hand over the other in a movement which, to William, was one of inexplicable desolation.

"I never denied you anything," said William.

He looked at Matthew's hands, and waited.

"I never asked you for anything," said William. He moved his head, as if to escape from some torment.

"I know," said Matthew, lifelessly.

"Yet, you want to go away."

The wind was struggling, loud against the windows once more. It was a threatening voice and, to William's ears, it had a portentous sound. Again, he moved his head in that search for escape.

"You want to leave your home, your family, your father, Matt. Why? Just tell me why?"

Matthew said to himself: I can't tell you. I haven't any words for you. You could understand, if you let yourself. But you won't ever let yourself.

He said: "Father, I want to go to Italy."

"Italy!" William looked up quickly. The pain retreated from him. He felt that he had been about to understand Matthew; he had known that he could not bear that understanding. "Why, of course!" he exclaimed. "It's your painting, isn't it, Matt? Well, why didn't you say so in the beginning? Of course, you may go to Italy. After you come home again, in the spring."

"No," said Matthew. "Not in the spring, Father. Now. It has to be now."

William smiled affectionately. "Genius pushing you, eh? I can understand that. But you can't break off your education in the middle of the year, can you? It wouldn't be the right thing. So, shall we plan for you to go in June, and not return until September? I might even go with you," he added, his smile indulgent. He felt that he had just escaped some awful revelation, and there was a kind of hysteria in him. "We'll travel all over Italy, Matt. Maybe Julie will want to go on to Paris, with your mother. Well, now, we'll make it a family party, Tom, and you——"

"No," said Matthew.

He stood up. He stood by his chair, his hands hanging at his sides. "You must understand, Father. You must understand that I've got to go away alone, perhaps for a long time, perhaps even for years. No," he added, "you won't understand. But I thought I ought to tell you, anyway. I'm going. I'll find some way, even if you won't help me."

William tried to get to his feet, but an overpowering weakness made him drop back. "You won't say why, but you want to leave—to leave everything I've given you, everything I've worked for."

"Yes," said Matthew.

William looked at the lamplight and firelight on the marble walls, at the scarlet curving of the draperies, at the rich rugs on the floor, the statues, the lamps, the priceless paintings, the ivories, the gilt on the green and red sofas and chairs, on the Venetian mirrors, the embossed figures on the mighty oval ceiling—at everything he had bought for his children. The great roaring had again invaded his mind. What was it for which Matthew was famishing? For William, though he had at first denied it, had seen the desperate, muted hunger on his son's face, and it was from this that he had turned away.

I ought, he thought confusedly, to have insisted that he go to church when he was a child, not just occasionally, but regularly. He ought to have had some religion. They all ought to have had some religion. I don't know. I don't seem to know anything anymore. But I think there is something in the Bible about children honoring their fathers and their mothers—perhaps in religion there is something for a man to hold to——

"I don't know anything," he muttered.

Matthew's pale yellow brows contracted. His eyes became curiously intent upon his father, as if seeing him for the first time. His hand closed over the back of the chair beside him.

William's head dropped. He shook it slowly from side to side, as if in sick denial.

"I never asked anything of my children," he said. "I knew you owed me nothing, and that I owed everything to you. It seems it wasn't enough." He lifted his head. He repeated: "It wasn't enough, was it, Matt?"

Matthew's hand tightened on the chair. Father and son regarded each other in a long silence.

"Tell me, Matt," said William, almost in a whisper, "where I have failed. Failed you, failed perhaps all my children. I want to know, Matt. I don't know how I've failed, but it seems I have."

Matthew did not answer. He did not, however, look away from his father.

"My whole life belonged to all of you. For me, there was nothing else," said William. It was hard and painful for him to speak. "You know that, don't you?"

"Yes," said Matthew.

"I've really had no other existence," William went on, in dull wonder. "Everything was only for you. I believed I owed you that, that every father owed his children that! Nothing was ever demanded of any of you." He paused.

The light which had come into Matthew's eyes had dwindled back to dullness again. He said: "Yes. That is why I want to go to Italy."

Once more William moved his head slowly from side to side in a distress for which he had no words or understanding. He linked his fingers together on his knee.

Matthew said: "I'll need very little money, Father." His voice was expressionless. "I don't want to 'travel in style'. I want to find some small place, and perhaps just live there for a few months or so, by myself."

William came briefly to life: "That's ridiculous, Matt. You're my son. I'll send you a good check every month. You'll live at the best hotels—see something of life." His smile was painful. " 'Very little money'! Nonsense. You can have anything you want. Besides, there are emergencies sometimes. Emergencies, too, have a way of avoiding anyone with a full purse. Now, where in Italy do you want to go? Rome? A young man like yourself would naturally prefer Rome. Do you remember that hotel, not far from the Borghese Gardens? What is that street? Via Vittorio Veneto? You'll meet many of our friends there, in the spring, after you've made your tour."

Matthew's fingers beat a slow tattoo on the back of the chair. Something which had been in him, briefly, had gone.

William became determinedly animated. "That girl you liked last summmer, Matt. Martha Pierce? Pierce, yes. Great friends of the Blakes, aren't they? Well, it seems to me that her father told me, last summer, that he and Mrs. Pierce and Miss Martha were thinking of touring Europe this spring. He owns all those mines—Pierce. I'll drop him a line in Pittsburgh, tomorrow, and tell him that I'd appreciate it if he would make a point of seeing you, in Italy—he and his family."

Matthew stirred. "Thank you, Father," he said.

Rome. He would not go to Rome. He would not see the Pierces. The very thought was a weariness to him. He forced himself not to think; if he did so, he would lose this precarious volition to go away.

He had to leave his father now. It was impossible to speak any longer. He almost cried: "Thank you. Good night." He ran as if a great danger were behind him.

William watched him go. He lay back in his chair, his arms dangling over the sides. A whirlwind of thoughts rushed back to torment him.

I have given my children what I believe, and know, every child should have, because it is his birthright; security, love, the satisfaction of all desires, a beautiful environment, sympathy.

All that I am, all that I had, I gave to my children. It was not enough. I had no more to give, but it was not enough. Why am I so tired? Why do my thoughts clot together in clumps of words without beginning or end? My sons are no longer children. They are making their own decisions, as I always taught them to do. Tom has made his decision; Matt has made his. It is only right. Why should they consider me? I am only their father, and I owe them everything.

But why are they so unhappy, so wretched? William opened his closed eyes on the terrible thought, which had struck him out of the darkness. Never bound, why are they slaves? "Lies, lies!" he cried aloud, furiously, as if answering a challenger. "They are happy. They aren't slaves. They have a right to choose, even if it hurts me."

He saw Thomas' face, big, coarse, sly, full of ribald laughter. That face did not warm him, now. He felt the vague, large movement of terror in himself. He saw Matthew, and the terror loomed larger. He saw Julia, so pale these days, so irritable, so silent. He saw Barbara, intense and quiet. O, my God, he thought.

"My God," he said in a loud dull voice. God. There was no God. Ursula had sometimes been successful in getting the children to go to church, to Sunday school. But he had always laughed at them, affectionately. Then, when they were old enough to oppose their mother, they never went. I was right, he said to himself. I was right—— But I have no one to talk to, no one. I have no one to help me.

Ursula. For the first time in many years he thought clearly of his wife, saw her face. In a few moments, when he was rested, he would go to Ursula.

The great clock in the hall boomed the hour, the quarter hour, the half hour, and then the hour again. Once more, it went its rounds; the snow battered against the windows. The house was silent as death itself.

William opened his eyes. He must have slept. He felt no refreshment. There was a weighty paralysis upon him. The enormous room was warm, but he was icily cold. Someone was standing beside him. It was Ursula. She was standing there, looking down at him, and from her attitude he knew that she had been there a long time. There were tears in her eyes.

He pulled himself up in his chair. She had been watching him, while he slept, vulnerable and broken and full of anguish. He forgot that he had wanted to see her. He saw only that she was old, like himself, and that she knew what he had been thinking of here all alone. It enraged him. He made a gesture of weak anger and dismissal.

"What do you want?" he asked. "Why can't you let me rest in peace?"

"Oh, William," she murmured. Her skirts rustled. She went away from him. He watched her until she had gone.

CHAPTER XLV

BARBARA LIKED silence. But she did not like the silences that filled her home. They were not like the silences of nature, a kind of harmony; they were the silences of those who lived alone, thought alone, plotted alone, slept alone. They were foreboding and dangerous.

The silence of the house, tonight, became more than she could bear. She thought of the dance tomorrow night, the celebration of the New Year, all the gaiety which money could buy, all the laughter which youth could evoke, and she turned away from the thought with distaste. After the guests would be gone, and the musicians, too, there would be silence again, and little cells where each member of the family would live, walled up in himself because he cared for no one else.

She went to the window. The snow fell faster now, swirling about in long white scarves, heaping itself upon spruce and weighted bush, blotting out the earth and the sky. Far away, the street lamps were blurs of misty gold, sometimes hidden, sometimes struggling clear of the pervading blizzard. The snow was like the silence of this house, absorbing everything, covering everything with motionlessness.

I must talk with someone, she thought desperately. Oliver. Where was Oliver? She had not seen him since dinner, and then he had hardly spoken to anyone. He had appeared unusually abstracted. Her brothers had disappeared, as usual, each to his own "den," and Julia had murmured something about preparations for tomorrow and had gone upstairs. Barbara had followed. For a long time, now, Barbara had been sitting here in her own room. Even Julia was someone to talk to, and she decided to find her sister. There was something she ought to say to Julia, who was becoming paler and thinner these days, and very quiet, her liveliness faded and dimmed. How was it possible for Papa not to see this? But surely, he was seeing. Very often, he looked at Julia distressedly, seemed about to ask her a question, and then did not speak.

But what could she, Barbara, say to Julia? She, herself, had never been taught gentle words, consoling words, or phrases of sympathy. The capacity was in her, but its outlet was filled with stones. Barbara let the draperies fall from her hands. She cared nothing, really, for her sister, just as no one else in this house cared for any other member. She had waited, for several months, to discover just how Julia would solve the problem of herself and Eugene Arnold. Apparently, in spite of what she had said so exultantly to Eugene, she had not truly found any solution.

I don't love Julia, thought Barbara. But I pity her. She thought about this for a few moments. In this house, pity was an alien thing. She shook her dark head impatiently. Yet something forced her now to want to go to Julia. How could she help her sister? Help. Again, this was an alien thing, this desire to help even where there was no love.

Barbara, to her own wonder, found herself knocking on Julia's door. She opened it. Julia was sitting on her bed, surrounded by a half-dozen or more beautiful new gowns, blue, pink, white, silver and gold. They lay heaped about her, in brilliant lengths, embroidered in seed pearls or shimmering silk. Huddled among them sat Julia, staring sightlessly before her, her fingers twisted on the gray flannel skirt which covered her knees, the firelight making her face very white in the dusk of the room. She had not lighted a single lamp.

She stared at Barbara with sullen distaste. "What do you want?" she asked, rudely. "Why didn't you knock?"

"I did. You didn't hear me, I suppose," replied Barbara. She closed the door behind her. Julia did not ask her to sit down. She continued to stare at her sister, repellingly.

"What do you want?" she repeated.

Barbara hesitated. She took a few slow steps into the room. Awkwardness brought a slight flush to her cheeks. She glanced down at the gowns on the bed. "Are you trying to decide what you are going to wear tomorrow night?" she asked. There was a slight stammer in her young voice. "I think the silver is very pretty."

Very suddenly, Julia stood up. She went to the fire, moved a fallen ember with the toe of her buttoned shoe.

"I'm not interested," she said at last. "I don't care." She looked sideways at her sister. "What does it matter to you, anyway? You didn't come here to ask about my clothes, did you?"

"No," said Barbara, seriously. "No, I didn't." The flush on her face deepened.

"Well, then, why did you come?"

Barbara stood in the center of the room, hopelessly. She

had no proper words. At last she blurted out: "I came because
I wanted to help you!"

Julia swung about quickly. Her back was to the fire. The
darkness hid her face, but there was a nimbus about her hair.
"Help me?" she repeated, incredulously. "And what makes
you think I need help?" Now there was something tense about
her, something almost fierce. "You don't know what you're
talking about, Barbie! Why are you annoying me, coming
here, sneaking into my room?"

Barbara's quick temper flared. "I'm not 'annoying' you.
I'm not 'sneaking'." She stopped. Her sister was watching
her with alert wariness and suspicion. Barbara detected fear
in the other girl. "Julie, you're not well, are you? I've seen
that for a long time. And—and that's why I thought—I really
did think—that I might be able to help you."

"You!" cried Julia. She burst out laughing. "How concerned
you are, all of a sudden. This is very funny, very funny, indeed."

"Yes," said Barbara, gravely. "It is very funny. It's terribly
funny when anyone in this house thinks about anyone else,
or wants to help. That's what's so wrong here."

Julia lifted a hand in an abrupt gesture. She let it fall
again. She said, with almost her father's own brutality: "If
I needed help, which I don't, I'd never go to you, Barbie."

Barbara considered this somberly, for a few moments.
She nodded. "I shouldn't blame you," she said, in a low tone.
"I couldn't expect anything else."

Julia watched her. But though she waited, Barbara had
nothing to add to this. Julia sighed in an exaggerated manner:
"Really, Barbie, you are so mysterious tonight. And I must
ask you to go. We'll all be up very late tomorrow, and I
was just about to go to bed."

The sensible thing would be to go, thought Barbara. Julia
was being even more unpleasant than usual.

But all this no longer mattered. There was an urge in Barbara,
a desperate pity. "Please, Julie, listen. I'm awfully sorry,
but I saw you and Gene Arnold, last May, up on the mountain.
I didn't intend to listen. I didn't want to listen. I heard everything you said. I couldn't help it."

Julia, on the hearth, was very still.

Barbara took another step towards her. She said, pleadingly: "Julie, you are so afraid, aren't you? You are afraid of
me. Don't be, please. I'd never tell anyone. I'd never have
spoken about it, even now, if you had found some way, as

you said you would. But you didn't find it, did you? And that's why I wanted to help."

Julia spoke chokingly, in the hushed voice of terror and hatred: "You sneak! You spy! What do you want?" Then, when Barbara, shocked, did not answer, Julia cried frenziedly: "Why don't you go and tell—him, or Mama? Why don't you go and ruin Gene, and ruin me? What are you waiting for? Did you just come here to gloat, before you told everyone? Well, go and tell," she continued wildly: "I don't care any longer. I can't go on like this. But when you tell, I'll leave this house and I'll never come back. Never, never!"

Barbara tried to speak, but it was useless. She could only think: This is the way we are, in this house. We know only hating and hurting and greed and cruelty. Because we were taught that we alone mattered, and that we owed nothing to anyone.

She held out her hands to her sister. She could speak now, haltingly. "Julie, please. Julie—dear. Do try to understand. I want to help you."

Julia put her hands over her face. She spoke from behind them, moaningly: "Go away. Please go away. I don't know why you came here. You don't want to 'help' me. You couldn't help, anyway, except by not telling, by letting me alone."

"I won't ever tell," said Barbara, wretched. "Please believe that. I'll go out of this room and I'll forget I ever knew anything about you and Gene. Can't you trust me, Julie?"

Julia dropped her hands. She moved aside a step, leaned against the side of the fireplace as if completely stricken and exhausted. "How could I ever trust you, Barbie?"

"I know," said Barbara. "It's almost impossible to believe that you could, isn't it? We haven't been sisters to each other. It's too late for that, for either of us. But you can trust me, Julie. Please don't hate me."

Something in the young girl's voice must finally have reached Julia. She opened the eyes she had closed so abruptly as if to shut out the sight of her sister. She stared at Barbara in the firelight.

"I've been sitting alone tonight," Barbara went on. "And I began to think of you, and I thought: 'I might be able to help Julie.' And that's why I came."

Julia continued to lean against the fireplace, without answering.

Barbara said, falteringly: "It's a very silly idea I have, but I must tell you. Papa is always trying to get you to notice some young man or other. Julie, why don't you say to him soon: 'Papa, you've brought Gene Arnold here so many times, and I don't know anyone like him. I think I could care for someone like Gene. Gene never looks at me. He doesn't know I exist. But I like Gene, Papa.'"

Even to herself, her words sounded childish and foolish. Yet Julia was listening. She was listening with deep acuteness. Now she laughed again, a hoarse, rough laugh.

"How silly you are, Barbie. If I said that idiotic thing to him, do you know what Papa would do? He'd ruin Gene. And Gene would never look at me again."

Barbara said, resolutely: "Papa loves you. He cares more for you than for all of us put together. You are diplomatic, Julie. Impress it upon Papa that Gene isn't in the slightest degree interested in you, or even that he avoids you. That will enrage Papa, that any man might not be interested in a daughter of his. Then, if he says he will transfer or discharge Gene, you can tell him what you've just told me, that you'll go away and he'll never see you again. You meant that, didn't you, Julie? Yes, you meant it. And Papa will know that you mean it."

Julia's hand gripped the corner of the mantelpiece. It was impossible to know whether she was giving this preposterous idea any thought, but Barbara was encouraged by her sister's silence.

Julia clasped her fingers tightly together. She whispered: "He hates Gene."

Barbara looked at her eagerly. "Yes, I know. But not so much, now. You've already done something to Papa, Julie. It's—it's tenuous. But you can manage it, Julie. I know you can."

Julia walked carefully away from the mantelpiece. She went to a distant corner and sat down. She rested her chin on her hand. She sat like that for a long time, while Barbara waited.

Then Julia said softly but piercingly: "I don't know why you came here to give me this 'idea'. And I'm not going to say whether I'll think about it or not."

"Julie!" exclaimed Barbara, impulsively, starting towards her sister.

But Julia raised her pretty delicate hand, as if warning her off, and Barbara stopped.

"It's nothing to you, Barbie. It's none of your affair. You've asked me to trust you. I can't. But I can say this, if you ever mention Gene to Papa I'll tell him how you moon over Oliver."

She moved slightly in her chair, and now her soft voice was full of detestation: "Oliver! Who knows who or what he is? Don't you know that Papa hates him, hates him more than he does Gene? Don't you know what he'd say if I told him you were gone on Oliver? Oliver—who might be anybody?"

Barbara was stunned. She could only stand there, and look at her sister. Julia began to laugh gently. "You didn't know, did you, that I've watched you, too? But I did, Barbie, I did. And I know."

She turned about in her chair and looked directly at Barbara. Her eyes glittered in the firelight. She chuckled gently. "Silence for silence, Barbie. That is how we must trust each other."

Barbara said, brokenly: "Oh, Julie. Oh, Julie, how terrible this is."

Something in the young girl's attitude, the droop of her shoulders, the bend of her head, the helpless falling of her hands, touched Julia's conscience. Something made her, if only briefly, ashamed and aghast.

"Yes," she muttered, "it's terrible. But that's the way we are, isn't it?"

Barbara lifted her head. She looked about her. She drew a deep breath. "No, it's not 'the way we are', Julie. It isn't the way I am, anymore."

She walked out of the room, her knees trembling. She opened the door, closed it, then leaned against it.

CHAPTER XLVI

OLIVER STOOD near a great spruce heavy with snow and smoked quietly. His shoulders were already white, and the brim of his hat was filled. He had had to leave the house, that house where it was impossible to think clearly, so permeated was it with the solitary hostilities and enmities that dwelt in it.

He had believed that if he could be by himself for a while some clarity might come to his mind, so that the fantasy in which he and Ursula had indulged early that evening would be dispersed by the cold wind of common-sense. It was not possible that he was really brother to Eugene Arnold. There had been, between himself and Ursula, an atmosphere of hysteria, a kind of hypnotic and mutual hallucination, born of uncertainty and the mystery of his beginnings. He had wanted to be assured that he was free to love Barbara.

The bitter white storm had not done what he had desired it to do. He had stood by this spruce for a long time, thinking and smoking, and the fantasy had become surety. Now, a dozen forgotten voices of friends of William returned to him over the years. "That boy of yours, Oliver, reminds me of someone. Who is it?" William had always replied: "I don't know. He doesn't remind me of anyone." Yet William had looked at the young boy, frowning. He, too, had seen a resemblance. To whom? William had, apparently, never suspected but he had, on those occasions, been colder than usual to Oliver, and there had been a gleam of aversion in his eyes. What am I thinking? said Oliver to himself, with detestation. It is all illusion. But he knew it was not.

There had been very few occasions when he and Eugene had been alone, even for a few moments. Suddenly Oliver remembered those occasions acutely. Eugene had barely spoken to him, but he had stared at him with those pale hard eyes, and there had been in them a sharp curiosity, the slightest trace of perplexity. He had been trying to discover why something about Oliver puzzled and annoyed him.

My brother, thought Oliver and threw his cigarette into

the snow with a gesture of disgust and repudiation. Since
Oliver had become a man, there had always been this antipathy
between the two. Then it deepened, became more intense,
as if something hidden in each of them had recognized itself
in the other.

For over a year, now, Oliver had been trying to find some
trace of the parents who had brought him to life. He had had
to move carefully. William was a director of the orphanage
from which he had taken Oliver. The other directors and
officers and managers were William's friends. Oliver had had
to approach them obliquely. But it had been impossible for
them not to guess for what he was longing. The orphanage
could give him only meagre information, if any at all. At
that time, over twenty-three years ago, it had been a small
and poverty-stricken little institution, supported by a grudging
public charity. It had had two old nurses, now dead, a female
manager, dead these past fifteen years, a charwoman and
a janitor. The last two were probably dead, also, for they
had been old when Oliver was an infant.

He had gone through the files of the Andersburg newspaper. He had found a single item which noted briefly the
fact of his desertion at the orphanage, and the date. The
police, said the newspaper, were trying to find the infant's
parents. He had been deserted at night. A man had reported
seeing "a female furtively leaving the door of the orphanage."
His mother? But the witness had been certain, in spite of
the feebleness of the one streetlight, that the "female" had
been an elderly woman. She had been poorly dressed, and wore
a shawl over her head. Later, the newspaper had noted the
fact that this deserted orphan had been adopted by William
Prescott.

As a lawyer, Oliver had access to the files of the local courts.
He had found his adoptive papers. "Parents unknown." But
one parent, dead now for twenty-two years, was no longer
unknown. He was Chauncey Arnold.

Had Oliver's mother been a servant in his house? Or
a shop-girl, a little milliner, a dressmaker? Any one of these
was possible. Oliver, oblivious to the storm, lighted another
cigarette, shielded the flame with his cupped hands. It was
little enough to go on. It would probably end in nothing.
Wasn't it wiser to let it end in nothing?

The truth, brought out into the open, might ruin him, might
hold him up to ridicule and wide public scorn. Scott, Meredith

and Owens was an old and prudent firm, full of honor, integrity and tradition. Meredith and old Scott were, themselves, Harvard graduates. They had received a letter of quiet but enthusiastic commendation from their ancient friend at Harvard, the dean of the Law school, who had written them in Oliver's behalf. He had been certain that they had made their dignified overtures to him in spite of the fact that he was of unknown parentage, and the adopted son of William Prescott. Insofar as Mr. Scott and Mr. Owens and Mr. Meredith were concerned, William Prescott did not exist.

The shadow of scandal, falling upon their junior, would horrify them. There was nothing the least unseemly in their lives; they accepted no sensational cases, only the dullest and most proper ones, estates, mortgages, sound partnerships. He, Oliver, was slowly winning their admiration and approval. But, if he once laid bare the truth, all would be lost. They would probably repudiate him, in the stateliest way, without regret or apology.

Nevertheless, he must find the truth, even if it ruined him. Something enormously important lay in that truth.

Now he was conscious that he was very cold, and that his shoulders were heavy with snow. He was about to turn back towards the house, which lay huge and dark behind him, when he heard the swift crackling of footsteps, as if someone were running towards him.

He stood still. The footsteps were light and quick; someone was in full flight. A footpad, a burglar? He was hidden by the tall spruce; in a moment the runner would pass him. He heard the wide branches of the spruce being disturbed; a shower of white snow blew up into the air. And then he saw that the runner was Barbara, her head bent against the wind. She was running as if pursued. She had stumbled sideways into the spruce, but it had hardly slowed her rush.

Oliver caught her by the arm. "Barbara!" he exclaimed.

Her round fur hat, her coat, her hair, glittered with the fine snow that had fallen upon them. Oliver saw, by the distant glow of the street lamps, that her face was distorted in terror, and that her eyes were flooded with tears. Then a fresh gust of wind and snow swirled between them.

"Don't be frightened, dear," he said. Something sinister had sent her out into this black and white fury. He felt her resist him for a moment; then, all at once, she was leaning against him and sobbing uncontrollably.

"Barbara," he said. He put his arms about her, held her close. "My poor child." Then he only held her strongly, putting his cheek against her forehead.

He let her cry, and said nothing, though he was deeply alarmed. It was not like Barbara to weep easily; he had never seen her hysterical. He felt her gloved hands clinging to him. She could not control herself, though she pressed her mouth against his shoulder in a wild attempt to stop her cries. He heard the smothered gasps and sobs, and they hurt him physically.

Now he tried to calm her. "Barbara," he said, urgently. "Dear, sweet Barbara. Try to tell me. Let me help you. What is it?"

He took her face in his hands. The tears rolled down her cheeks; her mouth was open in an expression of anguish. Impulsively, he bent his head and kissed her, first on her cheek and forehead, then on her cold lips. All at once, she was standing still and trying to see him through the swirls of snow.

She said: "What did you call me, Oliver?"

"What did I call you?" he repeated. He withdrew his hands. He looked down at her earnestly.

"You called me 'dear' and 'sweet'," she said. She was crying again, but softly now. "Did you mean that, Oliver? Am I dear and sweet—to you?"

He was silent. She took his sleeve in both her hands. "Am I, Oliver? Please tell me. I must know."

When he did not answer her, she shook him with a renewal of her wildness. "Oliver, you kissed me. You didn't kiss your sister, did you? You kissed me, didn't you?"

He took her elbows in his hands and held her tightly. "No, dear," he said. "I didn't kiss my sister. I kissed you, Barbara. Dear Barbie."

He glanced back at the house. It was almost lost in the storm. Here and there a rectangle of yellow light, blurred and misted, showed where it stood. "Barbie," he said, and then again, "Barbie."

She was only a young girl, and there, in that house, was her father, and here he was, with no name of his own and nothing to offer her, except, perhaps, hatred and violence and ignominy. Hardly knowing what he said, he exclaimed: "I don't even know who I am!"

She laughed and cried together, and leaned against him. "I don't care! I have only been afraid that you wouldn't want me, or that——" She stopped abruptly, and turned her head away from him in the deepest shame.

"Or what, Barbie?"

When she did not reply, he laughed a little, drearily. "Did you think I was your brother, Barbie?"

"Yes," she murmured.

He waited a moment, then drew a deep breath. "I see," he said. "You were afraid we couldn't be married. But we can, Barbie." Now he was astounded by his own words. "Barbie, we can't talk like this," he continued. "You are only seventeen. You don't know what you are saying. I was a fool, too, to say what I've said."

She clung to him again. "Oliver, I love you. Haven't you seen it, Oliver?"

Once again, he looked at the house. He sighed. "Yes, dear, I saw it. And I love you, too. I've always loved you, I suppose. But Barbie, I've nothing to offer you, nothing. And there is something that I must do that might make it quite impossible for you ever to marry me. I don't want to do it, but I must."

She had heard only what she wanted to hear. She threw her arms about his neck and kissed him again and again. The fresh sweet breath was against his lips. "Oliver!" she cried. There was so much innocence, so much passion, in her voice and in her kisses, that he was profoundly moved and shaken. He put his arms about her again. He wanted to return her kisses; instead, he said:

"Please listen, my love, my dear. I have nothing, I am nobody. In a little while, perhaps, I'll be even worse than a nobody. There's something I have to do. We must wait, Barbie, wait until you have enough judgment and understanding."

She heard him now. She leaned back against his arms and looked at him piercingly. "You think I am too young, don't you?" she asked. "I'm not, Oliver, not really. Oliver, I ran out because I couldn't stay in that house any longer. You must take me away, soon, or perhaps I'll have to go away by myself and never come back. I'm not hysterical. You must believe me."

He thought of Matthew, and though he was again alarmed for Barbara, he said: "I believe you. Yes, I believe you."

Her hands held the arms she was leaning back against. She said: "Oliver, will you marry me? Soon?"

"Barbie," he began.

She was speaking faster, and the clutch of her fingers was strong. "You said you have nothing, that you're a 'nobody'. Even if it were true, which it isn't, I wouldn't care. You have what you are, and to me that is so much that I feel ashamed to ask for it. Will you marry me, Oliver? Will you take me away?"

He tried to withdraw his arms, but she held them tightly about her.

"Do I have to wait until I know what it is you've got to do?" she asked. When he did not answer her, she said: "No. I won't, and I can't wait. Whatever it is, it'll mean nothing to me, Oliver, can't you see that?"

But he was looking beyond her, as if he had forgotten her. He was seeing Eugene Arnold. Barbara saw this, and her hands dropped from him. "What is it, Oliver?" she stammered. "Why do you look like that? You looked like——"

"Who, Barbie?" He regarded her with sudden sharpness.

She was shivering with the cold. "I don't know," she faltered, and even took a step backward from him. "I don't know. But it's someone I don't like."

He tried to make his voice indulgent, but the hardness was behind it: "And you've never before noticed what you thought was a resemblance to someone?"

"I don't know," she said, unsteadily. "Yes, I think I do know. I think I kept seeing the—resemblance, and I shut it out of my mind. I think that was because I didn't want to know whom you resembled. I still don't. I don't know what you're talking about!" she cried, with abrupt wildness.

She began to cry: "Even if you do look like someone I hate, it doesn't matter to me. Lots of people look like other people who are perfect strangers. What does it matter? What's wrong with you, Oliver?"

Eugene and Julia. He had forgotten Julia. Somehow, Julia would contrive to have Eugene.

Oliver suddenly remembered the girl who was staring at him so wretchedly. He was disturbed to see her in such misery and confusion. "Barbie, dear," he said gently, "you are quite right. It doesn't matter." He put his arm about her, held her tightly. "Barbie, will you marry me? Not right away, but in a few months perhaps?"

"Oliver!" She was stunned with joy.

"You mustn't tell this to anyone, Barbie, until we are ready, not even to your mother. You must promise me that."

"I will! I will, Oliver!" she cried.

She was like a child. She is a child, thought Oliver. But she is also a woman. No child could kiss a man as she had kissed him.

"Well, then," he said, affectionately, "it's all settled. It's very late. And you are shaking with the cold. Let us go back to the house."

He drew her hand through his arm, and they returned to the house together.

CHAPTER XLVII

THE COLD SPRING air numbed Oliver's face as he left the court-house. But he was both elated and satisfied. He had won his case, in behalf of the clients of Scott, Meredith & Owens, against almost insuperable difficulties. Mr. Scott had been very dubious; he had intended to present the case, himself, but had been stricken with influenza. As Oliver was familiar with all the details, he had asked him to take his place. Oliver had won. Mr. Scott, in his majestic way, would be more than pleased.

Oliver was still not certain that he would be able to retain his position when the truth was known. However, he treated himself to a good luncheon at the Imperial Hotel. He had almost three hours before court opened again. In the meantime, he had some personal business to do. That morning, before going to court, he had received two messages. One had been from his adoptive father, William Prescott, the other from Mr. Ezra Bassett. The one from William had disturbed him greatly, for he was apprehensive that William, the strangely intuitive, had guessed the secret engagement between himself and Barbara. In any event, the interview would hardly be pleasant.

He went at once to the great sprawling saw-mills, to which he was now a stranger. Under a pewter sky, the wide and curving river gleamed silver-gray. Beyond, the mountains raised rough brown heads in the pale spring sunlight. They were like the heads of enormous old giants, patched with white. About the mills and the barges and flat-boats drawn up at the docks there hummed an immense activity. Oliver could smell the clean resinous odor of lumber, could hear the screeching thunder of machinery. Business was good again, and Oliver was pleased; though, remembering William, he felt again a sudden pang. He looked up at the main building; the words, "The Prescott Lumber Company," had been newly painted, as if in exultant defiance of the prophesied "panic." The brilliant white letters blazed in the sunlight.

He was respectfully told by a clerk that Mr. Prescott had not yet returned from luncheon, and "Mr. Oliver" was requested to wait. The other clerks looked at him curiously. He sat in the waiting-room, and looked about him. The door was open. Across the hall was another door; it was shut, and on it was painted in gilt letters: "Eugene Arnold, General Manager."

Oliver stood up. He went across the hall, opened the door, encountered the surprised face of a reception clerk. "Mr. Arnold, please," said Oliver, abruptly. "Mr. Oliver Prescott calling."

The clerk scuttled to a distant door, opened it, disappeared. In a moment or two he returned, agape. "Mr. Arnold will receive you, sir," he said. Oliver went at once to the door, closed it behind him.

Eugene was sitting at his desk, a wide and shining width of clean mahogany. Everything about the room had his own aseptic quality, austere and barren. The bare windows looked out on the river, and so large were they that the view outside seemed an extension of the interior. For a moment or two, Eugene looked at Oliver in deliberate silence, then said, indifferently: "Hello, Oliver. You wished to see me?"

Oliver was perturbed. He did not know why he had come to this room; he had acted on impulse, and he was not given to impulse either by nature or by his legal training. He sat down slowly, watching Eugene very closely. He studied him with great penetration. Eugene, in return, just sat there, his pen poised above a sheaf of papers. Oliver saw the thin fleshless fingers. Involuntarily, he looked down at his own. Eugene's hands were almost colorless; his own were dark. Yet, they were the same hands. That face, with its lack of color, the skin parched and drawn about the tight mouth, might have been his own face, younger and darker and slightly fuller. Ten years younger, thought Oliver. As I grow older, we are becoming more and more alike. One of these days everyone is bound to notice.

"Father asked me to call in to see him," he said. "I'm in a hurry, and I thought he might be in here with you."

Eugene laid down his pen. There was a pucker of bleached flesh between his eyes.

"Well, he isn't here," said Eugene. He looked at his watch consideringly, all his movements neat and partrician. His clothing fitted him excellently; there were no blurred outlines about Eugene. Oliver saw his brother's thin broad chest and shoulders, so like his own.

Eugene was looking at him again, and again there was the

pucker between his light eyebrows. "Have you any idea why he asked you to come?" he said. "Perhaps I could help, and save him time. He isn't well, you know."

Oliver was vaguely angered. "I know that," he said slowly. Why hadn't anyone noticed that their voices at times were startlingly alike, expecially when he, Oliver, was annoyed? He smiled. Eugene was indeed disturbed, not only instinctively, but consciously. So far as he knew, Oliver had never before been summoned to these offices by William. He is trying to pump me, thought Oliver, with bitter enjoyment. He said: "After all, I ought to know whether Father is well or ill. I live in the same house with him."

Eugene said nothing. He stared at Oliver, thoughtfully. He is trying to read my mind, thought the younger man. He is good at that.

Then, as never before, he became aware of the controlled and silent power that was in Eugene Arnold. He had never underestimated Eugene, but he had not fully known him until now. A deadly man, he said to himself. He is like a big lean cat, waiting to strike in the dark with the most exquisite precision and deadliness.

Oliver thought of Julia, so pale and speechless these days that William was fearfully and angrily demanding of her that she see Dr. Banks, or, better still, that she consent to go to New York with him for an examination. On these occasions, Julia would either rise and go out of the room, still not speaking, or would burst into tears. Oliver, remembering this, looked at Eugene closely. Nothing was disturbing this man very much. He was not giving Julia any assistance. He would not endanger himself. Many men risked danger for women. This man would not.

He became aware that Eugene was still regarding him almost without blinking, and that he had been regarding Eugene in the same manner. Eugene frowned slightly. He said: "Tom is beginning to take many details off his hands."

Oliver had been so obsessed with this man whom he believed to be his brother that he momentarily was confused. He almost said: "Who?" He caught himself. "Yes, I suppose so. Good for Tom, and good for Father." His tone was sincere. "You haven't been to dinner recently, Gene."

"No," said Eugene, coldly. "I've been spending quite a few nights here, going over a few small matters."

Small matters! thought Oliver.

He looked about the large bare office. That there was some

conspiracy he had known for a long time; the knowledge had been intuitive. He would not find out about it here. Eugene was too brilliant, too clever, for that.

The door opened, and Tom entered with his usual big boisterousness. "Hey, you, Gene!" he shouted, before he realized that Oliver was in the room. His cunning eyes narrowed to slits, and his large, heavy face darkened. But he said, casually enough, in a lower voice: "Oh, hello, Oliver." He stood there, quite near the door, but still far off, and now there was a wary suspicion about him. His eyes slid from Oliver to Eugene, and back again, with great rapidity.

So, he's using Tom, thought Oliver. Or they're in it together. What is it they are "in"? Tom was still young; he could not conceal his uneasiness, his dislike. He even ran the tip of his tongue over his lips. His massive shoulders drooped slightly, as if he was afraid, and his nostrils widened.

"Has Mr. Prescott returned?" asked Eugene, with cool aplomb. "Oliver is waiting to see him. Your father asked him to call."

"Eh?" said Tom. He turned to Oliver. His ruddy color had faded somewhat. "He wants to see you? Why?"

Oliver stood up. "I don't know why," he replied, curtly. "That's why I came to find out. Didn't you know he'd sent for me?"

"No," replied Thomas, in the usual bullying tone he used towards Oliver. "I don't know all the old man's business." It was evident he believed Oliver to be lying, for he studied him craftily. "He sees you almost every night. Why didn't he talk to you at home?"

"Why don't you ask him?" said Oliver. Thomas jerked his head a little. He looked at Oliver, glowering, surprise glinting in his eyes. "What?" he muttered. "Oh. Well, if it's important to you, he's in his office now. We went out to lunch together."

He seemed bemused and taken aback. Very intently, he watched Oliver go to the door.

"Good-bye," called Oliver over his shoulder. He went out, closing the door decisively behind him.

There was silence in the room after he had gone. Tom still stood there, clenching his huge meaty hands, which hung at his side. Eugene watched him, calmly amused. When Thomas saw this, he said with low pent rage: "What're you laughing at? What's he doing in here, with you?"

"Oh, sit down and stop being dramatic," said Eugene. Thomas sat down. He obeyed Eugene automatically, as he had never obeyed anyone before. "Your father sent for him," continued Eugene. "So he came. It must be some private matter, of no particular importance. Perhaps your father is thinking of giving him a little business."

He tapped his fingers on his desk. "Your father does his business here, you remember. Calling Oliver here makes the call official. Why are you glaring at me like that, Tom? It isn't my fault that he came in here looking for your father."

Thomas rubbed his temple with his knuckles.

"He's sly," he muttered. "You think he's going to give up anything he can get? Lawyers are pretty shrewd, you know. Pa calls them 'the devil's race'. Think he thinks he can get—anything?"

"No," said Eugene. He spoke abstractedly. He turned sideways and stared at the gleaming river beyond. "I don't think he wants 'anything'. In fact, I don't think he'd take 'anything' —from your father."

"Well, he's a fool. He was always a fool."

Thomas waited for Eugene to answer. But the other man continued to look at the river. His sharp profile was outlined against a silvery light. "I've got it!" exclaimed Thomas. "Do you know something? He looks like you!"

The fingers that tapped on the desk, slowly and rhythmically, stopped. They lay on the wood; they curled a little, like a spring. Eugene turned again to Thomas, who was scrutinizing him acutely.

"I've wondered for a long time who he looked like," said Thomas, grinning. "It's you, that's who it is. Funny, isn't it?"

Eugene did not answer.

Thomas began to chuckle. "It's the funniest damned thing I ever saw! Old Oliver getting to look like you. Why, he even sounded like you, a minute ago!"

The idea amused him intensely. Then, after a long time, even Thomas became aware of something terrible in this room, and he no longer chuckled.

"What's the matter with you, Gene?" he asked, uncertainly. "Why do you look at me like that? Just because I said he's beginning to look like you?"

Eugene picked up his pen. He said, coolly: "Don't talk nonsense, Tom. I have a few things to check here. We'll go through the mills this afternoon."

Thomas got to his feet in his lumbering, awkward fashion. He was his father's heir, and Eugene was only William's employee. But during these past few months Eugene had begun to dominate him smoothly, subtly. Thomas knew this, felt it. It had never antagonized him, he was intelligent, he knew a master when he met one, and was prepared to follow, especially when the following was to his own advantage. "All right," he said, sullenly. "I'll go back to my office and do some little things, myself."

He stamped out, loudly, like a child who has been reprimanded by an inexorable schoolmaster. He glanced back once, Eugene was writing notes swiftly, his fair head bent over the papers. Thomas banged the door angrily behind him.

When he was alone, Eugene slowly and carefully laid down his pen. He sat with his hands on the desk, and again they were curled, like springs.

William, lowering and gloomy, faced Oliver across his own desk. He was aging fast, so fast indeed that he seemed older than his actual years. Something had broken in him since Matthew had gone away, or, rather, something had begun to seep away from him, like the slow leeching of blood.

"Why didn't you come to me in the first place?" he demanded, angrily. "Why all this sneaking around, asking questions in what you probably thought was a very bright and clever way, not likely to arouse suspicion? I could have told you what there is to know. You didn't have to go prowling around that asylum, sniffing up every tree, until the superintendent felt it incumbent upon himself to tell me. You had no right to humiliate me like this, make a fool of me."

"I'm sorry," said Oliver, quietly. "I can see now that I've been making myself a little ridiculous. You know I wouldn't want to cause you any embarrassment. After all, it was a long time ago."

"Yes," agreed William, still angrily. He paused. He regarded Oliver with unusual somberness, and now he was no longer infuriated. "Why do you want to know, anyway? Aren't you satisfied with things the way they are?"

Oliver said: "It isn't that. Please believe me. After all, it's a natural curiosity, isn't it? I'd really like to know who I am, whether I still have a mother or a father, or perhaps a brother or a sister."

William tried again to be enraged. It was a useless attempt. He looked at Oliver more closely. The vulnerable spot in him was touched. He said, roughly: "I don't think so. Yes," he added, "I can understand your wanting to know. I suppose it's natural. And you're dissatisfied, too?"

"I didn't say that, Father," said Oliver, quickly, full of

compassion. He tried to smile. "Put it down to my legal training, if you want to."

William managed a saturnine smile. He could not remember
having smiled at Oliver for years. "A good training," he even
managed to say, with heavy banter. "I know. I paid the bills.
And you've done well at it, I've got to admit that. Just heard
a report about you from old Owens last week. First time
the dried-up old rascal ever spoke to me without being spoken
to first. 'Wonderful mind that son of yours has,' he said."
William stopped. He frowned. "Well, you might have come
to me," he went on, hastily. His fallen cheeks and jowls had
mottled with color. Vaguely, he wondered why he should feel
this sad aching.

"I don't suppose there is anything to know, beyond what
I've already learned," said Oliver.

William tried for sarcasm. "You lawyers! Perhaps you've
suspected you might be a secret heir or something, eh? Hidden
away, so someone else will inherit? A wicked step-mother,
or something? Well, you're wrong."

Oliver sat up straighter. He spoke carefully. "No doubt
I am, Father. But is there anything else you can tell me?"

William leaned back in his chair, scowling. "I know what
they've told you. It wasn't all. Oh, I went into it before I
adopted you. Thoroughly. Wanted to be sure there'd be
no future claims." He stopped again, looked at Oliver as
if seeing him clearly for the first time in a long while. "No
claims," he repeated, almost inaudibly. "I didn't want that.
I wanted to be sure you'd belong only to me." Again, his face
mottled with unhealthy color.

Oliver was unendurably moved. He waited.

William said, loudly and harshly, pushing back his chair
so that it almost fell over with him. "Or perhaps you thought
you might prove I was your real father!"

"No," said Oliver, gently. He lied without hesitancy, out
of compassion. "I'd have liked to have found that out, if
it were so."

"Eh?" muttered William. He put his hand over the lower
part of his face, and his eyes, once so dominant, so powerful,
were the eyes of a broken old man. Oliver looked away. He
said: "You've given me so much. I don't want anything else
from you, Father. I've taken too much from you already.
I only wish I could return it in some way. You know there
isn't anything I wouldn't do for you."

William's fingers trembled about his lips and chin. "I

know," he said, then he dropped his hand. He sat upright. For a brief moment he was again the strong and dominant man of his younger years. He spoke concisely:

"There's just this you don't know. On the night you were left at the hospital, someone rang the janitor's bell. It was late. He was an old feller, that janitor, and he came sleepily to the door. There was a woman there with a child in her arms. Not a young woman. Just a poor woman, about fifty years old, in a shawl. She said she wanted to talk to the manager about leaving the child—you—there for a few days. The janitor let her come into the hall. He was still half asleep. He said he'd go for the manager. Then the woman said to him: 'The baby's name is Oliver.' Apparently she wanted to be sure he had heard her, for she took him by the arm, and repeated that."

"Oliver!" said the younger man.

William nodded. "Yes, that's what she said. I never liked the name, myself." Again he smiled gloomily. "He left her to call the manager. When he'd brought her down, the woman who had brought the baby was gone. She had left the child—you—on a couch in the hall. No one heard her go. Everybody was asleep. And that," concluded William, "is all there is to tell."

"And she never came back?" asked Oliver.

"Of course not. They looked for her. She couldn't have been your mother. She was too old. They examined your clothes. They were poor, but clean and warm. You'd evidently had good care, for you were healthy and plump, they told me. And you weren't afraid, so you hadn't been abused. A few months later I adopted you."

Oliver tried to smile lightly. "So I wasn't exactly left on a doorstep, as the story goes."

"No. But almost."

Oliver stood up. "Thank you, Father," he said.

William said, with annoyance: "And now, you've got to stop this nonsense. There's nothing more to find out. You're only irritating me, going about asking questions."

"I'll remember," agreed Oliver, somewhat ambiguously.

He walked back slowly to the court-house, thinking intently. At any rate, he had been given a name. Oliver. Oliver what? And then he had a most fantastic idea. He began to hurry. He reached the court-house in a state of breathlessness.

Within a short time he had found a copy of Chauncey Arnold's probated will. It was dated two years, or a trifle less, before he had died. It was a brief will, but a sound one;

at that time he had had a fortune, a position and a prosperous business. He had left his money to Alice. And then came a curious paragraph:

"Upon the death of my wife, Alice Arnold, the principal is to be divided between or among my issue, equally, without reservation, or prejudice, under any circumstances."

Now all the other phrases of the will were blurred away, and Oliver stared grimly at the last paragraph. "Between or among my issue." Chauncey Arnold, then, had known that another woman was about to bear him a child. He had not named her. He had not named any child, not even Eugene. He had referred only to his "issue."

Chauncey Arnold had been swept into bankruptcy. But he had left a sum in trust, and this had educated Eugene. No one questioned the will, or wondered at it. It had been assumed that Chauncey Arnold had had hopes that Alice would bear him more children. She had borne only one child.

Oliver was breathing unevenly. All at once he was certain that Eugene Arnold knew the exact wording of the will.

Oliver returned to the court-room, pale and stern.

CHAPTER XLVIII

IT WAS ONLY AFTER the court had adjourned that Oliver remembered that Ezra Bassett had sent a message asking the younger man to call upon him. It was odd. He could not remember that Ezra had ever spoken to him with interest or kindliness, or even noticed him. Then he remembered that of late Mr. Bassett had often followed him curiously with his eyes. An obscure excitement took possession of Oliver, but he repressed it. He found a telephone in the court building and called the bank. It was after banking hours; Ezra had probably gone home. But Mr. Bassett, he was informed by a clerical voice, would talk to him immediately.

Ezra's rich voice, cosy and warm, came to Oliver's ears in the friendliest of fashions. Indeed, he wished to see Oliver. "Quite important, my boy," concluded Ezra, mysteriously. Oliver replaced the receiver, looked at it with deep thoughtfulness.

He was admitted to Mr. Bassett's inner office, where he found the rubicund old banker smoking pleasantly before the fire. He took Oliver's hand; he pressed it warmly in his plump fingers, and his clever old eyes twinkled at the young man as if with affection. Oliver was not deceived. The smell of something queer was very strong in this room. He expressed gratitude for Ezra's offer of brandy. Ezra went to a locked and inlaid cabinet and drew out a musty old bottle and two small glasses. "Pleasant, this," he commented. "I've been hearing a lot about you lately, Oliver. Very good things. Been following some of your cases, in the papers. Real brilliance. Only last night I said to Mrs. Bassett: 'That young man is brilliant. He'll go a long way.'" He carefully replaced the bottle, and said, casually, "But then, anyone might have expected that."

Oliver became alert. He said, as if respectfully amused: "Why should anyone 'expect' brilliance, or anything else of that kind, from me, Mr. Bassett? No one knows who I am or where I came from."

Mr. Bassett put his keys in his pocket, chuckled. He came back to the fire, sat down. His comfortable paunch pushed against his waistcoat, which was of black silk. He smiled benevolently at Oliver.

"You've had a good education, Oliver," he said. "The best."

Oliver sipped at the brandy, which was most excellent. "Thanks to my father," he said.

Again Mr. Bassett chuckled. He held up his glass to the firelight, nodded his head as if satisfied, drank a little. "Oliver," he said, "you're a lawyer. I want to engage your services. In short, I want your advice."

Oliver said: "Thanks, Mr. Bassett. But Mr. Scott, or Mr. Meredith, or Mr. Owens, would have been a better choice, though I can't help but be gratified at your calling me."

"Nonsense," replied Mr. Bassett sturdily. He set his glass down on the table at his elbow. He put the pink tips of his fingers together. He studied Oliver. Then he began to nod his head. His next words, however, were very innocuous: "I want you, my boy. As I said, I want your advice. Strictly confidential, of course."

"Strictly confidential," agreed Oliver. He had not known what it was he had expected, but now he was aware of the deep emptiness of disappointment. "Anything said to a lawyer is sacred, as you know, Mr. Bassett. As sacred as what transpires in the confessional."

Mr. Bassett smiled. "Yes, I know," he said. "Sacred. I knew it wasn't necessary for me to remind you of that, Oliver."

Was there a warning in his voice, a suety threat? Oliver put down his own glass. But Mr. Bassett was beaming with paternal kindliness.

"It is, in a way, a very personal matter, Oliver, and, as I said, strictly confidential. It is also a matter of conscience. You would not think a banker would have a conscience, would you?"

"One is likely to encounter a conscience in the most unlikely places," answered Oliver, smiling.

"I must first tell you a rather sordid story," said Mr. Bassett. He took up his glass, and again examined it critically. "I reserve this only for those whom I know to have the most cultivated taste," he added, idly. "I suspect you have such taste, Oliver, though poor William is notably lacking in the appreciation of good liquor."

"Thank you," said Oliver.

Mr. Bassett touched a bell on the table beside him. At the hard clear jingle, Oliver started. A clerk came in. Mr.

Bassett said: "Curtis, you will please make out a check, as retainer, for Mr. Oliver Prescott." He turned to Oliver. "Say about two hundred dollars, Oliver?"

Oliver sat very still. He said: "Two hundred dollars will be quite sufficient, Mr. Bassett."

"Now, then," said Mr. Bassett. His voice had subtly changed. It had become less friendly. He clasped his hands over his paunch, looked dreamily at the fire. "A very sordid story, Oliver. It concerns an old friend of mine who died many years ago. Mr. Chauncey Arnold.

"An old friend," he repeated. He coughed. "Of course, you were only an infant at the time Mr. Arnold died, so you could not be expected to know all the details of the matter between your—father, and Chauncey."

"I know them," said Oliver.

"Indeed," murmured Mr. Bassett. He sighed. He looked at Oliver out of the corners of his eyes. "I suppose it was inevitable that you'd get to know them. And then, there was Gene Arnold. Very good of William to employ him. William couldn't have made a better choice. He has an instinct for the proper men."

Oliver's fingers tapped on the arm of his chair. Mr. Bassett was studying him a trifle too acutely. He was moving his eyes over Oliver's face, over his body, and then over his tapping fingers. Oliver immediately held his hand still.

"What do you think of Gene Arnold, Oliver?" asked Mr. Bassett. He was smiling oddly.

"I don't know him well," replied Oliver. "I've seen him thousands of times, I suppose, but still I don't know him well. There was never any—shall we call it rapport, between us, sir."

Mr. Bassett appeared vaguely amused at Oliver's words. But he only murmured: "Yes, yes, of course." He went on: "In spite of what some ill-natured people might say, Chauncey was no fool, except in one instance. He might have continued to display intelligence, if he hadn't been so self-indulgent in his later years, just before he died. You never saw him; he was a very handsome young man, at one time, very—er—vivid. We were children and boys, together, Oliver. Chauncey, however, later on, developed a tendency to indiscretion, and put on too much flesh. Moreover, he drank considerably." Mr. Bassett sighed with regret.

"Is that the 'sordid' story you wish to tell me, Mr. Bassett?" asked Oliver, after some moments of silence had passed.

"Eh? No, it was only a prelude, my dear boy. I just wanted you to understand Mr. Arnold's whole story, his background."

Again, Oliver waited. He seemed to have lost all senses but hearing.

"People are apt to be rather censorious about what they consider a man's loss of 'virtue'," Mr. Bassett went on. "We are coming on more enlightened and less rigid days; perhaps this is good, perhaps it is bad.

"Now, Oliver, you perhaps remember Mrs. Arnold?"

Oliver had a sudden vision of Alice. "Yes, I called her Aunt Alice. She was kind to me, and my mother regarded her as her friend."

Mr. Bassett nodded, agreeably. "Yes. They were what, in my day, we called 'great ladies'. Your mother, Oliver, is still a great lady." He paused. "Chauncey was devoted to Alice. And that is why he came to me, nearly twenty-five years ago, with a story that distressed him to tell and me to hear.

"In short," said Mr. Bassett, "it was the old, old story. The old story, this time with a slight variation. He was once a rich man. Alice had a personal maid, a quiet, demure little thing, a Mennonite. You know the Mennonites, Oliver? Full of integrity, rigid in their personal lives?"

Oliver could not speak.

For a moment or two, Mr. Bassett gave his attention to the fire.

"Her name," he said, "was Mary Bauer. She was eighteen years old and, in spite of her queer clothes and her little bonnets, a very pretty little creature. I saw her only once or twice. Big dark eyes, smooth dark hair, and the sweetest voice."

"In short," repeated Oliver, and his voice was hoarse, "it was the 'old, old story'. In short, Mr. Arnold seduced Mary Bauer."

Mr. Bassett coughed, as if hurt at such open vulgarity. "Dear me," he murmured, "for a lawyer, you are a very precipitate young man, Oliver. Let us say that Chauncey and the girl fell in love."

"A middle-aged man and a girl hardly more than a child!" exclaimed Oliver with loud bitterness. He caught himself. Mr. Bassett was smiling, and the smile was not agreeable.

"It happened that Chauncey was much taken by the girl," he said. "I think he even loved her. Yes, I am sure of that. I don't know how the whole thing happened, and especially when the girl came of such a God-fearing family, and people. But it did. Of course, none of us knew anything about it, not even Alice, I am certain. And so I was astounded when Chauncey came to me, quite in despair, and told me the girl was going to have a child. His child."

Oliver could hardly control himself. This pink old devil knew. He knew everything there was to know.

Mr. Bassett sighed. "When the girl found out, she told Chauncey. She also told him she was going away. Not to her home. She couldn't return there, she said. She would go away to some good friends of her family, in Greensleet, who would care for her, until she could work again. She was very proud; she came of proud folk."

Greensleet! A small town only thirty miles from Andersburg——

"In those days," Mr. Bassett went on, "thirty miles was a long distance. If friends or relatives in Andersburg had connections in Greensleet, it was as if they lived hundreds of miles away. Besides, Greensleet was a tiny village, twenty-five years ago. It had one small bank, the First National, one or two shops, and only one school. It was not even on a railroad spur. Backwoods."

He looked at Oliver's glass. "More brandy, Oliver?"

"No," said Oliver.

Mr. Bassett smiled comfortably. "Well, then. Of course, I was very disturbed when Chauncey told me the story. The girl would not accept money from him. She only begged him not to follow her, or to see her again. It was, she said, the only way she could protect herself. A very determined and resolute little thing, with character. So, she went to Greensleet, to her friends. And Chauncey came to me. Business was very bad. But he gave me three thousand dollars for the girl. He had promised her he would not see her again, but couldn't help being upset about her."

"Very kind of him," remarked Oliver.

"I was to send the money to the bank in Greensleet. I informed the bank that 'friends' were forwarding the money for Mary, friends who preferred to remain anonymous. The bank sent me a receipt." Mr. Bassett paused. "I have the receipt."

Oliver gripped the arms of his chair.

Mr. Bassett said, mournfully: "I came upon the story much later. It is all in my files, carefully locked away. Mary apparently found her 'friends' in Greensleet not too hospitable. At any rate, it appears that within six weeks she married a young ne'er-do-well of a farm laborer in that village, possibly with the idea of protecting her child. No one knew much about him, or his family. The bank had notified her, when she arrived in Greensleet, that the money was waiting for her there. She refused to touch it. At first. Then, one day she appeared at the bank, said she was going to be married and that she would take the money to buy a farm for her husband-to-be. That is why he married her, I suspect. She must have told him the whole story. In a way, she must have bribed him to marry her."

Oliver could see little Mary Bauer with deep clarity, a girl suddenly awakening to the realization that, unless she accepted Chauncey Arnold's money, her child would be born under dreadful circumstances. She had become afraid, not for herself, but for her unborn baby.

"Yes, yes," said Mr. Bassett. "Very sad. Very sad, indeed. She married the young man, they bought a farm. It was good property, but he was worthless." Mr. Bassett apparently brooded over Mary and her husband. He said idly: "His name was John Oliver."

Oliver stood up, involuntarily. Mr. Bassett had apparently not seen Oliver jump to his feet. He was too engrossed in memories of the past.

"I have all this information in my files," he said, meditatively. "All of it. Ah, well.

"Perhaps things might not have gone too badly, except for a most unfortunate circumstance. About six months after the marriage, the baby was born. Then, in the middle of the night, when the child was about a year old, the farmhouse burned down."

Oliver forced his voice through the stricture in his throat. "They died?"

Mr. Bassett shook his head. "No. John Oliver was a drunkard. He must have caused the fire. Mary awakened to find her bedroom full of smoke and flames. She escaped with the child, just before the roof crashed in. She slept downstairs. John slept in a room above. Apparently they did not live together. John died in the fire. The girl was terribly burned. But she had wrapped a blanket about the baby, and the child had not suffered."

Oliver listened with horror.

"The girl was given shelter in the home of a neighbor about a mile away," Mr. Bassett continued sadly. "It was winter. How she managed to find the house through the snow, in the condition she was in, I don't know. Fear for her child must have driven her. In any event, she collapsed at this farmhouse. They called in the village's only doctor. He told the farm-folk that the girl was dying. They then prevailed upon her to tell them the name of the friends who had originally been supposed to take her in and protect her. Again, fearing for her child, for she knew she could not live, she gave them the name. The friends came. They notified her family, who lived on a farm ten miles nearer Andersburg."

"Her family came?" said Oliver.

Mr. Bassett nodded. "Yes. Her mother and her father. She was the only child, this Mary, and the parents had married late in life. Grim people, I understand. Grim, unrelenting people, aghast at the story they were told. The girl begged them to keep her baby. They might have done so, had they not discovered that Greensleet was well aware that John Oliver was not the child's father. The child was an outcast; it was illegitimate. It had not even the humblest status."

And now Mr. Bassett turned his head on his thick red neck and peered up at Oliver. Their eyes met. Oliver read contempt on the smug old banker's face, a kind of gloating.

"To such people, attuned more to the Old Testament than to the New, the child was not only an outcast in the sight of man, but in the sight of God. He was as guilty as his parents. He could not be given shelter in a respectable home, where the name of God was sacred.

"So, one night, the grandmother brought him to Andersburg. Left him at the little orphanage we had then. She spoke to the janitor. She gave the old man a name, and nothing else. Then she went away. The child was called by that name."

Oliver sat down.

Mr. Bassett relaxed in his chair. "Let us be just to Chauncey. He never knew. I'm sure if he had, he would have helped the child. He never knew that the baby, left practically on the doorstep of the orphanage, was his. He died, without knowing."

"How did you know?" asked Oliver.

Mr. Bassett looked reflectively at his tensed fingers. "It came about very oddly. About twelve years ago, I received a letter. From the girl's mother. Mary's father was dead by this time. The mother was dying of some obscure disease, and probably her conscience had begun to disturb her. She had heard from her daughter that Chauncey had had money deposited to Mary's account in the Greensleet bank, money which had bought the farm. As natural executor of her daughter's estate, she had learned that I was the banker who had forwarded the money. So she wrote me. She enclosed two yellowed newspaper clippings. One was about the desertion of the baby, the other about its adoption. She wrote that her daughter had told her Chauncey Arnold was the father. For years, she said in her letter, she had pondered whether or not she should communicate with the man who had adopted her grandchild. But, for some hidden reason, she could not bring herself to do it. I gather she thought he ought not to know, that it was best he should not know, for, as she said, 'he must be a very kind man'."

Yes, thought Oliver.

"But the old woman was still wrathful against Chauncey Arnold. She hated him, with what our earlier writers called 'an undying hatred'. She could not forgive him. Apparently, she did not know he was dead. She thought he ought to be told, that he ought to be 'shamed', that her daughter must be 'avenged in the sight of God'. She did not want the adoptive father to be told. She urged me not to tell him. But Chauncey must know. He must see his child call another man 'father'. That would be his punishment."

Mr. Bassett got up heavily, went to his cabinet again, brought out the brandy. He filled Oliver's glass, and his own. He sat down. He drank meditatively. But Oliver did not drink.

"Naturally, I was greatly disturbed, my boy. Chauncey was dead. I knew the man who had adopted the child. What should I do? Should I open old wounds, cause misery and distress to my—friend? For, he, too, you see, hated Chauncey Arnold. It was a great responsibility. I felt unequal to it. What would happen to the boy, if my friend learned that his adopted son was really the child of the man he hated? No," said Mr. Bassett. "I was not equal to telling. Let the dead bury the dead."

No, thought Oliver. You did not tell because you felt it might some day be a weapon. A weapon against William Prescott. You have been hiding that weapon. You've waited for the time to use it. The time never came.

He said, roughly: "But you intend telling your 'friend'—now?"

Mr. Bassett gave him a hurt glance. "My dear boy! Certainly not! How could you think that? And for what reason?"

"You are waiting, then, for the time to tell Eugene Arnold who his brother is?"

Mr. Bassett sipped his brandy with relish. "Exactly," he said, imperturbably. He became thoughtful. "Or, perhaps better still, for the brother to reveal his identity to Gene."

Now Oliver understood it all. He got to his feet; slowly and stiffly, he walked up and down the room. Mr. Bassett watched him, smacked his lips over the brandy, and smiled.

Oliver stopped before the old man. "Mr. Bassett," he asked softly, "why have you told me this story?"

"Simple enough," replied Mr. Bassett. "I wanted your advice. Shall I tell this adopted young man of his real parentage?"

For a long time they looked at each other. The fire crackled. The short spring evening was darkening outside.

Oliver said: "No. Not yet."

Mr. Bassett nodded. "Good, but when?"

"When the time comes. You are waiting for the time, aren't you?"

"You are very astute, Oliver."

Oliver drew a deep breath. "You have everything, the letter, the clippings, the receipts?"

"Yes. Certainly. And the child's birth certificate, and Mary's marriage certificate."

Oliver took up his hat and coat. "Good-bye, Mr. Bassett. And, of course, this is very confidential. You made sure of that. Good-bye, Mr. Bassett."

Mr. Bassett coughed. "Er, just a moment, my dear boy."

They walked into the bank together, Mr. Bassett's hand on Oliver's arm. All doors were locked; the clerks were busy at their books. Mr. Bassett called one of them, and within a few moments he and Oliver were standing in the vaults. Mr. Bassett opened a certain box, while Oliver stood by. "This box is in your name, Oliver," said Mr. Bassett.

Inside, there was a yellow envelope, filled with letters and papers. Oliver took up the envelope, and balanced it in his hand. The papers that established his paternity.

CHAPTER XLIX

THE THUNDEROUS evening outside, this late May day, was not more thunderous than the atmosphere in the library of the Prescott house.

The western skies had resolved themselves into tumultuous masses of tumbling dark cloud, through which thunder-heads gushed upwards like enormous fountains of vapor, crowned and bursting with the gold of the falling sun. In the east, the skies remained bright, and the mountains stood in vivid radiance against the blackening western heavens. But it was a foreboding radiance, already dying abruptly on some of the purplish ranges. To the east, the city of Andersburg, lying in its valley, still glimmered distinct and detailed in the sun, though the shadow had begun to blur its distant outlines. All day, it had been unseasonably hot and humid and uneasy. Now, though the west churned in chaotic and livid cloud-shapes, what breeze had stirred through the streets of the city, and set the mountain trees to moving, had died away. Over everything lay a deathly hush. But the earth was disturbed. It filled the hot air with bruised scents, the sharp tang of grass, the smell of dust.

William had returned home slightly earlier than usual, though when Ursula had anxiously questioned him he had replied impatiently that he was perfectly well. The heat had tired him a little, had made him sluggish. He wanted to rest before dinner. He went into the library, shut the door behind him with a bang. Once there, his sudden activity had subsided. He had almost fallen into a chair. The windows faced the west. The room waited in pent darkness for the storm. William lit no lamps. He sat in his chair, his head on his chest. Inwardly, he was fighting, fighting his hopelessness, his intuitive sense that something was most dreadfully wrong with him, and with everything. Beyond the windows reached the wide vista of sky and mountain and cloud, lit occasionally by ugly flashes of lightning. Now there was a muttering, which seemed to come more from the apprehensive earth than from the sky.

A servant came in silently, carrying a tray on which there

was a bottle of the whiskey which William loathed, and a glass. She put the tray down near the exhausted man, and went out as silently as she had come. With a great effort William turned his head and looked at the whiskey. He grimaced. Then, with an even greater effort, he poured himself the prescribed amount, drank it off suddenly and quickly, to be rid of it.

It was then that the door had opened again, and Julia had entered, a slender pretty figure in the dusk. She had said in a low voice: "Papa? Papa, I must talk to you."

William had roused himself. He was no longer so tired. The sight of his favorite child stimulated him, gave him warmth and pleasure. Julia had avoided him for so long; she never came for him any more. For months she had been so silent, so pale. He had tried wheedling, love, fondling, teasing, urging, to make her tell him what troubled her so deeply. All had failed. Julia had coldly eluded him, had run away from him.

He had said: "Julie! Come in, my darling." His daughter had returned to him. She would tell him what harassed her; she would let him help her, as he had always helped her. He patted a chair near him. His manner was eager, humble, full of aching sympathy. She sat down, stiffly, on the edge of the chair. She sat there for a long time, just looking at him, while the lightning flashed outside and the earth and sky muttered ominously together.

She had begun to speak. She spoke lifelessly, but with distinctness, as if each word had been rehearsed so long that she could speak it without emotion. Even when the lightning lit up her figure, it was a figure of quietness, only the lips moving inexorably. Under the passionless words, William heard her despair.

Then he knew nothing but his own incredulity, his rage, his refusal to believe what she had been telling him, his repudiation. Long after she had stopped talking and was only sitting there waiting, he could not speak. He could only say to himself, over and over: No. No. No.

Finally, in a strangled voice he said: "I'll send him away. You'll forget him then."

"No, Papa," replied Julia, very quietly. "For, if you do, I'll go away, myself, and you'll never see me again. Never."

"Where will you go?" he cried. There was such a weight and pain in his chest. He fought against it. "Don't be a fool, Julie. What will you do, without money or home? Or, do you expect to go away with—him?"

"I've told you, Papa," she said, with dull calmness. "He

doesn't know. He never looks at me. You can't shame me like this, Papa. You can't tell him: 'My daughter loves you, and so you've got to go away.' Do you think I could live in this city, in this house, after that humiliation? Do you think I could live here, thinking of him, never forgetting him, knowing he was gone where I couldn't follow, where he would hate me if he saw me, knowing that I had ruined him for something which wasn't his fault?"

The choking sensation in William's chest was almost unbearable. He still couldn't believe. His words were incoherent: "I can't believe a daughter of mine—— You say he doesn't even know you—like—him. Haven't you any pride? What could you do, to make him notice you? Don't you know all about him, Julie? The son of a bankrupt, a worthless scoundrel ——"

"You made his father a bankrupt, Papa," said Julia. "I've heard that if a man ruins another man, he always hates him, out of self-defense."

"You are wrong, Julie." Now, when it was most necessary, he could hardly speak. "I hated him for the rascal he was. I didn't 'ruin' him out of revenge." He paused. He fought against the pain which clutched his throat and chest in such an iron grip.

"That has nothing to do with Gene. I love him, and he doesn't love me. I want him as I never wanted anything in my life, and if he goes away, I'll die, or I'll go away, myself." Julia spoke impassively.

"Julie! Do you know what you are saying? Shameless things, things no young or decent girl would ever say! Julie, is your father nothing to you? Don't you know or care about my feelings, when I hear my own daughter talk like a strumpet? You 'want' him, you say! Julie!"

Julia did not move. If he was fighting, she too was fighting, and now she was too desperate to care.

"You trust Gene, Papa," she said, implacably. "Only last night you were saying how much you rely upon him, and how well he is training Tom. I've never let him know how I feel about him. I still don't think he knows.

"Papa," she went on, without pity. "Even if I gave him encouragement, which I haven't, I don't think Gene would have me. Who are we? What are you, Papa? You are a successful business man, but who were your parents? Whom do we know, except your associates, your hangers-on, the people who think they can get something out of you? Those who come here for the summers, for the holidays, from Philadelphia

and Boston and New York—they don't know we are alive,
Papa, though this big house lies right under their noses, and
they can't escape seeing it. But Gene, Papa, is invited everywhere by those very people, who respect him, because they knew
his parents and know his background, and because he is
a gentleman."

The cruel and vicious words, spoken so quietly, so ruthlessly,
were like flung stones upon William's heart. He even lifted
his hand a little, as if to shield himself against them. Julia's
eyes gleamed upon him in the dusk.

All his love had come to this. His daughter sat at a distance
and struck him with the stones of her words, and her eyes
gleamed like stones, in the growing darkness. She hated him
—his daughter.

He could not speak. He could only sit crouched in his
chair, as if trying to protect himself from his knowledge of
his children. The love of parents was despised, because it
was given without selfishness, without demands, given from
the depths of the soul, given with the soul itself. No man,
thought William, with anguished incoherence, should ever
give his soul to anyone. He ought to have known that love
cannot be bought, not even with love, and that when one asks
for love one is the most contemptible of beggars, fit only
for ridicule and laughter.

Julia watched him, as he lay sunken in his chair, and exultation filled her. She had hurt him, struck him, shown him what
he was. He was such a fool, her father, such a maudlin old
fool.

She said, relentlessly: "If Gene ever cared for me, ever
married me, his friends would be shocked. They would say:
'How could he look at the daughter of William Prescott?
Who are the Prescotts? Who is this girl? They are nobodies.' "

William did not answer. Then she saw him, shrunken and
dwindled, his eyes closed. Again, exultation filled her. She
beat her small fists against each other in her lap.

"Do you know, Papa, why a few of the best people even
notice us? Because of Mama. Perhaps Eugene would remember
that Mama was his mother's friend. I don't know. Do you
think money could buy Gene, Papa? No!"

"Yes," said William heavily, from the depths in which he
was curled. "Yes. It could buy Eugene Arnold. You don't
know him. It could buy him." She hardly recognized his
voice, it was so thick and slow. "Yes, Julie, money could buy
Eugene Arnold. It buys every man."

"Then try to buy Gene for me, Papa," replied Julie, with

bitter contempt. She swung to her feet. "Try to buy him, Papa!"

With a terrible effort he moved in his chair. There was a taste like clay in his mouth. "Julie," he said. And then again. "Julie. Julie, my daughter."

"Oh, Papa!" she cried. "Can't you see? Can't you see that you're acting stupidly, foolishly, unreasonably? It's so very simple. I want Gene; I want to marry him. I love him, Papa. You have nothing against him, really. Have you? Have you?" she demanded, fiercely.

He said, after a little: "No. I have nothing against him."

"Then, Papa, why be so unreasonable?"

Unreasonable. He no longer thought of the repellent idea of his daughter marrying Eugene Arnold. All that remained to him was the knowledge that his daughter hated him, that he was nothing to her, that she had rejected his love as all his children had rejected it, and that she could strike at him with such malevolence and cruelty because to her his love was a base thing.

An overpowering pang of grief and desolation shook him. He must have the illusion of love. He must do something for Julia, so that she would look at him with tenderness again. He could not live without the lying love of his children. Again, he must heap their hands with gifts; he must buy them with all that he had. Otherwise, he would surely die, deprived and starving.

Inch by agonizing inch, he pulled himself up in his chair. He rubbed his face with his hands. Very slowly, he said: "Julie. You should have told me before. Why did you let yourself suffer this way? Haven't I always said I wanted to help you? Why didn't you trust me? Look, Julie, I still can't like Eugene Arnold. But perhaps—perhaps I have been unreasonable, as you say."

He fought back the pain, the sickness. He held out his hand to his daughter, as a beggar holds out a hand for bread. "Julie. I'll—try. I'll insist that that man come here. You're a beautiful girl, Julie. Any man in the world would want you. You're my daughter. And I have money, Julie. You can't help but get Gene Arnold, if you really want him, Julie. Even if he is so much older than you are, and is Chauncey Arnold's son."

It hurt him intolerably to breathe. "My daughter. I had hoped so much for you, Julie."

But now she had flung herself on her knees beside his chair. Her warm young arms were about his neck. She was kissing

him, and weeping, and làughing a little. "Dear, dear Papa!"
she cried, and her tears were on his cheeks. "Oh, Papa, forgive
me for talking to you like that. I'm just a nasty little beast.
Dear, dear Papa! How much I love you, Papa!"

He put his arm about her shoulders. He held her to him.
But his arm was cold and lifeless. The bread had been offered
the beggar. It had been sprinkled with the salt of unforgettable
cruelty.

He took the bread. He could not live without it.

He kissed his daughter. "Julie," he said. "My little girl.
My little Julie."

CHAPTER L

AT HIS RIGHT, as he climbed, lay the brilliant sea, shading from plum-color around the wild black rocks of the shore to a deep and glowing cobalt just beyond, and then to a fiery aquamarine as it approached the horizon to merge with a sky no less flaming. It was not a sea, this, so much as an element of light, liquid, ever-changing, bursting into jade spume as it broke upon stones, flowing in incandescence around the pale sheer cliffs. Matthew climbed steadily, if slowly, on the round black cobbles of the road, pausing sometimes to look over the low wall at the sea, at the light-filled sky. What had Fra Leonardo called this country? "This shining land, this singing land, this resplendent vision of Heaven!"

Not too far in the distance, Matthew could see Sorrento, a crowded chaos of tiny white and yellow and pink houses, incredibly perched like a flock of birds on the face of the mountain, roofed with red tiles blazing in a hot sun of polished brass. Behind him, on the face of the grayish-black cliff, lay the little village where he lived. At his left, a high wall climbed with him, tumbling with cataracts of white, pink and red roses and, above them, mounted the terraces of silvery olive trees and vineyards, and a scattered villa or two. Women and children passed him, bare-footed, ragged, smiling, herding loaded donkeys. Politely, they stopped to let him go on unhindered. They knew this American signore well, this man with the sun-burned face, the tall slight body, the reluctant smile. They encountered him towards sunset, every day, when the bells of the campanile shook their delicate joyousness over the sea, and Vesuvio, beyond the waters, lay, a darker blue against the lighted blue of the sky.

Now Matthew heard the songs of the fishermen as they left the coast for the waters. He saw the slim white sails of their little boats, floating out on the colored ocean. Italy sang with the voices of a people who, as Fra Leonardo said so lovingly, could laugh in the face of death and hunger, of war and ruin, and who knew that laughter and song were the only answer to the mysterious tragedy of earth.

Sometimes, on the terraces above the wall to his left,

371

Matthew saw the lemon and orange trees, sheltered under thatches of straw, and sometimes, when the sweet wind brushed his face, he could smell the almost unbearably poignant fragrance of their blossoms. Light, scent, color, vividness. He let them all pour into him, as a dying man gratefully allows life to pour into his body, revivifying him.

The narrow road dropped and rose. Between clefts in the falling slope at his right he caught narrow glimpses of some small, red-roofed house, nestling in the rocks on a lower terrace. Sometimes old open carts, drawn by donkeys, passed him, jingling. The drivers, old, too, removed their hats with the extreme courtesy of the Italian, and greeted the young man. He never rode in their carts, but that, to them, was of no importance. Their black eyes, in their sun-darkened faces, were gay with friendliness and kind acceptance. The American signore might be silent, he might reply to the gayest of greetings with only a smile, but one could see that he was "sympatico."

The road, as it climbed, twisted and turned, and each new vista was one of supernal loveliness. Poverty might be here, but never sadness, never the grave and somber gloom of an England forever doomed to seek power, never the sleek urbanity of a Paris forever doomed to seek sophistication. Italy could never again be sophisticated; she had passed that stage ages ago.

Now, as the road rose and bent, Matthew saw the narrow steep walls of the Monastero de San Francesco, seemingly part of the soaring brown cliffs. He saw the long narrow slits of its windows, its red roofs, its climbing staircases. About it and above it lay its vineyards, its orange and lemon and olive trees, its red-earthed gardens, all terraced, every inch meticulously cultivated. Its campanile joined the thronging of delicate bells from Sorrento; the air trembled with the sweet and joyous chorus. The sky became even more luminous, the sea drowning itself in waves of purple.

There was a gate in the high stone wall that protected the terraces and kept the mountainous earth in its place. Matthew opened the gate, climbed the ancient stone steps beyond. At a little distance he saw the pacing monks in their chiostro, meditating, their hands folded, their heads bent. They saw him, too; heads inclined, gentle smiles greeted him. He went on, behind the monastero, to the vineyards, the groves of trees, the gardens. Here he found Fra Leonardo, busily tying up vine tendrils, and singing hoarsely to himself. A hymn, possibly. Knowing Fra Leonardo, Matthew did not believe this. It was probably a ribald snatch from some opera, some love-song dedicated to life and joy. But God could not be annoyed, Fra Leonardo had once remarked. Music was music, and God was the spirit of music. He could be praised in the singing of "Celeste Aida," as well as in some chant invented by the cold Romans, a chant quite alien to this swooning warmth, this unbelievable color of earth and mountain and sea.

"I am so unorthodox," Fra Leonardo would say, without the slightest apology or regret. "The abbot is doubtless very much annoyed with me at times. But I sing, and if I sing softly, who knows what I sing to God?"

Fra Leonardo was very short, incredibly wide and fat, and very old. He was ball-like, in his dark habit. He waddled when he walked, for, as he confessed, he enjoyed food even if it was the simplest, and he especially enjoyed wine. When he worked, he tucked his habit high up into his rope girdle, so that his thick legs were shamelessly exposed and became brown in the sun. He also rolled up his sleeves, "to keep them clean," as he said. But he loved the sun on his arms. The other monks managed to toil more decorously clad, but Fra Leonardo was a peasant, and apparently the abbot had grown tired of rebuking him. The abbot, Fra Leonardo would sometimes say with serene pity, had been born in Rome. One did not expect much gaiety from Romans; they were cold, and they brooded, and they remembered too often the ancient grandeur of their City. Sometimes they were even foolish enough to hint wistfully that Rome, strong and dominant and terrible, might again be the center of a materialistic world. Such error, such childishness, Fra Leonardo would remark with a shrug of compassion.

In exchange for casual lessons in English, given as Fra Leonardo worked, the old monk had initiated Matthew Prescott in the dialect of "basso Italiano," softer, more liquid, more musical and expressive than the precise and foreign language of the hard and ambitious Italian north. He always waited, toward sunset, for Matthew. If the young man disappointed him, as he occasionally did, Fra Leonardo was very unhappy until the next day.

Now he saw and heard Matthew, and his brown and enormous face sprang into a gay cobweb of a thousand wrinkles. They greeted each other with immense and careful politeness. The other monks had gone; Fra Leonardo was alone. He well knew that this was because the abbot encouraged him in his cultivation of the rich American signore who, monthly, gave a vast sum to the monastero and the monastero school. The abbot, being a Roman, was shrewd and astute. Because of the signore he did not always insist that Fra Leonardo attend the evening meditations and prayers, for this was the hour the signore had chosen for his visits. It did not matter, Fra Leonardo would reflect. If there were stains on his soul, the abbot would have to answer for them, not he. The monastero was poor, and the school for the village boys needed the lire. The lire from the hands of the American signore were more than welcome; they had enabled the abbot to enlarge the school and educate more boys, and to repair the ancient chapel.

Fra Leonardo was bald; his skull was like a golden moon. His eyes, little and black and twinkling, looked on the earth and on men with the utmost compassion, love, courtesy, and tolerance. He had a wide and almost toothless smile and the Semitic nose of the true basso Italiano. Now it was red and peeling, and very much in evidence. It shone, as his face shone at the sight of Matthew.

"How pleasant to see you, dear friend," he said, in his deep old voice. "I was afraid you would not come this evening, and then I should have had to join in the meditations." He shrugged with eloquence. "That abbot has the eye of a vulture. He sees everything," he added, lowering his voice cautiously, watchful of the pacing monks in their chiostro. Then he was happy again. "I read that book of American poems, this morning, Signore, when, I fear, I ought to have been praying. I thank you from the bottom of my heart."

"I have sent for some more books for you," replied Matthew. "That book shop in Rome is very obliging."

He sat on a big warm stone and watched Fra Leonardo. Fra Leonardo tried to make up by toil for his lack of piety. He was worth three of the younger monks. He continued to work industriously as he talked to his friend. In his youth, he had hoped to be a priest. He had been taught to read and write by the old priest, now dead, in Amalfi, his home. But he was, as he said, such a stupid and impervious person. So condemned by God to a life of benightedness. To Matthew, however, his curious mixture of illiteracy, learning, wisdom and intelligence, was an eternal pleasure. There was a piquancy in their conversation which could never have been there had Fra Leonardo been an educated man. There were times when the old monk would give a dissertation on Shakespeare which was truly amazing, and then he would falter, and revert to the most unlettered ignorance. This sometimes disconcerted Matthew.

He had explained to Matthew that, though he could read and write fairly well in his native language, he had read few books. Matthew, who had never done anything before for any human creature, had been moved to send for packets of books from Rome. But there was so much to read! Some instinct told him that Fra Leonardo would rejoice the most in poetry, so Matthew procured for the old man the very best Italian translations of the major poets, living or dead. What the abbot thought of these books no one ever knew. But this was after Matthew, to please his friend, had begun to make his large monthly contributions to the monastero. At any rate, though the abbot was wont to look sternly upon the old monk when he passed him in the cloister, he said nothing about the books.

Fra Leonardo was overwhelmed with passionate gratitude when Matthew, on this evening, remarked that more poetry would soon be forthcoming. "Ah, you are so good to me, my son!" he exclaimed. "I can never repay you." He had a sudden disturbing thought. He knelt down carefully and examined a row of lettuce. "The abbot," he remarked, "has again suggested that you call upon him so that he might personally thank you for the lire you gave me yesterday, and on all those yesterdays."

"No," said Matthew. "That is impossible. I do not care to make the acquaintance of the reverend abbot. I wish to talk to no one but you. However, you will give him the expression of my deepest regard."

Fra Leonardo sighed, and nodded. "I have told him that the Signore is very reticent," he said. "I have also told him that the Signore has been ill a long time, and is uneasy among strangers."

"I am afraid that is not true," said Matthew, gravely.

Fra Leonardo looked properly rebuked. "Yes, yes," he agreed. Then, he slowly lifted his great head and regarded Matthew with compassionate keenness.

He observed, with a sudden bright twinkling of his whole face: "You remember, Signore, how I have always mourned that I could not teach the boys in the school, because I am so very ignorant. It has been my dream to teach. Only this morning, when I felt most sad, the abbot came upon me and asked me why I sighed. I confessed my dream to him. I was afraid he would laugh, though Romans, I have heard, are not given to laughter. But he did not laugh. He only gazed at me and said: 'My son, I send you out to the vineyards, and to take care of the vegetables, because you are a wise man!' A 'wise man', Signore! Was the abbot indeed laughing at me?"

Matthew stared at him with his large light eyes for a long moment or two. Then he said, in a low tone: "No, Fra Leonardo, he was not laughing at you."

He picked up a handful of dry red earth and let it sift slowly through his fingers. He sat there on the rock, dressed little better than a peasant in a coarse cotton shirt faded to an old blue, rough trousers, his bare feet thrust into leather sandals. His yellow hair was untidy; his fair skin was scorched by the sun. He appeared to have forgotten the old fat monk. He looked beyond at the sea, which rippled in brilliant green and gold and scarlet, and at Vesuvio, turquoise against a sky which had become pure lapis lazuli.

Fra Leonardo, lovingly heaping the earth about the new lettuce, remembered how Matthew had first appeared to him, three years ago. A young man with death in his face, the monk had thought with intense and simple pity. He had come, one sunset, and had looked high up beyond the wall to the terrace where the monk was working, and Fra Leonardo had greeted him merrily. It was evident, of course, that the stranger was an Englishman, or an American, or a traveler from one of the northern countries, so that the monk was not wounded when Matthew had not answered. He had only stood there, gazing upwards.

Fra Leonardo did not see him again for several days. Then, once more he stood there, looking upwards and, most amazing of all, he greeted the monk before the latter had had time to call down to him. Here, Fra Leonardo had reflected, out of his deep wisdom, was a very shy spirit, a spirit full of terror and illness.

It had taken nearly four months before Matthew had voluntarily opened the gate and climbed up the terrace. Even then, he had done so reluctantly and very slowly, glancing about warily and suspiciously. Fra Leonardo had received this extraordinary visit with the utmost poise and in the most casual of spirits. His manner implied that it was very customary for strangers to visit him, to sit down upon those rocks and watch him, speechlessly, to make no remarks at all, to remain unsmiling, and to go away without a word.

The village was small, boasted no hotel, and had practically no tourist business, for tourists overlooked these few houses, this poor monastero and school, in their haste to visit Amalfi, Sorrento and Capri. Who lived here but a few poor peasants and a few monks even poorer? In the little chapel there was not a single Titian, not a piece of marble touched by the magic hands of Michelangelo, not a mosaic worth a second glance, not an altar that could draw one admiring exclamation. The view? There were thousands of views in Italy. Italy was nothing but views, and the view here was not so good as the views at Sorrento and Amalfi. The beach was narrow and stony and uninviting. And so, it was very odd, said everyone, including the monks, that a rich American signore should take a very dilapidated little villa near the village, and live as poorly as any peasant.

An old woman cared very casually for his villa, bought his fish and cheese and wine and bread and spaghetti, and cooked for him. She, too, had a story to tell. The American signore had the most magnificent clothing, which he never wore. He had a gold watch and a diamond ring, and white silk scarfs beyond imagining, and underwear fit for the king himself. He also had much money; she herself had seen it. But he cared nothing for this. The older men nodded wisely. The American signore wished to live quietly. This was evident. He received few letters, but many books, from London and Paris and Rome. Perhaps he was a poet, like all those famous Englishmen who had lived at Amalfi and Sorrento. Perhaps he would make this village renowned, also.

When it was reported, a year later, that large boxes containing canvases and paints and brushes had arrived for the signore, the excitement was discreetly frenzied. But the signore, after examining them listlessly, had not opened the boxes. He had lived here three years and he had still not opened them.

To the people, it was not remarkable that he had accepted Fra Leonardo as his friend. It was quite in keeping with all the romantic tales and songs. It was very satisfying and poetic. The people began to look upon Fra Leonardo with respect, and so did the abbot, when the lire began to arrive, for the school and the monastero, via the soil-stained hands of the old monk.

But Matthew made no other friends. He began, however, to show slight signs of friendliness towards the villagers, when he finally discovered that they had accepted his presence and looked at him with kindness. Once or twice he was seen talking to a child, or playing with a dog or a kitten. Beyond this he did not go, not in all these three years.

Fra Leonardo, himself, never wondered why Matthew had sought him out. It was enough for the old monk that Matthew came and talked with him, and sat beside him until the evening star came out and the sea became the color of a ripe plum. He accepted these visits as one accepts all that life and the earth have to give, simply, with affection and pleasure.

Once, only once, had Matthew remarked haltingly that he, at one time, had had hopes of becoming an artist, of painting great pictures. It had been a delicate moment. Fra Leonardo had accepted this strange and involuntary confidence with simplicity, and had made no comment.

There will come a day when he will awaken, the old monk thought. There will be an hour when his spirit will come forth from its dark hiding-place. Not yet, not perhaps for a long time. But the day and the hour will come. In the meantime, I will pray for him, and leave him to God.

The monk prepared to leave his work for the night, but Matthew showed no evidence of going as yet.

"Did you like the poems of Walt Whitman, Fra Leonardo?" he asked. "He was a man like yourself, I think."

Fra Leonardo said enthusiastically: "How you flatter me, Signore. Yes, I had a sympathy with this poet. How beloved he must be in America!"

Matthew smiled faintly. "He is not beloved by many, I am afraid, though he is called 'the poet of the people'. Scholars call him so. The people, unfortunately, are not aware that he wrote about them, and for them." He paused, then asked curiously: "What did you like best in his works?"

Fra Leonardo became suddenly very grave. He wiped his hands on his habit. He looked at the sea, at the village below, at the mountains above. He said: "This I like best: 'Whoever walks a furlong without sympathy walks to his own funeral dressed in his shroud.' "

Matthew was silent. He stood up. "Good night, Fra Leonardo," he said, courteously.

The monk watched him go. He heard the creak of the gate. With sudden swiftness the evening fell. Fra Leonardo sighed. He picked up his gardening tools. He looked at the purple sky, and serenity touched him again. Murmuring his prayers, he moved slowly and ponderously towards the monastero.

CHAPTER LI

AS THE SUMMER advanced, the intensification of color in the mountains, on the sea, and on the earth, became almost too dazzling, almost too violent. The very air shimmered, refulgently. The sun broke upon the eye in waves of light, caught up the world in fiery hands.

One hot evening Matthew found his old friend sitting, gasping for breath, on the rocks where he himself usually sat. Fra Leonardo said apologetically: "I am afraid I am very old, after all. Today I did not rejoice in the sun. I panted in it."

Matthew stood near the monk, and regarded him uneasily. The big bronzed face had a livid cast.

"How old are you, Fra Leonardo?" he asked.

The sunken black eyes twinkled. The monk pushed his huge bulk from the rocks and stood up. "Pardon me, Signore," he said. "Please rest yourself. How old am I? I must confess that by the time the grapes are ripe I shall be eighty."

"Eighty!" exclaimed Matthew. "But that is not possible."

"The Signore flatters me." The monk nodded solemnly. He looked at his wide knotted arms, brown as earth. "One would not think I had lived eighty summers? No. I do not believe it myself. Eighty centuries, perhaps, but not eighty little summers. I think I have lived forever."

Matthew sat down slowly. The monk looked at the sea and then turned to look at the mountains, at the monastero, at the vines and the vegetables and the flowers. "It is not possible that I have seen this so short a time," he said. "I was young when Italy was young. I shall live as long as Italy, as long as the world, and even when the world is gone." The livid shadow left his face; there was a resolution upon it now, and joy. "One does not need a priest to tell one this. One knows, in one's heart."

Matthew followed the monk's slow and seeking gaze. The sea was pure gold, still and motionless, the mountains black and green and gray, the village below a mosaic of many vivid colors. Matthew waited for the old familiar lassitude to return,

379

the ennui, the weariness. But it did not return. He thought
to himself: I have not felt it for a long time. It has gone.

He smiled up at Fra Leonardo. "It is a pleasant thought,"
he said.

"Ah, no, Signore, it is a conviction from God."

What God? Matthew asked himself.

The monk said: "The God of all men, of all the universe,
Signore." Mathew looked at him in amazement, and this
amazement heightened when Fra Leonardo continued in a
dreamlike voice: "The Signore has said he does not know this
God, and so this God has no meaning for him."

The monk put his stained hands on his immense hips. Slowly, again, he drank in the sight of the sky and of the mountains
and of the sea. "The Signore has told me of India, and of
the religion of the people who live there, how they believe
that life is inseparable from pain, and therefore not desirable.
The Signore seemed to think this belief very wise. I do not
think it wise. I think it is illness. True it is that life is inseparable from pain. Even a child understands that. But if so, of
what importance is it? Pain is a small price to pay for living.
A broken heart or a broken fortune is bearable so long
as the eye can look upon the sun."

He added: "But the Signore has said that there are such
countless suns in space. That is an excellent thing. Nowhere,
then, is there darkness. Nowhere, then, is there death. No
eye can close without opening again upon the sun, somewhere,
sometime; no soul can ever be alone, ever be without God."

Matthew sat very still, his face averted. The monk turned
to him. "The Signore thinks I am an old and stupid man, without wisdom or knowledge? He thinks I am a child who speaks
childishly?"

"I did not say so," replied Matthew.

Fra Leonardo sighed. But he also smiled. "Ah, Signore,
you are young, and I am old in this world. It is only the young
who say: 'There is no God.' It is only the young who say: 'There
is nothing but pain and evil.' That is because their years are
few." He waited, but Matthew did not answer him. The monk
chuckled. "A young man once said to me with such weariness: 'I have seen everything.' And I replied: 'No, my son.
He who thinks he has seen everything no longer sees anything.' "

Matthew moved restlessly, without speaking.

"There are some," continued the monk, "who no longer
laugh, because they believe they have gone beyond laughter.
That is only because they have never laughed at all."

He waited for Matthew to speak. When the young man remained silent, the monk sighed, and now it was a sigh of sadness, without his usual humor. "I do not know why I speak so to the Signore, so impudently, for I am nobody, and the Signore is a man of learning and has seen the world. I must implore the Signore's pardon. I can only say that I have spoken so because there is an urgency in me, a hurry, as a man speaks who is closing a gate behind him and must leave his friend."

"Leave?" muttered Matthew, in confusion. He got to his feet. "You are not leaving?"

The vast old man merely looked up at him, smiling tenderly.

Then Matthew understood. He stood beside his friend, and his mouth opened in an involuntary expression of pain. "No," he said. "You are only tired, Fra Leonardo. The day has been very hot. Tomorrow, you will not be so tired."

"The Signore is right," said the monk, gently. "I am afraid I have disturbed him. Nevertheless, I am deeply touched that the Signore should be concerned whether I remain or not."

Once more, he looked at the surging glory and color all about him. "Ah, I have only one prayer, Signore, that I shall always see this place. How could I live without it, even in Heaven? There are times when I have thought of my years, and how it might come about that I should lie upon my cot, dying, and not see this sea again, this sky, this earth, but must die in my cell, which is filled with shadows."

"You are very melancholy, tonight, Fra Leonardo."

"The Signore must forgive me. Even I, who love God, have my sudden moments of sorrow and fear. It is a sin; I must do penance for this. But, Signore, I have often dreamt that someone would perhaps paint this for me, so that I could hang it upon the wall of my cell, and see it to the end! Doubtless, the abbot would object, and, then again, perhaps he would not. After all, I am an old man."

Matthew spoke painfully: "There are so many paintings of similar views. If you wish, I shall buy one for you. I shall send away to Rome——"

"But no, Signore. It would not be this particular spot, this one small vision of Heaven. However, I thank the Signore for his kind heart, and his generosity."

He sat down upon the stones. He seemed to have forgotten Matthew. His eyes drank in the panorama about him. He smiled, and sighed, and the rosy sky reflected itself upon his face.

After some time he murmured: "The Signore will return home some day?"

"No," said Matthew, quietly. Now it seemed to him most necessary to speak to this old man. He said: "You see, there is nothing for me at home. I was given everything.'" He tried to stop himself, but the words poured out swiftly and brokenly: "It is so hard to explain, for I hardly know, myself. My father gave his whole life for his children. Have I told you I have a brother and two sisters? No. I did not tell you. But all of us—we are nothing, because we were taught we were everything. We were given love, but no love was demanded of us, and so we had no love at all. I have told you that I cannot explain. It is only here.

"And so, it is impossible to return to a place where there is no love, where everything is given even before the asking. For when one has everything one has nothing. Is that not so?"

"Yes, it is so," murmured Fra Leonardo.

Matthew's voice hurt him as he went on: "You will say I am a most unnatural son, for I do not love the father who loves me. But he has debased himself in our eyes, because he asked nothing from us. I could not see him again, without remembering. It is not good for a son to despise his father; while I am here I can think of him as a noble man, as a man who lived only for his children, unselfishly and with all his heart. I can even think of him with a little love, and much sadness. But only if I do not see him again. You think I am heartless, Fra Leonardo?"

"No," said the monk, mournfully. "I think you are only suffering."

With deep eyes he watched the young man as Matthew moved away a little.

"I do not love my mother," said Matthew. "I was cruel to her, when it was not her fault. I wounded her, and it was not her fault. I cannot see her again, either. I only hope that she will some day forgive me. And there is my brother. If I never see him again, I shall forget I hated him. There are my sisters, and they are strangers to me. I have no home but here, Fra Leonardo, and no friend but you."

"You have God," said the monk.

Matthew shook his head impatiently. "Not yet, Fra Leonardo. Not yet. There will come a day perhaps——" He turned back to the old man, who looked up at him with profound intensity. "When I am in this place, and with you, and I have my books, and my thoughts, something stirs in me, something begins to live, very feebly—but it lives. I know I am not dead. Do you know how it feels, Fra Leonardo, when one thinks one is dead?"

"I know what you have felt, my son," replied the monk. "But you have not been dead. You have only been asleep."

"It might be that I shall awaken," said Matthew.

He said: "For a long time, after I came here, I saw nothing. You have made me see, Fra Leonardo. It still is very dim, but I am beginning to see."

"You see, Signore, because you have looked beyond yourself."

"No." There was vehemence in Matthew's voice.

"Ah, but yes. You have given us so many lire for the monastero and the school."

"I did it for you."

The old monk smiled wisely, and spread out his hands. "How you deny yourself, Signore! 'I did it for you,' you say, and just a moment ago you denied that you have ever looked beyond yourself."

The bells echoed over the ocean, whose wine-colored waters flowed far below. The mountains beyond rippled in gold. Fra Leonardo lifted himself heavily to his feet. He put his hand on Matthew's shoulder. "God be with you, my son," he said. "Good-night."

CHAPTER LII

REVERENTLY, as if the big canvas were the relic of a saint, the two monks lifted it in their arms and carried it towards the monastero, with Matthew walking behind them. He might have been amused, or impatient, had he known what they were thinking, these simple and sophisticated men: Ah, now the rich tourists would soon begin to come to this village! Soon, fame would descend upon it, for the great artist, Signor Prescott, had painted its incomparable view, and had deigned to live among its people! Amalfi! Sorrento! They were living on past glories. This village would soon lift its head proudly; it would be a shrine. A fabulous hotel, perhaps, to surpass anything that existed in Capri; a refurbished chapel! The old monks walked with assurance, lifted the canvas high.

The abbot, a stern and dignified elderly man, met the monks and Matthew in the cool blue shadows within the monastero door. He was a small man, but he had majesty and hauteur. He gave Matthew the faintest of smiles, saluted him in purest Roman, to which Matthew replied with brief stateliness. The abbot did not reveal his really enormous curiosity. While Matthew had been painting in the gardens the abbot had not allowed this curiosity to cause him to wander there—not even for a single glimpse. The abbot was not a simple man, nor one given to fantasy or romancing. He doubted very much that this village had sheltered a hidden artist, distinguished or destined to become famous, and the prattlings of his monks had irritated him. However, it had been written to him from the cities that Signor Prescott was reputed to be the son of a rich Americano. The abbot, always a realist, considered the fact with satisfaction.

Even now, as the monks carefully carried the canvas, the abbot did not allow his eye to scan the painting. Each evening, it had been brought, still unfinished, within the monastero: the next day it had been brought out, for the "master." The abbot had heard delirious rumors about its beauty and "genius." He had merely made his small stern face even more forbidding, and had turned away.

It was finished, now. The monks were bearing it through

the shadowy halls towards Fra Leonardo's cell, Matthew still
following. The abbot hesitated, then followed also. On strict
orders from the abbot, no one was visibly about. Nevertheless,
quiet and noiseless though the monastero seemed on this
early evening, the ancient building vibrated with ebullience.
The little procession wandered through a colonnade of white
stone pillars looking out upon the chiostro where the monks
paced. Not a monk lifted his head but, as they caught a glimpse
of the others moving in and out of the shadows of the pillars,
a wave of electrification passed through them.

The abbot murmured to Matthew: "Fra Leonardo has been
removed to a high cell, Signore, where the evening sunlight
can strike, appropriately, upon a certain wall."

"Thank you, my father," replied Matthew gravely. After
that, they did not speak. The abbot wondered vaguely whether
all this was not very irregular. It did not matter. He was really
attached to that simple old peasant, Fra Leonardo, so beloved
of the rich signore, who, to show his fondness for the monk,
had given so incredibly many lire to this monastero. The
abbot smiled slightly to himself. He had always suspected
that the lire had been a bribe.

By way of many winding staircases and corridors, clean
and austere, full of violet light, the procession had at last
reached the cell. The abbot, himself, opened the wooden door.
Instantly, the evening sunshine struck into the corridor, in
a wild blaze of glory. Fra Leonardo lay on his cot, eagerly
waiting for his friend. He did not immediately see the abbot
and the monks, and the burden they were carrying. He
cried: "My friend, my dear friend! See, they have been so
kind. They have carried my old carcass up here, where I
can see the sun, though, unfortunately, I cannot as yet see
the ocean and the mountains!" Now he became aware of
the others, and was much agitated.

"Calm yourself, my son," said the abbot, in a gentle voice.
"No, do not move. It is forbidden by the physician. Your
friend," he added, very kindly, "has brought you a gift, which
he himself executed, for you."

Matthew was already standing beside the cot where his
old friend lay, and he had taken the cold brown hand in
both of his. Two weeks ago, the monk had been stricken by
apoplexy and, for two weeks now, he had lain on his bed,
partially paralysed. There was no hope for him; the paralysis
was spreading upward from his motionless legs. His left
arm, too, was already helpless. But his mind was clear, he

could speak and eat, and drink a little wine, and even laugh as he waited patiently for death. The physician had expressed himself amazed at the old man's vitality and love of life, which kept death so resolutely at bay.

Yet in two short weeks the brown flesh had withered and shrunk; the huge dome of the skull now crowned a face which had fallen away almost to nothing. But the eyes glinted and danced and beamed with indomitable life.

"Dear friend," he said fondly to Matthew, "I wait each day for your arrival. Tell me, is the sea like wine tonight, or like gold? Is there a plume of fire over Vesuvio, or is the old devil sleeping this evening?"

"The sea," said Matthew, "is both wine and gold, and Vesuvio is sleeping, and the jasmine fills all the air."

"Yes," said the monk, with ecstasy, "I can smell it through my window. Tell me," he went on with some anxiety, "how is my garden?"

"Waiting for you," said Matthew.

The monk glanced down at the coarse blanket which covered his legs. "I shall soon be rid of these," he murmured. "I shall soon be free, and then I shall visit my garden and see for myself."

In the meantime, the abbot had, with silent gestures, been giving orders to the monks. One of them had climbed on a stool. There was the sound of sharp hammer blows on the wall, breaking into the monastero quiet. Fra Leonardo started. Matthew moved aside. "What is this?" asked Fra Leonardo, surprised. Then, he became aware that the abbot was still in the room. Respectfully, he faltered: "Father, I do not understand this. Why is Fra Lorenzo driving a nail into my wall?"

"Wait," said the abbot, with his frigid smile.

The evening sun struck vividly on the white plaster wall. Now the other monk was lifting the canvas and Fra Lorenzo, from his perch on the stool, was assisting. Fra Leonardo stared. He attempted to lift himself. The abbot, that most stately and aristocratic of men, went to Matthew's aid when the young man tried to lift the old monk to a sitting position. They dragged him to the head of his cot; they pushed a pillow behind shoulders still massive. He did not look at them; he was not conscious of them. He could look only at the canvas now being settled in that blaze of evening light upon his wall, that big canvas which seemed more like a window opening onto sea and sky than a mere painting.

Fra Leonardo lay on his pillows and in the arms of the two

men, perfectly motionless, all his life in his face. He could not speak; but slowly, one by one, the tears began to well from his eyes, run into the brown and sunken furrows of his cheeks, lie in the pits about his smiling mouth. He lifted his right hand and crossed himself; he smiled, and sighed, and panted a little. His tears ran faster.

The abbot straightened up, turned to the canvas. He was astounded. He was a cultivated man, well acquainted with art and artists. He could not believe what he was seeing.

The canvas had been painted from the gardens where Fra Leonardo had worked every day, and it had been painted from his favorite spot. Now before him lay, to the left, the tumbling purple shadows of the mountains against a western sky of medieval gilt, fuming in a drift of magenta clouds and reflecting itself in far waters of flowing gold. Closer, still to the left, on the dark mountainside, which was patched with green and silver, climbed the vari-colored cluster of Sorrento. Directly ahead, the deep violet waters of the nearer sea glided to the strong blue of Vesuvio, which was of such a brilliance that it dazzled the eye. The slender sails of the fishing boats floated out upon the ocean, touched with scarlet. In the foreground, the mountain fell briefly away; there was a red roof or two, the side of a pink or white wall, far below.

No one in the cell spoke. But all at once it was as though a signal had been given. The sweet far fluttering of campanile bells invaded the cell; a wind wafted in the scent of jasmine; the songs of the fishermen came faintly, sweetly, purely, from the sea.

"Magnificent!" murmured the abbot, overcome. The monks could only gaze, reverently, as at the manifestation of a Saint.

As the sunlight beat exultantly upon it, increasing its incandescence, the painting filled the little cell with radiance. Again, it was really a large window, obliterating the plaster wall.

Fra Leonardo lay there, and gazed with passionate absorption; he blinked away his tears. After a long time, he looked at Matthew. He tried to speak. No words could come from him. His cold fingers clung to Matthew's hand. His dying face brightened until it had a light of its own, so great was his joy.

"I did it for you, Fra Leonardo," said Matthew. "I did it only for you, to bring what you love into this cell."

As the sun changed and fell, outside, the painting appeared to change, also. The colors became more vivid, but deeper, as if creating a twilight of their own. The gold became more intense, the purple darker and stronger. It was alive, this canvas, thought the abbot. But his exigent mind was already racing. Was this marvel a gift to Fra Leonardo, his for what few days remained to him? Or would this gentleman leave it here in the monastero, for the wonder of visitors?

Fra Leonardo whispered: "It is for me, this, my son? You painted it—for me?"

"Yes," replied Matthew. "Only for you. And always, if you wish it, and the abbot permits, it shall remain here."

The abbot smiled. He said to the monk: "Through you, my son, a miracle has occurred."

Fra Leonardo, however, looked deeply into Matthew's eyes. He whispered: "Yes. Yes, by the grace of God, a miracle has occurred."

Sweat stood in big cold drops on his forehead. Matthew gently wiped them away. The living joy on the old man's face moved him as he had never before been moved. The life that had lain buried in him so long, under stones of selfishness and self-preoccupation, stirred powerfully, rose, and took hold of him with a kind of passionate exultation.

Fra Leonardo leaned his head against Matthew's breast, rested in the strength of Matthew's arms. His eyes clung to the painting. He did not speak again.

He died, a week later, with Matthew beside him. But, to the very last, he looked only at the canvas on his wall and, in the final moments, joy lay like the sun itself on his face.

Two weeks after the old man had been laid to rest in the monastero cemetery, Matthew came to the abbot.

"I came to ask permission, Father, to paint in these gardens," he said. "I shall continue to live in the village. There is much to paint there, also: the women at the well, the winding streets with their walls overhung with roses, the faces of the children, the fishermen, the monastero—so many things, endless things. A lifetime is not enough in which to paint them."

"Yes," said the abbot, who had begun to see what he had never seen before.

Matthew laid down a bundle of lire. "My father is a rich man. I understand that he has established a large trust fund for me, in the event of his death. I want nothing of money, just enough to shelter me and to give me food. Above these, the rest belongs to you and to the monastero." He sighed. "It was always Fra Leonardo's wish that the monastero have a finer and more beautiful chapel. Perhaps my money can

assist you in this dream of his." He looked away fr
abbot. He said: "And what I paint is for the monastero,
to be disposed of, or retained, as you may wish."

He added: "It is a very strange thing, but I do not believe
Fra Leonardo has gone away."

CHAPTER LIII

IT WAS TO SEE HER house again, as it used to be, rather than for any other and possibly better reason, that Ursula had come here this cold winter day. She came very often, sometimes twice a week, but Barbara was not deceived that it was affection that brought her mother, unless it was affection for the house. Or perhaps there was here some unconscious refuge, a return to days when life was not so mournful and so desolate.

Ursula, gaunt and haggard, sat in the little parlor and looked about her with something like a vague peace upon her features. The tired restlessness was diminishing moment by moment; the anxiety on her puckered mouth softened. She sat there, in her loosened sables, slowly removing her gloves. Her thin gray hair rose in a pompadour under her wide felt hat. It only made the face beneath it more old, more weary. The firelight glimmered on her gold wedding-band, on the gold watch on her jacket. Barbara, her gray eyes observant and shrewd, regarded her mother somewhat sadly. Her young face was very firm and mature; her posture, too, was firm and a little uncompromising.

Ursula continued to look about her, and to sniff unobtrusively. Yes, the house was the same; the scent of old leather and wax and burning wood brought back memories dear and sweet and calm. Even the light which came in the windows was the eternal light she remembered, a light dimmed and quiet. The panelled walls glimmered, as they had glimmered when she had been a girl. The crack in one of them gave her a peculiar sense of pleasant disorientation. It suggested timelessness to her, for she recalled noticing it as a child.

"Shall we have tea now, Mama?" asked Barbara, in her severe young voice.

"No, dear. Not immediately, if you please," said Ursula. She was content, for a while, to be home. She did not look at Barbara, nor at the baby on Barbara's knee. Perhaps, she did not wish to see her daughter fully and completely. Once, long ago, friends had told her that Barbara strongly resembled her; Ursula had dismissed this as nonsense. There had been a faint displeasure in her voice when she had lightly denied what was most evident, and they had not mentioned it again.

Barbara fondled her baby, who was almost two years old, abstractedly. He was very good, and very serious. He smiled at his mother affectionately, and if he was at all restless, he was well-trained enough to repress it. He had Barbara's eyes and coloring; he also had Oliver's gentleness of expression. He eyed Ursula, now, thoughtfully. He squirmed a little. He reached up and tugged at the gold chain about his mother's throat. She tapped his hand decisively. "No," she said, quietly but firmly. "Billy mustn't touch."

Ursula brought her gaze back from the windows and regarded her daughter and grandson. A slight frown drew her faded brows together. Barbara said, with loving inflexibility: "This is one youngster who is going to learn how to behave, if I have to spank him to a bright scarlet on an unmentionable spot. He's not going to be a brat, a curse to himself and a misery to others."

Ursula's frown deepened, and her withered cheeks flushed a trifle. She held out her hand to the baby. "Come to Grandma, darling," she said.

The baby stared at her hand, looked up questioningly at his mother. She put him on his feet, straightened his embroidered bib, patted him on the head. "Go to Grandma," she commanded.

He tottered to Ursula, carefully watching each step. He reminded her of Oliver, at Billy's age, when he had come to her across this very rug, seriously, but with a smile. She almost withdrew her hand. Then she caught up the child and kissed him with trembling lips. The child kissed her rather wetly, became engrossed in her watch, fingering it roughly. "Billy," said Barbara, with hard clearness. The child subsided upon Ursula's knee, lost interest, and yawned.

"He wasn't harming the watch," protested Ursula. The flush was still on her cheeks, and her tone was resentful.

"He has to learn not to touch what doesn't belong to him," replied Barbara. She met her mother's eyes straightly. "He has his rights, of course, but only when they don't infringe on the rights of others."

Ursula was silent. Barbara, she told herself, was hard. She was unbending. She was a wife and a mother, but there was something spinsterish and too decided about her.

Barbara could guess her mother's thoughts. She was saddened, but she was also indignant. She thinks I am implying a criticism of Papa, she commented to herself. Well, I am. Poor, poor Mama! Long ago, she made up her mind that nothing but Papa mattered, and she set herself up as a wall of protection between Papa and his children.

Barbara tried to quell her mournful indignation, to drown it in her pity. Oliver was always arguing with her, reproaching her that she was obdurate. Barbara sighed. But it was irritating, and regrettable, that a woman intrinsically as intelligent and as just as Mama could become nothing but a watchman for a man who had already ruined his children.

Barbara touched the bell-rope. "It's time for Billy's supper, and for bed," she remarked.

"Oh, it's quite early yet," murmured Ursula, holding the child to her.

Barbara glanced at the clock on the mantelpiece. "Five," she said. A little nursemaid came in. Billy, however, was not reconciled to going. With a child's acuteness, he sensed the current between mother and grandmother. He whimpered, hid his face against Ursula's breast. Ursula's arms tightened. "Billy," said Barbara, sharply.

At that loving but determined voice, the child lifted his head, gave Ursula a resigned smile, slipped off her knee and ran to his nurse. The girl bent with him, and the baby kissed his mother. "Good boy. Good Billy," she said, approvingly. "Now Billy will have his dinner and go to bed. Say good-night to Grandma, darling."

The child obediently uttered the equivalent of this, laughed, and allowed his nurse to carry him off. Barbara touched the bell-rope again. "It really is time for tea," she said, smiling.

But the subtle antagonism still pervaded the twilit air.

"He is such a good child," said Ursula, a little coldly.

"Thank you, Mama. But he isn't a good child by nature. No child is. He is just being trained as well as I can train him. He must respect others."

"You are such a schoolmistress, Barbie," observed Ursula, trying to smile.

"I wanted to be one." Barbara laughed. "I think I'd have been a good one, too. You see, I have no illusions about children."

The words had a strange echo in Ursula's ears. For an instant, she was moved to laugh with Barbara. Then her face hardened. A maid brought in the tea-tray. It was Ursula's own, as was the silver, the delicate old china.

Barbara competently poured the tea. Its fragrance mingled with the scent of the burning wood on the hearth, with the odor of ancient leather and wax. Barbara inspected the small cakes. "Bessie has given us her specialty," she remarked. She handed a filled and steaming cup to her mother. Their fingers touched. At the touch of her daughter's strong young fingers, the saddest of thrills ran through Ursula, the saddest of longings.

"How is Papa?" asked Barbara.

"He seems quite well," answered Ursula. Again, anxiety grayed her face.

"It is almost a year now since he had his last attack," said Barbara, comfortingly. "Let us hope he won't have another one, ever."

"He won't, if he isn't upset." Ursula glanced at her daughter sternly. "And that reminds me, Barbie. Why haven't you and Oliver and the baby been to see us for nearly a month? Your father remarked about that, only last night."

He doesn't really want to see us, thought Barbara, with renewed sadness. Nor do you, Mama, really. You come here only because of the house. Don't you remember, Mama, how wildly you opposed my marrying Oliver, because Papa was so furiously against it, and without any honest reason? Don't you remember that Oliver and I had to be married in an obscure rectory, with only yourself present, because Papa would not come, and Julie and Tom would not come? I have always suspected, Mama, that even you came only at the last minute.

But she said nothing to her mother. She merely poured hot water into the silver teapot.

"After all," said Ursula, "the baby is named after him."

Yes, said Barbara to herself, somberly. The baby is named after him. Oliver, poor darling, thought that would please Papa. Oliver, my love, you keep forgetting that you are only a pseudo-Prescott, and that Papa had hoped that a boy of Tom's would perhaps be named after him. You've made that impossible, Oliver, and Papa will never forgive you for it.

Barbara had learned tact and diplomacy, but all at once her mother's last words were too much for her young and restrained impetuousness.

"I never feel we are welcome—at home," she said.

"Barbie! How can you say that! How cruel that is, and how untrue!"

Barbara was already sorry for her lapse. "I never liked that house," she said, with sincerity. "And Mama, Julie and Gene don't like us. You can say that is 'cruel' and 'untrue,' if you wish, but you know the real truth."

Ursula's voice was somewhat unnatural and strained: "I can't understand, Barbie, why you are so hostile to Julie and Gene. You know your father always believed, and still believes, that sisters are fond of each other. You might help him——" Her voice broke.

"To keep his illusion, Mama?" Barbara sighed. "I'm awfully sorry. You know that Julie really hates me. She hates Oliver, too. She and Gene have quite taken over the house." Now she was reckless again, because of her hurt, because of the brutal insults that had been inflicted upon Oliver. "You and Papa are almost boarders in that house, and you know it, Mama."

"Oh, Barbie, how can you be so venomous? I'm not young any more; Julie has proved herself an excellent manager, and has relieved me enormously. And Gene is just like a son, to your father. No one could be more considerate, or kinder, or more helpful."

Ursula put down her cup; her hand was shaking.

"Yes," said the young woman. "Gene is all that. I admit it."

Ursula waited. When Barbara added nothing to what she had said, she exclaimed: "How sinister you make that sound, Barbie! Are you trying to quarrel with me?"

But it *is* sinister, thought Barbara. Aloud she said, hoping to be kind: "No, Mama, I'm not trying to quarrel with you. I just want you to know why Oliver and I don't come so very often. Let us grant that you and Papa are happy to see us. Julie and Gene are not. It would be a lie to deny that."

Now, in the dusk, her eyes seemed to grow larger and brighter, and more bitter.

Ursula was silent. She was, as Barbara knew, intrinsically a just woman. Her mouth drooped in a shame she could not repress. She tried to forget what had happened, but it all came back to her remorselessly: Barbara's marriage to Oliver, William's mad threats to "drive the rascal out of town," William's visit, in his madness, to Scott, Meredith and Owens, their cold rejection of his demand that they sever relationship with Oliver. And then there was she herself, Ursula, terrified for her husband, upholding him in his fury, almost savagely denouncing her daughter and Oliver—Oliver, whom she loved more than she had ever loved her own children!

She put her hand to her forehead to shield her eyes. She and Barbara had never spoken of these things; not once, in all these four years. There had been between them a tacit agreement that they should never be uttered aloud. Yet there was no forgetting Oliver's grief at William's rage, Oliver's bewilderment at Ursula's denunciations, even though eventually he had understood and forgiven. He had forgiven long before Ursula had come to visit her daughter and Oliver when they had lived in a small neat house in the suburbs of Andersburg. Oliver had received Ursula with his old fondness and gentleness. He had greeted her as if nothing had happened, when actually so terribly much had happened. She had come, she announced falteringly, to tell them that Julia and Eugene Arnold were to be married, that the "family" wished Barbara and Oliver to know "before anyone else," and that Barbara and Oliver must be present at the engagement dinner the following night.

Barbara closed her eyes. She had tried never to think of that dinner, but sometimes she could not help remembering. She saw her father again, ravaged and ill; saw her mother's sick and determined smile; she saw Julia's beautiful, gloating happiness, Eugene's elegant composure, Thomas' wide and jeering grin. When she had wished to marry Oliver, Papa had been beside himself, yet he was, apparently, quite reconciled to Julia's marrying the son of the man he had ruined, and had never forgiven. The injustice had burned in Barbara like acid.

She remembered, too, the grandeur of Julia's marriage. For Julia, no obscure and abrupt little wedding in a shabby little parsonage! Julia had had eight bridesmaids, dressed like a rainbow, and among them had been Mary Blake, who had married Thomas hardly a year later. Nothing had been spared for Julia. The gifts alone had been fabulous.

Forgetting everything in the turmoil of her embittered thoughts, Barbara exclaimed: "Oliver always 'understands'! Always, always! Sometimes I get so sick of Oliver's 'understanding'!"

Ursula dropped her hand, and looked at her daughter. Suddenly, she was an old woman. She said with quiet resolution: "Yes, Barbie, Oliver always understands. For you, that is impossible, isn't it?"

The dangerous and grievous subject lay there between them; they saw it, and turned away from it. Barbara, her voice shaking, replied: "I try, Mama. I really do try." Her eyes were full of tears. "But I can't help knowing about Julie and Gene, and how they dislike us. Please give Papa our love, and tell him we'll visit him soon."

And now she remembered Thomas' marriage to that artful and smiling little creature, Mary Blake. William had been sincerely delighted at this marriage. This, too, had been resplend-

ent. Barbara's mouth tightened. Not for Thomas a tiny
little cheap house in the suburbs. For their wedding gift,
his father-in-law had given the young couple a magnificent
mansion on the mountain overlooking Andersburg. All white
stone and marvelous gardens, filled with luxurious furniture
and other treasures, and already staffed with impeccable
servants, it stood on a terrace, arrogantly staring down at
the city. Mr. Blake, much to William's proud gratification,
had settled an income of fifteen thousand dollars a year on
his daughter.

It was shortly after that that Ursula had offered her house
to Oliver and Barbara. Barbara had immediately and cuttingly, wanted to refuse. She could not understand why Oliver,
with the slightest of gestures, had checked her, had expressed
his pleasure, and had kissed Ursula so tenderly. Oliver, and
his "understanding"! Sometimes it was more than Barbara
could endure.

However, though she had moved in rebelliously, she loved
the house, as her mother had loved it. Later, she realized that
Ursula could have given her daughter nothing more valuable.
She had given her the place which, to her, was the dearest
place on earth.

Remembering, the tears thickened in Barbara's eyes. She
could even be sad, now, that neither Julia nor Thomas had
as yet given William a grandson or a granddaughter.

Ursula was gathering up her gloves and purse. "Sunday dinner, Barbie?" she murmured. She paused. "Julie and Gene
are dining with Tom and Mary."

"Then we'll surely come," Barbara could not help saying.
But she smiled as she said it, and Ursula even smiled back.
Now an unfamiliar warmth spread between mother and daugh-
ter.

"And don't forget Billy," said Ursula, rising. "Your father
is very fond of the baby."

Barbara did not deny this.

She tried to think of some parting words that might make
her mother happier. In an enthusiastic voice she said: "Isn't
it wonderful about Matt! Papa must be so proud. All those
wonderful paintings, one even exhibited at the Royal Academy!
And that ovation given him in Rome, too!"

But she had not made Ursula happy, though Ursula smiled.
Ursula was remembering the many urgent letters she had written Matthew, especially since William's last illness, begging
him to come home for a few weeks. Invariably, Matthew had
replied: "It is impossible, Mama. I cannot go home, not even

for a little while. I have tried to explain. Please don't think I am cruel. It is something I can't put into words. I can only say—I am afraid. I'm afraid, even now."

Ursula said: "Yes, your father is so proud. You know, he has bought the painting which was exhibited in London. It is on its way here." What a struggle it had been to convince William that Matthew was enormously "busy"! William had been determined to visit his son. His own illness had intervened, and Dr. Banks had conspired with Ursula when he had informed William that "for some time," he must undertake no journey whatsoever.

Barbara gave her mother the warmest kiss she had ever given her. The two women clung together briefly in sorrowful silence. I, Barbara could not help thinking, am not doing so badly at this "understanding" business, myself!

Ursula drove away in her carriage, her gloved hand waving to her daughter, who stood on the doorstep where she, herself, had stood so many thousands of times. It was right, somehow, to see Barbara standing there. It was as if her own youth, unburdened by the years, confidently and bravely awaiting the future, stood on that threshold.

The future, thought Ursula. God help us.

CHAPTER LIV

JULIA FASTENED her diamond and topaz ear-rings care-fullly upon her ears. She stood up with a rustle of topaz skirts about her feet. There were topazes and diamonds about her white throat, and upon her arms. They complemented the rich light auburn of her hair, her amber eyes, the delicate flush of her cheeks, the whiteness of her lovely shoulders and breast, the brightness of her perfect mouth. Her eyes sparkled with gay satisfaction. She turned about swiftly, to laugh at Eugene, who was watching her from a distant chair.

"Well, do I satisfy you, Gene?" she asked, teasingly. Her love for her husband made her face radiant.

He rose slowly and came to her. He put his hands on her shoulders. "You always do, Julie," he said. He kissed her linger-ingly; her bare and perfumed arms went about his shoulders. "Oh, how I love you, Gene," she murmured. "Not more than I love you, my darling," he replied.

She withdrew from his arms. "I wonder how much longer we'll have to wait," she said. Now her voice was sullen and full of resentment. "It isn't fair."

Composedly, Eugene glanced with meaning at the closed door of their large and luxurious bedroom. He said, calmly: "I think we've agreed——"

"Not to discuss anything in this house," she finished for him petulantly. She kissed him again. "It isn't fair to you, Gene," she repeated.

Without answering, he picked up Julia's sable cloak and put it about her bare shoulders. "We are already late," he said. "The carriage is at the door."

"I'm ready," she said. They went out together, walked slow-ly, arm in arm, down the curving marble staircase. Julia looked at nothing but her husband, and he smiled down at her. They reached the bottom of the staircase. "Bother," said Julia. "It's late, and we'll have to say good-night to Papa and Mama."

They found William drowsing before the fire in the red and marble room. Haggard and exhausted, he sat slumped in his chair. Ursula sat near him, embroidering, her face pre-occupied, her hair gray in the lamplight. As Eugene and Julia entered, she looked up alertly, ready to indicate with an automatic gesture that William slept. She tried to smile, as Julia brought with her, into this enormous room, the glow and radiance of youth and beauty and vitality but, in Eugene's presence, it was hard to smile affectionately. She had been aghast when William had told her that Julia wished to marry Eugene Arnold. All her instincts had protested, wildly, repudiatingly. Hardly recovered from the marriage of Barbara and Oliver, William's savage treatment of his younger daughter and foster son, and her own shameful refusal of support to the young couple, she could not conceal her repugnance to this proposed marriage. She could not believe that William would countenance it, and had been stunned when he had assured her that it "pleased" him.

"But William," she had cried, "how can it 'please' you? What has happened to you?" She knew that something had indeed happened, for William, for all his expression of pleasure, had seemed ill and broken.

"I said," he answered, in an ugly tone, "that it is perfectly all right. What is the matter with Eugene? He is my general manager; he is invaluable to me. He has done well for himself. Fifteen years difference in their ages? What is wrong with that?"

William would say no more, but Ursula, remembering Barbara and Oliver, had been embittered and remorseful. She could not, at the time, reconcile herself to this new marriage. Even now, after almost four years of it, she could not reconcile herself to it.

Eugene stood beside his wife. At thirty-eight, his light hair had faded, become almost gray. His dry face never told anyone except Julia anything. Julia, beside him, was all sparkle and topaz flame and delicate life.

Glad that her father slept, Julia whispered: "Say good-night to him for us, Mama. Poor Papa. He needs to rest."

Ursula nodded. She lifted her eyes to Eugene. He was regarding her as he had regarded her when he was a child, with a curious interest, respectful and dignified.

Julia and Eugene went out together. The embroidery lay on Ursula's knee. She looked at the fire. William continued to drowse; once or twice he muttered feebly, as if in pain, and Ursula would start then, look at him with aching apprehension. How terribly he had aged! How weak he had become, more than was natural in a man of sixty. His big thin hands dangled over the arms of his chair; he had lost much weight. His frame had become almost gaunt. His hair was white, that hair which had once been thick and black. Yet, when he went to his offices life returned to him, if only briefly. He goaded himself beyond his strength, for something had broken him. He was proud of Thomas; Thomas had "brains." He knew more about the lumber business than did many lumber men twice his age. Thomas was a never-failing source of consolation to him. William often repeated that: consolation.

Dear God, she thought passionately, let him live—and die—deceived.

In half an hour, Oliver and Barbara and the baby would be arriving. She folded her embroidery; gently, she re-covered William's sagging knees with the afghan. She went out into the morning room, where she would receive Barbara and Oliver, as usual.

In the meantime, one of the Prescott carriages, with Eugene and Julia, rolled up the mountain road. Eugene had tucked the fur robe tenderly about his wife; her head, covered with a bright and sparkling scarf, rested on his shoulder. It was already dark, but the snow on the mountains glimmered about them. In the west lay a pool of cold saffron in which the icy evening-star glittered restlessly. The mountains moved and shouldered about the carriage.

In the closed confines of the carriage, Julia said: "And now, again, we'll have to pretend to Tom that everything is going famously, and that one of these days, soon, he'll be president of the Prescott Lumber Company! Oh, Gene, my darling, it is almost too much for me to stand, when you and I know that you, and you only, are going to be president! I love Tom; I've always loved him. But, after all, he is not you—you who deserve everything, and have worked for everything."

Eugene took her hand, held it tightly. "I've been patient for years, Julie, sweet. It won't be long, now. Just be patient. And, of course, Tom must suspect nothing; he has been working with me, and doing everything that I suggest. I like Tom. But not even Tom, I assure you, Julie, shall stand in my way."

He spoke with unemotional quiet, but Julie smiled contentedly. Then she frowned. "Why won't Papa give up? How long is he going to——" She paused as she restrained the ugly word, and replaced it with another "——force himself, when he isn't well?"

Eugene stared thoughtfully before him. "Your father," he said, "won't ever give up, not even to Tom. You know that. He's going to make Tom a vice-president. Harmless, enough, even in the jaundiced view of his officers and directors. But while he is alive he'll never resign the presidency." Again, Eugene tucked the robe about his wife. "Unless he is forced to do so."

"You can't wait much longer, Gene. You must do the forcing."

"You are certain you won't hold it against me, Julie?" But even as he asked this apparently anxious question, Eugene smiled curiously in the dusk.

"Oh, Gene, how can you ask such a silly question! You practically run the business now. Besides, it'll be better for Papa to resign. His health is declining every day. He'll be glad, in the end."

Again, Eugene smiled. They were now approaching the big white pile of Thomas' home. They saw it against the dying brass of the western sky.

"He'll be glad, in the end." Eugene considered his wife's words. It would be the end, the end for the Prescotts, father and son. He, Eugene, could depend upon Julia. She was with him. William had done his work well. He could expect from his children neither pity nor help.

The blaze of lights in the white house broke through the carriage windows. Julia turned to Gene. She stopped. Her mouth opened a little, and her brows drew together. She said: "Do you know, Gene, you look like that hateful Oliver! I've wondered for a long time whom you resembled. Now I see it. How nasty! How revolting!"

The coachman opened the door. Eugene did not reply. He said: "Here we are. Take my arm, sweet. It is slippery, here."

CHAPTER LV

"HOW IS PAPA?" asked Barbara, as she removed little Billy's bonnet and coat, and gave them to a waiting maid.

"Sleeping, or resting," answered Ursula. She stood beside Oliver, who had placed his arm about her shoulders. She felt its affectionate pressure. Once, she had been comforted by his touch; now she could feel only the heavy sadness of remorse.

Oliver gently removed his arm. He had kissed Ursula's withered cheek. Though he was filled with concern for her, he smiled. "I'll glance in at him," he said. "I shan't disturb him, if he's asleep. Let him rest until dinner."

Uneasily, Ursula watched him leave the room. Did he remind William of the latter's own secret regret and shame? she wondered. But nothing could ever be revoked. She said to Barbara: "Let us go into the sitting-room, and have a little talk until dinner-time."

Oliver moved silently towards the red and marble drawing-room. He stood on the threshold. Ursula had turned down the gaslights on the wall, so that the monstrous reaches of the room were in semi-darkness. He saw William at a distance, sleeping. He slipped into the room, closer to William, and looked at the fallen face, the hanging hands, the sleeping attitude of desolation and abandon. He had forgiven, but he could not forget that this man had attempted to ruin him. Oliver quite understood why. William had expected so much for his daughters, Though, to William, Barbara was the least of his children, still he loved her, and she was his daughter. He could not accept the idea of Barbara's wanting to marry him, Oliver, for whom he had developed such an inexplicable antipathy.

Oliver looked at his foster father with compassion. His eyes became stern. I shan't let them destroy you, Father, he said in himself. I'll stop them!

He stood there, and a certain ruthlessness tightened his face. It was then that William stirred, opened his eyes, and saw Oliver. In spite of the very dim light, he saw what there was to be seen in Oliver's expression. He raised himself a little. He said: "Oh. Gene." He was bemused from his sleep, and he thought it was Julia's husband who stood there, near him.

Oliver went to a wall and turned up the lights. He turned. William was sitting bolt upright in his chair, blinking. "It's Oliver," said the young man, quietly. "Good evening, Father."

William was staring at him, as if appalled. He could not speak. Oliver sat down near him, but not too near.

William almost whispered, hoarsely: "I thought you were Gene. Standing there. You looked like Gene——" He coughed.

"You were asleep," said Oliver. "And then I startled you." He tried to smile. "Were you expecting Gene?"

William put his hands over his eyes, drew them down over his face. He shook his head, as if trying to shake off something. He made himself say: "Yes. I was expecting Gene. And Julie. They were going out. They must have gone, not wanting to wake me."

His voice dwindled away. Once again, he turned his head, stared at Oliver as at a ghost. "There was something about you—perhaps your expression," he muttered. "It was like Gene." He could not glance away. Fascinated, he narrowed his eyes. "I never saw it before," he said, as if to himself. "But there it was."

"No," said Oliver. "It was just because you were just expecting Gene." He was alarmed.

William was silent. His complex and turbulent mind churned with his thoughts. He was not a man who ever examined his motives, or his impulses. Vaguely, he now wondered whether he had not come to have a repugnance for Oliver because Oliver, even as a child, had reminded him of Eugene Arnold. Oliver, personally, had done nothing; Oliver had never done anything to hurt or wound him. Yet, he, William, had injured Oliver in return.

Knowing the terrible tenacity of William's mind, Oliver's alarm increased. He said, quickly: "I came to tell you before I told anyone else, even Barbie. Scott, Meredith & Owens have made me a junior partner. It will now be Scott, Meredith, Owens and Prescott. I thought you'd like to know, Father."

"What?" muttered William. "I'm sorry, but I didn't hear you, Oliver."

Clearly, more loudly, Oliver repeated what he had said. Now William listened. He averted his head. Oliver waited. William weakly placed his elbow on the arm of his chair, and supported his cheek in his palm. In this position, his face was hidden from Oliver. He said, and his voice trembled:

"I congratulate you, Oliver. But it's no more than you deserve. 'Scott, Meredith, Owens and Prescott.' It—it has a good sound, Oliver."

A good sound. William repeated that to himself. He could hardly see, he was so blinded and moved. He had said what he could. But how could he say: "Forgive me, for I didn't know what I was doing? Forgive me, for all the years."

"Thank you, Father," said Oliver. "I knew it would please you." He added: "It all came about because the old gentlemen thought I did such a good job before the Supreme Court, in Washington."

"You'll always do a good job, Oliver," said William, painfully.

Again Oliver replied: "Thank you, Father."

"I—I am proud of you," said William.

Oliver could not answer.

William sighed, and the sound was almost a groan. "Oliver," he said, "I haven't much to leave you. I think you ought to know that. I've put everything into trust funds for my children. There are only a few thousands for you. It was wrong, cruelly wrong, I see that now. But, at the time, I didn't think. It seems to me now that I never thought much at all."

"You've done more for me than I can ever say," said Oliver, quickly. "If I could live a thousand years, and could give them all to you, it wouldn't be enough. I'll never forget."

He hesitated. Then he said with resolution: "Father, I've a strange thing to ask of you. I want to hear you say: 'I trust you, Oliver.'"

William's hand dropped.

"It seems to me, Oliver, that I've heard a lot of people asking me to 'trust' them."

No doubt, thought Oliver, bitterly. He tried to make his voice light: "Well, I'm asking you, too. The only difference, perhaps, is that you could really trust me."

William regarded him curiously in a short silence. "What is wrong, Oliver? Why do you ask me this?"

"There's nothing wrong. I asked you only because it would make me glad to hear you say it."

William shrugged. "Very well, though it's very odd you should ask that question. Frankly, I never distrusted you, though I don't suppose my trust is worth anything. All right, Oliver, I trust you." He aroused himself. "Is Barbie here, and little Billy?"

"Yes. I came in alone, to tell you about the junior partnership. They, and Mother, are waiting for you. Shall I call them?"

He went out of the room, returned with Ursula, Barbara and the baby. William's devastated face broke into a genuine smile of affection. He held out his arms, and his grandson ran to him with a gleeful shout. The child climbed upon his knee, wound his arms about William's neck, kissed him heartily. "You ought to have named him Oliver," said William.

Ursula flushed with embarrassment; Barbara straightened with affront. But Oliver smiled.

Oliver said, standing very near William, and speaking so low that only William heard: "I'll never forget your saying that, Father. You couldn't have said anything more kind, anything I'd want to hear more."

Knowing of the deep antagonism between William and Barbara, Oliver usually spent, before going to the Prescott house with his wife, at least fifteen minutes in what Barbara would call, wryly, "a course in manners." It was hard for Barbara, who had a forthright approach to the appreciation for reality, to have patience with a man who refused to face it. This had been the reason for the old hostility between father and daughter.

Barbara, still smarting from what she believed another affront to Oliver, was now in no condition to exercise pity. William liked to have little Billy at the dinner table. Sometimes, upon prompting from Oliver, Barbara permitted this. But tonight she curtly handed the baby over to a maid, with clear instructions that the child be kept out of sight until his parents were ready to go. William made no angry protest, as he usually did. He was too tired and too shaken.

This was not enough for Barbara. During the dreary dinner, she fumed silently and kept giving her father dark glances, refusing, in the meantime, to let Oliver catch her eye. When dinner was nearly over, she said to her mother, but with an air of significance which captured William's attention: "When Billy is old enough, he is going to Sunday school."

William said, coldly: "You are going to let him be taught superstition?"

Barbara almost snorted. " 'Superstition,' Papa! He is going, for his own sake, to be well grounded in religion. He's got to learn that there is an authority beyond his own desires and childish wishes. He'll learn that the church is the authority of God, his parents the sole authority in the household, and his teachers the unquestioned authority in school. This will give him a genuine feeling of safety, make him understand that he is only one atom in a world of people, and extremely unimportant in the large scheme of things. He must understand his unimportance, and that if he is to achieve any sort of personal distinction at all, he must do it by his own efforts, and within the frame of society as it is."

"A very Spartan idea," murmured Ursula, with a distressed glance at William, and a harsh glance at her daughter.

"There was something in the Spartan idea," answered Barbara, belligerently. Her cheeks were flushed. "The Spartan children were, at least, not parasites upon their parents; they understood they had to stand alone and work and fight well for themselves, or perish. That is the inexorable law of nature."

William's face swelled dangerously with dark blood. Oliver, like a fencer, stepped smoothly into the impending quarrel. He said: "Barbara sounds rather formidable, and most unmaternal. Actually, she's very gentle with Billy, and sometimes very sentimental." Barbara glared at him, outraged. Ursula, seizing the advantage, rose and said: "Shall we leave the gentlemen to their coffee, Barbie?"

Barbara was not prepared to leave the gentlemen at all, until she had avenged Oliver. But her mother was standing, and had turned very pale. Barbara mutinously stood up and accompanied her mother out of the room. When they were safely in the drawing-room, Ursula said to her daughter: "Are you deliberately trying to hurt your father, Barbie, who has been so ill?"

Barbara did not reply at once. Then she said, steadily: "Yes. Yes. He hurt Oliver, tonight. Oliver saved me. If it had not been for Oliver, I'd have been as bad as Julie—or perhaps worse. You, yourself, ought to be grateful to him."

In a strangely pent voice, Ursula said: "I think of nothing, nothing, but your father. He must be saved from the consequences of his own delusions."

After a while, when the women had left, William asked Oliver to come upstairs to his rooms. Oliver, surprised, followed his father. William shut all doors with an oddly secretive and impatient air. It was as if he was embarrassed. He went to a dresser, opened it, unlocked a box concealed there, and brought out a small object wrapped in a piece of silk. He sat down near Oliver, the object in his hand. All at once he appeared ill and overcome with despair. He looked at Oliver a long time before he said, feebly: "I've got something here. It's probably nonsense." He paused. "I know you try to 'spare' me, Oliver. It doesn't matter. Barbie's a good girl. Yes, a good girl," he added, with heaviness. "Like her mother. Sense.

They both have sense. Oliver, you'll take care of your mother, won't you?"

"Of course." Oliver was alarmed, but he smiled reassuringly. "You're just tired, Father," he said.

William stared before him. "Yes," he said. "I'm tired. Yes, I suppose I'm tired." He unwrapped the object, but he still concealed it with his hand. He coughed weakly. "I never told you—I never told anyone—very much about Dr. Cowlesbury. I tried to tell—— It wasn't any use. I couldn't. There are some things a man can't talk about."

Oliver waited, while William fell into silence. But he maintained an attitude of composure and interest.

Then William stirred irritably. "It's probably nonsense," he repeated. "I always thought it was nonsense, even when I was with the old doctor. But still——" He opened his palm and let Oliver see what was in it. It was a beautiful small crucifix of gold and ivory, exquisitely carved and pierced. "The doctor's," said William. He held it out to Oliver, and Oliver took it. "He gave it to me," William went on. "It was just before he died. He wanted me to have it. He was a Catholic." William smiled faintly. "He said it was blessed, or something. It was for my children, he said."

William stood up abruptly, and Oliver stood up, also. William eyed him almost irately. "It was what Barbie said," William remarked. "She probably wouldn't want it for little Billy, anyway. Children grow up—they haven't time for—God. No one has. I don't suppose anyone ever did, except people like the doctor."

Oliver could not speak for a moment. He said: "Barbie'll want it, for Billy. I'll want it, for Billy. It will mean something to him, I know. Just as it means something to me."

William was pleased. He forgot his embarrassment. But he said carelessly: "Well. It didn't mean anything to me." He looked at the crucifix in Oliver's hand, and his face changed. "Well," he repeated with a curious somberness.

He went as quickly as he could towards the door, and Oliver followed. William stood on the threshold for a moment, his back to Oliver, his head bent. "Forgive me," he muttered. And then he walked away, even faster.

CHAPTER LVI

IT WAS NINE O'CLOCK at night, on this evening in the middle of a cold and green April, but it was not dark behind the closely-shrouded windows of the offices of Scott, Meredith, Owens & Prescott. The hearth was heaped high with logs; the air simmered with the fumes of tobacco, the heat of the fire and the blazing gaslights on the panelled walls. There was even a fragrance of brandy in the atmosphere.

Nine old men, some of them very old indeed, were gathered in the large main office, and only one young man. That latter sat near the "three gray midgets," as Messrs. Scott, Meredith, and Owens were known among the more disrespectful inhabitants of Andersburg. But "midgets" or not, these gentlemen compensated for their size by the vastness of their integrity, by their reputation, their combined wealth, and their formidable dignity. Amazingly alike in physical appearance, though not even remotely related by blood, they sat in their majesty, unperturbed, quiet and dominant, each small gray head erect, each pair of shoulders high and broad and firm, each little face a very replica of nobility. They dressed alike, in dark gray suits, with black silk ties adorned with black pearl stickpins, small shoes miraculously polished. They wore the rings of their universities too, but no other jewelry. Near them, of them, sat Oliver Prescott.

In comparison with all this patrician and solid elegance, the six other old men, in spite of their excellent clothing, appeared a somewhat untidy crew. There was, perhaps, something a little too florid about Dr. Banks, Mr. Leslie and Mr. Bassett, something too artificial about the saintliness of Judge Muehller, something too sly and wizened about Senator Whiscomb and Mr. Jenkins. Perhaps their disheveled air arose from a certain disorder which pervaded them, a disorder of minds beset by fear and concern, for Mr. Scott had just finished reading to them a letter from the Northwest Lumber Company of Seattle, Washington. Certainly, even Mr. Bassett's and Dr. Banks' high and ruddy color had faded; certainly, Judge Muehller's atmosphere of martyred delicacy had been shaken; certainly, Mr. Leslie's brutal posture had become flabby. As for the others, consternation and dismay had blurred their ancient outlines and changed them into the very portraits of impotent old men, still savage, but robbed of cogency.

Mr. Scott looked with stately satisfaction at the letter he had just read. His associates looked back at him mildly; the others glared at him, aghast. Oliver waited.

A long and panic-stricken silence followed the reading. The officers and directors of the Prescott Lumber Company could not even glance at one another; the old lawyers held their gaze. They dared not look away from him, it appeared. He might, in another moment, reach over to his desk and bring out another paper of doom.

Dr. Banks' trembling hand passed over his white beard. He had trouble in finding his voice, and then he could only murmur: "Ridiculous. Impudent. Not to be taken seriously for a moment." His voice dwindled away.

"Not to be countenanced—impudent," murmured Mr. Bassett. Then he saw Oliver. His round face instantly turned malevolent. He stared at Oliver, and there was rage glittering behind his spectacles. He began to say something, then stopped. He began again: "Is it necessary, Mr. Scott, that Oliver Prescott be present? I have no personal objection to Mr.—Prescott, but under the circumstances——"

Mr. Meredith said tranquilly: "Mr. Prescott is our junior partner. In a few moments he will address this meeting and inform you gentlemen of certain other facts."

"He is——" Mr. Bassett started to say, then once again halted.

Oliver's quiet voice completed the sentence: "Mr. Scott, Mr. Meredith and Mr. Owens are already aware, Mr. Bassett, of a certain conversation I had with you a long time ago. I have not 'betrayed' you, as you seem to think, for there was nothing, really, to betray. In a little while, you'll all know how the facts of my own case can be used in behalf of all of us, and of the Prescott Lumber Company."

His three old partners gave Oliver a benevolent smile. Mr. Owens touched his arm lightly. He spoke: "Gentlemen—Mr. Bassett, we have the highest regard and affection for young Mr. Prescott. We regard him as a son. We beg all of you to treat him as if he were. Later, you will understand."

Now the attention of the officers and directors of the Prescott Lumber Company was turned incredulously upon Oliver. He met the combined assault of their eyes without embarrassment, returned it calmly. If he felt contempt for them, he did not show it.

But Ezra Bassett could not control himself. He turned to his fellow officers and directors and said, slowly and loudly: "Gentlemen, I am in possession of certain facts of my own. Something's smelling very bad in here just now. I ought to have told you of it before, I presume. Nothing legally prevented me. I am not a lawyer." Now he shot Oliver a look of the purest malignancy. "I ought to have told you that this—that Oliver Prescott is the illegitimate son of Chauncey Arnold. He is Gene Arnold's half-brother."

Again, an astounded silence fell upon the room. Mr. Bassett's friends stared unbelievingly at Oliver, who remained composed. They blinked their eyes at him; they strained forward to see him more clearly. He folded his arms across his chest, crossed his knees. One or two of them took off their glasses, polished them with white handkerchiefs, put them on again, and resumed their piercing scrutiny of the young man.

Mr. Bassett chuckled. "I have all the evidence, and so has he. He can't deny it."

The old lawyers smoked their cigars tranquilly; they exchanged the slightest of smiles.

Oliver said: "I don't propose to deny it, Mr. Bassett. I propose to use it, as you once suggested that you and I might use it."

Mr. Leslie broke into a loud guffaw and struck his knee with his clenched fist. "God!" he exclaimed. "What a scandal this is going to be! It'll shake Andersburg from east to west!"

Mr. Meredith waited until the disturbance had subsided. He said with serene sternness: "Gentlemen, I assure you that if you attempt to injure Mr. Prescott, you'll regret the day. For you see, gentlemen, my associates and I summoned you here in all mercy, and only after long pleading on the part of Oliver. He wants to save the Prescott Lumber Company. It is in our hands to destroy it. He wants to save it because of Mr. William Prescott. However, should you, beyond these doors, communicate to anyone one word of a certain unfortunate circumstance, then I say with all sincerity that I hope you have, beyond your holdings in the Prescott Lumber Company, private fortunes sufficient to sustain you for the rest of your lives."

"What do you mean, sir?" stammered Judge Muehller.

Mr. Meredith shrugged. "I propose that Mr. Prescott now address you. You will, I am sure, hear him out in silence and in courtesy."

Almost squeaking under the shock of what he had heard, Senator Whiscomb said: "I refuse—I don't intend—I don't know what this is all about!" Frantically, he looked from one old man to the other, a long stare of terrified dismay. "This is too much for a man my age to have to listen to—Chauncey Arnold's son! The Company. What is all this?"

Mr. Owens addressed Mr. Bassett: "Plotters always make the very serious mistake of believing that they alone plot. Personally, I dislike that word—'plot'. Our firm, sir, has never engaged in anything nefarious. We have never attempted to blackmail——"

"Blackmail!" stuttered Mr. Bassett.

"Blackmail is what I said, sir," replied Mr. Owens, with cold severity. "What else would you call your attack upon our junior partner? Or would you prefer to call it malice, or hatred, or simply plain cruelty? What had you to gain? You thought you could injure him, debase him in our estimation, hold him up to ridicule in the sight of this city? You have heard Mr. Meredith's warning. We, too, are old men. We are fast losing our patience. In spite of our affection and regard for young Mr. Prescott and our promise that, for the sake of Mr. William Prescott, we'll assist him in the saving of your Company, we shall, if we hear any further attack from any of you upon our junior associate, be compelled to ask you to leave immediately, and to take the consequences."

Dr. Banks and the others listened in dazed incredulity.

Again, Mr. Scott looked at the paper in his hand. "Be sure, gentlemen, that the Northwest Lumber Company would not have written me of their desire to enter the Western and Eastern lumber markets, and would not have suggested that they wished to absorb the Prescott Lumber Company, had they not had reason to believe that it is possible to do so. I might reminnd you of a certain passage in this letter: 'We have, as our objective in this, the avoidance of the increasing danger of competition, and the elimination of smaller competitors, thus stabilizing control of the lumber business in general in the important areas.' I need not remind you, gentlemen, that the Northwest Lumber Company is the largest lumber company in this country. It is 'big business', gentlemen. The Prescott Lumber Company was once 'big business', also. It is not so, now. And we have it in our power to eliminate it entirely, instead of permitting it to become a subsidiary of the Northwest Lumber Company."

"A subsidiary!" exclaimed Judge Muehller, freshly appalled.

Mr. Scott smiled gently. "But I am infringing upon Mr.

Prescott's own territory. Oliver, will you now address these gentlemen?"

Oliver stood up without haste.

"Gentlemen, Mr. Scott has not told you the date of the letter from the Northwest Lumber Company. It is dated six months ago." He paused. "Since that date this firm has been in communication with them."

He waited. No one spoke. No one averted his head. The fire crackled and the gaslights flickered a little.

."At the very beginning, I want to say this," went on Oliver. "I want to save the Prescott Lumber Company, and for only one reason: for the sake of my foster father. He is dying. He may die tomorrow, as Dr. Banks can tell you: he might live another six months. Longer than that, I believe, he cannot live. Dr. Banks, may we ask your professional opinion?"

Dr. Banks bridled. He turned to his friends. But they only returned his look questioningly. He coughed. "A physician should never be called upon to give his opinion to anyone save his patient, or his patient's family. His opinion is sacred."

Oliver smiled. "Under the law, I am a member of Mr. Prescott's family."

Dr. Banks pretended to reflect upon this. He was extremely frightened. Angrily, he said: "Very well. I am violating no confidences, I presume, when I say that Bill cannot live more than six months. Of course, that is only my opinion. I won't bore you with the recitation of certain symptoms which have—ah, disturbed—me, but I can give it as my opinion that Bill Prescott will not see the year out."

Mr. Leslie said brutishly, shifting his bulk in his chair: "You're almighty concerned with this, aren't you, Mr. Oliver Prescott?"

"I am," replied Oliver. "I am concerned to the point where I'll do anything to save this Company, in order that my adoptive father may die in peace. But if I'm to save it, you'll have to help me, though, under any other circumstances, you'd refuse. For, you see, your refusal would mean your ruin."

Again, he studied them. "You are all old men, very old men. Still, you want money. Your minds are so fixed upon your money that you have forgotten two very vital things: Eugene Arnold, and Tom Prescott. You have forgotten that Tom Prescott is married to Mary Blake, and that behind Tom and Mary are the Blake millions."

No one answered him. The old lawyers smiled.

"Temporarily, at least, you might forget Tom, except in connection with Eugene Arnold. But Eugene Arnold you must not forget. You must not forget that he hates my foster father. You must not forget the very evident fact that he wants the Prescott Lumber Company for himself, and that he intends to have it."

"A lie!" cried Mr. Jenkins, speaking for the first time.

Oliver smiled again. "Mr. Bassett," he said, "won't agree with you, will you, Mr. Bassett?"

Mr. Bassett flushed crimson. His friends as one man turned to him. Sweat had burst out upon the old man's face. He said, regarding Oliver with hatred: "No, I don't agree with Jenkins." He took out his handkerchief and rubbed his damp forehead. "It's only an idea of mine, perhaps, but I've been watching Eugene Arnold. It came to me years ago that he wanted the Company. I think it came eventually to all of us. But he can't have it. There's no way he can have it!" he added, shrilly.

"Yes, there is," said Oliver, composedly. "There are the Blake millions, and Mr. Blake is very fond of Tom. You see, Eugene has for years been playing a fine game. He's convinced Tom that he is his friend, that his sole desire is to see Tom president of the Company, and that he is working with Tom to that end. He is using Tom. It is possible that he'd even allow Tom to become president. The pleasure of torturing my father, the humiliation of my father, and the sight of his agony at discovering that his son had betrayed him, might be too delicious a dish for Eugene Arnold to reject.

"But with Tom as president, should Eugene permit Tom to become president, there would always be Eugene Arnold behind him. I happen to know that he has an alternative, however. He would permit Tom to be president only if that alternative did not mature. It won't, gentlemen. But Eugene doesn't know that, not yet.

"Gentlemen, as I go on speaking, you must not, for an instant, let Gene out of your minds. If there is a villain in this piece, it is Gene Arnold."

"Your brother," said Judge Muehller in a gently dreaming voice.

Oliver repeated: "My brother."

He drew a deep breath. "I might say, at this time, that my father, on the occasion of his learning, two months ago, that Tom would be a father in less than seven months, has already assigned ten percent of his holdings to Tom." He added, in a low tone: "That was Gene's suggestion to Tom, when Tom told him that his father had asked him what he would like in celebration of the news."

The Senator exclaimed: "How do you know all this? How do you know all these things?"

Oliver was silent for a few moments. He then said: "About five months ago I had to tell my mother a few things. She thinks only of my father. I had to persuade her of the plot which is developing against her husband. I had the facts by then, and she finally believed me. And so, she told me. She told me all she knew, and all she suspected. Because she was terrified."

"A woman's suspicions are never to be relied upon," said the judge.

"Perhaps not—always. I verified these. But I am ahead of myself. I want to go into the background of this whole thing with you. You will see, then, that I know everything."

"Rather a preposterous statement, for a man who is exclusively a lawyer," remarked Dr. Banks with inimical softness. He waved his hand: "Pardon the interruption, dear Oliver. Pray continue, and enlighten us, especially about the lumber business."

Oliver studied him for a moment. "I may be a lawyer, sir, but I undertook, as an extra-curricular activity, the study of the lumber business. I thought, more than five years ago, I might have need of the information. I wasn't mistaken.

"You see," he continued, "I never trusted Eugene Arnold. You may call it intuition; you may call it a certain—understanding. I knew that the Prescott Lumber Company, and Mr. Prescott, were in danger. Men like Eugene Arnold never forget. And, so that I could follow Eugene further, it was necessary, first of all, that I become familiar with the lumber business.

"I don't have to recall to you gentlemen what has been happening in America since Mr. Roosevelt became President of the United States——"

He was interrupted by a raucous interjection by Mr. Leslie: "Roosevelt! That swine! Too bad he wasn't shot, instead of McKinley! He's a destroyer of free enterprise, that's what he is, the enemy of American prosperity, which is the result of big business. Look what he did to the Northern Securities Company! Interfering rascal! Anarchist! No wonder we have labor troubles." He glared at Oliver. "I suppose you intend to give us, as the background for some muddled plot you have in mind, a discourse on the fine qualities of Roosevelt, who is wrecking free enterprise."

Oliver smiled. "No, Mr. Leslie, I don't. I don't intend to talk about big business. I might remark that if anyone here is at all muddled, it isn't me. You see, it was the protection of small businesses like the Prescott Lumber Company which became the concern of the President. The Northwest Lumber Company is big business, for it intends, as you can see from its letter to us, to 'eliminate competitors.' But Mr. Roosevelt is inclined to look on the Northwest Lumber Company with some kindness, for it has promised to aid him in his determination to conserve our forests, which are in real danger of being destroyed. Selfishly, or with real sincerity, it has entered, with the President, into a plan for the conservation of our natural resources. It is going to coöperate with him in the North American Conservation Conference, to be held within a year or two. Again, for some reason, probably financial, it has even succeeded in interesting Mr. Jay Regan and his associates, who are normally against conservation of any kind. I'll come to that later, however.

"Mr. Prescott was once strongly in favor of the conservation of our lumber resources. In that, I think he was a pioneer. But I don't have to tell you what happened to Mr. Prescott a few years ago. I'd like to believe that you gentlemen," and here Oliver's face hardened, "are guilty of the change in my father's attitude towards the conservation of forests. But you aren't guilty of that, though you didn't object, of course, to my father's abandonment of that sensible and patriotic idea."

He paused, and looked aside for a moment. "Well. You all know the change. My father became reckless. He was obsessed by the idea of providing large estates and trust funds for his children. It became a phobia with him. Everything else was forgotten. So, recklessly, in order to make money very fast, money which was deposited in the untouchable trust funds set up for his four children, he decided to throw out conservation.

"So obsessed did my father become with his plan to make his children financially invulnerable that he sacrificed everything. He lost his boldness in enterprise. He lost initiative, invention. Finally, large portions of his salary were also thrown into the trust funds."

Now he looked piercingly at each of the six directors and officers. "It is just a thought of mine, but I'm sure you are aware that Mr. Prescott has very little money of his own left. Yes," he added, with quiet bitterness, "I'm sure you are. Just as I'm sure that Gene Arnold has kept you informed."

"Look here!" blustered Mr. Jenkins. "You can't throw assumptions around like that, insulting assumptions."

Oliver turned his attention upon him with the utmost acuteness. He nodded. "Perhaps, you, Mr. Jenkins, and one or two others, aren't aware that—some—of you know these things. Am I right, gentlemen?" he asked, looking directly at Mr. Bassett, Judge Muehller and Dr. Banks.

Mr. Jenkins, Mr. Leslie and Senator Whiscomb, mouths open, eyes widened, swung upon the doctor, the judge and the banker. These last, attacked with such suddenness, shrank.

"Eh!" said Mr. Leslie, vindictively. "Is something going on here we haven't heard about? What is this about you and Gene Arnold—Bassett? Banks? Muehller?"

Oliver interrupted smoothly: "Gentlemen, it is possible that this is just imagination on my part. After all, you are all officers and associates, aren't you? You wouldn't plot against your friends, would you? Just for money?"

Dr. Banks, wounded and outraged, broke out in a loud sonorous voice, as he faced Mr. Jenkins, Mr. Leslie and the Senator: "Of course not. Intolerable even to suggest it. We're friends together, aren't we?"

"Are we?" said Mr. Jenkins, his wizened face screwed together cunningly.

"We are, indeed," said Mr. Bassett, the second to recover from the staggering attack.

Oliver interposed: "I've been mistaken, then. Please forgive me. Shall I go on?"

The doctor, the banker and the judge, still sweating with fear, looked at him hatingly, but with new wariness and respect. The others, with quiet savageness, divided their attention between Oliver and their friends. Scott, Meredith and Owens, though they smiled pleasantly and happily in the background, were temporarily forgotten.

"So," said Oliver, satisfied that his coup would serve to mitigate hostility from Mr. Bassett, Dr. Banks and Judge Muehller, "we have this situation where my father has brought the Prescott Lumber Company to a very dangerous pass. It isn't expanding. It is shrinking; it is about to dwindle into a sixth-rate company. It isn't your fault. It is the fault of my father's obsession. He knows he is ill; he's known that a long while. He is marking time, and has been doing so for years, just to build up those trust funds. Gentlemen, how are your dividends?" he asked abruptly.

Mr. Leslie said sullenly: "You know so much, you ought to know what they are. Rotten. But you can't blame Prescott for that," he said, angrily. "It's that Roosevelt, and the panic he's started, with his interference with business, and his coddling of labor, and his fight with Wall Street."

Oliver shook his head. "It isn't Mr. Roosevelt's fault that Prescott is in such a bad way. I'm sorry, but you've got to blame your president, though I ask your charity and understanding.

"Now we come to the actual and imminent danger. We're in the midst of a 'silent panic.' Before the year is out we are going to have a real panic. Why? That is a question you'll have to ask Mr. Regan, Mr. Morse and Mr. Rockefeller. It is also a question you should ask the speculators on the Stock Market—the small as well as the big speculators. Overexpansion and reckless speculation brought the crash in the Market less than thirty days ago. It will result in a real national panic within the next few months.

"It may surprise you gentlemen to learn, later, that it will be Mr. Roosevelt's anti-trust laws which will prevent hundreds of small companies from going bankrupt, being absorbed, or disappearing entirely. It won't, however, save the Prescott Lumber Company from bankruptcy, disappearance or absorption, because the fault lies in its president.

"Let us get on. Gene Arnold knows all this. He is also determined that the Prescott Lumber Company shall not be absorbed by any larger company. He has a lot of very brilliant plans. He'll let the company approach bankruptcy, he thinks. And then he'll step in. Either with his dupe, Tom Prescott, and the Blake millions, or with his own friends. I might say, gentlemen, that these friends do not include you, the officers and directors of the Prescott Lumber Company, though it is barely possible that he has persuaded you to the contrary."

Again, Dr. Banks, Mr. Bassett and Judge Muehller could hardly suppress their agitation. So intense was this agitation that they forgot three others were watching them with baleful suspicion. They looked at one another, and each face was a study in consternation, dismay or fear.

Oliver allowed a few moments to pass in a pregnant silence, for he had a fine sense of timing. When he spoke again, everyone started.

"Perhaps some of you know that Mr. Regan holds, as collateral, twenty-eight percent of the stock of the Prescott Lumber Company personally owned by my father. Yes, I see that you know. I am using my imagination again, very impertinently, when I suggest that some—or all?—of you have had this 'n mind, possibly with the idea of buying this stock from Mr.

Regan, and then, with the stock you already possess, of ousting my father. You don't have to protest; you don't even have to feel guilty. It is all 'business', and I'm not reproaching any of you. For I understand, you see, that my father, because of his health, and because of the many things he has done to build up private fortunes for his children, is no longer competent to run the Prescott Lumber Company."

He paused, and waited until he had the attention of everyone. "Eugene Arnold has visited Mr. Regan very recently, with regard to the stock Mr. Regan holds."

"What!" cried several voices, incredulously. "Where would he get the money?" "Who's behind him?" "How do you know that?"

Oliver replied: "Where would he get the money? Keep your eye on Gene, gentlemen. He has friends. Again, not you, any of you, in spite of any secret idea any of you might have. He isn't interested in you. He told Regan that you were decrepit old men, that you won't, naturally, live much longer and that, in some way, whether you live or not, he'll be able to get rid of you. I won't go into the full details. They aren't necessary. But they are true. Mr. Regan told me all this, himself."

"What!" they cried again, stunned.

Oliver nodded. "Please let me continue for a moment. Gene's friends include some of the wealthiest people in Andersburg, and some of the 'outsiders'. They are impressed with his brilliant mind, his astuteness, his tremendous ability. They are prepared to back him. But Gene is too clever to rely wholly upon promises, however enthusiastic. If his friends won't help him buy that stock, Mr. Blake will, through Tom. In that event, he'll force Tom upon you as a sort of dummy president, while he, himself, will be the power behind Tom. Eventually, he'll find a way to oust Tom. I haven't the slightest doubt of this. In the meantime he isn't, of course, interested in you. You've served your purpose. You'll be forced out, by threat of bankruptcy, if you don't follow. Eventually you'll be forced out, anyway, most probably by a sudden and crippling fall, within a few months, in the value of the Prescott stock you own."

He allowed the terrified old men a long time to digest this. They forgot the dangerous division which, fifteen minutes ago, had arisen between them. Now, in their overwhelming alarm, they were together.

"Yes," said Oliver, softly, breaking the silence, "you are in extreme danger. I tell you this, for I need your help."

Stupefied, they looked at him, unblinkingly. "Yes, gentlemen, your help. Though I'm a peaceable man, I might add that I demand your help. You'll be saving yourselves by helping me; you'll be saving the Company. In a few moments, I'll tell you what you must do.

"I said that Mr. Regan told me all that I've told you. You may think I'm flattering myself when I say that I impressed Mr. Regan very favorably. Perhaps this is because Mr. Scott, and Mr. Meredith, and Mr. Owens, are old and very close friends of Mr. Regan's."

Mr. Scott cleared his throat delicately, and nodded, when the six officers and directors turned to him as one man.

"Yes, indeed," he murmured. "Mr. Regan and ourselves are old, old friends. Known each other since boyhood." He chuckled gently. "Jay would do almost anything for us, within reason, of course, and provided it gave him a little profit. But, forgive me, I am interrupting our dear young friend, Mr. Prescott. However, I might add that Oliver impressed Mr. Regan on his own account. He owes nothing to us."

Oliver bowed to the old men, ceremoniously, while the others watched, still in a state of stupefaction.

"Time is growing short, gentlemen," Oliver resumed briskly. "I had a very interesting and satisfying talk with Mr. Regan. To make it brief, Mr. Regan has promised me that he will sell the twenty-eight percent of my father's stock to no one but the Northwest Lumber Company. He won't sell it to you, or to Mr. Blake, or to Gene. I have his solemn promise." He smiled slightly. "There's a profit in it for Mr. Regan, too. He is interested, to some very impressive extent, in the Northwest Lumber Company. Moreover, I believe an arrangement has been made between Mr. Regan and the Northwest Lumber Company to the effect that the Company will open a large and active account with Mr. Regan."

He sat down, imperturbably. He folded his arms upon his chest. "Suppose you gentlemen consider all this, very carefully, for five minutes. Consider all its implications."

They considered it. In the meantime, Oliver exchanged glances with the three old lawyers, who smiled their affectionate approval of him.

Then Mr. Leslie spoke harshly: "What's in it for us?" The five others stirred, and looked towards Oliver.

Oliver stood up again. "A lot, gentlemen. The saving of a great part of your personal fortunes. Did I forget to tell you that I have visited the offices of the Northwest Lumber Company? I see I did. It was a very interesting and congenial visit. They understood everything. They have deputized me to tell you that if and when they take over the Prescott Lumber Company they will increase the Prescott stock twenty-five percent, and will exchange it for an equal amount of Northwestern stock of the same value. And, gentlemen, I am sure you know what the value of Northwestern stock is today."

"Incredible!" gasped Dr. Banks.

Now six faces began to glow with astounded delight, avarice and eagerness. The six old men gazed at Oliver as at a glorious vision which had promised them fresh fortunes and profits.

"I can hardly believe it," muttered Mr. Jenkins.

Judge Muehller gleamed with saintly admiration. "Oliver, you are a clever young man; I might even say, a most admirable young man."

"If these are all facts," said Mr. Leslie, in a shaken voice of hope and doubt.

"They are all facts," said Oliver. "Within a day or two, we'll be glad to show them to you, in black and white."

"My dear Oliver," said Mr. Bassett, with the deepest affection, "you have asked us to 'help' you. We need not say that we'll be only too glad to do that. But tell us."

"Yes, indeed," chorused the others, richly. The old lawyers regarded them with the utmost pleasantness and interest.

Oliver waited for a moment. His face became grave and sad. "It won't cost you anything to help me. For, you see, I am thinking only of my father, William Prescott. It will cost you only a little charity, a little pity, a little understanding.

"You realize, of course, that he is only too aware of the condition of the Prescott Lumber Company and that, though he has brought about its imminent ruin, he still hopes some way can be found to save it for his son, Tom. As far as the company is concerned, he is realistic. That is why he is in such present despair. And so, I ask you to visit him very soon, as soon as possible, and to inform him that in the event of his death you intend to vote his son, Tom, in as president of the Company."

"But that's impossible!" exclaimed Dr. Banks. "That whipper-snapper!"

Oliver nodded. "I agree. But you can lie, can't you, in the name of charity and human compassion?"

Dr. Banks subsided. He beamed at Oliver. "Of course, my dear boy. We understand. Certainly, in the name of kindness—old associates, naturally. Human feeling."

"Of course," echoed the others, tenderly.

"A Christian act," said Judge Muehller.

"Poor old Bill," said Mr. Jenkins fervently.

"Can't help but pity him," said Mr. Leslie.

The strain was beginning to tell upon Oliver.

"Thank you, gentlemen. I knew you'd understand."

"What about Gene Arnold?" asked Senator Whiscomb, viciously. "He'll be kicked out, won't he, that rascal?"

"No," said Oliver, quietly. "Though Mr. Regan doesn't like him, and the Northwest Lumber Company, knowing what he is plotting, is not inclined to view him with kindness, they understand he is a very valuable man. I agree with them. I agree with them that the Prescott Lumber Company, as a subsidiary, will prosper under Gene as general manager. They are interested only in profits, not in personal matters, gentlemen. Very regrettable, of course, but I'm sure you understand."

"If that's the way the Northwestern wants it, then I suppose that's the way it ought to be," agreed Dr. Banks, assuming a stern, resigned air. "I never trusted Gene, however."

Oliver could not help smiling. "You were very astute, Doctor."

He hesitated. "My father will die soon. I have something to suggest. This is most important. Nothing must be said to my father about the Northwest Lumber Company. He is not, under any circumstances, to know. It would break his heart. The Northwest Lumber Company's negotiations with all of you will go on with the utmost secrecy. They understand. They know that my father now goes to the office only three half days a week, and that he is failing rapidly. With your help, my father can be protected from knowing anything."

As if at a signal, the six old men rose and went to Oliver with their hands outstretched. They shone with virtue and happiness. He took each hand and shook it. If the bitterness he felt showed in his eyes they did not see it. He let them clap him upon the shoulder, paternally. He endured their touch, their closeness. He accepted their congratulations on his "wisdom," and "charity," and their general joyous approval.

When the hubbub had subsided a little, he threw a very potent explosive among them.

"I almost forgot, gentlemen. There is another little matter. The Northwest Lumber Company intends to have me represent them as a director on the Board of the Prescott Lumber Company. I am sure you gentlemen will have no objections."

The change that came over them was ludicrous. The three old lawyers craned forward from their chairs in order to enjoy this.

"You?" stammered Mr. Bassett.

"You?" faltered the others.

"Yes, gentlemen. I."

He smiled at them, coldly. "It won't be so bad. You see, they intend to send one of their best men here, as president of their new subsidiary. A very able man. You'll like and trust him. I know him well. His name is Kenneth McCord."

He added: "Almost my sole duty will be to watch Gene Arnold, though I promise you that I'll do my best by the company, too."

After the six old men had gone, Mr. Meredith put his hand on Oliver's shoulder. "Dreadful old scoundrels," he remarked. "I never liked them. Three of them aren't even gentlemen. You ought to have allowed us to do as we originally intended, Oliver."

"But there was my father, sir," replied Oliver.

"Yes, I suppose so," Mr. Meredith sighed. He smiled. "Sometimes the quality of loyalty can be strained. Nevertheless, we like you for it, dear boy."

Oliver was thinking, with really passionate relief: Now I shan't have to ask him to remember that I hoped he would trust me.

CHAPTER LVII

THE SMALL MAHOGANY clock on the mantelpiece in Dr. Banks' library struck a sweet and melodious nine. No one heard it. There was a tension, a hidden malignancy, a savage meanness, here in this room, and a small and malicious triumph. Oliver felt it all and, reluctantly, he had to admit that Eugene Arnold was a better man than any of these little old men who were gloating over him in this silence; better because he had stature and boldness and daring and distinction. Eugene could look at the ruin of a whole lifetime and retain his composure and pride. He might have been a plotter, but he had been a large plotter. There had been a purpose in Eugene's evil, and that purpose, reflected Oliver, had possessed a kind of dignity, for it had been based on an undeluded love for a father.

Oliver could even feel a sort of regret for his brother. He hated to see something of magnificence, however inimical, destroyed. He could for a moment, wish that none of this had ever happened; to be marked as in league with these ancient blackguards revolted him. What Eugene had heard, this past hour, had not diminished his elegance, had not crushed him. He looked before him, thoughtfully. Oliver had an involuntary impulse of pride in his brother, which he could not suppress.

He said: "It's no use, Gene. You can't do anything about it. You can't hurt my father, now. And," he went on, raising his voice, "if you should attempt anything in revenge, if you should decide to do a little imitation of Samson, if you should put Tom up to anything—though it could only end as we intend it to—I'll have to step in again, personally."

Eugene did not move his body. He only turned his long narrow face towards Oliver. "How?" he asked, with interest.

Oliver hesitated. He looked at the old men, who were listening with absorption. He moved in his chair so that as much of his back as possible should be towards them. "I'll tell Father that you are my brother," he said.

He had known that he might have to say this, though he had also hoped to be spared it. But he had been forced to speak, for he had followed Eugene's thoughts perfectly.

423

He had also wondered how Eugene would take this news. Calmly, incredulously, or with cold contemptuous denial? He was certainly not prepared to see Eugene's eyes fix themselves upon him curiously and with detachment.

"You don't believe it?" asked Oliver.

Eugene's pale mouth puckered meditatively. He still looked at Oliver with interest. "Yes," he said at last. "I believe it. I didn't know, until comparatively recently, and even then I didn't have the facts. Before my father died I was alone with him for a few minutes. He then told me that he had a child, somewhere. He didn't know whether it was a boy or a girl. He asked me to find that child." Eugene smiled. "He wanted me to give his other child help, when and if I could. My mother was never to know."

He said, when Oliver did not speak: "You have the facts, I suppose?"

"Yes," replied Oliver, rather indistinctly.

"Then, there is no reason to doubt. After all, you are a lawyer. You wouldn't say that, unless you could prove it."

"No." Oliver could not look at him now. "But what made you suspect it, yourself?"

Eugene smiled again. "It was inescapable. Even Tom began to see the resemblance. I saw it, possibly long before anyone else did. You see, I have a photograph of my father, when he was a very young man. And you resemble him more than I do. I think it was about eight years ago when I first noticed that resemblance. Still, there was a very good chance that it was all coincidence. You say you have the proof?"

"Yes," repeated Oliver.

The old men sat entranced. Two or three said to themselves: Yes, he's just like Chauncey at his age, or younger.

"My father told me the name of the mother," said Eugene. "You have her name?"

Oliver's eyes narrowed bitterly. "You still hope it is all coincidence, don't you, Gene? Well, it isn't. The name of my mother was Mary Bauer."

Eugene nodded slightly. "Yes, that is correct, then."

Something was hurting Oliver. He did not examine it. He went on quickly: "If you should go to my—father, in your long vengefulness and with the sole purpose of causing him suffering, to tell him what his son and you have plotted to do, even though you have failed in it, then, in my own vengefulness, I'll have to make him suffer even more. I'll tell him that he adopted the son of the man he hated most in all the world. Do you know what will happen then, Gene? He still has strength, and he's indomitable. He'll get out of his bed, to destroy you. He'll get help, too. He'll get help from me. For please understand, I have only to say the word and the Northwest Lumber Company will kick you out."

Eugene nodded again, thoughtfully. "Yes, I can see that. But what of you? What will Mr. Prescott do to you, when, or if, you tell him?"

"He can't hurt me, Gene," answered Oliver, sadly. "No one can. But he can hurt you. He'll forget that you're Julie's husband. He's always instinctively distrusted you and detested you. You can't deny that. He'll realize he can't injure me. You'll be the only victim. He wouldn't stop at anything. Of course, there is Julie's trust fund. Would you like to live on that, and on what you've saved? All the rest of your life, Gene, and do you think that Julie would like to know that I am your brother? Julie's never liked me, you know. In fact, I believe she hates me."

"Yes," said Eugene, as if they were discussing the most abstract of subjects. "All that you say is true."

Oliver continued: "It's no use, Gene. You can't lift a hand against my father, or against me, without completely wrecking yourself. I have control over your future. And, as I told you a short time ago, the Northwest Lumber Company believed me when I told them you would be invaluable. They hope to gain your complete loyalty. I think they will. After all, they are not William Prescott. And there'll be many opportunities for you, later, as you have doubtless been thinking, yourself. The Northwest Lumber Company always advances its able men, and you'll be one of their best."

Eugene considered all this with detachment. Once or twice he nodded. He said finally: "I suppose I owe you something. You could have demolished me entirely, couldn't you?"

"Yes. But that would have been stupid. I don't like to 'demolish' anything, and I'm not spiteful. Even you aren't, though you are a cruel man. You've wanted to kill my father, or cause him to suffer enormously. Because of your own father. I can understand that."

Eugene asked with faint interest: "What do you intend to do about Tom, after Mr. Prescott dies still believing the lie these gentlemen are going to tell him? Not, I admit, that I care about what happens to Tom."

"We are going to elect him second vice-president," said Oliver.

Eugene smiled with cold enjoyment. "Excellent," he murmured. "In that position, he can't do much mischief."

"I suppose it is superfluous to ask," said Oliver, "but I'd like to be sure. Tom doesn't have any idea that his father has already forfeited his stock to Mr. Jay Regan, does he?"

Eugene's faded brows lifted in contempt. "It is indeed superfluous. It is also a stupid question. If Tom had known—and you can be sure I did everything I could to prevent him from knowing—he'd have tried long before this to buy back that stock with the Blake money. It was most necessary for me to keep that knowledge from him. His father, naturally, never told him. He had too much pride, and wanted his son's 'respect' too much. Then, when Tom had married Mary Blake, it was too late to buy back the stock."

Oliver sighed. "Well, your job now, Gene, is to keep Tom quiet, to keep him persuaded that you'll both have to wait a little longer. You'll have to invent some reason."

Eugene gave him a bland look. "Are you threatening me?"

"Naturally," answered Oliver.

Eugene lifted his head in a small but expressive gesture. "You can be certain of one thing, and that is I am not a fool. As you informed me a little earlier, I've been using Tom, for my own purposes. I can go on using him, though in a somewhat altered way. I'll keep him quiet until his father dies. Of course, he is going to be slightly furious when he is robbed of the chance of confronting his father with the announcement that he is a better man than Mr. Prescott, after all, and that he has been unanimously elected president of the Company while his father is still alive. For the reason that his father is a failure."

CHAPTER LVIII

OLIVER PRESCOTT was in conference with Mr. Meredith when a clerk entered with a card for him. "I'm very busy just now," he said. Then he glanced at the card. He looked at Mr. Meredith without expression. "Eugene Arnold," he said, and stood up. He told the clerk to send Mr. Arnold into his own offices, and went there himself.

Eugene was waiting for him in the pleasant office, into which the July sunshine streamed warmly. One of the things which had always impressed Oliver with reluctant admiration was Eugene's calm self-possession under all circumstances, his balance and judiciousness. He wondered, a trifle drily, whether he was not more impressed by them since he had discovered that he, too had all these in some measure and, in a certain sense, from the same source. Nothing, thought Oliver, could put Eugene out of countenance. He accepted a cigarette from his brother, allowed Eugene to light it. If anyone was in the least strained, it was not, it annoyed him to admit, Eugene. He wondered what had brought the older man here to see him, and he was immediately on his guard.

Apparently Eugene felt this, for he smiled.

"We haven't seen much of you for the past couple of months," he said. "In fact, I haven't seen you at all—since April."

"I've been in Washington a great deal," replied Oliver. "And whenever we have visited Father and Mother, you and Julie have been out."

Eugene's smile became less tight. "Strange, isn't it?" he murmured.

Oliver could feel himself coloring. "Barbara has seen her sister," he said, coldly.

Eugene inclined his head. "Lawyers seem to work at night a great deal," he remarked casually. "Mrs. Prescott often remarks that you visit Mr. Prescott frequently during the day."

"Yes," said Oliver.

"The Old Man is failing. Sad, isn't it?" said Eugene.

There was something out of tune here, reflected Oliver. It was not like the meticulous Eugene to use Tom's vulgar phrase "the Old Man." Oliver must have betrayed his vexation, for Eugene added: "You're wondering why I am here. Believe me, it is just a friendly visit. Unless you are very busy?" he added.

He is goading me, thought Oliver. He was about to say, very abruptly, that he was indeed busy, when he became aware that Eugene was watching him with close curiosity and with not so secret amusement.

"I'm not too busy," he said, rather curtly. "But I am surprised. You did say 'friendly visit,' didn't you?"

"Yes, and I meant it. It's almost five, anyway. I was passing, and I thought I'd drop in to see you."

"Go on; be friendly," said Oliver. He could not help smiling a bit.

Eugene turned his head a little; the sunlight made his pale eyes glint. "I never thanked you, I am afraid."

"Don't thank me. The Northwest Lumber Company is our client, and I did the best for them as such in recommending that they continue to have you act as the general manager of the Prescott Lumber Company."

"With a large increase in salary when the merger takes place," Eugene added. He looked at Oliver directly, and his amusement was no longer even slightly concealed. "Come now, you know very well that they could have replaced me, and would have done so, at a word from you. They have very fine men in their organization." He waited. Oliver said nothing. "It couldn't have been because of any—shall we say—family feeling?"

Oliver said: "Because Julie is my wife's sister? No."

Eugene actually laughed. " 'No,' " he repeated. "You don't like Julie, and the dislike is heartily returned. Incidentally, Julie doesn't know as yet, about the approaching merger."

Oliver's hand began to tap on the top of his desk. Eugene saw that impatient and annoyed motion. Oliver saw him looking, and held his hand still. Eugene leaned back in his chair, and spoke meditatively: "You wouldn't be the lawyer you are if you were fundamentally sentimental, and if you weren't also a realist. Good lawyers never fool themselves. You don't. At least, not most of the time."

"I don't know what you're talking about, Gene," said Oliver.

"Oh, yes, you do. You know that if you didn't have me kicked out it was because I'm your brother."

Oliver looked away.

"Sentimental?" said Eugene, softly. "No, not exactly. Brothers have been known to outbest each other, to hate each other, even to kill each other. Brotherly love, in the closest sense, is quite a rarity, especially if one brother has more money than the other."

"What are you getting at?" asked Oliver, sternly.

Eugene said: "If a brother of mine stood in my way, I'd knock him down. So would you, in a certain sense. And, in that sense, you did, though your reasons, I know, were really quite virtuous.

"You see, both you and I grew up believing we had no one. I don't count my mother as anyone, because she didn't like me, and I am afraid I didn't like her, either. We were both lonely—you and I. We had no brothers and no sisters. After my mother died, and in spite of our mutual sentiments towards each other, I became even more lonely. I'd never cared for anyone except my father, and he died when I was only twelve."

Oliver waited for Eugene to continue, but he did not go on. Oliver said: "I still don't know what you're getting at."

"Don't you? I thought good lawyers were very acute. I'll put it more simply. There's a streak of sentimentality in everybody. If I'd grown up with a brother I'd probably hate him by now, in the normal fashion. But not having had one that I knew of, I'd often enjoy a little self-pity. As you did."

Oliver was about to deny this angrily, and then he said to himself: That's true.

"You were an adopted son, and you had sisters and brothers, under the law. But you were lonely; you were left out. As I was, too. We both worked alone. We both lived alone. We had no one. I think you found that out very vividly when you married Barbie—even from the woman you call 'Mother'."

Oliver's face darkened. Eugene nodded, satisfied. "You see? You haven't forgotten. You are what is known as a 'good' man, and so you've forgiven. But you haven't forgotten."

"This isn't getting us anywhere," said Oliver.

"I don't know about that, Oliver. Anyway, I wanted to thank you for instructing that pink old rascal of a Bassett to let me see copies of the documents you have."

"You didn't come here today to suggest that we become good and affectionate brothers, did you?"

Eugene laughed again. "Not as baldly as all that. But I'll admit that I'm not sorry, now, that you're my brother. If you were such a one as Tom Prescott, I'd be damned sorry." He waited for Oliver to comment, but the younger man merely stared at him with narrowed eyes.

It became evident to Oliver that Eugene was enjoying himself, but his voice was quite grave when he said: "I've always been ambitious. I'll go on being ambitious. Just as you will, too. You know, without my telling you, that I've not only been ambitious but that I've had another motive in trying to get control of the Prescott Lumber Company."

"I know. You like neatness. And you wanted your revenge, didn't you, Gene?" Oliver looked away. "You didn't get it, but that didn't seem to disturb you too much. I've got to admit I've admired you for that. You didn't 'avenge' your father, if you'll permit a little theatricalism."

"No. But you did," said Eugene.

Oliver jerked his head back.

Eugene said, gently: "It was accomplished, after all—by a son of my father. As you have said, I like neatness."

Oliver stood up. Eugene stayed in his chair. Again, his eyes were glinting.

"We don't like the Prescotts, do we? We married two of them, yet even if we are—attached—to these two, we have no respect for the Prescotts, have we? We know what the whole family is; we know what the sons are. You're looking forward, Oliver, to the day when we can both tell Tom Prescott what's happened to him. He's ambitious, too. You are going to enjoy that day, aren't you? Just as I am."

"Yes, but not for the same reason! I'm going to enjoy it because of what he tried to do to his father." Oliver's voice was contemptuous. "It happens that I——"

" 'Love' Mr. Prescott?" finished Eugene. "But you're human, too. You have your resentments. You'll do what you intend to do to Tom, even though he's Mr. Prescott's son. And the reason's not entirely virtuous."

He stood up, also.

"And now I'll tell you something else: You've always pitied Mr. Prescott. Don't you know there is an element of egotism in pity? We sympathize to some extent, with those we consider our equals or our superiors, but we don't 'pity' them.

"I never pitied William Prescott. For I knew him for what he was, which you never did. I knew he was a genius; you didn't, did you? I admired him, you didn't. Even remembering his infernal obsession about his children, I can still admire him for what he was. He was a great man."

They looked at each other fixedly.

Oliver said: "There are values beyond your understanding. We may use the same words, but we mean different things."

"Perhaps. You're a lawyer, Oliver, and you ought to know. But it's still true that you never knew William Prescott; that you only pitied, that you never admired him. None of his family did. I think he's beginning to understand that now. It's a terrible thought for a man to have when he's dying."

He picked up his hat. "Good evening," he said.

CHAPTER LIX

EVEN THOUGH, for the past three weeks, William had been ordered to remain in bed, he would not permit a nurse in the house to take care of him, nor would he follow his doctor's orders. Each afternoon, unassisted, panting and sweating with weakness, he would force himself out of bed, and go to a chair by the window, where he would sit, trying to subdue by will-power alone the agonizing pound of his heart. He would not admit to himself that he was gravely ill, that he was most certainly dying. Once in the chair, he would look out over the pleasant July gardens, the grass and trees, and, very slowly, he would be able to catch his breath. Sometimes he fell asleep, sitting there, and Ursula would find him so. But she never permitted him to guess that she had seen him, and would only reenter when she was sure he had awakened and had laboriously returned to bed.

Then she would come in, quite casually, to discover that he had shaved and washed himself and had changed his night-shirt. She would ask him how he was; he would reply impatiently. Sometimes, while speaking, he would pause a moment, anxiously listening to his own voice, suspecting a dwindled note, a faint gasp between words. Then he would make his voice stronger, and more brusque. That damned Banks! If he, William, wasn't ill by now, this bed-squatting would surely make him so! He'd give himself a day or two more, to get back his strength, and then he wouldn't permit himself the luxury of lying here like an invalid but would return to the office immediately.

It was that heavy cold he had had in the spring. Sometimes you couldn't shake off such things readily. They lingered, sapping your strength. William would cough quite convincingly. Ursula never made the mistake of adjusting his pillows, the sheet, or the light silken shawl which covered him. She would sit down at a little distance in the great ponderous room, and nod her head, knowing that her husband was watching her closely. She would keep her face casual, and agree with him, while all the time her anguished mind kept crying to itself: No! You can't die, my darling! I won't let you go.

She would bring him the evening paper. She would watch while he struggled to a sitting position, and not let him suspect that it was almost more than she could bear to see his shrunken pallor, the beads of sweat on his forehead, the livid tint of his face. She would pretend not to hear his hurried breathing. She would only sit there, an aging woman full of sorrow and despair, while he glanced through the paper and muttered to himself about some fresh enormity on the part of "that rascal, Roosevelt." After a while she would order tea for them both. She had hoped, in the beginning, that he would talk to her then. But, though he drank the tea, he would continue to look through the paper, frowning. Silence would fill the room, except for the rustling of the trees outside, the distant whirr of a lawn-mower, the voice of a gardener, the singing of birds. The sun would send into the room broader and broader rays of rose and gold, until finally they would reach a large painting on the wall opposite the bed. Then William would put down his paper and, forgetting that Ursula sat there at all, would look steadily and smilingly at the painting. Some of the light would seem to be reflected in his eyes.

It was a painting of an old monk, standing in a garden of brilliant sun and flowers, with terraces of olive and orange and lemon trees rising behind him. His habit was tucked up in his rope girdle; his thick brown legs were bare, as were his arms. He stood in a very glow of flame and radiance, so that his dark face shone and his black eyes seemed to sparkle vividly. The intensity of color about him appeared to emanate from him, as if he were the sun, itself, and all this incandescence part of substance and flesh. He was a living presence in this room, a presence of warmth and fire and vitality, his full mouth vivacious, his bald head glistening. He gave the impression that he was about to laugh, or to speak, for one of his hands was lifted, expressively, and one shoulder half-raised in an eloquent shrug. He was, it was evident, a gardener, yet there was a passion and mobility about that old sturdy body, and in the lines of those massive arms and legs, and in the huge curve of his belly.

The painting had been set in an ancient Venetian gold frame, elaborate and intricate. At the bottom was a small golden plate: "Fra Leonardo." In the corner of the painting itself were very small black letters: "Matthew Prescott."

William would look at the painting for a long time. It was as if he drew strength from that smiling painted strength, life from that colored flesh, hope from those black eyes. He would sigh a little. He would say aloud, but to himself: "Fra Leonardo. A monk." Then, after a moment or two: "My son." The last words were almost indistinct; they trembled slightly.

Ursula would think of the daily and frantic cables she was sending to Matthew, and of the silence which had followed all but the first two. She would think of those cables of Matthew's in reply, of the four repeated words of them: "I can't go back." Bitterness would overcome her, tears would rush from her eyes, and she would get up and go from the room. She knew that William never noticed her going. He would look only at the painting, until the closing dusk blurred it out.

"Your father is dying," she cabled every day. But now there was no answer. "My husband, my darling, is dying," she would say to the hot closed stillness of her room. But there was no answer. She said this, with her eyes, to her daughters, to her son, Tom, to Eugene, and still there was no answer. There was an answer in Oliver's eyes, but she would not receive it. For she was full of grief and anguish and terror, and she was all alone, and the silence of her children was paradoxically, easier to bear, than the comfort she refused from Oliver.

She had helped Oliver, in his effort to save her husband a last suffering. But, strangely, in these tormented days, she could resent it that it was Oliver, who was not William's son, and not hers, who was protecting William. She was all emotion now; sorrow had overwhelmed reason and kindness and understanding. If even one of her children had expressed sadness she would have broken down and wept, and been comforted. She wanted no comfort from Oliver. When she saw him, she remembered that she had had, for the sake of her husband, to assist Oliver in the forthcoming defeat of her son, Tom, and so storm-wracked was she that she could feel a thrill of hatred, a repugnance full of unreason. In the shadow of Oliver, Barbara hardly seemed her daughter. She, also, was in the conspiracy, and upon Barbara, too, Ursula could project her hatred.

"I wish Mama would give me just a single opportunity to comfort her," Barbara would say, when she and Oliver had returned home. "She sits there so stiff, and with such a rigid and forbidding face, that I can't say a word. I tried, once, but she only stared at me as if she hated me."

"Your mother is a proud woman," Oliver would repeat, over and over, trying to control his own wretchedness. "She's very strong. She doesn't want that strength touched; she's afraid it will crumble. She's just trying to warn you off, Barbie."

But he knew he lied. He knew all about Ursula. "Help her by being as matter-of-fact as possible, sweetheart."

In the evening, Eugene and Julia would visit William. He would look only briefly at Eugene. But when he saw Julia the lividness would fade from his face, his eyes would brighten, and he would put his hands on her pretty shoulders when she bent to kiss him. Sometimes she would visit him during the day, too, but not often. She had many social engagements to fill, and her father's love for her was becoming an uneasy and irksome thing. She had received from him all that he could give her; his hands were empty, now. The odd uneasiness she was feeling these days was nameless. It stayed with her even when she had left William, and she was less zestful with Eugene, even less tender. Often, when alone with Eugene, she was irritable, and would fall into a sullen silence.

Tom came two or three times a week with his pretty and vacuous little wife, who always looked on the bright side of things and was full of eager sentimentalities. She was not very intelligent; she always assured Ursula and Julia and Barbara and Tom and Oliver that "Father is really so much better every time we see him."

She could not understand her witty Tom, who was usually so fond of her, and whose child she was carrying. He was very attentive to her, particularly in the presence of her adoring but sharp-eyed parents. But lately, and this hurt and puzzled her, he had fits of silence and sulkiness. He was an active man, yet even little Mary had a dim understanding that activity was something different from the restlessness which Tom was displaying.

Oliver, watching Tom and Julia closely at the Prescott house, had decided that these two ignoble plotters were finding their father's illness tedious, and that they were impatient for his inevitable death. Lately, however, he had not been so sure, and this had disturbed him. It was certainly not in his plan that they should suffer real anxiety, or the faint beginnings of remorse and self-disgust. There was even an evening when Oliver saw Julia give her brother a somber and brooding glance, full of aversion. Tom had caught that glance: he had flushed, and his big coarse face had thickened. He had got up then, muttering something, and had left the room.

As for Barbara, in whom tenderness and concern for others had been nourished no more than they had been nourished in her sister and brothers, she had no means whereby to express her misery, even to Oliver. Once or twice she had wept, though she had proudly controlled her tears almost immediately.

Her only link with tenderness was her husband and child, and even with them she was occasionally reserved. Knowing her father's vulnerability to love, she is afraid for herself, Oliver would think, sadly.

Dr. Banks, though always richly cheerful with his patient, held out no hope to the latter's family. The end might come at any moment. It could not be long postponed. Dr. Banks had called in an eminent heart specialist from Philadelphia. The verdict had been confirmed.

The days went on, and William steadily lost strength. During the last three days of July he remained in bed, looking at the painting on his wall, lying in emaciated exhaustion and motionless for hours. Nurses came in now. He no longer protested. There was in his eyes a dull withdrawal, a terrible sick patience. But still, he spoke very little to Ursula. He could speak only a few words even to his children. When they left, he immediately fell into a deep sleep. Ursula could hear his hard and painful breathing even in her room, where she lay all night, tense and unsleeping, dry-eyed and dry-lipped, listening to the wind in the trees, waiting for a call she knew was coming. During these hours she sometimes drowsed fitfully, awakening to the muffled sound of the nurse's footsteps in the hall, and finding herself braced like steel against her pillows. Only when the footsteps retreated, and William's door closed softly, did she relax. Then pain would run through her body, and she would turn her face to her pillow, but not to weep. There were no tears in her. There was only an anguish beyond thought or expression, an anguish so vast that she seemed surrounded by it, breathed it into her lungs, expelled it only to feel it gain power within her. And, over and over, to herself she would say: No. No. Her eyes would follow the path of the moonlight along her wall, until it paled and the sunrise would stream red against it. And she would say to it, aloud now: "No. No."

William lay sleeping, under the influence of the sedative which had been administered to him at midnight. He was dreaming. It was a very vivid dream, and he did not once suspect that it was only a dream. He was hurrying in a gray world, and he was full of pain, which had taken the form of a tortured thirst. The ground under his feet was broken and cracked, bleached like sand, but hard. Behind him, about him, and in the distance, the wilderness stretched away without a horizon. The sky was gray glass, without sun or moon. There was no sound; even his feet, stumbling upon gray stones, made no noise. The deathly plain that lay everywhere about him had been sucked dry of everything but silence. No hill, no house, no tree, no grass, could be seen anywhere. Only this pallid wilderness without end, without beginning.

There was something he must reach, he thought in his dream, something which would quench this thirst which was now a fiery agony. A well? A stream? A river? He did not know. But he had to find it, or he would die. He would surely die, he said aloud, but his voice had no sound, either.

And then, in the distance, he saw the fountain, a thin gray shaft, wavering in the shifting gloom. He knew it was a fountain. He hurried faster. He reached the fountain. But the shaft was broken; it stood in a heap of stones faintly glimmering like skulls. There was no water in it.

He stood there and looked at the empty fountain. There had never been any water there, he said to himself. It was all a lie. It was always a lie. He had come to the end. There was no going on, for there was no hope of water except in this fountain which, he now saw, had never contained water.

The nurse was shaking Ursula, who had fallen into a stupor of exhaustion. Becoming aware of the nurse's anxious hands, she sat up immediately. "I've called Dr. Banks," whispered the nurse quickly. "I think you ought to go to Mr. Prescott immediately, Mrs. Prescott. I'll wake up one of the maids and send for your children."

Ursula flung herself out of bed, caught up her crimson dressing-gown, and raced out of the room like a young girl. Her heart was beating suffocatingly. She could not think. Her knees bent under her; the few short steps to William's room seemed a league.

It was quiet in the room except for William's long and rasping breaths. He seemed to be still sleeping. Only a night-light burned on a distant table. Ursula bent over her husband. His face was the color of earth, and covered with a film of moisture. His mouth was open, as he struggled for air.

Ursula knelt down beside the bed. She put her head on William's pillow; his labored breath blew against her gray hair and cheek. It was not warm, that breath, but cold. She put her hand over one of his, and it was like ice, and wet. Now she was in darkness, conscious only of that dying wind against her flesh, and of the dying hand she held.

Someone touched her head. A hand lay upon it, comfortingly. But, in her dreadful paralysis, she could not move. She had no strength to shake off the consolation of that hand, which had begun to smooth her hair tenderly. She could not even moan or cry out. Then she heard a hoarse and gentle voice: "Ursula."

The hand lay heavily upon her head, and she knew it was William's hand. But still for a long time she could not move, and not until the hand fell away. She lifted her head, and her wrecked face was illuminated by the faint light. William was smiling at her. Now she became aware that his harsh breathing had softened, was almost normal. His eyes, sunken far back in his head, were tender and grave.

"Dear Ursula," he whispered. A shadow ran like a wave over his face.

"William," she said. Then: "Oh, William. Don't leave me, William."

The gravity increased in his eyes. His words came very low and haltingly: "The will. Don't mind the will, Ursula. I—didn't know."

She caught up his hand and held it to her numb lips. "I love you, my darling," she said. "Don't leave me, William. I have no one but you."

An expression of wonder brightened his eyes. He lifted his weighted hand and laid it against her cheek. "I have no one but you, Ursula," he said. "I never had anyone, but you."

She could not bear these terrible words. Her throat could hardly move, but she finally managed to whisper: "The children, my darling. They're coming."

He looked beyond her. She did not know that Eugene and Julia were already standing at the foot of the bed. But she saw William's face had become stern and remote. She saw that he looked away.

"I've been cabling Matthew," Ursula whispered, and her voice was a low grating. "I—I've had a cable. He ought to be here in a day or two. Perhaps tomorrow."

William smiled at her, and again touched her cheek. "No," he said. "There isn't any water."

She thought his mind was wandering. She looked about wildly for the nurse. The room was unnaturally dim about her. Two shadows approached her. She stammered: "Bring him water."

William said: "I have asked Oliver to take care of you. Go to him and Barbie, my love. There isn't anything for you here."

He shut his eyes. Frantically, she pressed her mouth against his. His lips were cold and dry. But she could feel that he was trying to return her kiss. Then his eyes opened. "Poor Ursula," he said. "Forgive me."

She did not know that she cried aloud: "Don't leave me! Wait for me, William." Hands were lifting her. She tried to fight them off. She tried to cling to the hand she held. It was cold now, and limp. William's eyes, open and staring, looked before him. But now they did not look at the painting on the wall. They did not look at the shadows beside his bed.

White sleeves and white hands were drawing a white sheet over William's face. It was then that Ursula screamed once, and loudly: "No!"

She stood there, supported by someone's arm. She heard Eugene's voice: "Let's take her back to her room, Julie. And you stay with her."

A great cold silence and calm fell upon Ursula. She pushed away the arms about her. She heard a sharp sob, and then the sound of weeping. She turned around and saw Eugene and Julia. She looked at them. She stepped back from them. She continued to look at them. Eugene was very pale. Julia, her bright auburn hair hanging in disheveled beauty far below her waist, had buried her face in her hands. She was sobbing. Ursula listened to the sound, and the great cold silence in her strengthened.

She turned, and very steadily, her head held high, she went out of the room. She went to her own room and quietly lay down on her bed. She could feel nothing.

Oliver found her there. Barbara was with her sister. Oliver had begged her to let him see her mother alone. He sat down beside Ursula. He said, and his voice shook: "Poor Mother."

He took her hand. He said: "He asked me to take care of you."

"Yes," said Ursula. Her lightless eyes turned upon him. A spasm ran over her face. She said, as William had said to her: "Forgive me."

Then she saw that Barbara, very white, her face streaming with tears, was entering the room. Ursula watched her calmly. All at once something broke in her and shattered, in overwhelming pain. She held out her hand to her daughter; the motion took her last strength. Barbara bent over her, lifted her in her strong young arms. Her tears wet Ursula's face; Ursula could taste the salt of them.

"Dear Barbie," she whispered. "Oh, Barbie, my dear child." Her head fell on Barbara's shoulder, and she closed her eyes.

CHAPTER LX

THE AUGUST WIND, warm, fragrant and soft as silk, blew through the opened windows of the Prescott house. The massed trees, a hundred different shades of rich green, whitened and ruffled slightly in the wind, glittered as the sun struck them, clamored in a gentle chorus. The sky poured out its light, locusts shrilled loudly; from the road outside the gray walls of the grounds came the clatter of passing carriages, the very occasional roar of an automobile. It was a gay and joyous day.

But in the Prescott house grief moved heavily and silently. Ursula sat with her two daughters and her son in the dimmed library. Consoling guests had gone; the servants had been told to admit no others. Ursula had asked her children to remain with her, and they sat here, not speaking, only waiting. They looked at their mother, grim and white-haired and haggard, thin to emaciation.

Since William's death, almost a month ago, she had not cried, and her eyes, sleepless and dull, were dry as paper. Her cracked lips had a mauve tint. Sorrow lay on her face, but it was a bitter sorrow, desolate and forbidding, and as cold as a wintry day.

Much of Julia's auburn and rose-tinted beauty had dimmed during these past weeks, and her black frock only emphasized her pallor. She twisted her hands together upon her knees. Her face was sullen and tired. Thomas, too, was pale, his large coarse face sulky, his cunning eyes fixed upon his mother. Barbara sat near Ursula.

Ursula looked at them all, slowly and fixedly. She said, at last: "I asked you to be with me today, because I have a few things I want to tell you. We all know the terms of your father's will. It was made several years ago. He spoke to me of it, just before he—died." Her taut and wrinkled face moved slightly. "He left all he had to you, with the exception of this house, and a small annual income for me. He left me the house."

She paused. Her voice was very quiet and without emotion. "That will, as I have said, was made several years ago. He had a lot of money, then. He died almost bankrupt. Because,

440

during thesse past years, he poured all he had, all he could make at the cost of his health and his life and his peace of mind, into those trust funds for you. When he died, there was practically nothing left. Over the years, from the time we were married, he gave me a very large allowance. I saved much of it. So, with careful investment, I now have nearly two hundred thousand dollars."

She waited for some comment. No one spoke. Julia, however, stared at her mother with intent interest and thoughtfulness.

Ursula began to sigh, but she dared not sigh; she dared not weep. There was in her too much agony, which she must keep imprisoned.

"The house," she said, "is heavily mortgaged, of course. When your father made that will, he believed that he would in time be able to lift the mortgages. He left the house to me, expressing the wish that his children should live here also. This house was his dream; it was the house he built for his children; he thought they loved it as he loved it. Your father," added Ursula, in that terrible, quiet voice, "was a very tragic man. He loved you. He thought you loved him."

Julia looked down at her hands; Tom thrust out his thick lips and squinted his eyes. Barbara dropped her head.

"I can't afford to keep up this house," said Ursula. "I am letting it go. None of you wants it, I am sure of that. I don't want it. It was my home all these years. But I don't want it. And I know that your father would want me to let it go. At the last, it meant nothing to him, for he knew that his whole life had been wasted, and that this house was a house of lies and cruelty and duplicity and ingratitude. That is what he died with: the knowledge of what this house really was, of what his children were. No one," added Ursula, "ought to be punished like that, when he is dying."

Thomas said in a queer voice: "I don't ever want to see it again, either. I'll never come here again."

Ursula looked at him. Something ran over her face, a sort of dull surprise and wonder. She looked at him for a long time. Julia began to cry, softly. But Ursula did not turn to her.

"Tom," said Ursula. "I know what you tried to do to your father. He knew, too, I am afraid, in spite of what Mr. Bassett and Judge Muehller told him two weeks before he died: That the Board of Directors had had a meeting and had decided that, in the event of your father's death, they would make you president of the company. They told him that, because Oliver

forced them to do it. You know all about it. Gene's told you.
It's all out in the open, now. Oliver discovered all your treach-
ery, all that you and Gene intended to do; actually, all that
Gene intended to do to your father, and to you."

She stopped. Thomas' pallor did not diminish. He was not
angry, or humiliated. But he could not meet his mother's eyes.
His mouth became somber and tired. Again, this surprised
Ursula.

Thomas said: "It doesn't matter. I mean that, Ma. It
doesn't matter. I—all I want to do now is to get out of Andersburg. Mr. Blake's made me manager of his mines. I never
want to see this town again." He looked at Julia. For an instant,
viciousness passed swiftly over his face, then faded into heavy
weariness. "I don't care about anything. I'm going out of
here, and I'm going to forget."

"Yes," said Ursula. "You'll go away. But you, Tom, and
all of you, won't ever be able to forget that you killed your
father. You despised him because he loved you at the expense
of his whole life; you plotted against him, you and Julie. Because
he loved you—you thought he was a fool. And you were quite
right. A man who loves his children as he loved you should
be prepared for betrayal and cruelty and grief and contempt.
But you have lost more than he has."

Julia cried drearily. Her mother looked at her in a moment's
silence, untouched. "Cry, Julie," she said, without passion.
"It's too late. You think you'll forget, too. You won't. You'll
remember even more, when you have children of your own."

She turned to Thomas again. "Yes, your father understood
everything, at the last. You can thank yourselves for that.
Your wife is going to have a child, Tom. You love your wife;
you'll probably love your child. You'll remember your father
when your baby is born, and you'll keep on remembering when
you have other children, too, and you'll remember when you
are dying."

Thomas said in a loud harsh voice: "I won't enslave myself
for the damned kids! I won't be that much of a fool!" And
then he caught his breath, stood up and walked to one of
the windows. He remained there, his back to the room, his
big hands thrust into his pockets, his massive shoulders droop-
ing. Ursula's brows drew together as she watched her son.
She clenched her hands on her knees. But she still spoke steadily: "The Prescott company is gone, for all of you, even though
Gene remains as general manager. It's gone for your father's
sons. I think he knew that, before he died. I only hope that
it didn't matter so much to him, at the last."

Thomas said, his back still to his mother: "I don't care. I hope—he—didn't care, either. I'm not going to deny that we were rotten children. We were. I'm not going to defend ourselves by saying he made us that way, though he did."

Ursula said: "You say you're not going to 'defend' yourselves. You are trying to do just that. In spite of what you say, you are blaming your father. Perhaps when you were children, and so dreadfully and dangerously indulged, there was some excuse. But you aren't children any longer; you haven't been children for years. You aren't imbeciles. When you had grown up, you might have had some pity. You have minds and understanding, and you might have had some pity."

Julia said, brokenly: "I can't bear this house. We can't live here." She spoke incoherently. "Papa always wanted us to have anything we wanted. He told us that parents owed that to their children. And so, when we took, when we demanded anything, we thought we had a—right."

"You are a liar, Julie," said Ursula. "You are a woman, and you've been a woman for years, and you know you didn't have a 'right.' "

Julia cried desperately: "You talk of cruelty, Mama! You are being cruel, yourself, now!"

At the window, Tom moved restlessly. "Shut up, Julie," he said loudly and dully.

Ursula went on: "You knew, for a long time, that your father was dying. It meant nothing to you. Save your tears, Julie. Save them for your children, when they forget you, or leave you lonely, or pretend false love for you, or break your heart."

She said: "There is an old German proverb: 'Every man is every other man's devil'. I can say, with reason, that children are their parents' devils. They never let them forget that they, too, were once children of fathers and mothers."

Barbara, the controlled and silent, spoke now: "Oh, Mama."

Ursula looked at her. The bitterness was still in her eyes, but it softened slightly as they turned on Barbara. "You were a very cold girl, Barbie. You didn't love your father. But at least you understood enough not to exploit him and betray him. And you were the only one he spoke of before he died. He must have known more about you than I knew."

Barbara's eyes filled.

Ursula continued: "Five hours after your father died, I received a cable from Matthew. He said that he 'felt' he could come home to see your father; he wasn't 'afraid' any longer, he said. I cabled him back and told him his father had died.

Then he wrote me. He asked me to come to Italy and live with him."

Julia wiped her eyes. She faltered: "Gene suggested to me that I ask you to come and live with us, Mama. I—I think we want you to do that."

Thomas came back to his chair. He settled himself in it ponderously. "No," he said, "she ought to come to Mary and me."

Ursula smiled. When her children saw that smile, they looked aside. "No. I'm going to live with Barbie and Oliver. I'm going to live in my old house again. *My* house. But I don't think I'd want to live there, except alone, if it weren't for Oliver, and little Billy. I'm sorry, Barbie. I'm going to live in my house again because your husband is there, and your father's grandson."

Barbara's tears came faster. Ursula said: "You, Tom, and you, Julie, detested Oliver. But Oliver was instrumental in saving Gene's position, Julie, and if your father had any peace at all, Tom, it was because of Oliver. You'll never like him—but that's something else for you both to remember, too."

She sighed, and her voice broke: "It's very strange but, when it is suffering or desolated or ruined by its own evil, the world always says: 'The younger generation will save the world for themselves and for their children. All our hope is in our children.' But the children become men and women, and they don't save the world, they don't save themselves, they don't save their children. The hope is a lie. Men have to lie to themselves; there'd be no living without lies."

She lifted her hands, let them fall again. "There's nothing more to say. I had to tell you all this, because, you see, I'm lying to myself, also. For I want to believe that you'll teach your children that there is no hope for anybody, except in himself, and no hope for the world, except in each man's responsibility towards his neighbor. All the evil that ever came to any man, to the whole world, comes when men say to themselves: 'I, but not my brother.' You won't teach your children that. And so the terribleness of the world will only increase."

She stood up, then, and left the room, tall and thin and straight, and she did not look back.

PROLOGUE

ALL THAT HAD to be done was done.

The Prescott house had been sold, and sold at a great loss. The neighbors could not afford to buy this house, and keep it from destruction. No one in Andersburg could afford to buy it.

The swart walls would be torn down. The marble would be carried off. The treasures and the rugs and the pictures and the furniture would disappear, be bought by strangers for the decoration of the houses of strangers. All that William Prescott had loved, had gathered together for his children, would be lost. Julia and Thomas and Barbara would buy nothing, for they wanted to forget. Because of what they wanted to forget, they wished nothing of this house to remain.

Ursula could now say to herself: "Let them forget. Please, God, let them forget. Let them forget everything but a hope for their children."

Her bitterness was gone. She had her sorrow now, huge yet in some way comforting. She could remember that William had loved her, and that he had thought only of her before he died. It was enough for her. It was enough for all the rest of her life. In the end, she thought, there is only a man and his wife, even if one of them is dead, and the other is left, remembering.

She would take nothing with her from this house but Matthew's painting. In her first anguish, she had believed she would sell it. Then she knew that William would want her to keep it, even if she kept nothing else. It was strange that one so still and retreating as Matthew could have painted anything so strong and vibrant, so surging with life and so powerful. It was very odd but, finally, the painting reminded Ursula of William, and not of her son.

The weary work of months had been completed. It was winter, now. In a few days it would be Christmas, Christmas again, in her old home, with Oliver and William's grandson. There would be a tree for the baby, and laughter, and love and festivity. One did not die, even if one wished to die.

In a few moments, Oliver and Barbara would arrive for

her. She would go away with them, to her house, where the fire would be burning on the old hearth, and the smell of leather, and the lamps, and the panelled walls, would remind her of her father. Had August Wende had hopes for her, Ursula, too? Had he thought his hope of the world was in her? Poor Papa, thought Ursula, standing alone at the leaded window, and looking out at the dark night and the snow.

There was little Billy, waiting for his grandmother: little William Prescott. He was sturdy and young, dark-eyed and full of eagerness. What would the world do to him? What would he do for the world? Everyone spoke, now, of a century of comfort and progress, of peace and enlightenment, of the banishment of hunger and war and injustice. In less than two weeks it would be 1908. The Panic was passing. Perhaps, if one lied to oneself, one could believe that a "new era" was indeed coming, when all the old cruelties would be buried, all the old hatreds forgotten.

Perhaps it would indeed be possible to believe in that ancient salutation to the world: "On earth peace, good will toward men!"

Ursula began to weep, the first tears she had shed for her husband.